Loving and Learning

JUNE
BARRACLOUGH

Loving and Learning

ROBERT HALE · LONDON

© June Barraclough 1999
First published in Great Britain 1999

ISBN 0 7090 6441 1

Robert Hale Limited
Clerkenwell House
Clerkenwell Green
London EC1R 0HT

2 4 6 8 10 9 7 5 3 1

Typeset in North Wales by
Derek Doyle & Associates, Mold, Flintshire.
Printed in Great Britain by
St Edmundsbury Press, Bury St Edmunds, Suffolk.
Bound by WBC Book Manufacturers Limited, Bridgend.

A tous mes amis français – et à la France, en reconnaisance des jours heureux de ma jeunesse que j'ai passés là-bas

J M B
Aix-les-Bains mai 1997 – Londres mars 1998.

L'Oiseau Bleu

The lake lay blue below the hill.
O'er it, as I looked, there flew
Across the waters, cold and still,
A bird whose wings were palest blue.

The sky above was blue at last,
The sky beneath me blue in blue.
A moment, ere the bird had passed,
It caught his image as he flew.

Mary Coleridge

Part One
1825

Chapter 1

Huntingore Hall 1825

Georgy paused for a moment and looked back to the house, then over the lush green fields, before she entered the orchard. All these fields around her home, lovely Huntingore Hall, belonged to her father, Christopher Crabtree. Even when she was scarcely more than a toddler she had been especially fond of the orchard. It lay to one side of the house, beyond the kitchen garden, and she had imagined that the words 'crabapple tree', referred to Crabtree, even the trees being named after her father.

She still loved the orchard and often went there for a moment's peace and quiet, just to be by herself. Surely at the age of – just – eighteen, that was not too much to ask? The Hall and the home farm lay on level land between Wetherby and York, but the pasturage sloped down to the valley where wound the river Wharfe on its way to meet the Ouse.

Having ascertained that she would be alone in the orchard and that there was nobody working nearby, Georgy went to walk under the old apple and pear trees. The foamy blossoms of spring would set over the next few months and there would be the whole of summer for them to wax large and sweet, unless there was unseasonable cold or, even worse, strong winds.

The April wind could always sneak over from the hills, though on the whole the house and land were reasonably well protected. A long, tree-shaded drive led to the Hall from the lane that turned off the road to York, which wound round into the distance: The 'Over the Hills and Far Away' road, Georgy always called it.

In the distance she could hear her ten-year-old cousin Jack

bawling his head off. Jack's voice! How did poor Edward Walker stand it?

Georgy had found a wonderful friend in Mr Walker, the tutor to her cousins, John and Nathaniel, but it was something that concerned him that she must now think over.

She stopped her pacing to lean against the gnarled trunk of a very old apple tree whose trunk had been warmed by the spring sun. She wished she could stop worrying and give herself up to Nature and the pleasant air, for she resented the necessity for a period of deep reflection. The 'problem' had probably been growing for the last year, but only yesterday had it been forcibly presented to her as such by her father.

Her thoughts would not settle. Why should her papa believe that Edward Walker had designs on her? She liked Edward, respected him, might even – though she would hardly admit it to herself, and certainly not confess it to anyone else – be a little 'platonically' in love with him. Well, with his *mind*. He must be about thirty-five, not an age girls of eighteen would consider for a husband or – she considered the word daringly – a lover.

Georgy had always disliked thoughts of husbands, who appeared to do nothing but take away the youthful bloom of friends a little older than herself, but she had always been fascinated by Love, not necessarily connecting the two. A good thing she had not blurted that out to Papa yesterday or he would have been even more horrified. Even her best friend Abigail Strang had been unsettled by Georgy's remarks about marriage.

She moved away from under the trees and went to stand near a hawthorn hedge by the gate to the paddock they called the Far Lawn. Here there was an old wooden swing, made by her father when her brothers were little boys, and still used occasionally by their sister.

Both her brothers were away, Will in the army and Benedict at Oxford. Her cousins, Jack and Nat, were much younger, staying at the Hall only because their mother, Georgy's Aunt Charlotte, her father's youngest sister, was ill. The boys' father had died in one of 'Boney's' campaigns when the boys were only babies, and Georgy was sorry for them. Being sorry, however, did not preclude immense irritation. Aunt Charlotte had never known how to organize them to do anything sensible, and they had run riot since they had been despatched to the Hall. She hoped that her aunt would soon get over the illness which had been variously described as 'extended mourning', 'low spirits' and 'rheumatism'. Her own mother would also be mightily relieved when the boys departed, for they gave the servants a good deal of extra work.

She forced her mind unwillingly back to the scene with her father as she went up to the swing and gave it a preliminary twirl before sitting down. The wood was still a little damp from the dew. She did not begin to swing but used it as a seat, keeping her feet on the ground and moving it slowly from side to side, forwards and backwards, with the rhythm of her thoughts.

The boys must have been almost two years now at the Hall, and Edward Walker had arrived not long after them. When Aunt Charlotte recovered, the boys and their tutor might return to Westmorland, or the lads might be sent away to school. In either case she would lose Edward Walker's company and very much miss her conversations with him. She had learned so much since Edward had come among them. Sometimes she thought she was the only person in the household who wanted to go on learning, and she was now too old for the schoolroom, though eighteen was not really very old. But she ought by now to have acquired all the 'accomplishments' she would need for the battle of life, a battle she guessed had not yet begun.

She had loathed almost all those accomplishments which she had been expected to have acquired from her governess. Miss Langdale had departed last year the day after her seventeenth birthday. She loathed them because she was so bad at 'accomplishing' them, especially sewing and embroidering. Indeed, she had not 'accomplished' anything in those subjects, and also considered herself to be a mediocre pianist, a messy water-colour painter, a singer who could not keep in tune, and a hopeless if lively dancer.

Miss Langdale had not taught dancing – that had been Monsieur Delapole at the Assembly Rooms, and he was connected with the only subject she had enjoyed and was good at: speaking French. Apparently she 'had an ear'. Why she should be able to imitate the sounds of a foreign language when she could not sing in tune was a mystery. Miss Langdale had been astonished, for her own French was heavily accented, if fluent. But Georgy had begged the dancing master to talk to her in his language, and he had obliged.

13

Until she got to know Edward Walker, Monsieur Delapole had been the only young man – and he was not so young – with whom she had ever had a rational conversation. Then Edward – or Mr Walker as she was supposed to address him – had come to teach the boys, and she had discovered that one of his many accomplishments was that he too spoke the French language, and much more fluently than she did, having lived for a time in Paris.

It was true that Edward was probably older than the dancing master – or as old – but that did not matter because of his possession of a *mind*. Her own had blossomed in the conversations and even the arguments they had enjoyed together. They had talked when they took the boys for walks or when she went up to the schoolroom with a message, and in the evenings in the library if her parents were away on a family visit. Never, never had he 'tried anything on'; she very well knew the servants' phrase, and even realized to what the words might refer. At first she had made no connection between a certain strange activity she had once glimpsed occurring under a hedge, and the idea of love between men and women.

It had been one summer, three years earlier, that Georgy had almost disturbed two outdoor lovers; they had certainly disturbed her. She had been fifteen at the time, walking at the edge of Holm Wood, and it had been the sun shining in the near distance on a bare female bottom that had alerted her. Although she had turned round and crept away into the thicket, and then run back through the woods, her heart beating wildly, that sight of a man and a woman had left her feeling oddly uncomfortable, both mentally and physically. They had not heard her or seen her, she was sure. She had known instinctively, even then, that this was to do with the way the human race perpetuated itself. Like dogs and horses! She supposed that it must also have *something* to do with finer feelings or why should they talk about love and marriage in the same breath?

Yet, when she came to think about it, 'love' was not the right word for what she had seen and the idea that her father might ever imagine that her talks with Edward Walker could lead to such carryings on was inconceivable! Not that Papa would ever say anything indelicate, and Mama was even worse, never coming to the point of any criticism of her daughter's conduct. Why, she and Edward had even talked of 'love' – it had to do with the poetry

14

they were reading – and all had remained rational and pleasant.

Now it had all gone wrong. On their return from a visit to Charlotte a few days ago, her mother and father had been very angry when Hargreaves, one of the older maids, had reported that the tutor was 'paying far too much attention' to Miss Georgina.

Georgy had always got on well with the servants; Hargreaves was her only failure, and she had no idea why. Why should Hargreaves want to spoil her innocent pleasure? She was aware that Hargreaves had really meant that *she* was paying too much attention to Mr Walker, but she had not dared to say that, had put it the other way round.

Yesterday evening her father had asked her to come into the library, where he wished to speak to her in the very room where many of the most agreeable conversations with Mr Walker had taken place. Papa had told her in no uncertain terms that what he called their 'too friendly relations' must cease. Edward Walker, if not exactly a servant, was in the family employ and it was not seemly that she should be too friendly with him. The lessons had been all very well – but now she was too old for them.

Georgy had been so furious she could hardly speak. Then she had burst out with: 'He is an educated man, Papa, and even if he were a servant, he is an intelligent person. I suppose you would think M Delapole was a "servant"? Well, last winter I had conversations with *him* too! And now I want to learn all the things Miss Langdale could not teach me.'

'There are plenty of books here for that,' replied Christopher Crabtree, somewhat discomfited, for he did not like arguments and was not usually an unreasonable man. Georgy understood that he was frightened she might truly entertain 'unsuitable' feelings for the tutor. But he had as far as she knew said nothing to Edward himself, which was odd. Perhaps he was embarrassed? He would certainly not want to get rid of Mr Walker, which would mean finding another tutor for the boys. Jack and Nat were such tearaways only Edward Walker could control them, so his continued presence was necessary to her parents' peaceful existence.

She would have to tell Edward about the conversation with her father. Perhaps they could laugh about it? The scene had upset her, not least because she had sensed she would soon be even less free than heretofore. She felt like running far away – except then she would never see Edward again. The one person from whom she might ask advice was the one person who could not be asked.

She sat on the swing and tried to imagine what Edward would say if presented with the problem as if it belonged to someone else.

Did she entertain 'unsuitable' feelings for him? It was hard to know what 'suitable' feelings were. She presumed the kind of decorous chit-chat that passed for conversation among some of her friends and their beaux was what Papa would not have minded? Maybe it was that he did not like his Georgy to be too serious about anything, especially about poetry and ideas? Now that the matter had been dragged into the open however, it had made her even more determined not to lose Edward's friendship. Did not Father see that the more he forbade it the more she would resist?

She vowed to speak to the tutor that very evening; she must discover what he knew. She was aware that emotion often clouded her judgement but she was smarting from the injustice of her father's attitude.

Papa and Mama would be going out to dinner that evening to the Wilkinsons, who never invited her to their gloomy old barracks of a manor house on the York road. She would plead a headache and pretend to retire early, having first made sure that Edward would be down in the library at eight o'clock when she had something of importance to communicate. What, though, could she – or should she – say to him?

Once her brother Will had said to her: 'Don't you realize how your determination looks to Papa? He is not used to women who are direct in their speech.'

It was true that Mama usually got her own way through a side-ways approach. *She* never raised her voice.

'How could I be like that?' Georgy asked herself. 'I was not *made* like that – it is not in my nature!'

Her 'nature' was something she regarded as almost a divine gift. Why else should she be compelled to argue, to disagree, except that she was being true to herself, to this 'nature' of hers?

When she had spoken of this to the tutor, he had commanded her to write an essay about Nature in general, and she had been surprised in conversation with him afterwards – after he had corrected her efforts – to discover he thought there were many natures similar to hers.

'Even a divinely ordained temperament needs the curb of reason to make it effective,' he said with a smile. Oh, he was so good for her.

Another time, at a house party, on a visit to an uncle who lived near Malton, usually an event she found tedious in the extreme, her cousins had invented a game to while away the long evenings. It consisted of describing others without naming them and then making the rest of the company guess who was being described. Georgy had heard herself last year described as 'talkative', 'changeable', 'obstinate', 'over-imaginative' and even 'giddy', by her cousins and their friends.

She had been amazed. What *they* called talkative, *she* would have called fluent; what *they* saw as 'over-imaginative', *she* would have called 'possessed of a lively imagination'; *their* 'giddiness' was surely 'vivacity'. She was not a giddy girl; but a serious-minded one who tried not to let it show when she found herself in uncongenial company. She was not a Lydia Bennett, indeed not.

From all this it can be seen that Georgy had quite a high opinion of herself.

As far as any childhood is ever happy, Georgy Crabtree's had been happy. She had been on the whole an optimistic child; this positive side to her character had not deserted her in adolescence. Although not uniformly sunny, her temperament stood her in good stead when she was fourteen, fifteen, sixteen, even if she was regarded by her parents and relatives and governess as 'a rebel'. They chiefly meant 'unladylike'. Georgy was never loud or unmannerly, but she did defend herself and her own opinions with some vehemence.

Ben was her favourite brother, a tactful young man who understood his sister and often sympathized with her. He did not possess her hot temper, or the irritability of their brother Will, but was rather a peacemaker. Georgy loved him and wished she did not cause him to worry about her. He had told her that he sometimes did.

'Don't do anything rash,' he had said before he went away.

'I'm always very careful,' Georgy had replied, 'I'm not likely to jump off a haystack or try to ride Molly bareback, or swim across the river at spate – you know I am a bit of a coward about such things!'

17

She was wilfully misunderstanding him for she knew he had not meant acts of physical daring. Her 'rashness' was likely to come out in arguments with their father or intense irritation over any attempt to curb her doing what she wanted. Not very terrible things, but unusual things she had read about – usually in French – in her grandfather's books. Her father had never stopped her reading them, although she used her reading as ammunition for argument.

She read of ladies who had 'salons' where young men gathered to talk. How she would love to be like them! Papa had just laughed at her. She dreamed of emotional excitement, so that when she first heard of the Revolution, that had happened in France during her father's own early youth, she had at first discounted tales of The Terror, wanting only to find out about women revolutionaries.

Edward said that once you upset the *status quo* you might unleash terrible passions and even more terrible actions. He was still a 'radical' , he said, but chopping off people's heads had not been the right way to go about improving society. No wonder the English were at present so against change; no wonder the 'evangelicals' were in the ascendant.

Edward's arrival at the Hall had been the answer to her prayers, but she had been careful from the very beginning to dissimulate as far as possible her delight in meeting a man who knew about the world. Of course, she had not found out everything about him straight away; her discoveries had happened only slowly. She knew now that he had lived in France, had read widely, and had educated himself, risen from what she imagined had been a materially disadvantageous position in society, so that he had to earn his living as a tutor to richer families. She was sorry for him.

Only recently had she discovered the extent of his knowledge of France and its literature. But from the very start she had liked him, right from the day she had been allowed to take French lessons from him after begging her father. The dancing master had gone away and her governess gone to another family and there was no way of practising her accomplishment.

Georgy was a girl whose quick sympathies led her to go by first impressions. She imagined that so far she had been proved correct in her assessments. She liked words; she liked ideas; she knew she was clever, though only recently had she realized she must hide this 'cleverness', or make herself unpopular. The family were the middling sort; her mother came from a family of East Riding gentry who had married into a certain modicum of wealth earned through West Riding industry, wealth that seemed set to gather more to itself now that it had become established.

Georgy knew she was not rich by the standards of London society, or some of the members of her mother's own family, but she had the right connections to marry well, and it was this desire of her parents that she marry in the not too distant future that was the reason for her most adamant refusals and rebellions.

Edward Walker was quite aware that matters had come to a head over the servants' tittle-tattle, though he did not yet know about the scene in the library between his employer and his pupil. He had always behaved most circumspectly, and he was aware that Georgy admired and respected him. That everyone thought she was 'in love' with him, annoyed him.

As he came down the stairs from the schoolroom at teatime on the afternoon of Georgy's orchard thoughts, she passed him going upstairs and muttered: 'Be in the library at eight o'clock – I have something to tell you.'

If he had been asked to describe Georgy he would have called her ardent, generous, intelligent and independent. He alone recognized the passion in her that she did not even know she possessed. She was not perhaps an exceptionally beautiful girl, but she was a highly unusual one. All he had suppressed so successfully in his own nature was there in her. She was perhaps less sensitive than he had been himself in his youth, certainly more sociable. He knew in his bones that she would give the wrong impression to others, especially to young men who were less honest than himself. He had tried to warn her of the difference between talk and action, telling her that young men thought young women of spirit were there for their delectation or taming. He did not put it quite like that but she understood with her mind even if her heart rebelled, thinking, surely love is what both young men and women want?

Together they had read the latest poetry. She had already discovered Byron for herself. He had spoken to her of Wordsworth, whose poems he had loved for many years. She responded quickly to her reading for she possessed strongly individual perception.

Edward did not regard Georgy as headstrong so much as imbued with youthful hope, but he told her she should practise observing others more closely and herself less. He had hated saying this, but it was for her own good. He knew her for a loyal, dependable and conscientious young woman, but it was clear to himself that not only did he find her charming but that he also found her attractive, might even be 'in love' with her. Not a soul knew, and he was determined he would never use her own admiration for him to influence her feelings for him. Not a drop of excessive feeling had he ever allowed to appear. He knew she liked his company but he imagined that his attraction for her was only an intellectual one. He had been careful never to give the slightest hint of any interest he might have in her other than that suitable between a teacher and a pupil, knowing only too well what even the mildest flirtation could lead to. In his own young days he had suffered from being in love with an unscrupulous married woman who had led him a dance before going off with someone else.

In any case, there could be no hope for him: he had no useful 'connections', and earned his own living, and even if Georgy came one day to feel more for him as a man than as a fount of knowledge, how could he marry her? The Crabtree dowry would not be given to a humble tutor. He would not declare himself, unless when she was of age she spoke to him first. At present she was too young; later, someone else would marry her. Even if he succeeded in publishing his critical studies – especially his book on Wordsworth's nature imagery, to which he was devoting himself in his spare time, that would cut no ice with her father. What was he thinking of? She had never even tried to flirt with him – that was why she was so refreshing! But he did so *like* her . . . .

Georgy had for the present given her mind into his safe keeping, and that had been enough. He was a scrupulous man and he truly cared more for Georgy's happiness than for his own. She had been almost sixteen when they had first met and it hadn't taken him long to discover her real worth. Balancing the conventions and the impulses of his heart with the need for Georgy to be free, and for her never to suspect his real feelings, had been a difficult business, but he thought he had succeeded.

20

Now her family had apparently got this idea that he was 'encouraging' her. What was he to do? Georgy had most likely – and most injudiciously – told her father how 'interesting' she found his mind.

He groaned as he prepared to meet her clandestinely in the library for what he had decided would be positively the last time they would be alone together. Mr and Mrs Crabtree had taken fright, and he could understand their feelings. He had done nothing unchivalrous, but he was determined that his fancy for her would not be revealed, nor to what extent he admired her spirit. He feared they would eventually send her away to be 'polished', and he very well knew what that might mean.

Even a spirit like Georgy's could be crushed. The world would *tweak* her into place; what a suggestive word, he thought: flattening, pinching, fitting her into a little space, pulling, pushing, plucking till her mind was of the right sort for polite – and respectable – society . . . .

From his top floor back window near the staircase to the attics he had seen Georgy enter the house, so he went down and knocked at the library door. Even though it was only Georgy, he was nervous. Rumours flying round the servants' hall had been reported to him by Jim the coachman who had said 'that cat Hargreaves' was spreading gossip about him and the young lady.

He was no kind of suppliant though. He didn't want to leave, but if they didn't want him to stay he could up and go; doubtless there were other – and nobler – families who needed tutors for recalcitrant offspring.

Georgy's 'Come in!' sounded nervous too, but when she saw him she rose, and as soon as she began to speak he saw she was indignant.

She sat down and beckoned him to be seated too and began with no preamble.

'Have you heard what they are saying? That I have been making a nuisance of myself – it isn't true, is it? Tell me it is ridiculous.'

He looked at her levelly. 'Begin at the beginning – who has been saying this – and in what connection?'

'Papa got me here yesterday evening and said he had been told – by Hargreaves of course, the snake! – that we were "seeing too much of each other". Oh, it made me *so* angry! – then Papa said I must not have any more lessons with you—'

Edward cleared his throat. He felt rather angry himself. 'Did he say why?'

'Oh, just you were paying too much attention to me – as though anyone can learn anything from someone who doesn't pay attention to them!'

'Georgy,' said Edward after a pause. She was quite pale now. 'You can guess what this is about? What they might think?'

'You don't need to tell me – I am not stupid,' she flashed. 'And it is all a pack of lies—'

Well, that was something. The idea that he might find her body attractive was obviously far from her thoughts, never mind any notion that he might have an ulterior motive for finding her pleasant company. And he had not had another motive; liking her, finding her an apt pupil, considering her as the owner of a lively mind were enough. The fact of that mind's embodiment in the flesh of a young woman was of secondary importance just now.

But he could not say this to her. They were already treading on dangerous ground.

'What exactly did your father say?' he asked, looking her squarely in the face.

'That – that you are – paying me too much attention ... because I had made a nuisance of myself. Has he said nothing to you?'

'No – and he should have done!'

'That is strange – but I suppose he might be embarrassed? He says I must stop my lessons with you – I am too old for them now. But they will certainly not want to get rid of you – they'd never find anyone who'd stay with the boys! Who would put up with them?'

She dared not say that she guessed Papa feared Edward might have had 'designs' on her. No, what she must say was that Papa regarded him as a servant. That was easier to say, easier to counter. She could not say that Papa suspected *she* might be in love with *him* – he had not said so but she had known he was thinking it.

'I was angry with him because he talked of you as though you were a servant like Hargreaves—'

'That does not worry me, Georgy – you know I have much sympathy for servants!'

'But did you not realize any of this? All the servants must have heard Hargreaves – and they will all know Papa was talking to me here last night—'

'If that's true they'll know we are together now.'

'I'm not a prisoner! Papa has never been really unreasonable before – and – and I cannot bear it if I cannot go on with my talks and lessons—'

'Georgy, be reasonable. Shall I speak to your father, tell him . . . .' He was going to say 'we have acted perfectly innocently' but that might be giving her the wrong ideas, so he went on 'that I know he has allowed you to have lessons with me for longer than most young ladies?'

She was silent, so he went on: 'In any case you know you can carry on now with your reading alone. Let him cool down for a time, and let us wait and see.'

'I will try,' she said pathetically, and never had he longed more to take the child in his arms. But that would be against the spirit of his even deeper feelings for her.

If Georgy had hoped they might laugh together over it all, her thoughts when she finally got back to her room were not at all mirthful.

She even shed a tear, but it was a tear of rebellion.

One day at the end of the following week, after spending as much time as possible reading in her room, Georgy was once more commanded to see her father, this time in his tack room. He was polishing some harness, liked doing such practical things. He looked up.

'You're to go on a visit,' he said with no preamble. 'Your aunt Caroline and uncle Clive, your mama's cousins, are at their London house and your mama thinks it time for you to acquire a little polish. So at the end of next week you'll go to town!'

There was nothing she could say; he had made up his mind. Saying it was mama's idea was cowardly.

She managed to tell Edward Walker as he came back from fishing with the boys, their Saturday treat. 'I am to go away to Uncle's in London! His wife's servant will accompany me there on the Mail from York. What can I do?'

'But this is good news indeed!' said Edward who, truth to tell, felt slightly relieved on his own account, if at the same time sad at the idea of Georgy's absence. 'You will be able to see the way the world is – make new acquaintances – and did you not once tell me your uncle was an Oxford man? It will be a great adventure – you will meet new faces.'

'Very well, Edward,' she replied furiously. 'I know my duty. *They* just want me to find a rich husband – *I* intend to meet interesting people for their own sake.' But she could not help feeling secretly a little excited.

Edward reflected that they could not have gone on as they had, now that she was eighteen . . . . Georgy must find new friends, make her own way.

But she had no idea how much he would miss her.

Chapter Two

London

Ten days later Georgy found herself seated next to her aunt's maid Matilda in the Mail that plied regularly between York and London. The coach and four made a great deal of dust and noise as it clattered down the Great North Road. Georgy had set off at six o'clock that morning, in the Northern Post, which was the quickest coach. Even so, it would take twenty-five hours to reach its destination. There were frequent daytime stops to unload the mail, or change horses, and an hour or two in the evening at an inn for food. The passengers got little sleep. They could have alighted and slept one night at Stamford and taken the next coach in the morning but that would have made the journey much longer. Everyone was talking about the 'rail-road' that had apparently just been invented; people were saying that one day you would be able to get to London in half the time taken by the horses.

Eight passengers sat and sweltered now inside the stuffy coach that looked so handsome on the outside, all black and maroon. Clothes became crumpled, hands dirty. Georgy was glad that her best clothes were all packed in her trunk which was roped, with other people's, on the top of the vehicle. In the trunk she had, along with her ordinary dresses, her new cotton summer dress that had a pretty pattern of blue and yellow flowers with lace at the hem and the sleeves.

She had never before worried much about clothes, seeing them as a necessary evil, but this dress was so pretty – and even quite *décolleté* and she knew she looked well in it. Mama had been talking about having another silk pelisse made for the winter too. It seemed that her daughter was suddenly grown up. Did she realize she was being sent away in case she developed 'unsuitable' feelings for Edward Walker?

Georgy had no idea whether her father had yet said anything to him. She rather thought not; if he had, she felt sure Edward would have told her. All he had said to her when they had met on the lane, this time quite by chance, his two pupils running on ahead of him, was:

'Don't take it amiss if I say again that you must not give the wrong impression to people, Georgy.'

'You mean I am too much of what they call a "bluestocking", and Society won't like it?'

What Edward had meant was not that, but that she had so much natural verve, whether it was discussing books or being 'enthusiastic' over nature or music, and was so open and friendly – and talkative – that young men would easily come to the conclusion that she was 'forward' and try to take advantage. He had tried so many times in so many different words to tell her this, for he knew her to be *au fond*, intense and serious minded. The seriousness was all very well – but the intensity ought to be kept within bounds.

'Oh, don't worry about that – it will be a change for them! Just be careful not to give too much of yourself away!'

She had pondered this. Sometimes she had wondered if Edward had imagined she was like Mary Bennett in her favourite novel *Pride and Prejudice*. But it was not *Mary* Bennett who was likely to wear her heart on her sleeve!

Georgy's 'uncle' Clive was her mother's cousin, the son of her mother's aunt Mary Ann who had married a rich city merchant. Clive too had married a rich lady, Caroline Edmondson, and they lived in London and Bath as well as owning a small property in Sussex.

Georgy had only met 'aunt' Caroline once before, when she was a small child – it seemed years ago, but she remembered her well and she knew from her parents that she was a gentlewoman who did not flaunt her wealth. On arriving in London at 27 Montacute Square she had expected that this time the lady she must call 'Aunt' would look much older. But what seemed aeons ago to Georgy was only a few years, or Caroline had worn well. London appeared to suit her. It was Georgy who felt old and stiff after her long journey. Uncle's carriage had met them on Cheapside where the Mail stopped and she had stared around her with avid interest at the streets and the horses and the crowds. Such crowds! She had sniffed the mixture of horse dung and river water that permeated the place, if not quite so much on Montacute Square, which was tucked away quite near the park.

Coming down to dinner for the first time after Matilda had helped her dress and done her hair for her – with ringlets over the forehead – Georgy had intended to keep quiet and observe the others unless she was asked for an opinion. There were only four of them at the meal, her Uncle Clive, his wife Caroline, and a lady introduced to her as 'my sister' by Caroline. Georgy thought she heard a French name. Madame de Something, she thought her aunt had said, but the lady was addressed as Camilla. Now, *she* looked much more fashionable than her clearly older sister Caroline.

Georgy had been hungry before they sat down but found it hard to eat and talk at the same time and her uncle did ask her so many questions about her family and Huntingore Hall. How had the shooting been last year? What was the state of health of her various relatives? How well had the home farm done in the previous harvest?

She did her best to answer, thinking of the women at home who hoed in the fields. What a world away from these smart ladies.

'Farming in general is in a bad way,' said Clive.

That was what they always said, she thought.

'Still enjoy your riding and your long walks?' he asked, remembering how when she was a very small girl he had seen her on her pony, and how even then she and her brothers had gone for long walks around the countryside.

The ladies spoke less but left a good deal of their supper on their plates. Uncle Clive drank wine and there was a footman waiting on them.

'Come, do have some more fish – or do you not like fish?' Aunt Caroline said at one point. 'Clive, my dear you must allow our young guest to finish her supper and keep your queries for later.'

Georgy was grateful, attacked her fish and then her pheasant, and finally the elderberry water-ices with gusto.

After the meal, the ladies adjourned to a small withdrawing room where a tray with a silver coffee-pot was brought in by the same footman. Uncle Clive had stayed in the dining-room to finish his wine. It was all new and strange to Georgy. Her own parents did not drink wine as a general rule at home, only on special occasions, but here she had enjoyed her first glass of claret.

'It is French coffee,' said Caroline as she poured it out from the silver pot into tiny white china cups decorated with pink rose-buds.

'I hear you speak French?' said Camilla.

'Oh, yes – but not perfectly,' answered Georgy, and then Camilla turned on a positive spate of French.

'I am your aunt's younger sister' – she rather emphasised the *younger* – 'and my husband is French. They call me Camille in France but my sister prefers the English version.'

What could Georgy say to this?

She murmured: '*Vous demeurez en France, Madame?*'

'*Mais oui. Nous avons une petite propriété en Saône et Loire – pas loin de Mâcon. J'ai deux enfants, Mademoiselle.*'

'Speak English, do dear,' said her sister with a slight yawn.

'I am looking for a young English person to help look after my children,' pursued Camilla, or Camille, now in slightly accented English which Georgy was sure was added for effect. 'Your Papa did not mention this to you?'

'No!' answered Georgy in surprise. Was that why they had invited her to stay with them? To see if she was 'suitable'? It may have been just what Papa was looking for on her account – and something he imagined would please her too.

'You mean – in France, Ma'am?' she asked in English.

'*Certainement. Alors, nous verrons* – we shall see?'

Shortly after this exchange Georgy went to bed in a small pink room at the top of the narrow house. She could hear the night watchman at first but soon fell asleep, for she was really tired.

After breakfast next morning she learned from Aunt Caroline, whose sister was apparently out shopping in The Quadrant on Regent Street that Camilla's French title was Madame de Marceau, that her husband was the son of a count, and that she was soon to Return to France to rejoin her children who were at present staying at home with their father and the servants in Burgundy.

'She wants them to speak English as well as they do French,' explained Aunt Caroline. 'My sister met her husband, Augustin de Marceau, over here in London when they were children. His family are *émigrés* from The Terror. When all that, and Boney, was over – more or less – the family returned to France – must be about ten years ago, along with my sister who had just married her husband over here.'

'How old are the children? What are their names?' asked Georgy. She liked children on the whole, her cousins Jack and Nat apart.

'Well, there is Lucie Augustine Gabrielle – curious mouthful, isn't it! – but they call her Lucie. She is nine, I believe, and her brother Thibault is two years younger.'

Then Caroline went on to speak of her sister's French relatives – there seemed to be a whole host of them, beginning with the count and countess and their other children and numerous cousins. Georgy was quite bewildered.

So far nothing definite had been said about offering her this post of 'English governess' to the children. Perhaps they thought she might consider it beneath her? Papa must have really wanted her away if he was prepared to allow her to be a sort of servant? But it would get her to France! – and they were not treating her like a servant here, more like a daughter. Camilla, though, was another *tasse de thé*. Georgy was not sure if she trusted her.

When that lady returned from her shopping, Georgy was invited into her room for a real dish of tea.

'Come, tell me all about yourself,' said Camilla. 'I hear you are a bookworm.'

Now who could have told her that?

'It is true, ma'am, that I love to read – indeed I have read some of the French poets—'

'Really? Well, then, I can tell you that my husband has a distant cousin who is a poet! I believe he is now famous – I cannot remember the *exact* relationship. In France they are very family minded, you know, and I have met many relatives. They often pass by our little place on a visit.'

'What was the poet's name?' asked Georgy.

'Alphonse – he was in Savoy for a cure and, what was the story? He met a lady there whom he saved from shipwreck on the lake and she became his inspiration. She died, of course.'

Could she be speaking of the famous Lamartine whose

Méditations Georgy had read with Edward Walker only a few months ago?

'Is his name – Lamartine?' she asked.

'There you have it – Lamartine! You must forgive me. I am not a great reader of verse myself. I believe he is becoming quite well known?'

'And you have *met* him?'

'I was introduced only last year to his wife – she is English, you know. It was when we were in Savoy ourselves – we go for the waters and for the air. I did not meet your poet but I particularly remember his wife, being English myself. You are not a Catholic are you?' she asked Georgy suddenly and answered her own question 'No – you can't be – dear Clive comes from a Protestant family, naturally. I "went over" – I believe the poet's wife did too. I seem to remember we talked of it – and of her daughter who was only a baby. They lost a little boy.'

Georgy was hanging on every word. 'He wrote a wonderful poem – about a lake,' she said.

'My dear, you must recite it to us all! I'm sure you *can* recite it, *n'est-ce pas?*'

Now what was she getting herself into? It was true she knew several, if not quite all, of the verses by heart.

'Remind me – I must hear your French!' Then Camilla rose, yawned, and said she would have a rest, London was so tiring.

Georgy departed and decided to look for the library – if there was such a thing here in this grand house.

She took the book she had found in a small book room – you could not call it a library – up to her bedroom. Used as she was to the vast number of books at Huntingore Hall, collected by her grandfather, Georgy knew her way around such places, and it was clear that Uncle Clive was no reader. There were several books of travel, however, some of them with the name *Theodore Edmondson* inscribed on their fly leaves. That must be Aunt Caroline and Madame de Marceau's father's name? The book she had chosen looked new, smelt of printers' ink, Georgy always sniffed books when she was about to read them. This book had maps and was about mountains. One chapter was entitled *Wanderings through the Kingdom of Savoy* and this she read avidly. Savoy was where the poet had met his great love and also where Madame de Marceau had said the family went for 'the cure'. Apparently it had been annexed during their Revolution by the French, but things were now back to normal, with a new king.

She remembered what Edward had told her of that book of poems that included *Le Lac*. It was quite new; he had bought it in London though it had been published in Paris. Now she fell to wondering when exactly the poet had met his lady love by the lake. There was something about that same lake here in the book and she read on with enthusiasm. The region was described lyrically by the gentleman whose 'wanderings' had led him there: it must be a beautiful place. She'd like to go there, oh she would!

She only just managed to wash her hands and comb her hair before she was summoned to dinner, which was early because the family was going to the theatre. They had explained that next time she could go with them. All she could think about was, The Lake, The Mountains, The Poet .... In other words: Abroad! Would she be asked to take up that post they had mentioned or was that just a casual reference that had nothing to do with her? And if they did want her, would Papa allow her to go?

She bit her lip – it was so provoking not to be free, to have to ask permission to live the life you wanted to live. But she was prepared to look after children if she could thereby see more of the world.

Abroad, who knew – she might even meet the Poet!

She was to discover quite soon that the idea had already been mooted to her parents, though nothing had been said to her except that she was to go on a visit to her relatives in London. Papa must want her well out of the way of Edward Walker to consider her going abroad. He'd think it was killing two birds with one stone – pleasing his daughter and getting her away from the Hall . . . .

Her French was tested by Camilla de Marceau the very next evening. Georgy wanted to ask her, if you want me to speak English to your children, why should I need to speak French? But she said nothing, feeling her fate hung in the balance.

They were in the drawing-room and they had visitors – Clarissa and Robert Bond – who were Uncle Clive's cousins, and their daughter, a Mrs Robinson, who looked very discontented. Having once been presented to them, Georgy was then ignored. She had seen the women arrive, very fashionably dressed, in pelisses with five tiers of lace frills, three rows of lace at the collar and enormous straw bonnets heaped with flowers and ribbons. No wonder they needed a maid to redress their hair after these appendages were removed.

The men went off and then the women's talk was of maid servants. Georgy learned that Madame de Marceau had an ancient maid in France called Eglantine and a younger one named Célanie. They helped to look after her children, she said.

'So you have not yet found an English maid to take back with you?' asked Mrs Bond.

Georgy's ears pricked up at this. She was seated on a spindly chair and felt she was on show though nobody had addressed a remark to her so far. Was it really a maid they wanted, not a sort of governess? She thought Aunt Caroline looked uneasy.

'That reminds me,' said Camilla, 'Georgy speaks French – and she can recite us all a poem – written, she tells me, in the little place we often visit on holiday.'

Oh dear, how was she to get out of this? She doubted Mrs Robinson or her parents spoke that language. Aunt Caroline saved her by saying: 'I think Georgy would rather recite to us privately, Cam!'

'In France,' said Camilla, 'ladies are always prepared to entertain a salon.'

Soon after this the family left – they had to make a call upon another relative, they said. Georgy had the impression they were a little overawed by the two sisters and the opulence of the furnishings, which were indeed lovely – a mother of pearl mirror, a Turkey carpet and gold and white sofas and chairs.

'Now!' said Camilla. 'Strike whilst the iron's hot! Mademoiselle, *avancez* – we beg you to recite a few verses of the great poem!'

Georgy 'advanced', cleared her throat and began: 'It is a sad poem but I will do my best.'

She cleared her throat: '*Le Lac*', by Alphonse de Lamartine – from his *Méditations*:

> *Ainsi toujours poussés vers de nouvaux rivages*
> *Dans la nuit éternelle emportés sans retour*
> *Ne pourrons nous jamais sur l'océan des âges*
> *Jeter l'ancre un seul jour? . . . .*

Several more verses followed, but Georgy wisely judged it better to omit some of them.

'Capital!' said Uncle Clive who had come into the room once his female relatives had left it.

'Excellent, my dear,' said Aunt Caroline.

Camilla smiled. Was she reserving judgement?

'I'm sorry – I know my accent is rather English.'

'No, it is good – for a person who has lived only in this country. I believe you have a flair for recitation,' said Camilla.

Georgy did not know what to make of her Aunt Caroline's sister. She appeared bored, often looked at you without smiling as if far away with other thoughts, but then she would obviously make an effort to be agreeable. The praise of her own French accent was not excessive. Georgy would have felt awkward if the lady had said 'perfect' or 'remarkable'. If, however, she did want her to help with Lucie and Thibault she had better know what she was letting herself in for. She had no fear of a foreign country, or of a different way of life, or of unknown children, but she knew that the most important thing if you lived in someone else's household was whether you found your employer agreeable. Still, so far she had not even been asked! She had better possess her soul in patience, as her old governess used to say.

Nobody had so far mentioned the name of Edward Walker, the hidden cause for this unexpected holiday. She wondered if her father had hinted anything to his wife's cousins. Knowing him, he would have probably been vague and said something about bad influences and his little girl needing a change . . . .

Next morning, when Georgy was just about to come down the two flights of stairs to the little breakfast room, she heard her name called.

Camilla de Marceau was standing at the threshold of her bedroom, a room on the floor beneath Georgy. She was dressed in a long silky mantle thrown over what looked like complete nakedness. Decidedly, people in London were less averse to showing off their charms. Of course at home it was usually far too cold!

Georgy advanced down the flight of stairs and as soon as she stood enquiringly at their foot, the lady said: 'I had a dream,' and yawned.

Really? Was that all?

Then she beckoned her: '*Avancez*, Mademoiselle. I have just

33

had a strange dream and it has made my mind up for me! How would you like to accompany me back to France in a few weeks? Would you be partial to taking the post I spoke to you about?'

Georgy's heart began to beat somewhat rapidly. She swallowed, got out: 'I should have to ask Papa,' as a way of stalling. She was blessed if she were going to appear to jump at such a chance. There might be snags? Of *course* she wanted to go – even if it meant she'd miss her lessons with Edward. But they were going to end in any case . . . .

Had it all been decided when Papa wrote to Uncle Clive? Was the 'French test' just to make her think she had a choice in the matter – and that they did too?

'I want an English girl, but she has to be able to make herself understood in my children's first language – the servants do not speak English. I think you will do!'

'If Papa agrees, I should be grateful for the opportunity to see the world,' said Georgy.

'Yes, yes – but it will be hard work, you know – I don't give the care of my children to any Mary Jane!' She changed tack and stood looking at Georgy for a moment. 'Are you conversant with the work of Monsieur Rousseau?'

Now why on earth had she asked her that? A noble family was hardly a hotbed of revolutionary zeal?

'He is no longer in fashion, but I believe young people need a guide, a friend who will make sure they are happy! I am often too busy with my husband's cares, and the servants, to see to other than their physical needs.'

'I have heard of *Emile*,' replied Georgy carefully. 'Would you require me also to teach the rudiments of Nature Study?'

'Oh, that and lots of other things – until they are old enough to have a proper tutor.'

'I am only just eighteen, Madame. I could teach what I know, but I fear I am no needlewoman nor could I teach dancing or singing—'

'We can talk about that later – now I must dress. You may write to your Papa.' And with this she shut her door carefully behind her.

Georgy ran down the rest of the stairs in a confusion of excitement and anxiety, and could scarcely swallow her breakfast, which like everything else in this house was lavish: hot and cold rolls, a choice between tea, coffee, and chocolate and two sorts of cake.

It would be work for a year, her aunt said later on when Georgy asked her advice. 'It is indeed a beautiful part of the country, and the château is delightful. They sometimes travel into the mountains of Savoy in summer,' she added. It would indeed be an opportunity for her to be 'finished' and see the world, as well as improving her French. 'Also, you will meet gentlefolk,' Aunt Caroline went on, 'There are not so many families of the right kind near York,' she added, so that Georgy knew that her aunt knew about the contretemps with Mr Walker. 'I shall write to your papa in the same packet – when you have finished your letter, give it to me and I will see that it is taken off. But I feel sure your papa will agree!'

Georgy still found a small pocket of reluctance in her heart. She had the feeling that her parents would be glad to see her away for a year, by which time Edward would most likely have gone back to Westmorland to Aunt Charlotte's. Well, it was only for a year, wasn't it? – after which she could return and show them all her new worldliness. She meant, show Edward she had grown up.

It was Edward Walker who had spoken to her of the *philosophes* and of the rebel Jean-Jacques Rousseau and his theories of education. She could not imagine that the philosopher was writing for such as Madame Camille de Marceau who was a Catholic and therefore *bien-pensante*. But there was no denying the influence of literature. Edward had spoken of such theories because he was attempting to put them into partial operation with Nat and Jack. Not that he seemed to have had much success. But he was no fool; he had explained there was a large gulf between theory and practice. In other matters too, in spite of being an 'idealist' – or perhaps because of it – he was a little cynical. One day he had even remarked in connection with the poem Georgy had so recently recited, that: 'The best thing that comes out of the love of poets is a poem!'

But Edward was a man and a man could roam freely and experiment with life, even if he were poor. Not for the first time she wondered at his background. Somehow she did not see him as the son of a really poor man. True, he had no fortune but she had the impression that that was his choice, that he had quarrelled with his family and been cast off. If only she could speak to him now about the offer. He would give her the best advice. She resolved to write a note to him, but the problem would be how to get him to read it. It could not go in the packet with the letter to her papa? Then she had an idea. She would write an ostensible demand for a list of useful books and ask her father to give it to him. Surely he could not object to that? At the bottom of this she would write what she wanted him to know and would ask his advice. Her father would never bother to read it through.

Dear Mr Walker,
I should be grateful if you would advise me concerning what to teach two French children of our own language. I expect I shall be principally with them for *conversation*, but it would be as well to be prepared. There is a girl of nine and a boy of seven. I assume they will do the globes and the study of nature and some drawing and they have a teacher for dancing. The girl has learned some music and plain sewing from a teacher in Mâcon.

She carried on in this vein for a few more lines and then added:

'What do you think, Edward? Am I sensible to accept this prospect? The lady spoke of Rousseau and his theories – but she is a fashionable lady! If you do not think it a good idea, then I shall not go. I will not be 'got rid of'! But as you know, I do want to improve myself, and it will be a wonderful opportunity for me to speak French, *n'est-ce pas?* I return on Thursday to prepare for the journey but there is yet time to change my mind and Papa even now may be deciding to keep me at home. Meet me in the orchard the morning after my arrival home and tell me what to do.
                                        Your sincere friend Georgy.

She added a few extra lines after this about orthography and French history in case her papa was curious and looked to the end of the missive.

Georgy returned home a few days later with Aunt Caroline's maid to prepare for the possibility of a lengthy stay abroad.

Her papa turned out to be very willing to give his permission for her to go to France, saying only: 'So long as you want to go, my dear?'

36

She knew her mother would be more reluctant to lose her for a year but would be thinking of clothes and other practical details, and she was not wrong in her surmise.

She stole out of bed early in the morning the day after her return and went into the orchard. The dew was still on the grass and there was the delicious scent of May blossom drifting over from the fields. Would there be such blossom in France?

Must she really go far away? Was she mad to agree? Would Edward Walker have heeded her message? They had glimpsed each other last night but it had been late and she was tired. Now she had slept well and her spirits had rebounded with all the elasticity of youth.

She pushed open the little gate and saw him half-way down the orchard, leaning arms akimbo against a medlar tree. She approached quietly, not wanting for a moment to let him know she was there. He was looking away from the house into the distance and she stood watching him.

Then he turned towards her. 'Hello, Georgy – playing hide and seek? You thought I hadn't seen you!'

'Thank you for coming out,' she said humbly. 'You got my letter—?'

'Indeed, and I have compiled a reading list for you.'

'So you think I ought to go?'

'I know you *must* go – you will learn a good deal, and return a young lady.'

'Am I not a young lady now?'

'Not quite—'

'I want to go – but I shall miss – certain things—'

'I should make a virtue of necessity if I were you,' he said deliberately keeping the tone of his remarks light and bantering.

'Will you give me your advice? You know France – and the world. But I expect I shall be cloistered in a family—'

'What is she like, your Madame de Marceau?'

Georgy considered. 'Difficult to describe. Good-looking, and rather changeable, I think. But she seems to like me and I suppose I can be of some use.'

'Remember, it is not as if you depend on her for your bread – if you don't like it you can always come home.'

'But that would be cowardly – and anyway even if I came home – *he* won't let us go on talking to each other,' she added in a rush.

37

'I expect I shall be gone in a year or two myself,' he replied, ignoring the opportunity to speak more frankly. 'But remember, if you are in any difficulty you can always address yourself to me – I mean that.'

'What sort of difficulty?'

'Well, you said you wanted advice and I would advise you to say very little – except to your charges – you can say a lot to children if they like you. It is the young sparks – the young men, of whom I would earnestly ask you to beware!'

She looked at him in surprise.

'Young Frenchmen – even gentlemen – are more inclined to flirt than we English, Georgy. Remember, flirtation is all very well but do not take them seriously. You are very young.'

'You sound like my father!'

'I'm sorry – I don't mean to.'

How could he say that he hated the idea of her far away talking to other men, young or no. They would soon discover she was a passionate sort of girl, he thought.

He changed the subject. 'I don't know how much you remember of what has happened over there in France since Waterloo? Did you know that a new king is about to be crowned this very week in Rheims?'

'No, I did not,' she answered, surprised.

'Last year old Louis XVIII died. He wasn't a bad old stick.'

'What is the new king called? Why did they bother to have a revolution if, after all that – and Boney – they've got their king back?'

He laughed. 'You may well ask. The new king – an old man already – is the Bourbon Charles X. His son was assassinated a few years ago – but there is a grandson.'

'Do you think the people I shall stay with will be Royalists?'

'I should think so if they were *émigrés* – but Louis the Eighteenth of recent hallowed memory was a sort of constitutional monarch. You said the family had returned to their estates in Burgundy?'

'Yes.'

'I expect that would be in 1814? Well, how interesting – there is a new book whose first part came out recently over there – a history of the Dukes of Burgundy—' She saw how animated his face became when he could tell her about a book. 'And they say

38

Thierry is preparing a new book on the Norman Conquest of England,' he went on. 'Still I don't expect you'll see a copy – did you say the family also went to Savoy?'

'Yes – for their holidays – a sort of water cure, I think.'

'Well, well, you will appreciate our friend Lamartine's little holiday town. Don't forget Savoy is not French – but of course they do speak French there.'

'Oh dear, I wish I had paid more attention to my history lessons,' she said gloomily. 'Still, I did recite the poem we read together – *Le Lac* – somehow poems are easier to remember than kings and revolutions!'

'I expect your family will be pious,' he said. 'Like all the old *émigrés* who want to turn back the clock. They will bring about another burst of anti-clericalism – France is always at extremes. Your family will be for Charles X, the new king, all right, so you'd better say nothing rude about him. Still, they are not so mealy-mouthed as we English are becoming!'

'How do you know so much?'

'You forget I was once in Paris and met one of our spies before Waterloo!'

He had never told her so much about himself, though she already knew that at its beginning he had been in favour of the Revolution in France. He was more moderate now, and she too was horrified to read about what The Terror had brought to some of the French.

She asked him: 'May I write to you? Will you write to me? I shall tell no one if you do.'

He looked at her solemnly causing her to drop her eyes. 'Very well. I shall expect long and interesting missives that I shall hoard for future publication!'

'Let us say a first goodbye now,' she said. 'I promise I will write. I leave in a sennight, I believe.'

'Good-bye, Georgy – but I shall see you at table and be able to ask you to pass me the salt!'

'You are never serious,' she said.

Oh, but I *am*, he thought as she put out her hand to him impulsively. 'I have a little book for you, which I shall wrap in brown paper. You are not to open it until you arrive in France,' he said.

'Oh! Thank you. Will you leave it for me in the library before I go?' How stupid that she could not even publicly accept a book from him. But she did not want to get him into trouble.

In readiness for Georgy's visit to France, Mrs Crabtree had already commandeered her tried and trusty dressmaker Miss Amelia Chistopherson to sew three new chemisettes, of fine lawn, of cambric and of muslin, with embroidered collars, to go under Georgy's white cotton morning dresses. Then she was to have two new summer evening dresses, also in cotton, one of them dyed in the new colour, lavender. It had a lace frill at the hem and the sleeves were in frilly puffs. It was as if she was 'coming out' in Society: her mother was determined to be generous, but there was not much time to do all this sewing if she was to leave at the beginning of the second week of June.

Her mother offered her also one of her best paisley shawls. Georgy had never taken much interest in her clothes and was not going to begin now, but was suitably grateful. She was measured for one of the new pelisse dresses for special occasions which necessitated many more tedious hours of fitting, and several even more tedious hours of sewing. Miss Christopherson could not finish it all on time without help, so all the females of the household were conscripted. This dress was of deep blue silk lined in white, and when it was finished, only the day before her departure, Georgy could not help admitting it was beautiful, even if, when she looked in the long pier glass, it showed her a self she had never seen before, and the padded hem weighed her down a little. Her mama had found the pattern in one of last year's French fashion plates, and Georgy could not help thinking it was too good to wear, but she would take it in her luggage, 'for best', not go away in it. For the long journey she needed plain clothes, so would take her old ones, since mud and rain could hardly spoil *them*.

'You will have to wait for another evening dress once we know your circumstances,' said Mrs Crabtree. 'Until then the cotton ones will do very nicely. You will acquaint me with what you need once you have seen what is worn over there? They may have a dressmaker – Papa could settle the bill . . . .'

'Oh, surely, Mama, in the country I shall not need an evening dress?' objected Georgy. 'The children will be my responsibility – not dances with grown ups!'

Mrs Crabtree sighed and supposed there was at least something to be said for an unworldly daughter. Not that she had ever imagined Georgy had intended anything but a mental friendship with Mr Walker. It was too absurd of Christopher to be worried, unlike him. It would do Georgy a lot of good to get away and see a little more of the world – and would also improve her French, which was never a bad thing if you wanted a good *parti*. Georgy could never be said to be vain, but she must learn to be a little more aware of the conventions. If she chose to go around in plain cotton shifts and woollen shawls, her new employers would soon tax her with it. The French were, as far as she was concerned, an unknown quantity, but everyone always said how fashionable they were. Better someone else to put the finishing touches to her daughter. Georgy would take more notice of strangers than of her own mother.

Apart from the family and Edward Walker there was only one person whom Georgy would miss and she was away in Scarborough with her parents. Abigail Strand and her sister Lydia had been fellow sufferers at dancing classes during Georgy's childhood. Their papa was a successful barrister and they lived in an old mellow-bricked house a few miles away. Georgy liked Abigail, who had a calm and unruffled attitude to life. One thing about her was that she never judged people. She had always listened to Georgy's ramblings in childhood and later, and taken her seriously. If she disagreed with Georgy she would only say something mild. Lydia had been more sarcastic and critical, smarter than her sister and more ambitious.

'Girls should not interest themselves in romance, but be the object of it,' was one of Lydia's clever sayings.

But Abby was now engaged to a young solicitor who had often been called upon by Papa Strang in his chambers in York, a certain Hugh Thompson. Georgy feared there might soon grow up an unbridgeable gap between her and her old friend. It was her experience that girls changed when they got engaged; past friendships often receded for a time into the background. Abby might very well be married by the time she herself was back in England. She did not want to lose touch with her, for she had been really close to her at school, so she scribbled a note telling her of the momentous step in her own fortunes and added her address in France.

Perhaps Abigail would have a honeymoon in Paris, by which time Miss Georgina Crabtree might also be there, one of a salon of intelligent people .... She spent a few moments thinking about this, imagining herself established in Paris and showing her friend around, then brought herself out of her daydream. She was not going to France to conduct a salon or join Parisian society but as a humble mixture of distant relative and governess.

At last the day came when she was to travel once more to London. Papa was to accompany her this time, in the Mail, and hand her over to Madame de Marceau who was herself to leave for France a day or two later with her maids and trunks and paraphernalia – along with her new English governess. The journey over to France would be long, but Georgy was looking forward to it, especially to crossing the Channel. Once in Burgundy, in Saône et Loire, several days out from England, they were to change from the diligence to the de Marceau family carriage which would be waiting for them. These French diligences were said by her father, who had once travelled abroad, to be less comfortable than the English mail coaches.

'But you will not mind that – you are young,' he said.

He appeared to have forgotten why he was despatching his only daughter abroad and by now Georgy was looking upon it as an adventure not a punishment. Papa however did say that if she were overworked or in any way 'put upon' she must let him know. She was not a servant!

When the day came, her mother said a tearful goodbye. Georgy managed to appear calm, though she did not feel at all calm inside.

She looked up at the schoolroom window: Yes, there was Edward Walker with his two pupils, the boys both waving lustily. The little parcel he had promised her was in her reticule. Well, she had told him she would write to him *poste restante*, and he had promised he would reply to her at the château in Pinac-Les-Saules, which was the name of the de Marceau estate. Her father had not forbidden her to write to Edward; that she might do so had probably never entered his head. But if anyone imagined they'd be exchanging love letters they would be wrong. She just wanted to keep in touch with his thoughts, especially if she were to be preoccupied looking after children, even half French ones.

Even so she did feel a little sad, and looked forward to opening his present.

Chapter 3

Le Château de Pinac-Les-Saules

Georgy thought that in England you would not call this 'château' a castle. At home, castles were large and very old. This one was not far from a small village of thatch-roofed houses, most of which had wooden benches outside where the oldest male inhabitants sat and puffed their pipes. On the way, there had been hills and meadows, streams and woods, fig trees in gardens, vines in smaller fields; it all looked a prosperous part of the world. She was told that a little further away there were much larger vineyards. Camille also told Georgy that the de Marceau family used to own many of them, but the Revolution had taken them away and given them to the communes and then to businessmen in Mâcon who were against the 'aristos'.

Mâcon, the nearest large town to the south, had never been Royalist. During the last thirty years these new wine-growers had made money, especially since the first wine auctions had been held at the Hospice de Beaune a year after the *émigrés* had returned. The Count de Marceau had decided it was not worth trying to get them all back but his son Augustin still had hopes of owning some of the better vineyards again one day.

'Not that he knows much about making wine,' added Camille with a shrug. 'He was away in London for much of his childhood and until he was thirty!'

Pinac-Les-Saules was much smaller than any castle Georgy had ever seen. It was more like a manor house, though the style was quite different, the ceilings higher, the rooms larger. It was a pleasant building though, with a large mansard or attic floor, where her own bedroom was to be found, a little tower at one end and a large kitchen garden. At the front were bushes of Celestial roses with their grey-green foliage and pale pink blossoms. They had some of those at home in Yorkshire!

For the first few days Georgy was busy unpacking and trying to break the ice with the children Lucie and Thibault. 'Augustine-Lucie-Gabrielle', being two years older than her brother, was the more amenable. Georgy also wrote a dutiful letter home to reassure her parents of her safe arrival. It would indeed already be known to them, since Camille de Marceau had immediately written to London to assure her own family of it. The Channel crossing had taken eight and a half hours, but Georgy had not been seasick.

She took up her pen the next day to begin a letter to Edward Walker. The more she thought about it, the more she wondered why her father had never rebuked the tutor for 'taking liberties'. Maybe it was because he had not really believed he had? Or Edward had not told her what her father might have said to him?

Papa had obviously believed it was she herself who had been flirting with him. That made her angry.

She was well out of it away from them all.

Dear Edward – or shall I say *cher Monsieur*?
First I must thank you for the book. You could not have chosen better and I only hope you did not lose your own copy to me? I read a little of these *Premières Méditations* every evening. I have learned more verses of *Le Lac* by heart.

She looked up. She wanted to say: 'the poems remind me of you,' but that would be a little too embarrassing, since most of them had love as a subject. It was not that she thought of Edward himself romantically, but he understood her feelings, and doubtless the feelings of Lamartine himself. She went on:

The children eat the last meal of the day with the grown-ups and go to bed at an hour we would call late, and I must soon see their hands are washed before dinner, but having half an hour's freedom I am beginning my first letter to you. I shall describe a few 'impressions' of the kind that would not interest Papa and Mama.

44

We arrived at this 'château', which is quite a way from Mâcon, only three days ago and I am still dazzled by the journey. I wish I had time to describe it all to you, but since you have been to France I expect you can imagine it for yourself. After a good night's sleep I was immediately given the two children to amuse! No rest for the wicked, but so far they appear to be quite reasonable children. Nothing like your own charges, I am thankful to say, though the boy can be a little sulky. The girl, Lucie, is beautiful – a really lovely child with dark ringlets and a heart-shaped face and the biggest eyes you have ever seen. She was quite shy at first but I think I am gaining her confidence. The husband has so far not made an appearance. I thought it a little odd that he should not be here to greet his own wife. I know Papa would have been if Mama had been away so long – but *autres temps autres moeurs* . . . .'

(Later) – I had to break off, and am endeavouring to finish this by the light of a very small candle in my room. It turns out that Monsieur de Marceau is already in Savoy taking a cure for his *foie*. I could not think why he should go to Savoy for his *faith* but then realised they meant his *liver*! I can understand about half of what they say but am determined that within a few weeks I shall understand everything. At least the children understand *me*.

I have already met several friends of the family who seem to drift in and out of the house all day, or arrive in their chaises for a gossip. There is a near neighbour called Hortense Vivier who seems to be somebody's great-aunt. She is always talking about her sister's clever grandson Louis-Marie, (fancy boys being called Mary!), and there is a sort of bailiff, but the servants say he is rich, a Monsieur Jacques Cellard.

The family are to go to Mass tomorrow so I said I would accompany them. I have nothing against Catholics. As you know, I am a Pantheist, like Rousseau.

I gather Monsieur de Marceau is sincerely religious. Madame de Marceau, whom I shall henceforth call Camille when I write to you, is said to be quite pious – '*assez dévote*' but that may just mean that she follows the conventions. I wonder if she changed her religion just to please her new family? M de Marceau returned suddenly yesterday. I do not think his wife expected him and he was very out of humour. At dinner he was talking about his father's estates – at least I think I understood it aright. The family had hoped for the undoing of some land settlement made during the Revolution when their lands were confiscated and they fled to England. I asked Augustin de Marceau how many French people had emigrated. He looked surprised, as if the teapot had spoken (though they do not have a teapot) and after a pause he replied, 'I believe over seventy thousand.' I had not known what to expect but certainly not this rather sallow testy person who fusses a good deal. He looks much older than Camille and scarcely notices his children. He shook hands languidly with me when I was presented to him and thereafter proceeded to ignore me. Well, that may be a good thing; I shall be able to come and go a little more easily if he is not on the look-out for me doing my 'duties'.

Later, his wife told me that people like her father-in-law had not received adequate compensation and there were hundreds of lawsuits going on between returned *émigrés* and the government. I gather they hope the new king will be more generous. Old Count de Marceau was condemned to death but escaped before the sentence could be carried out. Enough of these weighty matters . . . .

I hope soon to take the children on an 'English walk' – that is, to gather wild flowers. Apparently they do not do that here. I have noticed lots of other little things that are different, apart from the food and the wine. They eat a good deal of dark bread and many little round goat cheeses, and sausages and cured hams, and grapes and other fruit, berries and apples and lemons. We have eaten aubergine flan, *terrine de légumes*, and a dish called *tarte jardinière* with asparagus and carrots – all delicious – I did not know vegetables could be so divine – it must be the butter they add! There are fish caught by a servant called Dominique in the small lake nearby – trout, and a sort of tench or perch I have never eaten before that is simply delicious. There is always a stoup of Burgundy, both red and white, on the table and I have taken to wine-drinking immediately, never having drunk such wine before. Up till now I had only tasted a mouthful of claret, and once a thimbleful of Papa's sherry, but not this mellow ruby liquid that goes down so well with the food, or the lovely fruity cold white wine. The children's mama laughed and said I must be careful not to get too great a liking for it or I would be fat before I was forty, not to mention the dangers of drunkenness ... I saw she was teasing me.

The food is what Camille de Marceau calls simple fare but to me it is ambrosial. I have become acquainted with red and green

peppers and olives and many herbs. Garlic flavours dishes wonderfully, and everything is cooked in olive oil; even the chicken from
the farm is basted with it. Of course we have carrots and cauliflow-
ers and onions and apples at home, but not in such abundance.
The asparagus is new to me and the tomatoes and beans taste quite
different – sweeter and redder and greener. The family do not eat
mutton because the pasturage nearby is not suitable for sheep but
they eat a lot of under-cooked beef! It does not taste much like the
roast beef of Olde England. But in general I love the food – it is
not just the taste, but the colour of it, the way it comes to table in
little casseroles or dishes, and you eat one thing, then another, that
charms me. For the first time in my life I am looking forward to the
next meal! Do you know there are peach trees in the orchard – I
gather they will be *white* peaches, like I have never seen before!
They are said to be delicious. I was told I could eat as many as I
cared in August but to see that the children did not overeat.

Except for the Countess's room where the *mobilier* is gold and
curly and decorated, the furnishings are not grand – they say the
family had to start up again when they returned after The Terror
and that they lost a lot of furniture and plate and tapestries. But I
like the country furniture; it is simple and sturdy. We eat – the children and I – off plates with bluebirds painted on them. I said to
them that the bluebird meant happiness – they did not know.

There is the same policy towards my *reading* as towards my
eating. I had not seen many books lying around, and there is no
library as such, but Camille asked me the other day if I would care
to read some of the books her sister had sent on for her. 'I am not
a great reader,' she said, 'but you are welcome to borrow anything
you care to.'

You can imagine how delighted I was. I feel sure that Aunt
Caroline is more intelligent than her sister, my employer, certainly
more of a *reader*, so her taste will be good. I do not mean that I
dislike Camille, who will one day, I suppose, be *Madame la Comtesse*,
for I find her fascinating, but she is so unlike myself or anything I
could become! She slept for most of our journey from England,
said she had a headache. I could not have slept however tired I
was . . . .

(Even later) – This letter threatens to become a novel itself. I
shall send it with the other mail tomorrow though Lord knows
when you will receive it. The great news is that scarcely have I

arrived here than I am to journey with the family *next week* over to Savoy – to Aix on the shores of the very lake of the poem. Augustin de Marceau goes back to Aix tomorrow and we shall rejoin him there. Can you believe that I might even see the Poet! We are to stay until the end of August.

It is strange – scarcely am I become used to this house than I am to leave it for over two months.

In haste –

Yours ever,

Georgy Crabtree.

PS I have been asked to address Camilla as Madame in public but I may call her just 'Camille' in private. She prefers the French name. 'After all, we are distant cousins by marriage,' she said, 'and "Madame" sounds so formal to us English. My husband would prefer to hear you call me Madame, but when he is not there, you need not!'

She has just informed me that *He* – I mean the Poet – will certainly be in Aix very soon. Is that not exciting?

Georgy was in fact enjoying what was to her a new feeling, that of being regarded as an adult. *That* was what she had wanted at home – she saw it all clearly now. She had wanted to be *in charge of herself.* Here she was in charge of two children, and did Camille de Marceau's bidding but Camille treated her as grown-up, and therefore received her devotion.

Camille said that her husband awaited the arrival in Aix of his wife and children with some impatience. He did not like travelling with the children and it was chiefly for his benefit that they all went to Savoy. He was already well established at the pension where they were all to lodge. Georgy had already had the impression he liked his comforts and did not relish being disturbed in his routine. Their arrival – a little late on account of a broken wheel – had put him out, delaying his evening bath, perhaps accounting for the testiness.

Their pension was to be found in the centre of town, very near the thermal establishment. Everything in it appeared plain and serviceable, nothing showy. Georgy was told by Madame de

Marceau that all the furniture in the pension was called 'Savoy Empire'. Georgy had a tiny room next to the children's, furnished with a small bed, a table, a glass, and a chair. There was a crucifix on the wall but there was also a desk, which pleased her. Here she could sit to write her letters, if her duties ever allowed of it. There was so much to do, even with the help of the maids they had brought with them. Camille and her husband had their rooms a floor below hers, and they all dined at a round table in a simple room with a balcony that overlooked the square. The food was ample and simple served on dark brown plates that looked very countrified. There were a few engravings on the walls – one of the Roman arch that was just round the corner from the pension – but nothing to catch the imagination.

Georgy would sit on after the children had gone to bed and Camille was out with friends or 'resting' at the thermal establishment, and think about the Poet or dream over his book of poems. The children were tiring, however good they were, and she needed someone to talk to who was older than nine. Sometimes Célanie, one of the maids they had brought with them from the Château, would come up from the kitchens for a chat. Célanie gossiped a good deal with one of the pension servants, Madeleine.

'I miss Eglantine and that's a fact,' she would say. Eglantine had been left in charge of things in Pinac, being older and more responsible. Georgy found the maid's French a little difficult to understand but picked up many crumbs of information about the family from her. She had the impression from what the maid let slip that her employer, Mme de Marceau, was a little bored. Surely there was more to do here than in the depths of the country?

More often than not though, Georgy would say good-night to Célanie, go to bed looking forward to reading one of the books she had brought with her, and then fall asleep very quickly over it.

Aix: Sunday 10 July 1825
Dear Edward
It seems an age since I last wrote. I have not gone to Mass with the family today – enough is enough! – and I wanted to catch up on my letters, and also be alone for a short time. I find I do need a little time alone to remain rational. I am writing at the desk in my little room here. The pension we are staying in is quite near the one in which the Poet and his family usually stay. There is a court-

yard inside the building and a wooden gallery on the first floor, almost like a chalet, with a view over the lake – which is about half an hour's walk away. Unless it is misty, which fortunately it has been for only one morning so far, whenever you look over in its direction, there is always presented to your view a strange jagged line of mountain against the sky. They call it *la Dent du Chat* – the cat's tooth.

I have not yet set eyes on The Poet but it is true that he will soon be here in town – along with his wife and little daughter. I went down to the lake yesterday with the children and recited his words aloud to the summer sunshine. I could not have believed the place could ever be other than sunny, or produce feelings so despairing . . . .

I must describe the town to you for I do not believe you have ever been here? If my letters bore you, regard them as my diary for I have scarce time at present to write both to myself and to you!

The streets are kept fairly clean in order to attract the visitors who come for their health – the thermal baths are the *raison d'être* of the place. The baths contain both sulphur and alum and this morning I watched animals being cleaned in the 'horse bath'.

All around the town, which is built on a hill that stretches down eventually to the lake, there are vineyards and meadows and orchards which we saw when we came here in the carriage. It is quite a noisy place with many inns and hotels and 'cafés', though I suppose it is less so in winter when all the visitors have gone. There is the smell of the water everywhere, a sort of sulphurous odour that is not unpleasant. There are long rows of poplar trees from the cobbled square in front of the town 'château', all along the lane to the lakeside. It's quite a long walk – over a mile. On the way you can look at the rocky beds of the streams that lead to the lake, and the walnut trees planted near them, sometimes with vines trailing in their branches.

The lake is lovely – quite large, with wooded hillsides on the other bank. Since it is sunny, with calm weather, the waters are a bluey green. I took the children down yesterday again to play on the shore and they sent the carriage for us on the way back since it is too far for their short legs. *I* was quite tired too – children are very exhausting, I find, and I sleep very well!

I was told that, ten years ago, various members of the Bonaparte family stayed in the town. Two were Joséphine and her daughter Queen Hortense of Holland. She was married to Louis Bonaparte, the younger brother of Boney. I do not dare to call him Boney here. However much these Royalists disliked him and were glad to have a Bourbon king back on the throne I think they were also very proud of their little ex-Caporal – at least whilst he won their battles for them.

Savoy is now returned to the brother of Victor Emmanuel, one Charles Félix. I never knew much about these foreign royalties but tales about them make me think they lead more exciting lives than our old King George ever did. The French are always asking me about our Royal Family and about the aristocracy. I know little and care less, but I do not like to hurt their feelings when they take such interest in Perfidious Albion. When they say to me 'Your Prince Regent', they mean our present King – and they always add 'He behaves more like a Frenchman.' I would not have thought he was a person anyone would be proud to be like!

Camille said this morning that a new 'cercle' had just been created in the château in the centre of the town, a sort of club for the rich foreigners who visit the place for their health. Plans are afoot to call it the Royal Foreigners' Club. Céline, another house-maid at the pension, not to be confused with our Célanie, says that there is a gaming circle at the Hotel de la Poste where the 'invalids' go to play games of chance, but this new club according to Camille, who had it from her husband, has a *library* (!) a billiard-room, newspapers, a reading-room, a ball-room and a tiny theatre, as well as a *salle de jeu* for games of chance, and evening concerts. Of course these things are not for young women, or even for women at all, who are only admitted with their husbands and then only at certain times.

I shall add to this missive later – just now I must take the children for their 'constitutional' . . . .

. . . There is an old Roman arch just near where we are staying and they say there are several statues from 200 BC being looked after by some nobleman. I never before realized how close the past is. I know, at home, the past on the moors is much older – from before the dawn of civilization, but here it is *human* past and I have the feeling that the people here were quite civilized when we in Yorkshire were dancing round in woad. I may be wrong of course, I usually am, so forgive me . . . .

When she had been baptized Georgy had been given the female equivalent of the name of both the reigning monarch and his son, but the family held no particular brief for the Hanoverians. Edward Walker had opined that they were for the most part an uneducated and boring bunch. Georgy was patriotic, loved England, or at least that part of it to which she belonged, but was more interested in English poets than English royalty. Now, if they were to ask her about Shakespeare, or Lord Byron, who had perished only the previous year, she would be delighted to oblige. She did know something about the poetry of her own country, not just about Monsieur de Lamartine and his poems. In her reticule she had the precious volume Edward had given her as a keepsake before she left, her little copy of the *Premières Méditations*, so that she might consult it whenever she had a spare moment. She was also reading when time permitted *A History of the Town of Aix* that she had found in a cupboard at the pension. Here she discovered that the ruins of the 200 AD baths – a vast complex – had been found in 1772 underneath the Pension Perrier! They said the water that still gushed up near there was extremely hot. There were both hot and cold baths at the thermal establishment where those taking the cure stood whilst servants poured buckets of water over them. It did not tempt Georgy at all. She had no fervent wish to bathe or be showered with the hot spring water, and it was not considered suitable for the children either.

Anyway she was healthy.

She took her book once or twice to the square near the poplars and read about the past of the place she was in. The Barbarians had sacked the town, but it had recovered, at about the time the last Romans left Yorkshire. Then there seemed to be a long gap. But in 1718, by the Treaty of Utrecht, the Duke of Savoy had received the title of King of Piedmont and Sardinia, and in the last half of the last century, around the time her own parents were born, Victor Amadée the Third had constructed this new thermal establishment.

So many stray facts like this went knocking round in her head, but she realized how very ignorant she was of so many things. The more you knew, the more you knew you did not know . . . . She soon finished the book and wished she dared ask Monsieur de

Marceau if he would borrow another for her from the new 'Cercle' library.

She liked to walk as well as to read; there was little to do in the small amount of free time allowed her but to walk, and read – and write her letters.

'I hope you are not too bored?' said Madame de Marceau one morning.

'Oh no! How could I be bored? There is so much to see and to learn,' replied Georgy enthusiastically.

Camille laughed. Georgy almost asked Camille if the place bored *her*, but thought she had better not enquire.

Camille was thinking, we are lucky with this young woman.

There was a new park where Georgy accompanied the children when the others were at the thermal establishment, and sometimes she would sit on a bench there, as the children played. She had thought of sketching the trees, but knew her attempts would be no more successful than those of her attempts to sketch St Mary's Church in the square across from the château.

Nobody had ever questioned her accompanying the family to church, though they knew she was not of the Faith. She would rather go with them than attend some dull respectable Swiss Calvinist place. When in Rome . . . If they went to Geneva she might visit a Protestant church, she supposed, just for the experience. M de Marceau, the children's papa, was supposed to be very religious, but Georgy had revised her opinion of Camille and come to the conclusion she was not. Perhaps her own family in London had not been very pious.

She was trying to finish her letter to Edward Walker; there was so much she wanted to say.

> Yesterday, Camille as I now call her to myself, since Madame de Marceau is such a mouthful – was talking to a woman friend of hers about the Poet. Monsieur de Lamartine is some sort of cousin of the old Count, twice or thrice removed, and she was certainly having a good gossip about him. I am not sure I understood it all. I was not supposed to be listening, but you cannot help hearing when the windows are open on to the inner balcony and the person in the room below has her windows open too! She was being indiscreet, for she hinted he was 'not always a virtuous young man.'

Somebody had told her that the Poet had had a son with a
woman who was married to a friend of his! This was some time
before the Poet was married and before he met the Lady of the
Lake. I do not know whether or not to believe it . . . .

On reflection Georgy scored out the last five lines; you could
not write such things to a man, she supposed.
She went on:

Camille will read a novel occasionally. She read a novel by Jane
Austen in French, with illustrations, called *La Famille Elliot* because
she says she must improve her *French!* I realized it was the novel
Persuasion. I do not expect you to have read it. Usually it is ladies
who read novels, but I think it is quietly brilliant, even in French.
There is nobody here with whom I might discuss the ideas that
come to me from reading. Camille finishes a book – and that is
that. I would love to hear the Poet speak of poetry, but I wish *you*
were here so that I might have a rational conversation.
  I hope my epistles do not bore you too much. I expect they may
since you know about the World and I am only just beginning in it.
  People here gamble a good deal. The maids tell me of the sums
of money lost overnight. Everyone in the town seems to know their
guests' business! I suppose there is more gambling than at home,
though Papa always said there was much gambling in York, if not
as much as in London ... I believe that Monsieur de Marceau
gambles, and his wife does not like it . . . .

Georgy put her letter aside, feeling a little disloyal to literature,
and wishing she might quote a line from M de Lamartine: *Un seul
être vous manque et tout est dépeuplé* – would be more than a slight
exaggeration. It was not true either; she did not miss Edward in a
sentimental way, only his conversation, and encouragement, and
his lively mind.

It was all very well writing to Edward Walker and describing the
weather, which was excellent – warm but not overpoweringly hot;
or describing the way the peasants looked as they worked in the
fields; or the delicious silk gowns of the rich visitors; or the flowers Lucie and Thibault gathered in the meadows near the lake; or
how the stars looked on a clear night; or the effect the smell of

incense and candles had on her at mass in the little church in the square; or the pension meals, which were ample, if not quite so tasty as at those at the château; or the furniture of Savoy Empire style in the rooms; or the pension itself which, like most of those in the town, was built around an interior courtyard, a wooden balcony linking all the rooms on each floor. It all interested her, but the most important parts of her letters were her descriptions of her own reactions to everything in this new country, and why should Edward Walker be interested in *them?*

One morning she and the maid Célanie walked with the children to the village of Tresserve on a little hill a mile or so away. Georgy had been told that the Poet had actually composed his 'Lake' poem here under the shade of some chestnut trees! It was here that he and his love had been wont to walk and sit. Georgy very much wanted to drink in this atmosphere.

When they arrived, the children naturally wanted to run up and down and she found it hard to concentrate on the poem with Thibault's shrieks and shouts ringing round them. At least the child was now less sulky, but you could not concentrate on atmosphere with Thibault around. Savoy appeared to have released his energies.

Another day they walked to the lake shore. Lucie consented to having a large sun-bonnet tied under her chin and was given a little sketch-book and a piece of charcoal to amuse herself with. For a girl of nine she was precociously clever but did not seem to be vain.

The children's English was improving by leaps and bounds. In exchange they told Georgy the words for the flowers and insects she knew only by their English names. Thibault wished to paddle in the lake but Georgy had been told to take care, for the lake shelved quite deeply not far from the shore. Fortunately, Célanie was there to help, so she and the maid had perforce to play a game of hide and seek until they all threw themselves down exhausted.

Georgy had brought her book of poems with her and managed to reread *Le Lac* as she looked at its blue summer ripples. She decided that the poem was not just about the lake but paralleled its different weathers through the changing moods of the poet. No sooner however had this thought begun to crystallize than Thibault disappeared and she had to get up and go to look for him. Not much chance of reading when you were in charge of a seven-year-old boy. On finally coming across the boy throwing pebbles into the lake round a bend in the shore Georgy put her book away for the day.

'Your papa will take you out in a rowing-boat,' she promised the child.

'Ah, he will let the servants do that!' said Célanie. 'Monsieur is not strong and the children give him a headache.'

Perhaps he was just lazy, not liking to exert himself, thought Georgy. She could not really blame him.

The day after the visit to the lake shore, Georgy received a reply from Edward Walker to her first letters. It was brought by the count's servant among the papers and messages for the family that had arrived in Pinac since they had left for Aix.

Monsieur de Marceau himself presented it to her: 'A letter from England,' he said in English, a language he spoke quite well though never now to his wife. Georgy wondered not for the first time why he could not speak it to his children instead of keeping her in the family for that purpose. But Augustine de Marceau took little interest in his daughter and spoke to his son usually only to tell him to make less noise.

She had no time to read the letter until after supper. Camille and her husband were out together for once at the Circle, so she looked forward to an hour or two's peace in the pension.

Dear Georgina

I was glad to hear from you with all the details of yr. long journey and yr. impressions of France. Now you will be in Savoy and I trust still enjoying the novelty of a new place. All goes on much the same here. Your papa and mama miss you, I think. Yr. cousins continue also with much the same habits, but you will not want to hear about that I am sure.

I wonder if I ever spoke to you of the *Philosophes* – the great men of the Enlightenment, who are still needed in this new age? I was reading the other evening the programme of one French nobleman who was guillotined for his pains by those he had considered his friends. Idealists are always destroyed when they try to join themselves to Revolution, as I have often told you. You do better to stick to your poets. After sketching the unregenerate past, this noble Marquis had a programme for the future not unlike that of many of the people a relative of mine once met in Paris. I believe I may have spoken to you about these men – and women – of the Enlightenment? But all came to naught when the idealists were vanquished by the men of violence.

I hope that you are not finding your Royalists too dreary for you. But I don't think you will, for you have the temperament that always finds interest in the lives of others, however different their characters from your own. Be careful, Georgy, not to be led astray by extremes in any camp.

I should be pleased to hear more from you on the family and your impressions of Savoy though letters are taking two weeks or more to arrive. Take the opportunity to experience the Catholic Church. It is not so powerful in France as once it was, but let us hope that the excesses of The Terror have perhaps been a salutary lesson for both the believers and the *sans-culottes*.

Your own country still fears rebellion, as well it might, but I do not think we shall have such scenes as once took place in Paris. Rather our 'revolution', now that men like Wilberforce have had their way, has been a puritanical one, enjoining upon all Englishmen pious and godly behaviour.

I wonder if you will meet your Poet – whose work I much enjoyed reading with you. I hope the little book is still absorbing you. It seems I cannot help wishing to educate!

For which you must forgive your faithful tutor

Yours ever

Edw. Walker

She was a little disappointed, but what had she expected? He certainly took an interest in her opinions.

Chapter 4

Marianne de Lamartine was to arrive in a few hours on the main square of Aix where she would lodge at the Pension Perret. As well as its many rooms above, it had a café on the ground floor and a room that contained what its proprietor was pleased to call 'My exhibition of Natural Sciences'.

Jean-Jacques Perret had little to do with the organization of the visitors' and pensionnaires' lives, for his three formidable sisters were in charge of all that. He was more often to be found talking in the café, where he employed a head waiter named Jacotot, one of the most popular men in Aix, liked both by its inhabitants and its visitors. Jean-Jacques knew all the gossip and kept an eye on the ups and downs of the emotional stock exchange.

Marianne, who was born Mary Ann, needed a change as much as her husband did, and she would be accompanied by little three-year-old Julia. For the present, however, Julia's papa, Alphonse de Lamartine, was walking alone by the lake.

Although she said nothing, he knew his wife could not help but feel his past should have been consumed in his *Méditations* and no longer hover like an unsubstantial wraith over their lives. It had given him for one thing the notion that their daughter should be named Julia, the English version of his beloved Julie's name. That had been a mistake, almost cruel of him, he felt. Pray God Julia would stay strong and healthy, for she was their only child now. Their first child, a little son, had died in his second year.

Nine years ago he had walked here with Julie Charles, his 'Elvire'. Eighteen months later, she died in Paris.

Nine years ago: the same lake, the same vines, walnut trees, meadows, mountains; the same sky, the same light and shade . . . . Except that it was never quite the same, was constantly renewed.

If anything could make him feel sixteen again it was this lake, this light, this sky . . . .

He often thought how cruel fate had been to allow him to help save Julie Charles from drowning, only to have her die so soon afterwards of that 'decline' already in evidence when he met her, for she had been an invalid. Indeed, they had both been in Aix for their health; only he had recovered. Julie's decline had been years in the making, had been the reason for her coming to Aix. His own suffering from palpitations had driven him to take the cure in the same place, stay in the same pension . . . . Fortunately he had never suffered from the consumption that had killed his Elvire and had also put an end to the lives of two of his young sisters last year. 1824 had been a terrible year for the family, especially for his mother. The two girls, both only in their early twenties, had died within a few months of each other.

Julie had been his inspiration; his feelings for her had breathed life into all his first collection of verse, poems that had made such a stir, made him famous – and not only in France. Two years ago now he had brought out a second volume and was now publishing longer poems. He had not been idle: only two or three months ago he had published a poem to the memory of Byron, perished last year at Missolonghi, and followed it with a long religious poem. Oh, he was ambitious but poetry was not the whole of his life; he wanted action too.

What had Julie, apart from her manifestation as Elvire, really been to him? Because their love had not been given the opportunity to last, it had an eternal existence as a passionate romance. They were using the word 'romantic' about him now, as well as about his writing.

Elvire would go on living in literature, but if his wife only knew it, in no way had Julie been the most passionate of his real life erotic attachments. She would remain an inspiration; one day he might even write the story of their meeting in prose rather than verse. Her memory would always remain fresh, he was sure of that, for other memories had stayed with him of other loves, earlier passions more innocent, later ones more sensual.

If he was walking alone here by the lakeside now, just for an hour or two, it was not to think of Julie, though it might seem he returned to the place precisely to do that, and luxuriate in melancholy.

He found himself thinking of all the many women he had desired and the several with whom he had been in love; it was a self-indulgence, but it was only for this little period by himself before the others arrived. Afterwards he would return to the pension to carry on his family holiday.

There had been Lucy, and Henriette, before his little Neapolitan Antoniella, who had died when she was only twenty-two. He seemed to remember that was in 1816, scarce ten years since, the year before Julie herself had died – but his chronology was always weak. Sometimes his life appeared in bright scenes linked by months of desolation and he wondered where he had been, what he had been doing.

It must be thirteen years ago that he had left Italy, but as the years had passed, because Antoniella too had died, she had remained especially present to his mind. Just as he would never forget his love for Julie, so he would never forget his feelings for Antoniella, and hers for him. One day he might even write about her too, as he had written about Julie! He would have to find another name for her.

After the Italian girl, there had of course been Nina de Pierreclau; and Nina's son Léon, was also his own son, the person on whose account he felt the most guilt. He must now be twelve years old? Would he ever dare tell his wife about him? Léon and Nina were at present far away in the Argentine, but one day in the not too distant future he would have to do something for the boy. He had no other son now but this bastard one, with whose mother he had never been in love. Nina would not go into a decline – she was far too robust!

But it had not been Antoniella, nor Julie, nor Nina, who had preoccupied his senses the year before he married his English Mary Ann, whom he would see within an hour or two.

The Italian Princess Lena de Larche had been the most passionate woman he had ever known, and the most beautiful, and he had been told that she wanted to see him again. He was waiting to hear if he had been appointed secretary of the French Legation in Florence, where ruled the great Duke of Tuscany. If he were – and he wanted the post very much – he would be sure to see Lena. But he was determined not to succumb, he would resist her enticements. He had sworn that was all over: the wildest sensual episodes of his man's life, absorbing his body and soul even more than the little Italian girl of his young manhood. He remembered the violence of the passion Lena had aroused in him – *she* had seduced him! But even to remember was dangerous . . . . Six years, was it, since he had met her? Three years after Elvire had died? Strange how, like Antoniella, Elvire in death was closer to his *spirit* than the vibrant Lena, whose presence could yet reanimate all his urgent desires, bring back to life his passion. She was beautiful and she was intelligent ... from the very first day of their meeting he had been overcome by dizzy desire and an overwhelmingly violent need, the more ardent since it was involuntary, nothing like the love that had been aroused in him by Elvire here by the lake. Lena had been – still was – for him the epitome of voluptuousness and mysterious glamour; Lena was the one who had scorched him! Why had he suffered such extremes of desire when he made love to her? He had never felt such passion before or since. Sometimes his life, his good sober life, seemed pointless when he could not possess her for ever. But in the end he had forced himself to give her up as a mistress. He felt no guilt over his sensual dereliction, only an enormous disquiet about his own sensual appetites.

No – no – no! – he must not think of Lena. He was married, and all his passionate attachments and even his *petits amours* were perforce over. Marriage had saved him from himself, had put order into a dissolute life. He would always admire and appreciate Lena's beauty – would even like to keep her as a friend, if that were possible, though it might take a good deal of persuasion for her to agree. Was it ever possible for a sincere friendship to rise from the ashes of a sensual passion? He would have to share her with her circle of admirers for she did not lack male company, beautiful as she was.

Their mutual passion had been too physical, too all-engulfing, too *mad* to have lasted at that pitch. Lena would have – indeed had – worn him out. He must try not to remember their month together in Burgundy where she had followed him, and they had stayed together at that inn, must not think of that bedroom with the sky-blue curtains . . . .

In any case their love affair would have inevitably ended. Even if he had not married a year later a woman who was as intelligent if not so beautiful. He must stop thinking about women and think about his happy childhood in Milly, an infancy he wanted to recreate for his little daughter. His father had been forced to retire there after being condemned to death, as so many had been, but saved at the last moment by the decree of 9 Thermidor.

He must not think about those times either; he must concentrate on his little family and their future.

One day he intended to enter public life – it might be sooner rather than later, if his submission to the government to represent his country in Florence succeeded. Tuscany was not Revolutionary Paris, but Tuscany and Florence held Lena; he must not return to thinking about what he had lost, must direct his thoughts to his future career. He was thirty-five; it was about time he had one. Whilst waiting he would continue to write, for words came easily to him. He was a lucky man. He knew he was handsome too, but tried not to be vain; that he was beloved by his family, a good horseman, a man with a good reputation, all that counted, even if few people knew of his deeper insecurities . . . . Yes, he would continue to do what he was best at – writing – and look forward to public service.

He threw a pebble into the lake. It made the tiniest plop and then the waters closed over it as it rejoined the millions of other pebbles down at the bottom of the deep waters.

Lena would not die young. Like Nina only in this, she was not the kind of woman to go into a decline. But, full of life, and will, and beauty as she was, he'd never write another poem directly to Lena, or about her. He had already used his experience of passion with her in his poem *Enthusiasm*, written when he determined to abandon that part of his life dedicated to passion and to devote himself to his forthcoming marriage with Mary Ann. As for Nina, she had interested him at one time, though he now regarded his affair with her as a mistake. But in the unaccountable way of doing things that Nature had, his own lust and Nina's mild adultery had led to Léon. He was determined not to let the child suffer.

All these philanderings were over, all over; he might have learned his true nature through Lena, but that sort of love was too consuming, would swallow up all the rest of his life. Even before he met her he had already sworn to cease his endless promiscuity. Two years after meeting her he was married, three years after he was a family man.

He threw another pebble and murmured to the waves: *I am a*

poet with two collections of verse under my belt and others to appear any moment.

Answer came from the lake: *The past is the past, however much you may dip into its deep well for your writing.*

But just now and then, to hold on to his inner life, he would allow himself to remember his first thirty years, and the act of memory would bring them all back again, and bring back his loves, Lena the most dazzling of all. Forgive me that weakness, he muttered to himself. You must live now in the present – and the future – for the sake of Mary Ann and little Julia. You are an honourable man and they depend on you.

Neither must he think about his sisters' decline and death, or the death of his own baby boy. Such things were tormenting and he must cheer himself up for the sake of others.

He turned and walked away from the shore. He would concentrate this summer on repose and on planning new work. There were letters to write, books to read. Young Victor Hugo had written to him again, calling him his 'idol'! Ridiculous! but if people saw him as an innovator ...? He had appreciated the energy of the *Odes* of the twenty-year-old Victor, who was most decidedly set for fame, no doubt about that. Fancy a young poet of only twenty-three being 'poet in residence' at the coronation of Charles X! Was he jealous of him?

But was he not himself already a chevalier de la Légion d'Honneur, making up a little for his failure to become a member of the Académie . . . .

The fresh air had done him good ... and the hour or so alone. He had sorted out his priorities and made a few promises to himself.

His servant would still be waiting on the lane with the carriage but he intended to make his own way to the upper town. His dear dog Fido was being brought in the other carriage with Marianne and Julia. How he looked forward to a reunion with him: he'd exercise him down here tomorrow.

Alphonse walked over to the servant and told him to return to the pension, then he made his own way there. As he passed by, several people turned to stare at the tall handsome figure. Some might even know who he was, may even have read his verse.

Georgy Crabtree saw an excessively good-looking man in his mid thirties, wavy-haired, with a straight nose, small ears, hair curling on his forehead, a mobile mouth, a smile on his lips, but with an air of separateness about him, as he turned into the street behind their own pension.

She knew immediately who it was.

Georgy had been much preoccupied with the children. Thibault had run a temperature and a cold and consequently whined a good deal. It had been pleasant to go out for walks with Lucie alone, but then she had caught her brother's chill, so Georgy had perforce to occupy the little boy, who was easily distracted. She read him English fairy tales as he was not well enough to be up to the *Petit Précepteur*, whose vocabulary they were struggling through.

A day or two after Georgy's sighting of the Poet, the little girl was still convalescing, and they were all eating luncheon, an ample repast which always began at twelve o'clock sharp, when Camille de Marceau turned to Georgy, saying:

'I have had a note from our English neighbour, the one who is married to Monsieur de Lamartine. She invites me to take a dish of English tea with her tomorrow afternoon at the Pension Perrier. Would you like to accompany me? Ladies always take their maids on such occasions and mine would be tongue tied in English. Célanie can look after the children instead for an hour or two.'

Georgy thought, as her *maid*? Well, I suppose I would go as the dog to meet *that* lady! I wonder if her husband will be there? As she was trying to assemble French words to express her delight, for Camille always spoke French at table, the lady went on:

'I thought, she might like to have a little conversation with you. I don't know how many other women she will have invited. I didn't go last year, but as her husband is a distant cousin of Augustin's, I cannot get out of it!'

'Will Monsieur accompany us then?'

'Oh dear no! Men don't go to such simple occasions. I expect he will be at the Cercle as usual.'

'So M de Lamartine will not be there either?'

'I should not think so – though they say he prefers to live quite simply when he is here in Aix.'

'I should love to accompany you,' Georgy replied.

Dear Edward,

I had almost finished my letter to you when yours arrived here. I'm sorry I haven't replied before now, and I enclose it with this one. I was delighted to hear from you, but I am so busy looking after the children here in Aix that I fall asleep as soon as my head touches the pillow and can read and write only in the afternoon. Thibault takes a little nap then so that he is not too tired to eat his dinner in the evening. Their mother insists on this – it helps to keep her servants happy, I expect.

The great news is that the family of Lamartine: the poet, his wife, and his daughter are now all lodging in the town, and my employer has been invited to Madame de L's afternoon-tea gathering at their pension! Camille has asked me very kindly if I would like to go along with her – as a sort of companion – since Madame de L. is English and might like to meet another English person.

I can't help wondering if He might be there. Shall I dare tell him I have read *Le Lac*? (that is if I am allowed to say a word to him!)

In the moments I have had to myself and sometimes when I have been walking with the children, I have been thinking about Life. There is so much to see even in a little place like this – with people going on with their lives knowing nothing about England or probably even their own past. It is Time that is the Great Enemy, I think – as the Poet said. It will *not* come to a full stop for a while so we can all stay the same for a bit. I have always felt that. I don't want things to change, yet I know they must because of all that is wrong with the world, all that you have so often spoken to me about. I was reading a *revue* that was left in the salon by one of the other guests, or should I say 'patients'? They were writing about Byron, who is all the rage here, and called him a 'Romantic'. I don't really understand what that means. Does it mean that what Byron writes has no foundation in reality, or just that he has a sort of imaginative extravagance? I think I remember your telling me once that your favourite Coleridge used that word of poetry, if not of himself, and now it is all the rage.

Byron was not religious, was he? I have been thinking about that too – having been a few times to Mass here with the family. It is all very beautiful, but does not seem to connect with what I feel about God. I think it is the women here who are the ones who are religious.

65

Other times I think about the tiniest atoms that all make up the world, lodged in cells like those in a honeycomb and I think how they all fit together, and wonder if there is a pattern to it and a pattern in our brains? I am remembering Cowper's: 'The cells where Mem'ry sleep ...' What a lovely thought!

I wish I understood more about all the new inventions too. I'm sorry if I sound tipsy – or mad – but there is nobody here to talk to about such things . . . .

She put down her pen. She supposed she really did write nonsense? Edward Walker might not mind – he had previously enjoyed that sort of conversation with her. She would finish her letter when she had seen the Poet.

Chapter 5

The great day came when Georgy walked along with Camille de Marceau to the Pension Perrier to Marianne de Lamartine's At Home.

'She was really a Mary Ann,' Camille was saying on the way there, 'but like myself she is trying to be *complètement française.*'

Georgy was nervous, hoping against hope that the lady's husband would also be present. She had even ventured at luncheon to say once again to Camille that she would love to meet the great man.

'*You* have met him, Madame. Is he handsome?'

'Oh, terrifically,' said Camille rather absent-mindedly. She added as she slowly swallowed a grape: 'My husband tells me he resembles his own mama who is a very handsome lady – he met her a year or two ago in Mâcon.'

To meet a poet's wife was doubtless enough of an honour for a young provincial English girl, and with that Georgy might have to be content. She found it hard not to betray her excitement as they arrived at the Pension Perrier and were ushered up a wooden staircase, from which you could see a sand-laid inner courtyard. The house was larger than it appeared from the street. The staircase led to an open landing and a balcony that went round the whole of the first floor.

They turned left and went past two or three doors before Camille knocked at the next one. It was opened by a thin girl with frizzy hair who curtsied and said: '*Entrez, si'l vous plaît.*'

Camille handed her her card. They could hear the girl talking in a high voice from inside the inner door and the murmur of a low-voiced reply. Then she opened the door to them again and they went in.

There was a tall lady standing by the table, a lady with an oval face and thick brown wavy hair. She was wearing a pretty blue cotton dress with a lace frill at the hem, perhaps a little formal for four o'clock, but then, as Georgy knew, the English tended to suit themselves.

Camille de Marceau performed introductions, saying Georgy was 'a young English relative who is helping me with the children.' Georgy performed her best curtsey.

The woman had a kind expression on her face, though it was perhaps a little sad. She had a high forehead, calm brown eyes, slightly flushed cheeks and a long nose. Her neck too was long and graceful. When she spoke Georgy could see that two of her front teeth were slightly crossed. She tried not to stare, but it was exciting to see what sort of woman the Poet had married!

An inner door opened and another woman came in with a little girl. This was Julia, a lovely little creature about three years old. Her fine baby hair was in fat little ringlets and she was wearing white pantaloons and little pink slippers.

'Bonjour,' said Georgy.

The little girl looked surprised. After a pause she said: 'Hello.'

'She speaks English as well as French,' said her mother. Nobody else seemed to be expected – were there to be no other guests?

'Do you always speak English to her then?' asked Camille.

'Oh yes, Madame. Her father wishes her to speak both languages, and I am sure he would like her also to speak Italian one day too! That is my husband's favourite language!'

Little Julia de Lamartine was tall for her age and very pretty, with dark deep-set eyes, a straight nose and a rosebud mouth. Did she look like her father? wondered Georgy.

'Your cheeks are quite flushed, my dear,' said her mother and drew the child to her. The maid, or nanny, stood by respectfully.

'Oh, Madame Lamartine,' said Georgy impulsively, 'my young charge, Lucie, Madame's daughter, would love to play with your little one, I am sure!'

Both Camille and Marianne de Lamartine looked rather surprised that the English girl had spoken, and in French too.

'Perhaps she is a little young for Mademoiselle de Marceau. I will ring for tea,' said Marianne. Inclining her head gracefully towards Camille, she said quietly, 'I am so glad you could come. None of the other English people is here at present and there is a cold going round among the Savoyards which I feared Julia might catch, until the other guests called off their visit for another day. There is just one young man I am expecting – a distant relative of my husband's – but he may have forgotten . . . .'

'Yes, my children have had this very chill,' said Camille sitting down at a little table. Georgy remained standing, smiling at Julia.

'You may bring your daughter to see Lucie whenever you wish – she has now recovered from her chill,' said Camille.

Marianne inclined her head gracefully.

'I was going to ask you to show us some of your sketches. I told my young companion how well you drew and painted,' said Camille, trying once more. Her compatriot was rather reserved, but it was probably shyness.

'Oh, I have nothing new. I am intending this summer to sketch my daughter,' said Marianne. 'Tell me, Madame, have you read anything of interest recently? There seems little here in the Cercle library.' She was clearly making an effort.

So she was a reader, thought Georgy. Camille looked a little blank but hastened to say that Georgy was the bookworm. She appeared to be making a big effort to present her 'maid' in a good light!

They went on to speak of the curate at the church in Aix and Georgy realized the lady was truly religious. Intellectual, but religious. She must keep quiet, hold her tongue, for she had remembered that the lady had turned Catholic when she married the Poet. How truly religious was *he*?

She liked Marianne de Lamartine, half listened to the women's conversation as she took Julia and sat with her in the window to amuse her with a book of fairy stories she found on the table. She was a bright child, asked many questions. Georgy had just begun to tell her the story of *Little Red Riding Hood* when there was a knock at the door. The maid appeared at the inner door of the chamber and Marianne signalled to her to answer the knock. A thin pale young man was standing on the threshold.

'*Entrez-donc, Monsieur*,' said the hostess, and then, hurriedly to Camille, as the maid ushered him in: 'He is the son of a distant cousin of my husband – who I gather is also great-nephew to your husband's Aunt Hortense. I had hoped he would join us – and here he is.' She presented him to the rest of the company, Julie included, who clapped her hands, probably pleased to see a young man, her father being the only male she saw much of. Georgy looked forward to speaking to Aunt Hortense's 'clever great-nephew' of whose brilliance she was always boasting.

'Monsieur Louis-Marie des Combes – Madame de Marceau – Miss Georgina—' She turned to Georgy: 'You must excuse me – I don't know your English surname.'

Well, she certainly wasn't being treated as the maid. Perhaps it had just been one of Camille's jokes? Louis-Marie bowed low and Georgy felt he might snap in two.

The pension servant then wheeled in a kettle that had had boiling water poured into it in the kitchen. The young man being disposed in a high-backed chair, Mme Lamartine busied herself brewing the English drink.

'Have you tasted tea before?' Georgy asked the young man.

'Of course.' He inclined his head. 'My mama made me drink it last year to purge the blood.'

Tea as a medicine was a novel idea, though Georgy already drank a lime-flower tisane.

'Oh dear, have you been ill?' she asked before she could stop herself. She was aware that she tended to ask personal questions of new acquaintances too early on in the proceedings. But the young man did not seem to mind. He started a reply at the same time as his hostess.

'Louis-Marie had the fever last year—'

'All my family have suffered from distemper of the blood—'

'But you are better now – from the fever?'

This Louis-Marie had a crumpled face; he needed smoothing down, as you might do a screwed up piece of paper. She thought, he needs a magic potion to set him to rights again. Was a 'distemper of the blood' a serious matter? Fevers were serious.

Mme Lamartine said a little too quickly: 'You are quite recovered now, Monsieur, I believe?' and Georgy saw her glance quickly and involuntarily at her little daughter. She must be especially worried lest her only surviving child caught an infection.

Julia said, 'Please, man, do you know Red Riding Hood?' Louis-Marie looked puzzled.

'Le Petit Chaperon Rouge,' said Georgy.

He smiled and he had quite a pleasant smile. 'Oh – yes, of course – my nurse used to read to me from Perrault when I was a baby—'

'I am not a baby,' said Julia firmly.

'Oh no, I did not mean it was just a story for babies!'

Georgy was thinking: Madame doesn't want to let her daughter out of her sight or she would not have her stay for this grown-up tea-party even if the French were less inclined to banish their children to the nursery for meals.

'Shall I take Julia for a walk?' suggested Georgy to Camille in an undertone. 'The fresh air—'

'Wait, we shall drink our tea first – her mama will probably send her off to the kitchens in a moment to drink her milk.'

Georgy took up the picture book and showed it again to the child. Camille was now trying to find something to say to the young man about Great-Aunt Hortense. Their hostess was also able to discuss the young man's family, which she did in detail.

After a preparatory clearing of the throat, Louis-Marie, who Georgy thought must be about twenty-five, ventured: 'Shall we have the pleasure of seeing your distinguished husband, Cousin Alphonse, this afternoon, Madame?'

'He will return at six – it is his usual custom.'

'Then I shall hope to greet him. It is two years since my family saw his parents and all his sisters in Mâcon. Papa and Maman wished me to convey their good wishes to you both. I had a letter from Mama only yesterday. She hopes Madame de Cessiat and Madame de Coppens are well.' He paused. 'We heard the sad news last year of Césarine and her sister – Madame de Vignet and Madame de Montherot. Little Sophie is, I believe, not yet married?'

'No, Sophie is still recovering from her sisters' deaths,' replied Marianne stiffly, 'and my husband is still mourning his two sisters.'

Georgy wondered what the poet's sisters had died of. Since Louis Marie was still looking expectant and Marianne was obviously unwilling to enlarge upon their tragedies, turning to Louis-Marie Georgy put in her own oar.

'Your own family do not come to Aix?' she asked him.

'No, no – only myself – to take the cure. *They* are all hale and hearty. Only *I* have the misfortune to be a sufferer.'

Georgy knew they were supposed to feel sorry for him and she did, a little, but he had been tactless over the dead sisters. What really ailed him? Maybe he was like her Aunt Charlotte, suffering from low spirits, if not rheumatism.

'I hear the baths are excellent for rheumatism,' she said to Marianne as soon as the thought came into her head.

'Indeed they are,' replied that lady as she began to pour from an English teapot.

'And for the liver and spleen,' added Louis-Marie earnestly, determined to show he was the expert on the Thermal Establishment.

The maid was now handing round small shallow cups of pleasantly scented tea and a plate of tiny macaroons.

'*Maman*, I want some of those,' said Julia, pointing.

'You may have *one*, chérie.'

'And the drink! The drink!'

'You are becoming too excited. Joséphine, you can bring in Julia's milk.'

Louis-Marie cleared this throat and said: '*Chère cousine*, would you mind very much if I too reverted to childhood and drank a cup of milk?'

'Why no, of course not – it is good for building the bones. Joséphine, fetch two mugs of the fresh milk they brought down from the farm today.'

'Thank you – I do find English tea rather strong. I prefer lime-flower – and camomile in the evening.'

He might be only twenty-five but he talked like somebody twice that age, thought Georgy. The same thought must have flitted through Camille's head for she raised one eyebrow, a trick she had, and allowed her glance to rest upon Georgy for a moment.

'And you, Mademoiselle?' said Louis-Marie, once the ladies had drunk their tea and nibbled their macaroons and he had sipped his milk as if it were ambrosia. Julia had been taken out of the room by the maid to wash her hands. 'Are you also an admirer of my cousin's verse?"

She did not reply at first but the two women were now engaged in quiet conversation, probably about the dead sisters or the duties of mothers, and she was left by the window with the young man.

Decidedly an odd tea party. She asked the young man: 'M de Lamartine is *your* distant cousin but he is the distant cousin of M de Marceau as well – how are you related to each other?'

'I am a cousin on my mother's side – she is cousin *germaine* to Alphonse's father. M de Marceau is related to Alphonse through his father who is related to the poet's mother. On the other hand my father is nephew to Tante Hortense – whom I believe you may have met?'

He said this quite pleasantly but in a rather pedantic way. Georgy was to discover that whatever you asked Louis-Marie was given due consideration before a lengthy and instructive answer followed. Still, it was useful to learn all these words for relationships.

'Have you come across the verse of my cousin M de Lamartine, Mademoiselle?' he asked.

'Yes, Monsieur, I have read your cousin's verse,' she admitted.

'He is translated into English?'

'I'm not sure – I read the poems in French.'

He did not ask her at first what she thought of them but said, 'Yes, you do speak our language quite well. You are here for the cure?'

'No, I am engaged to speak English to Mme de Marceau's children.'

'And you have a little leisure in which to read and perfect your French grammar?'

'Not much – but I read the *Premières Méditations* before I ever came to France. My – tutor – introduced me to them. Have you read any of our English poets?'

'Your Lord Byron of course! I write a little myself,' he added with an air of modesty she could not help regarding as false. Why did she come to such swift judgements of others? It was a fault. She resolved to like this young man who could not surely be as boring as he looked, if he read Byron and dabbled in verse himself?

'Have you published? Perhaps you have had advice from your illustrious relative?'

He answered the second part of her question. 'Certainly he has advised me to wait before committing my words to public print – after all he was thirty before his own first volume appeared!'

'Then you have time enough.'

'I should like to read some of my verse to you Mademoiselle. Do you ever walk by the château in the evening under the poplars? Several of my co-pensionnaires are wont to take a stroll there after supper when the weather is fine – and some of the young ladies come with their chaperones—'

'Oh, I am needed after supper to help my charges to bed – you see I do not only speak English to them! But I do walk from time to time under the poplars in the square – our pension is quite near. Or I take the children for walks in the park during the day. I like to get some fresh air, and as I am not exactly a servant I do not have to work every minute of the day! The weather has been so marvellous for walks!'

'Then I shall look out for you – it is a pity you do not take the baths – they would do you much good—'

'I think poetry does me more good,' said Georgy.

Just then, footsteps were heard on the stairs and the door was quietly opened. A tall man was standing under the lintel.

'Alphonse! How very nice – you are early,' said his wife, 'and so you may greet our visitors,' she concluded, perhaps reminding him in case he had forgotten.

'We were just about to go,' said Camille.

Louis-Marie was looking overcome, staring at M de Lamartine with a look Georgy could only describe as one of hungry worship.

Introductions were again performed: much bowing, curtseying. She could not help staring herself at the tall handsome figure who appeared neither shy nor put out and who said, 'I apologize for disturbing your party.' He had an easy manner but under it she thought she sensed a certain distancing, a certain wariness. What should she say to the great man now she was in the same room as genius?

Her mind was a confused mixture of his words about love and the sight of his wife sitting there, and his little daughter. The ordinariness of the scene, even its banality – all that talk of tea and cousins – contrasted with the impassioned stanzas she knew so well.

'Where is Fido?' asked Marianne.

'I sent him to the kitchens for a bone.'

'My husband goes nowhere without his dog.'

Georgy knew you could not suddenly start talking to a poet about his poetry. She was no one to him, just an English girl who knew more about him than he would ever want to know about her. Why indeed should she think she 'knew' him because she and Edward had read *Le Lac* together and she had learned so much of it by heart? A poet had to have an ordinary life too, like other people, she realized suddenly. Apart from his talent – or genius – he was a man like others; his words were not *him*. Yet a poet wrote for others, not just for himself – or why would be bother publishing his words?

M de Lamartine sat down, stretched out his long legs in their elegant moleskin trousers and smiled at the company. Then: 'Where is Julia?'

'With Joséphine – she has had her milk,' answered his wife.

It was true, he was excessively handsome.

His distant cousin Louis-Marie was still staring at him intensely. Eventually Alphonse sensed his concentration and asked politely how were Cousins Léonie and Gustave.

'They are well, sir and I hope you too are in good health?' Oh Lord, was he about to mention the two dead sisters?

But even Louis-Marie sensed it would not be a suitable occasion to mention such things, though it was clear that talk of health was more than a convention for the young man.

'Passably,' replied the poet. 'Are you taking the cure, Madame?' he said turning to Camille.

'We come for my husband,' she replied shortly. Then, thinking perhaps she had seemed offhand, she added: 'I do take some baths – I suppose it does good?'

'And your husband – Augustin – is well?'

'Tolerably.'

Georgy hearing all this thought, well, the poet's health is passable and the count's tolerable which comes to much the same thing. But the poet looks much healthier than my employer. I wonder what he came here for in the first place? Surely his lungs are not affected?

'And your little ones? I seem to remember your husband telling me last year of your son's measles. I have not yet seen Augustin at the Club.'

'Thibault? Yes, he was ill, but is now completely recovered. The children have had colds but that is quite usual.'

Oh dear, Georgy reflected, his little boy died. Was it something the baths could have cured? Marianne was looking a little strained, probably overhearing this conversation as she busied herself preparing a tisane for her husband.

Camille too sensed dangerous territory and was quick to add: 'I brought over my young English relative to meet your wife. She is helping me with the children. She speaks English to Lucie and my son.' Now for it, thought Georgy.

He turned to her. 'I am pleased to meet you, Miss,' he said in strongly accented English.

Georgy inclined her head. Her curtsey when he arrived had probably not been noticed. She found herself thinking how odd it was that he had married an Englishwoman. You could understand Augustin doing that because he had been exiled in London. But Alphonse de Lamartine looked so French!

It was now or never. She took her courage in both hands and enunciated in perfect French: 'I feel honoured to meet a writer whose work I have studied at home in England.'

He looked surprised, but whether at her speaking French or her having read his verses she was not sure.

'And you speak our language well. Tell me – they read me much in London? I was in London a few years ago but my book had hardly travelled there at that time.' He looked suddenly shy but pleased.

'Oh, I do not live in London, but my ... tutor, in Yorkshire, gave me your *Premières Méditations*, to read – he knew your work as I imagine many people do now.'

'Georgina appreciates poetry,' said Camilla. She was still making every effort to be pleasant and helpful to her. It was to occur to Georgy later that she might be storing up goodwill in case she needed an ally in future.

Lamartine inclined his head to Madame de Marceau and smiled. Georgy could see that he found Camille attractive. But he got up and put his teacup back on the buffet.

'Don't get up – I'm afraid I must leave you now.' Perhaps he was feeling inspired and would go to his room and write.

'And we too must leave,' said Camille briskly.

Then the maid appeared at the inner door leading Julia by the hand.

'Papa, papa!' The child ran up to him, arms outstretched and Georgy saw his face soften. It was a mobile face; she could easily imagine him reduced to tears or fears.

Louis-Marie coughed a little ostentatiously: 'I hope to see you at the Cercle, cher cousin. Monsieur, Mesdames.'

He made his farewells and included Georgy but ignored the little Julia who said after he had gone out: 'Papa, do you know about Red Riding Hood? The lady told me.' She pointed at Georgy.

Lamartine smiled and said: 'Ah, Julia if you are a very good girl I will tell you the story of the Sleeping Beauty!' He took her up in his arms. Georgy was relieved. If you had thought Monsieur de Marceau was typical, you would not believe any member of the French gentry or nobility recognized his own children, never mind embraced them and talked to them.

Soon afterwards, Camille and Georgy said goodbye too, Julia pulling at Georgy's hand and repeating '*Chaperon Rouge, Chaperon Rouge.*'

Georgy shook hands with Julia's noble father and Camille thanked Marianne for her kind hospitality and hoped she would accept her own in the near future.

It was over! She had met him. She had seen the Poet and spoken to him: he had even spoken to her. He was human.

Over the next few days Georgy was to go over and over in her mind everything that had been said. She could not wait to finish her letter to Edward, but was kept so busy with the children that there was little time.

Was she a little disappointed that the Poet had not looked different from other men? Had she expected him to look like an immortal among mortals? She had a little feeling that although he was modest about the lyrics – which he had once told a critic he could write quickly, without revision – he also had other ambitions elsewhere. Towards the end of their time in Aix Camille was to tell her he was to travel to Italy in the autumn to be Consul in Florence.

She remembered Edward saying ironically: 'The best thing about a poet is usually his poem.'

Poets lived in the day to day world along with everyone else, but poets of thirty-five would never reveal their innermost thoughts to unknown English girls who had better worship words rather than people. If only they could have spoken of time and death and love, despair, loss and consolation! Instead, they had spoken of Red Riding Hood and avoided the subject of death: his sisters', his little boy's . . . . He had not suffered those wounds when he wrote *Le Lac.*

She tried to imagine him rowing a boat to rescue the lady he had met in Aix in 1816 but could not.

That same evening, Camille spoke of their visit to her husband.

'Oh, Alphonse is such an idealist,' replied Augustin. 'I saw him just now this evening for the first time this year at the Cercle. He never says much – sits reading the reports – Italian newspapers chiefly.'

'Perhaps he's bored here,' said his wife, 'but he's a good family man – I could tell that.'

M de Marceau looked uncomprehending. Then: 'Naturally; all his mother's family are strongly religious. Alphonse, like his mother, is no exception. He also used to worship the trees, I hear, when he was not reading Rousseau.'

'He sees good in everyone, I imagine,' said Camille.

Camille was actually wondering whether such a man as Lamartine understood the depths of human depravity. There were rumours about his previous love-life which she had no intention of discussing with her husband.

'Aymon – he knew him well when they were boys – told me once that Alphonse was very spoilt as a child,' added Augustin.

'Of course, with all those sisters,' said Camille, unpinning her long hair.

'He never had to suffer – *his* parents didn't have to uproot themselves,' said Augustin bitterly. He still felt angry about the Revolution that had plucked his parents and grandparents out of France and sent them over the Channel.

Camille was thinking what a handsome youth the poet must once have been – he was still very well set up. Just think, *she* might have married such a man if she'd been in the right place at the right time, as Mary Ann Birch had been. She sighed.

'Aymon said he was a dreamy youth,' continued her husband who seemed to want to continue his analysis of the poet. 'Very much the young master and always with a book in his hand. Even reading on horseback. That reminds me, Thibault must soon start to ride the horse I'm having brought over from Mâcon for him.'

Now his son was the young master of a château, he thought, but it did not assuage his feelings of having been cheated of a comparable childhood inheritance.

'You could see he loves dogs,' murmured Camille, thinking he must have loved women too even if he'd come to a full stop with Mary Ann. What was it about certain marriages that made men unreachable, even men who had formerly enjoyed many women? Lucky Mary Ann. Not that she completely regretted her own marriage but she dreamed still of passionate love.

78

Aloud, she said: 'His wife was pleasant to that relative of your aunt's, Louis-Marie—'

'Ah, he too was at the Cercle yesterday – such a bore! The man is always ill.'

Since her husband was also a hypochondriac Camille forbore to comment. In her own experience the bad qualities so easily seen in others were usually those one possessed oneself.

She knew that a good deal of gambling went on at the Cercle and hoped her husband had not been at the gaming table. Last year when the club members had rented the château in the town from the marquis and added the café, the concert hall, the orangery, the ball-room, the billiard-room and the reading-room it was obviously the *salle de jeu* that had attracted the visitors – the gambling-room was more popular than the other rooms put together.

If rumour were to be believed, her husband's cousin Alphonse was not averse to trying his luck there too. She imagined he always needed money because he loved the good things of life as well as being generous towards others. She also guessed that it was partly her money that had swayed him to marry Mary Ann Birch. However, they seemed happy enough.

Chapter 6

Georgy went on thinking a good deal about the Poet, as she still thought of him, now that she had seen him in the flesh. She still found it hard to reconcile the idea of a man, a married man, a father, who was taking a cure for whatever was thought to be wrong with him, and the person who had written the lines she had committed to memory.

Did poets ever talk about their verse, or was it a part of themselves which was for public consumption only on the printed page, safely laid away for posterity? He did not seem like a famously successful poet, though he was handsome and had seemed pleased when she told him people read him in England.

A few days after their visit to the Pension Perrier, whilst Lucie and Thibault were having their siesta, she took the slim volume of the *Premières Méditations* and sat on a bench under the poplars in the square near the pension. There were several groups of people walking up and down under the trees.

She reread one or two other favourite poems. Georgy had always liked elegies; indeed until last year her favourite verse had been that perfect *Elegy in a Country Churchyard* of the poet Gray. But there was no doubt that this much younger poet saw many aspects of life in much the same way as she already did herself. His verse though was much more personal than Gray's, more like her favourite's Byron and Shelley ... dreamier and gentler though ... more tender perhaps than Lord Byron. He continually asked himself questions about life without supplying any answers. These questions made him sad – as they had occasionally made her sad. But had not poets always been concerned with questions about time and death and love and the evanescence of life? Lost love and lost time?

Edward had told her they were living at a time of great change; everything was being challenged.

Was it just that Monsieur de Lamartine wrote about such matters in a more approachable way?

She sighed involuntarily, thinking of the Revolution that had uprooted Monsieur de Marceau and his family and led him to meet Camilla. Without that same Revolution *she* wouldn't be sitting here in a foreign country thinking deep thoughts!

Georgy smiled at herself, which she often did. Many people would think that talk of revolution, or even of elegies, was not the business of a young woman. *Her* business was to fall in love and get married and produce more children for the world. Not that she had any real objection to all that, but there were other things that interested her as much or more. Now, if she were to meet someone like the Poet, but younger, nearer her own age, someone with whom she could share her thoughts ... she might feel differently?

She was roused suddenly by a green ball that bounced near her feet. She looked up from her book. A little boy ran up and she scooped up the ball and threw it back to him.

There was always life going on – you couldn't sit and think for long; you had to join in. She turned the page.

What had the Poet to say about God? Her employers had been very insistent that he was a religious man. Was he not more concerned with life down here on earth than in heaven? Did he not address himself to time rather than to the Christian God whose church was only a hundred or two yards away over at the bottom of the square? Or, if he addressed God, was it not the God of the lake and the trees and the sky, the god of 'Nature'? He looked for religious consolation, but he found that consolation in his love for nature, and in his love for his Elvire . . . . People were the most important things – and the memory of the love felt for them. She knew Mr Walker preferred Wordsworth, who also addressed himself to Nature. Shelley though, now *he* spoke about youth and love and she loved his poetry best.

'*Bonjour, Mademoiselle,*' a voice cut into her reverie. She looked up. It was the young man they called Louis-Marie who was standing looking at her earnestly.

'Oh! Bonjour, Monsieur.'

'You were deep in thought – I must not disturb you,' he said, but made no pretence of moving away.

'*Ah, oui* – I was thinking about English poets,' she answered.

'Of which poems were you thinking? Quote me some of their lines!' he said imperiously, and sat down beside her.

He appeared more self-confident than he had been that afternoon at the Pension Perrier. She understood; she was only an unimportant English girl whom he could impress. She tried to suppress such an ignoble idea, but he *was* the sort of man who thought he was doing you a favour by talking to you in a 'serious' way.

He sat down beside her. What a nuisance!

> '*Oh World! O Life! O Time!*' she declared.
> '*On whose last steps I climb,*
> *Trembling at that where I had stood before,*
> *When will return the glory of your prime?*
> *No more – Oh, never more! . . . .*'

'How well you recite – I am afraid my English is not too good. You must translate for me. I assume it is Byron?'

'No, it is not. It is Shelley, who was drowned three years ago—'

'I thought he was not regarded as a suitable person for young women to read?'

'I'm sure you're right,' she answered ironically, but Louis-Marie only looked puzzled. 'Anyway, what he says is a little like Monsieur de Lamartine, you see.'

'*Ah oui?* I see you have his first book on your lap. I was going to suggest to you that we walked a little way under the trees – you have no chaperone?'

She rose, tucking the book under her arm. 'No – and I'm afraid I have to go back. I came out only for half an hour while my charges were sleeping. I needed fresh air.'

'Perhaps if you came tomorrow we could continue our conversation? I should like to introduce you to my friend Amaury Arnaud. He too is a poet.'

'Thank you.'

He bowed, and she turned and walked back quickly to her pension. She would read in the little courtyard until the children woke up.

In the evening she finished – at last – the long letter to Edward Walker, taken up whenever she had a moment away from the children. Camille appeared to trust her completely with Lucie and Thibault, which made Georgy a little anxious.

'They'll come to no harm if you keep an eye on them,' said Célanie.

'I worry lest they might rush out of the pension and be crushed by a horse's hoof or a carriage!' said Georgy. 'It's different from living in the country.'

'You could always be chased by a wild boar,' replied Célanie. She was teasing her, but Georgy had never before felt responsible for anyone and it was rather overwhelming. She had begun to feel much older since she had begun to work with the children.

In her letter to Edward Walker she had tried to express her feelings about the man Lamartine, along with some tentative conclusions about the kind of poetry he wrote. Mr Walker – Edward – would probably find her comments jejune. Criticism did not come easily to her.

Is it easier to write of the man, than the Poet? I do not know M de L well enough to give a considered picture and am not likely ever to know him better, but as you once told me about Rousseau, I feel he is a 'soul searcher'. Whether he is still full of sorrow for the woman he met here and lost through death I do not know. Yet I believe he would always be the sort of person who *liked to write about what he had lost.*

He was very charming – I could not make up my mind whether he loved himself as much as he loved others! I think he is perhaps the sort of man who has been spoilt a little by his mama. He obviously adores his daughter and is very sincere. I expected him to be 'natural' and he was *sans façons*, as the French say. Although he was very polite, I felt that he was self-absorbed – perhaps he was once shy? I suppose all writers are self-absorbed? M de Lamartine is not a gloomy person but I guess he is often sad about his little boy that died. My 'employer' said afterwards that though he is very serious, people say he sees everything through rose-coloured spectacles, prefers to be unaware of the iniquity of mankind because he is such an *optimist!*

For the rest you will have to wait for me to read more. I see already that he elevates Beauty, as do the English poets to whom you introduced me last year. I think he prefers to shed light on everything rather than envelop it in a sort of Byronic darkness. His verse is so harmonious – I wonder whether the noble Lord would have found it too "sweet"?'

When she had finished her letter she felt she had done her best to convey her fugitive thoughts. Edward Walker could make what he would of them. It was always hard work to sum up impressions. She'd have found it difficult to describe how she judged Augustin de Marceau and his wife. How well did anyone know anyone else? The children she could understand better. Were first impressions anyway to be trusted?

She had said nothing yet to Edward Walker about Louis-Marie. You really ought not to discuss one man with another. Her first impressions of the younger man had not been favourable – but she told herself she was being intolerant and over-critical. He had seemed to want to be friendly, and he was so far the only person of her own age she had come across since her arrival in France.

Her old tutor was very likely bored by all her literary outpourings, if too polite to say so? Not that she would ever have written of such things to her parents or even to her best friend Abigail Strang. She had better commit all these lucubrations to a journal, must not burden Edward Walker with them. She would see if she had enough money to buy a book for this purpose. She had brought a few French sovereigns with her, for her father had given a few guineas to Cousin Clive for this purpose, and he had exchanged them for French francs with his sister-in-law Camilla. Georgy received only a tiny allowance for her work with the children. Still, board and lodging – and such good board and lodging – all cost money.

I am perhaps seen as the governess, the poor relation, she thought. Yet they do not treat me as a servant. It is a difficult position. She had noticed that Camille made favourites of some of her servants, especially Célanie, who said philosophically: 'Women need women to confide in.'

The next morning Georgy took her letter, along with a shorter one to her parents, to Monsieur de Marceau who was lying languidly on a sofa reading the Despatch before he departed for his shower. He promised to send it on with his own letters to Paris, thence to London, and Yorkshire.

Yorkshire seemed so far away and for a moment Georgy indulged in a little nostalgia for the fresh air and bare moors of her birthplace. But she was not really homesick, wished only that she could magic herself just for a few hours across the Channel – and be back in time for supper. Then she heard Thibault wailing in the distance. She never had much time for introspection. Probably a mercy, she thought, as she dashed up the wooden stairs to the children's room.

'She took my horse!' he sobbed. Lucie was sitting at the table holding the plush horse and staring into its eyes.

'I only wanted to see if I could make him breathe!' she said.

'You can pretend he does,' said Georgy, taking the animal and restoring him to his rightful owner who pulled his ears and then threw him across the room, saying:

'You are not to play with Lucie! She is a bad girl!' Lucie was in fact a very good girl and Thibault was jealous of her accomplishments.

Order was finally restored by Georgy sitting them both at the table with their copy books. There was always something new for her to learn as well as them. She would ask the children the French names for certain animals and flowers and it pleased them that *they* could be *her* teachers.

Her standby was *Questions on Common Subjects*, the book by Mrs Richmal Mangnall, brought with her from England. She had to be careful, for reading through it one day in order to prepare the next lesson, she had discovered the pages on French history were rather biased in favour of the English. There was a good deal about Captain Cook, of whom she discovered her pupils had never heard. But she also learned much herself from the redoubtable Richmal. How ignorant she was; she had never realized that the king who was executed in 1793 was brother to the recently deceased Louis.

On 12 April 1814, the race of Bourbon reassumed the government of France; and on 4 May, Louis, XVIII, brother to Louis XVI, was welcomed to Paris, as the rightful possessor of the throne, by an immense multitude. Napoleon Bonaparte was conveyed to the island of St Helena and there ended his eventful life . . . .

Well, that might meet with the approval of the Royalists among whom she now found herself, for some appeared to think that old Boney had eventually succeeded in taming the worst excesses of The Terror. Others though – the Liberals – believed that Napoleon had betrayed all they had hoped for from the

Revolution. And now there was yet another Bourbon on the throne! Another brother. She sighed. Politics led one into deep waters. Brought up as she had been to loathe Napoleon, it was difficult to appreciate his good points from whichever French side you were on. Some thought he had ended the Revolution and made life safe, but then discovered he was ruthless in eliminating rivals. The Jacobins disliked him because he had become reconciled with the Church, and then got himself crowned Emperor – which was not what they had fought the Revolution for. Boney had wanted to govern the whole of Europe from his own throne. He must have been a very clever man, a hard man, an efficient man, the sort of man she did not like – but she imagined some young people might think of him as an inspiration. It was because they envied his power. She had heard Edward Walker grudgingly admit that Napoleon had succeeded in founding a new system of law and a new system of education, and wasn't that what old England needed?

She looked down again at the Mrs Mangnall on her lap, who was coming in very useful in explaining simple things to children. It was good for her own French that she had to turn the woman's English into her charges' first language. That morning she was to explain how candles were made and then they would copy some English words from the *Petit Précepteur*. Fortunately the pictures in the little book had their titles in French. All she had to do was show them the watering-can, the jug, the tortoise, and the ostrich. Thibault copied the pictures and Lucie wrote the English names in her neat flowery hand. She had learned to suppress her own boredom, and once the children were in bed there was always *Redgauntlet* to read, which Papa had sent her from England. She wondered idly what Walter Scott had thought about Boney.

After luncheon that day, a simple Savoyard meal of bread and Reblochon cheese and fruit that Georgy took alone with the children, Camille returned from her morning 'cure'. The afternoon was sunny but not too hot and Camille suggested she take the children for an 'English' walk in the park.

To get there they had to walk across the main square by the poplars, and it was just as they had turned towards the road that Georgy saw the familiar figure of Louis-Marie coming towards them from the other side. Thibault was watching a recalcitrant horse refuse to budge in the middle of the road and for a moment they were all standing stock-still.

Oh dear, the little Frenchman was bound to see her. Bother, she thought, I don't really want to talk to him. It was a mercy she was with the children. She had already discovered that children could occasionally be useful. You could talk to them at gatherings when nobody else said anything to you, and they were capable of dispelling the domestic 'atmosphere'. This happened occasionally when Monsieur de Marceau and his wife were engaged in some argument, for Camille was not one to sit down under criticism from her husband. Georgy often wondered about them. Once, long ago, had they been in love?

Louis-Marie was walking with another youth, a taller man dressed in a green velvet cap and white silk cravat. She looked the other way, but it was no good. She knew Louis-Marie had seen her. She bent to adjust Lucie's hair ribbons as he came up.

'And are these your little charges?' he asked in his light voice.

'Curtsey, Lucie,' she whispered. 'Thibault, shake hands with Monsieur de Combes.'

'I don't know who he is,' said Thibault crossly, his attention still on the horse.

'May I present Monsieur Amaury Arnaud,' Louis-Marie went on.

The other young man, who had a little orange flower in his button-hole, was also looking at the stationary horse himself. He said: '*Enchanté*,' but did not look it. At least, thought Georgy, this young man will not want a walk in the park with infants.

But she was wrong, for he suddenly turned his attention from the horse and said with perfect solemnity to Thibault: 'Naturally you don't know me – but I can see you like horses?'

'Yes, I do,' said Thibault. 'And I am to have a horse at home!'

Louis-Marie was trying to look interested but was clearly bored.

'We were just going to the park – sometimes there are riders there,' said Georgy hastily. Lucie was pulling on her arm to cross the road.

'Here!' said the new young man, 'I think you had better cross over here. There are carriages coming in every direction.'

Georgy grabbed Thibault and they followed the young man who was weaving across the street to the entrance to the mown fields and groups of trees they called the park. There were a few seats, occasional hawkers, pedlars, vendors of sweetmeats.

When they arrived at the other side of the road she turned and saw that they were being followed by Louis-Marie. His more quixotic companion was now well ahead. Decidedly it was not the done thing to be accompanied by two young men – it made her feel like a nursemaid with 'followers'. But Amaury Arnaud waited for them all to come up, and when they did he smiled, saying: 'I feel like a little stroll myself.'

Louis-Marie wiped his forehead with a large pocket handkerchief. 'You permit us, Mademoiselle Georgina, to walk along with you?' he managed to get out. He was not such a quick walker as his friend who was now once more striding ahead. 'I'm afraid I do get rather breathless,' he apologized.

Thibault said: 'I want to go with that other man to see the horses.'

What could she say? She replied to Louis-Marie: 'Thank you – you may walk a little with us if you wish.' His friend had not asked permission, was obviously more casual. 'You are both welcome to help entertain the children – it is their afternoon treat,' she went on. Louis-Marie shrugged his shoulders slightly. But after all, he was a sort of relation, a friend of the family.

Amaury turned round again to see if they were following him, paused, and waited once more for them to come up together by the path under the trees.

'It is a change from our promenade under the poplars,' he said, and smiled.

'The children cannot walk as quickly as you,' she said, 'but thank you for making a way for us across the street. I always worry that they will run ahead of me and fall under a carriage.' He was a decidedly unusual sort of man, she thought, and she had the impression that Louis-Marie was a little put out.

Lucie had brought a ball with her and for a time they all, except for Louis-Marie, who sat gloomily on an iron bench, played at throwing it to each other and trying to catch each other out. The children were delighted as they ran around, becoming very excited. Georgy was just going to say they must not get overexcited when Amaury held up his hand and said: 'Listen . . . .'

They listened.

Thibault exclaimed, 'It's the horsemen!'

In the distance they heard the beat of hooves.

'They'll pass us on the path behind,' said Amaury.

There came into view a detachment of Charles Félix's militia in scarlet and white uniforms, a standard-bearer holding up the banner of the Kingdom of Savoy with its white cross on a red background, the soldiers' silver swords clanking at their sides.

Thibault was thrilled. He jumped up and down in his excitement and Lucie held up her doll to see them. Georgy noticed the horses were what you might call a mixed bunch. She had always been promising that they would see the soldiers on horseback one day, and here they were. Louis-Marie stood with them watching as they passed.

'A subject for an epic?' he murmured.

Georgy looked at Amaury who was staring into the middle distance. He had curly dark hair and very dark brown eyes, an aquiline nose and full mouth. *He* might be a poet – and would probably be a better one than Louis-Marie.

Just as she was thinking this, Louis-Marie said: 'We are both to recite some of our verses at the *Cercle* tonight.'

'Oh, you write too?' she asked Amaury.

He shrugged his shoulders. 'If I write about these soldiers it would not be to praise them,' he said.

Louis-Marie looked uncomfortable. How close were they as friends? Maybe Amaury was not such an impassioned Royalist as himself.

Lucie, who had been listening, said: 'Will you write about the horses, Monsieur?'

'I might – but now I must leave you, having been reminded that I must put together some work! See you later *mon vieux*.' To Georgy and the children Amaury bowed and said: 'Thank you for the pleasure of your company,' and then he was off.

'I really must take the children back now,' said Georgy. Louis-Marie looked discomfited to find himself in the middle of a park with a young woman he did not know very well and two little children.

'Are ladies allowed at the *Cercle*?' she asked him as they made their way back to the square, the children now dragging their feet.

'Oh,' he answered, surprised. 'They come with their husbands of course – but never unaccompanied unless it is to the Salon de Dames for wives of members.'

He did not offer to take her. Not that she could have gone in any case, but he might have been a little more chivalrous about it. He obviously did not want her any better acquainted with his friend's poems, she thought.

Georgy found the interesting face of Amaury Arnaud was hovering behind her eyes as she fell asleep that night.

The next morning the children's lessons were taken as usual in the small sitting-room. Their father insisted his offspring work for two hours every morning even on holiday. Georgy wondered whether their mother agreed with her husband. It was surely rather unusual for a seven-year-old and a nine-year-old to work every day of their summer holiday? She tried to imagine her cousins at home being asked to open their books if they were on holiday in Scarborough, and knew they would have rebelled. But after all that was what she was here for, and there was still plenty of holiday left before they would return to the château.

Augustin de Marceau claimed the baths did him good, although Georgy thought he looked just as pasty-faced as before. Camille on the other hand glowed with health. She had made new friends among some of the other wives and mothers. There was a little ante-room where they all met for a chat after their shower and then they would go to the *salon de dames* in the *Cercle* for coffee. Georgy wondered if Camille had ever met Louis-Marie's friend Amaury but was too circumspect to ask. She had undoubtedly been impressed by that young man. The very next morning Camille received a note from Louis-Marie. She looked up from her coffee and yawned. Her husband had not yet break-fasted. Georgy had heard him come in late from what she guessed must have been the gaming tables.

'M des Combes wants to know if he may call upon us tomor-row,' said Camille, reading the note. 'What a bore – I shall ask my husband to entertain him – after all he is his relation!' She looked sharply at Georgy. 'Perhaps it's you he wants to see!'

'We saw him yesterday in the square,' said Georgy. 'He was with a friend and they walked a little way with me and the children.'

Camille continued to look at her speculatively. 'We are not in England, you know – young French ladies do not usually walk in the town with young men.'

'He was only being kind – they helped us cross the road,' said Georgy. 'And I am sure he has no particular wish to see *me*.' She was in fact not sure at all, expected the young man would arrive with a bundle of poems for her delectation.

Camille sighed. 'I suppose I should have asked him here formally after we met at Marianne de Lamartine's. Then it would have been more correct for you to acknowledge him in the street. You must not forget that I am responsible for you, *ma chère*.'

Georgy felt rebellious. Even if she had no particular wish to see Louis-Marie and talk to him, the idea that her liberty might be curtailed or constrained because of what was the 'done thing' was unpleasant. But later she reflected that Madame de Marceau was happy for her to take the children off her hands, knew perfectly well that she took them walking in the park, and sometimes walked alone without them on the streets of the little town. She was only saying what she felt she ought to say.

The next afternoon was arranged for Louis-Marie's visit, although Monsieur de Marceau had flatly refused to take tea with his distant relative, implying that such entertainments were woman's province. He had repaired as usual to his 'club' at the *Cercle*, where his wife had been earlier in the day, in a different room and with her women friends.

'You will please help me entertain the young man,' said Camille to Georgy. 'Lucie and Thibault can stay with Célanie who is to bake some cakes this afternoon. It will please them to assist her.'

Georgy was never sure when her employer was speaking ironically. She still found Camille difficult to understand, such a mixture she seemed to be of kindness and imperious commands.

At four o'clock Louis-Marie was shown into the tiny salon of the pension. As Georgy had expected he had a sheaf of papers under his arm.

'*Ah, chère Madame!*' He bent over Camille's hand. Georgy avoided this by extending her own hand and grabbing his for a brisk shake. Once settled with his glass of milk – he had once more refused tea – Louis-Marie looked at them and complimented them both on their healthy complexions.

Camille was amused. The young man appeared to have learned the art of flattery at his mother's knee.

'I wondered if you were going to attend the concert?' he said, after wiping his mouth with his pocket handkerchief.

'What concert is that?' asked Camille.

'Next week in the *Salle du Cercle* – it was only advertised yesterday. A few musicians from Lyon will play and sing extracts from opera and chamber music. I thought it might interest you.'

'I shall have to consult my husband,' replied Camille. 'I am not very musical – but Mademoiselle Georgy might be interested.' She turned to Georgy with a slight smile that said, What did I tell you? He is after you! That is why he has come.

But Georgy, who never passed up a musical invitation, was interested. Especially if Amaury Arnaud were to be there, though she could not mention this to anyone.

'Thank you,' she said cheerfully. 'If you can spare me one evening I should be delighted to listen to music.'

'Why yes, *ma chère*,' said her employer, 'I am sure you must have a little entertainment now and then.'

Thus it was arranged. Louis-Marie never got round to reading them any of his verse, for at five o'clock Camille intimated she must leave to meet a friend and the children could be heard asking for Georgy. She could hardly ask Louis-Marie if his friend might be going along with him.

She found herself thinking again and again of the handsome young Amaury. He had never appeared again in the square, alone or accompanied, though she had twice taken her book there for half an hour, to sit reading on a bench near the church or by the fountain.

She found herself wondering if she had imagined he had looked at her in a specially interested way that afternoon when they had met. If he had, he had made no effort to follow up any interest. For the present she was stuck with Louis-Marie, whom she determined not to encourage even if he had asked her to the concert. She would concentrate on the music.

The following week it seemed that half the 'patients', or visitors, to the town were attending the concert. It was decidedly the chic thing to do. She had dressed in the famous cotton evening-dress with the frill and hoped it would do. Camille cast a critical eye over it, pulled at a few flounces, and then pronounced her '*très anglaise*'. Georgy did not know whether, from Camille de Marceau's lips, this was a compliment or not.

The morning of the concert, Camille had dropped a grenade at breakfast. 'My husband has decided to leave Aix earlier than he intended and wants all his family back at the château next week. His parents are to visit us there in early September, so I am afraid our holiday will be cut short.'

Oh well, if that meant she would never see Amaury Arnaud again, it also meant she would be rid of Louis-Marie.

Louis-Marie had kindly provided her with a programme and they were seated in the small theatre with a raised platform at one end where the musicians were already assembled waiting for their leader. Georgy wondered if M de Lamartine might be found here at this humble provincial entertainment, but he did not appear to be attending. He probably heard plenty of music in Paris.

She had not been able to help herself looking round for Amaury Arnaud, though she had said nothing to Louis-Marie about him. So far there had been no sighting, so she composed herself to be agreeable to Louis-Marie. He was not an easy person to amuse. Why had he asked her to accompany him? She made a shrewd guess that he wanted to be seen with a young lady, and she would do. He was being excessively formal. Perhaps he had really hoped Madame de Marceau would appear with him as his rich relation? That would undoubtedly have raised his standing. She did not know why she harboured such uncharitable thoughts about the poor man, whose guest she was after all, and resolved to thrust them out of her mind.

The concert began with the overture to *Der Freischütz*, rather thin in tone perforce, as the orchestra was small. Georgy enjoyed it, and it was followed by a minuet from one of Haydn's early piano sonatas. This was pleasant. If she suspected it was not played faultlessly, she did not know enough to pronounce upon the matter. Louis-Marie leaned his head on his hand and looked soulful. Then a middle-aged man sang an aria from *The Barber of Seville* and here they were already at the interval.

The *salle* took about 150 people and it was hot. Georgy was glad of her escort's suggestion that they might walk in the open air. All the rest of the audience had had the same idea.

Just as they came out of the inner door of the theatre and crossed the corridor with the crowd towards the outer door she thought she glimpsed Amaury. Then he disappeared.

On returning to the concert she saw that there were seats behind the orchestra. She looked over towards them, somehow sure that the young poet would be found there. She tried narrowing her eyes to see if she could make him out.

Some opera 'ariettes' were to follow. Her programme told her that they were 'direct from Milan' by a very young composer named Bellini.

The platform was now cleared for other singers and now Georgy could see that it truly was Amaury at the far left hand side at the back of the platform, sitting next to a young lady.

After the first ariette, which was delightful, she whispered to Louis-Marie: 'Is that not your friend sitting behind the string players?'

'He said he might come,' said that young man. She wondered who the lady was and was just about to ask, since there was a slight lull in the proceedings, when the music started up again.

At the end of the concert they stood in the corridor in the press of people and slowly made their way outside once again into the fresh air, Georgy hoping she might see Amaury coming out.

A man turned as he came out of another door further down the building, and she glimpsed a coat tail belonging to a masculine figure who – she was sure – had an orange flower in his button-hole. Louis-Marie was in front of her and she turned round again to see if she could make out the woman Amaury was with. She caught only the glimpse of orange silk before being forced to follow her escort.

The night was warm, the full moon serenely above the crowded little streets around the square. It would have been delicious to cross over to walk in the park as many were doing. But Louis-Marie deposited her at the pension without more ado. She thanked him profusely, wishing with every word that she might explore the town alone, and come across the handsome face, even if its possessor were with a woman.

M de Marceau's decision to leave Aix before the end of August had been sudden. There was much to see to before they left, and Georgy's juvenile charges were fretful. Like most children, and Georgy herself, they did not enjoy being uprooted. She had hoped she might by chance catch another glimpse of Amaury Arnaud in the street, and wished desperately that they might stay on a little longer in the town. But apparently M de Marceau's parents were firm in their resolve to visit the château in early September, and their word was law.

Louis-Marie called once before they left, but she could not arouse his suspicions by asking him outright if Amaury was still in the town. She longed to ask him also where Amaury lived. Perhaps it was in Paris – and if so she would never see him again.

'I have great hopes of a visit to my Great-Aunt Hortense in the not too distant future,' stated the other young man. 'So we may soon see each other again!'

The news came that M de Lamartine and his wife and daughter were also to leave the town at the end of August, a little after the de Marceau party. Georgy had hoped to see the little Julia again, but it was not to be, for Marianne, invited on a return visit to Camille, had pleaded a slight indisposition.

The next day there was another note from her to Camille to report great news: 'My husband has been appointed to the post of French chargé d'affaires in Florence: *Ambassadeur Extraordinaire –* at the court of the Duke of Tuscany! We shall all be going there very soon. It is what we were hoping for,' she wrote. 'We must be in Florence by the beginning of October and there is much to do.'

Georgy felt sad that she would never see them again either.

Part Two
1825–1826

Chapter 1

Autumn and Winter

They had been back in the Château de Pinac-Les-Saules for a week, when the threatened arrival of Augustin's parents, the Count and Countess of Marceau, materialized. Uprooted from Aix, a place she had loved, Georgy was feeling restless. She found the count and his wife a gloomy couple who yet seemed to feel it necessary to lead an active social life before they succumbed to old age. Once she had been introduced to them, they took no more notice of her, for which she was grateful. They made a show of petting their two grandchildren, but were soon tired by the children's presence.

Georgy noticed that their daughter-in-law found them a trial, but Camille could not be faulted for doing her best to entertain them. From what she let drop now and again she had clearly never warmed to them. Now she saw herself, in their eyes, as the 'eccentric Englishwoman' their son had unfortunately met when the family was in exile.

Augustin fussed formally round his mother but appeared to have little to say to her. Perhaps he was trying to make up in public for what he did not really feel. His father was a man of the pre-Revolutionary years, who had decided everything could now go back to what it had been before The Terror. Father and son were often closeted together, discussing finances, Georgy assumed, since that was what men usually discussed in private.

After a few days of decorous walks round the estate and long, silent meals – they appeared to have taken the habit of silence from their long forced stay in England – they began to plan a round of visits in their son's carriage, their own needing to be

99

replaced. Georgy reserved her final opinion of the older de Marceau generation until she might be better acquainted with them.

If the grown-ups gallivanted around the countryside, it would give Georgy at last a little time at the château alone apart from the children and the servants. She looked forward to relaxing a little and not having to be on her best behaviour. Until they went home she would employ her free time catching up with letters from England. One from her best friend Abigail Strang had been waiting for her on her return from Aix and there was always a letter to write to her mother. She had neglected writing to Abigail during the last few weeks and was still waiting for a reply from Edward Walker to her long collection of epistles from Aix. She was not yet ready to write another long missive to him, somehow not wishing to tell him about the handsome Amaury. If she mentioned the young man he would think she had done more than talk to him one afternoon and glimpse him one evening at the theatre.

And that *was* all that had happened!

'My employer is my great-aunt's daughter-in-law's sister,' wrote Georgy to her best friend Abigail, before trying to describe Camille. 'Now you will be none the wiser! Lucie asked me one day if Thibault and herself were related to me, and I explained I was their Aunt Caroline's mother-in-law's great-niece – which fascinated Lucie and enabled us *all* to learn some new vocabulary! 'You see you can still teach me as much as I teach you,' I said to Lucie. She is a very nice little girl and very bright and helpful. I wish I could say the same of her brother. He is not difficult or too boisterous but *is* inclined to sulks . . . .'

It was difficult to know what to write to Abigail. If they were together at home she'd find plenty to say to her, but her home, and Abigail's in York, were far away, her friend's preoccupations possibly now very different from her own.

She decided to write a little more about Camille. It would be a way of sorting out what she thought of her. There hadn't yet been any time to write her diary, though before she left Aix she had bought a thick black-bound exercise book for the purpose.

'Madame Camille de Marceau is extremely good looking, of medium height and blond. Her character is a mixture of agreeableness and occasional reserve. I find her a little baffling,' she wrote.

It was true that Camille could also be frivolous. She liked to say she was empty-headed, very unlike 'My clever sister Caroline.' But she was generous, if changeable, and was affectionate towards her son. She seemed to be a little more wary of Lucie, for the little girl was clearly intelligent, and perhaps took more after her Aunt Caroline than her mother.

'Camille is not aristocratic, but she is rich, her family fortune coming from the City of London,' continued Georgy.

Had Camille ever been in love with her husband? Was she still? She couldn't imagine that Augustin had ever fallen in love, and she found him even harder to understand or describe than his wife. He appeared stiff, unable to show emotion, but she thought Camille usually took her husband for granted. Then she would suddenly make a fuss of him, and he accepted her efforts complacently. Georgy could only guess that he had spent a difficult childhood in London and had married to escape his parents. Before their arrival, all she had heard of *them* – mostly from Caroline Bond in London – inclined her to assume they were people who would never come to terms with the loss of their estates and who would have much preferred their eldest son to marry an aristocratic Frenchwoman, even if Camille had brought a large *dot*. Camille herself would not be a member of this minor French aristocracy if she had not married Augustin de Marceau. Rather she'd be living in the English countryside amongst dogs and horses, and distributing a daily helping of good works. Here in France there was less scope for charity. The surrounding countryside was fertile and vine-covered, but the peasants lived a rough sort of life, and there seemed much less contact between them and the big house than there would have been at home.

She told Abigail a little of all this and ended her letter with a slightly ironic description of Louis-Marie. Should she mention Amaury Arnaud to her friend? No – she'd wait and see how long her feelings lasted. She might never see him again, in which case she would look rather stupid.

Hortense had returned to the bosom of her sister's family, who lived not far away. They all spent a good deal of time travelling round staying with each other. That happened at home, of course, but her own parents entertained more in the evenings and had more friends who were not family. Here in France the visits were only between relatives, however distant they were in consanguinity or residence. Georgy wondered if Camille found her life boring. She did not read and did not play the pianoforte, but she did ride.

It was on her return one afternoon from a ride in the nearby forest, that adjoined the estate of Aunt Hortense's other great-nephew, that she said: 'I saw your Louis-Marie today!' Georgy realized she was teasing her, but then Camille added: 'He was out riding with a friend of his – a very good-looking young man.'

Georgy's heart leapt, but she looked down at the handkerchief she was supposed to be embroidering for Lucie and affected a lack of interest. Fortunately she never blushed, was more likely to turn pale if she was excited.

'You told me you saw M des Combes with a friend in Aix, didn't you? Was he a Monsieur Bonaventure?' pursued Camille.

Georgy's heart sank. 'No, I believe he was a Monsieur Arnoux or Arnaud,' she said after a pause.

'Oh well, he can't be the same person then. Unless … well, I'm pretty sure Louis-Marie said the young man's mother was Madame Bonaventure. They told me he's staying with her in a house a few leagues from Pinac. I didn't even know that house was inhabited again. We never see our neighbours. But now I come to think about it, I feel sure I've heard something about that family.'

Georgy asked: 'What kind of thing?'

'Can't remember. I must ask Augustin. Now, tomorrow we are going to Mâcon and will stay a few days. My *belle-mère* wants to see an old friend of hers in the town. The children won't be going, so they will be in your charge. Célanie will cook for you.'

Georgy said: 'Did Louis-Marie invite himself over here?'

'I was forced to extend an invitation. I said, "when we are back and the old people have gone". I don't think I could manage him along with his great-aunt and my in-laws.'

Oh well then, thought Georgy, he won't be bringing another handsome young man here yet.

In this she was partly right, partly wrong.

The grown-ups had departed in a cloud of dust from the carriage wheels on the sun-baked drive, for it was still quite warm and they lacked rain.

Georgy felt her new responsibility. Camille must trust her if she left the little ones with her, even if it were only for a few days? What if one of them fell ill – or had an accident? But there was a horse in the stable and the male servants were used to riding to the apothecary. She could even ride there herself at a pinch. She had never particularly enjoyed riding but at home the men rode everywhere across country.

Célanie and Eglantine told her not to worry. 'She used to leave the children with us when Monsieur de Marceau was away in Paris last year and she was invited over to La Poissonière,' said Célanie.

They were sitting in the kitchen that overlooked the *potager*, the kitchen garden, and Georgy was keeping an eye on the children who had been allowed out to run around for half an hour.

'Where is La Poissonière – who lives there?' she asked idly.

'Oh, that's Monsieur Cellard's estate – you saw him here before you went to Aix—'

'Yes, I remember – he is quite well-off, isn't he?'

'They say so, though he's only the bailiff when all's said and done,' replied Eglantine, whilst Célanie pursed her lips and said nothing. Georgy wondered what she had against Jacques Cellard.

That evening the children were put to bed after many outdoor games that had produced much laughter. Hoping to tire them out, as there were only two of them Georgy had taught them leap-frog. Then they had played hide-and-seek in the barn and stables, eventually ending up in the house for one last game which enabled her to explore the upper rooms with their mansard roofs. Some of them were dusty and empty.

'I will teach you blind-man's-buff tomorrow,' she promised them. She intended also to teach them cricket, which was played by all the village children at home, girls as well as boys. The wickets would be a problem.

'Do all young English ladies play so many games?' asked Célanie.

'She is not so far from childhood herself,' said Eglantine to Célanie.

The next morning dawned; once again the weather was warm and sunny. After their English lesson – though Georgy thought they learned more English from playing games with her, and wondered whether Monsieur Rousseau had advocated games-

103

playing – Célanie took over and Georgy went for a little walk alone by the pond.

The water was very low and she amused herself skimming pebbles over its surface. On the far side of the pond the trees joined those by the side of the drive and became a little wood that stretched for a mile or so. She wondered if any of the trees were the same as those at home. For a few moments she tried to imagine what they were all doing at Huntingore Hall. The few months since her arrival in France seemed more like years. She was being well treated, even if she spent most of her time with the children, and she thought that she was making some progress, even with Thibault. She was also making good progress in speaking French, learning new words daily.

There would soon be the harvest and especially the *vendange*, or wine harvest, to look forward to, then her first winter abroad, before a new spring. Vaguely imagining the next few months, and just about to turn and go back to the château, she thought she heard a horse's neigh coming from the ride in the woods. She shaded her eyes from the sun and looked across at the entrance to the glade. Soon a horse did appear, ambling slowly along, its rider holding his reins loose.

Oh no! surely Louis-Marie would not take it upon himself to ride over when he had been told the family was away? But no, she was sure that the rider was not that gentleman. She waited for him to come round the pond before she saw with a lurch in the region of her heart that it was his friend. Amaury Arnaud was indeed the rider. She'd recognize him anywhere.

Did he know she was at the château, or was it just a young man spending a pleasant morning exploring the countryside?

She waited for him to come up. He must have seen her. Should she pretend she did not recognize him? What should she say to him?

The horse, a grey mare, trotted up and stopped a few yards away from her.

'Well, if it isn't Louis-Marie's English friend!' he said.

'Didn't Louis tell you I was with the de Marceau family?' replied Georgy. 'I believe my employer saw you a few days ago?'

'He may have done,' he said carelessly. 'I'm thirsty – can your servants give me water – and the horse too?'

'Of course. I was just about to go in and resume my duties. You remember Thibault and Lucie? Thibault would like to see your horse, I am sure! His own has not yet arrived though he has been promised one.'

'Then he shall. I am staying with my mama two leagues away, but I needed the exercise. Louis-Marie was busy with a sonnet but sends his regards.'

She thought she detected a slight tone of disparagement in his voice, but she took her courage in both hands as she asked him: 'Did you enjoy the concert?'

'Ah yes, the concert. You were there?'

'Yes – I was with your friend.'

Louis-Marie must not have told him who was accompanying him. She did not say, 'And *you* were with a young lady,' and he did not elaborate.

Thibault and Lucie came rushing out of the house when they heard footsteps on the gravel outside, but stopped in their tracks when they saw the young man. Georgy went into the house to find Célanie.

'I hope you don't mind,' she whispered to her. 'This young man – M Arnaud – is a friend of M Louis-Marie. He is thirsty, and so is his horse.' She was a little uncomfortable. A young visitor did not usually come into a house when the owners were away, and he had only a tenuous acquaintance with the 'governess'.

However, Célanie went out with her, took a quick look at the young gentleman, and pronounced: 'You are welcome to water your horse, Monsieur. Jean will see to it. And there is the pump round the back if Monsieur wishes to drink. Mademoiselle Georgy will show you.' They led the mare round to the stables.

Thibault ran up to pat the animal. 'I remember you,' said the child. '*Your* horse is not so handsome as the ones we saw in the park!'

Amaury replied: 'That is because I am a poor man, *mon brave!*' and Thibault looked puzzled.

Georgy could not help looking at Amaury as he laughed and joked with the child and the stable boy. Then he drank copiously from the spring water in the courtyard, cupping the silvery liquid in his hands and ending up wiping his face with them, and she tried not to stare.

He was so handsome! Was it just chance that he and his horse had needed exercise and that he had vaguely remembered Louis-

Marie telling him that the family of de Marceau lived not far away? He could not have ridden over because he wanted to meet the English governess again. It was more likely that he had enjoyed playing with the children in the park and knew they lived in this direction. Young men though, however agreeable, did not usually bother about children. This young man was now talking to her two charges with every appearance of ease.

'Mama and Papa are visiting Mamie,' said Lucie confidingly. 'But they'll be back soon, I expect.'

'Oh, what a pity I shall not see your mama,' he replied.

'Célanie and Georgy are looking after us,' said Lucie.

Amaury looked directly at Georgy and smiled. 'Then I hope you are both behaving yourselves.'

Thibault said: 'I want to go on your horse,' but Lucie pursued: 'If you come again we can play hide-and-seek.'

'I don't expect Monsieur Amaury wants to play that,' said Georgy. 'It is not a game for grown-ups.'

'But we play it with you,' said Lucie.

'Georgy is not grown up,' said Thibault, 'except when she gives us lessons!'

'Thiby, you are not to call her Georgy – you know what Mama said? We have to call her Miss,' said Lucie.

'I'm sure,' said Georgy to Amaury, 'that Monsieur and Madame would be pleased for you and Louis-Marie to visit them when they are returned. Indeed, she has mentioned that to me.'

'You do not have many visitors?' asked Amaury. 'I believe my mother mentioned one or two mutual friends. A Monsieur Cellard? He has two sisters whom I met last year – Pascale and Cécile.' His mare was now looking around her with curiosity.

'Oh, I don't know – there is always the family – and our few near neighbours. Yes, I have met M Cellard. He has not been over yet – we are not yet settled back here. I suppose you are in the district only as an extension of your holiday? Are you not usually in Paris?'

'Oh, my mother likes to move around. We rent a house here, a house there,' he said carelessly. 'She likes the present one.'

There was no mention of a father in all this, but Georgy repressed her curiosity.

'You enjoyed Aix?' asked Amaury as they walked the horse back in the direction of the woods, the children following with shrieks and runs like darting minnows.

'Hush, you will startle the horse!' said Georgy to Thibault; then, turning to Amaury: 'Yes, I loved it. There is less to do here, though I like your countryside.'

'What is your horse called?' asked Thibault.

'She is called Jument – because she is a mare.'

Georgy saw that he was skilled at juggling and dividing talk with more than one person at once, yet what did she really know about him?

'Have you any brothers or sisters?' Lucie asked him. Trust children not to be inhibited in their questions.

After a pause he answered: 'Yes, there is my brother Thierry – but he is only four – and I used to have another brother in Paris.'

'I should like to go to Paris,' said Thibault, patting the mare vigorously.

'Oh, I'm sure you will one day. And you, Mademoiselle,' he asked, turning to Georgy, 'Do you know Paris?'

'No – only when we came through from England.' She was thinking, if he has a brother of only four, his mother must still be quite young. Yet he is – what? Twenty? Twenty five at most.

'Then you must spend more time in our capital on your return. How much longer are you to stay with the family?'

'Oh until next spring, at least—'

Lucie, listening intently, said: 'She will stay till we speak English properly.'

'I must be off now. You can say *au revoir* to me in English!' He swung up on to his horse.

'Good-bye, Mister.'

'Good-bye, horse,' said Thibault.

'*Au-revoir!*'

He bowed slightly from the saddle to Georgy and they all stood watching and waving as the mare trotted away in the direction of the wood.

He turned and waved before disappearing under the trees.

'The young man who called this morning looks a bit healthier than that Louis-Marie,' said Célanie.

They were drinking their soup in the kitchen, Georgy having dismissed the necessity for a special place to be laid for her in the dining-room. The children ate their supper in the schoolroom, after which she usually read them an English story. Even the simplest required much explanation and translation. She could not understand why their parents, or at least their mother herself, could not have extended their English vocabulary for them. She had gathered from Célanie that Madame Camille had not liked babies and that her husband had at first preferred her to speak French even to her own children. He must have relented enough to have allowed her own arrival here – but maybe she was only on sufferance? Perhaps Camille had never really consulted him over her plan for a young Englishwoman to join their household for a time?

She replied to the maid's question: 'Yes, he does – but they must be about the same age.'

The older maid, Eglantine, was sitting in an old high-backed chair darning the children's clothes. 'I believe that young man's family once lived in the Château de Souillères' she said, after a pause whilst she threaded her needle. 'If his mother's the same lady I'm thinking of. But there was some upset – I can't remember exactly what – or we were never told – something to do with them taking the wrong side in the Wars – or before – I'm not sure. I think it was her father or her grandfather there was the talk about – I seem to recall that his name was d'Aubigny.'

Georgy wanted to know everything she could about Amaury Arnaud. But she did not want to let the two servants guess how interested she was. She had learned that lesson in England. Not that she was likely to get to know him the way she knew Edward Walker, but she might allow herself the day-dream of *one day* getting to know him better. Oh, he had probably just visited the château on the spur of the moment! The countryside must be rather boring for a young man who was at home in Paris? She wondered how long his mother had been renting the house beyond the forest.

'Was her father a Republican?' she asked Eglantine.

'As to that, I don't know – there were lots of *them* around – our family was for the King of course – but you'll know that. My grandmother worked for them, you know . . . .'

She was well-launched now on tales of 'her' family and Georgy found them fascinating. Such conflicts had been so much longer ago in her own country, though she remembered her father telling her about those in Yorkshire who were for Cromwell, including his own ancestors, good Puritan stock that they were.

She put away thoughts of the handsome Amaury until she could be alone in her room. Then she could indulge herself, remembering his voice and his face and his hands and the way he had glanced at her. There was nobody in whom to confide; Abigail Strang was far away, so she had better confine her thoughts to her new diary. So, on the evening of the day of Amaury's visit, Georgy began to try to write down her impressions of the young Amaury. After reading through the first page, however, written, naturally, in English, she suffered a kind of embarrassment. It would be easier somehow to write in French – but then it would not be safe here from prying eyes. She turned the page, and began to reread Lamartine's poem *L'Isolement.* She would copy it out: poetry gave a better expression of her state of mind than her own clumsy words. Like Shelley, Lamartine seemed to see himself as a dead leaf borne away in the wind. She turned back to the line she already knew and loved:

. .*un seul être vous manque, et tout est dépeuplé!*

Now it seemed to have an additional resonance. Was she being ridiculous? Today she had spoken for precisely half an hour to Amaury Arnaud, interrupted continuously by Thibault and Lucie. But her *feelings* were not ridiculous. If only she could see him again to talk at length about life and poetry . . . . The kind of conversation that with Louis-Marie was a purgatory would be delicious with the other young man ... and she felt sure Amaury Arnaud's verse would be better than his friend's.

She tried to think what Alphonse de Lamartine had been like at twenty or so – young, beautiful and melancholy, and mentally she compared Amaury with him. It was true that Amaury did not seem an excessively melancholy fellow, but she knew by now that poets did not always show their real feelings; you had to read their poetry to understand them. She must not make a romantic hero of Amaury, she scolded herself.

Not for the first time she remembered Shakespeare's words: *Oh the difference between man and man!*' Edward Walker had said, when they read these words, that the remark also applied to women. But she did not want to think about Edward; he seemed remote, far away, from another life . . . .

She realized she could easily sit for hours thinking about the handsome Amaury, but she also knew that she would never be allowed to indulge herself in this way – which was maybe a good thing. She could not linger long in her room with her thoughts; something would always interrupt them, so they were even more precious when they were saved up for a moment's solitude.

At the back of her mind, Georgy consciously placed the possibility of another visit from the young man under the heading: Something to look forward to. She had always used this method of calming herself or cheering herself up. Amaury might never visit again … she might never see him again – Oh, God! That was surely not possible? But so long as the possibility endured, the thought could keep her going for the time being.

The rest of the family would soon return. Meanwhile, the next day the children pestered her pleasantly.

'Don't you wish Monsieur Arnaud would come here again?' said Lucie. 'He's a nice man.'

Georgy concurred.

'I wish he would let me ride his horse,' said Thibault.

'Perhaps he will – but your papa is to buy you a pony, isn't he?'

'I don't want a pony,' said Thibault scornfully. 'I want a horse.'

'He is too small for a horse, isn't he, Mademoiselle Georgy?'

Georgy saw a squabble advancing but by now she had learned how to distract the adversaries. 'I thought you might like to fish in the pond this afternoon? Or would you rather go for a wild-flower walk?'

Fortunately they both said the pond.

The four de Marceaus, the elder couple and the younger, returned home the next day. The children greeted their mother, and Thibault consented to receive his grandmother's caresses without too much ill grace. Georgy was relieved that the matter of a horse was not immediately broached by Thibault for she could see that his father was preoccupied. After dinner he disappeared into his study with his own father. The old lady, saying she was tired, went to bed. Camille and Georgy were left alone in the small salon.

'My husband will be obliged to go to Paris very soon on business,' said Camille. 'And he does not wish me to accompany him.'

Georgy considered that his departure would at least precipitate that of Camille's in-laws, with whom she would obviously not wish to be incarcerated over the next few weeks. Camille implied this when she said with a satisfied air: 'Augustin can accompany his parents on their journey home.'

Georgy very much wanted to tell her mistress that she had had a visitor but did not quite know how to begin, without making the matter appear more important than it probably was. She was given an opening by Camille's asking suddenly: 'Did you have any callers? Monsieur Cellard? Louis-Marie des Combes? Aunt Hortense?'

'No, Louis-Marie did not call, but his friend – whom I believe you met last week – was riding in this direction and called to water his horse.'

'Monsieur Bonaventure, is it?'

'No, I was told his name is Arnaud – Amaury is his *nom de baptême.*'

'Ah yes, I remember, it is his *maman* who is called Madame Bonaventure. Odd. She must have been widowed and remarried. She has never taken a house in the neighbourhood before. How old is the young man?'

'Oh, about twenty-four or twenty-five – about the same age as Louis-Marie.' She tried to remain impassive.

Camille said: 'I suppose we must sooner or later entertain Hortense's cousin – and he can bring his friend along if he is still in the district.' Georgy was pleased.

The next day Camille received a letter which she read and then tossed on to the small table where she kept her pen and paper and a few miniatures of her family. Célanie was washing the children's hands before they settled down to work in the schoolroom and Georgy was helping Eglantine fill the vases in the small sitting room with late marguerites, her own idea. The French did not appear to go in for many flowers in the house.

Monsieur de Marceau could be heard in the garden shouting to his servant, for he was preparing a trunk of papers to take to Paris.

'It's from Louis-Marie – how that young man does cling! Still, I said we would invite him over here and I shall keep my word.'

'Does he mention his friend, M Arnaud?'

'Yes, he says they would both like to visit and his aunt may come too if they can harness a small carriage for her. *Zut alors!* If Hortense comes we shall never get rid of her!'

But the first visitor after M de Marceau's departure for Paris in pursuit of his father's – and therefore eventually of his own – estates was neither Louis-Marie nor Amaury.

Georgy was in the garden gathering herbs for Célanie when a horse and rider appeared at the stable entrance. She took no notice; it was not Amaury. After a few moments, the horseman appeared and Eglantine let him into the house by the side door. Georgy thought she had recognized Monsieur Jacques Cellard who had visited the château during her first week in France. She bent back to her work of tracking down the various herbs Célanie needed. There were some that did not grow at home in Yorkshire: too cold, she supposed.

Monsieur Cellard was a tall, burly, large-featured man of about forty-five with springy dark hair. He looked a thorough-going countryman and somehow, Georgy had thought, not very French – or what she had assumed was a French appearance. Apparently as well as acting as bailiff around the place, and working also for other owners of property, he had a farm of his own a few miles away. He was also called upon, as Georgy was to discover, to cast accounts for Camille.

A little later she heard the murmur of conversation from the open window of the small sitting-room at the corner of the house. Camille must be going through the books. M de Marceau often left business instructions with his wife who pretended she did not understand them. Georgy believed she understood more than she might admit, knew full well the state of their finances and was aware of what needed to be done on the land.

She went round to the kitchens at the back with her trug of herbs. Célanie was making coffee on a little stove.

'Would you mind taking this into the mistress?' she said, 'Monsieur Cellard likes his coffee hot and I've my hands full with the *déjeuner.*'

Both she and Eglantine often asked Georgy to help her with such things. Georgy did not mind at all, though she knew her family would not expect her to undertake what were after all domestic services. But she liked to be of use. Children surely belonged to domestic services too. Anyway, it helped her learn more French.

Camille never stood on ceremony when she was in charge of

the house. This did not preclude her occasionally becoming irritated with the servants, but they appeared philosophical about it. Georgy supposed they preferred an all too human mistress to her cold husband.

Georgy knocked at the door. She knew that servants did not usually knock but she was not a servant.

They both looked up as she advanced with her *plateau* on which were two white cups of steaming coffee. Camille was sitting at the window seat, by a little table on which stood her portable desk. She kept this in her room under a special lock and key. Now it was open and there were papers with seals and ribbons spread out on the table. They both looked up as she entered the room, and she had the feeling that something had just been said that was not to do with business.

But then: 'You could exchange those guineas for Napoléons,' said Jacques Cellard. 'The rate of exchange is favourable to England at present.'

'Thank you, Georgy,' said Camille in English. 'Where are the children?'

'They are waiting for me in the schoolroom, Madame – I have set them some copying from *Le Petit Précepteur*. Célanie thought you would like your coffee here—'

'Thank you – you can put the tray down on that table near the screen.'

Camille was looking well this morning. She was wearing a deep pink shawl over her paler pink day-gown, but her hair had not been properly dressed.

'You have met my English cousin?' she said to the man.

She must regard him as a gentleman, thought Georgy or she would not have bothered to say this.

He inclined his head and said: 'Of course, Mademoiselle,' but he did not get up.

Georgy said: 'Shall I pour your coffee?'

'Oh thank you – and then you must go up to the children.'

She poured them both a cup of coffee.

A warm Indian summer breeze was coming through the casement, disturbing a few curls on Camille's forehead. Jacques Cellard smiled at Georgy and then looked down at his papers. Camille sipped her coffee.

Georgy beat a retreat upstairs where she discovered Thibault with a page of spidery ink-blots intended to represent a bird. Lucie had copied out neatly:

> *The bird is perched.*
> *I have peeled that apple.*
> *It is dinner-time.*
> *What seed is this?*
> *Mary is making sweetmeats.*

'Now you can both tell me what all that means,' said Georgy, 'and then we can go and see if Eglantine is making sweetmeats!'

It was hopeless trying to teach them together. She looked at Thibault's drawing of a robin and persuaded him to write *rouge-gorge* and *robin* underneath his messy effort.

Tomorrow she would go back to Mrs Mangnall's *Questions.* Lucie had been interested in the French kings, but Thibault was more interested in *Questions on Common Subjects*, and seemed to enjoy Georgy's explanations. Relying heavily on Mrs Mangnall, she tried to explain such things as how candles were made, or of what ivory, or indigo, or cork, or flax, consisted. She had discovered quite a few things she had not known herself, or had forgotten. The only trouble was that she often did not know what these things were in French. But Camille usually did and did not mind being asked, though she said some of the things were confined to England – rhubarb for example.

Georgy was rather dreading *How gunpowder is made*, and thought she would give it a miss. She knew only too well the sort of things that interested Thibault.

Fortunately he was not yet quite up to reading it for himself.

Chapter 2

After Monsieur Cellard's visit nobody came for several days. The weather was still balmy, and Georgy did her best to amuse the children out of doors whilst they could still enjoy it. Camille went out once or twice in the small carriage. Then, at the end of that week, some of the smaller vineyards began their wine harvest. It was explained to Georgy that the wine made in the *domaine* was mostly local – *vin du pays* – but that Monsieur de Marceau had also invested in several larger vineyards further to the north-east, nearer Beaune and the Côte d'Or. She thought it odd, that he did not supervise the *vendange* himself, but Camille explained that M Cellard was very experienced.

'Augustin came late to it all,' she said, 'but he will probably call in to see the main harvest on his way back from Paris.'

Whenever Georgy was released from her tasks for a few moments, or for half an hour in bed at night before she fell asleep, she day-dreamed over Amaury Arnaud. She was distressed that, however hard she tried, she could not envisage his face exactly in her mind's eye. It was perhaps worse the harder she tried, for sometimes, out in the garden with the children or doing some task for Célanie in the kitchen, a sudden snatch of profile, a curve of a cheek, a stray wave of brown hair would come to her, only to fade away when she tried to keep it behind her eyes. She took to describing her feelings for him in her journal, writing in English. Camille was not likely to be interested in her diary. She was amazed at her own imagination: a dream Amaury floated over her as she wrote. Was it all in her mind? Did he care for her a little?

On the Sunday she went to church in the village with Camille and the children and here too she found time to think about

Amaury instead of following the others in prayer. The candles and the incense created an almost hypnotic atmosphere, very conducive to fantasy.

The next morning she was in the schoolroom with the children trying to explain the mysteries of long division to Lucie and teaching Thibault his tables when she heard voices through the open window. Thibault immediately got down from his chair and rushed to look out, saying: 'Perhaps he's brought the horse again!'

'Thibault come back! You haven't finished your work—' But she was just as eager to know who the visitor was and was disappointed when the child turned saying, 'It's not him – it's Louis-Marie,' and her heart slid down back to her boots.

Camille would entertain him, she thought, but she would not be able to escape him if she took the children downstairs. Still, perhaps Louis-Marie would know where Amaury was or if he intended a visit.

When she calculated that it was time for their glass of fresh milk, brought in by the Jean from the farm at the bottom of the fields, Georgy accompanied the children to the kitchens. She could hear a murmur of voices from the salon. The door opened and Camille called:

'Georgy, your friend is here! If you are having your milk I am sure he would like a glass.' Her *friend* indeed. And, being English she was perfectly aware of the word *milksop*. Did she mean to be a little malicious to them both?

Louis-Marie appeared and bowed, and she murmured a good day, before leaving the children with their mother and going off for the milk.

On return she found Camille sitting in a high-backed chair, a piece of embroidery on her lap, trying to thread a needle. This was the first time she had ever seen her employer doing such a thing. She must be feeling excessively bored. Thibault and Lucie gulped down their milk and stood staring at the young man. Louis-Marie uttered a few commonplaces, but he was obviously not used to children.

'You were in the park with us,' said Thibault. 'Where is your friend? Will he come to see me?'

Louis-Marie cleared his throat but Camille interrupted whatever he was going to say.

'Thibault, now you have finished your milk you may ask Célanie to play ball with you both in the field.'

He finished off his drink rather noisily and was off like a shot, only too pleased to escape. Reluctantly, Lucie got up as well. She would have preferred to listen to adult conversation, but followed her brother. Then Thibault returned for a moment, poking his head back through the door, and said to the young man: '*Is* your friend coming again with his horse?'

'Just what we were about to discuss,' said Camille.

When Thibault had disappeared again she turned to Georgy. 'Apparently Monsieur Arnaud will soon be off to Paris, but I thought it would be pleasant for us to entertain him here before that. Louis-Marie tells me he will be driving over to Madame Arnaud's – or rather Madame Bonaventure's – tomorrow and will take an invitation to luncheon.'

'It is most kind,' murmured Louis-Marie, wiping a moustache of milk from his upper lip with a large pocket handkerchief.

Georgy guessed that Camille wanted to find out more about this mysterious Madame Bonaventure. What better way than entertaining her son, then later extending a separate invitation to her?

'I believe your friend is also a poet?' pursued Camille, taking up a strand of pale pink silk and threading her needle with it.

'Oh, Amaury favours the lyric effusion,' said Louis-Marie. 'I myself incline to the epic.'

Camille was trying to look suitably impressed. Georgy wanted to giggle. She had better be nice to Louis-Marie though, for through him she might see Amaury again.

'I am writing a poem on the subject of Charlemagne,' the young man went on.

'That must be a very difficult subject,' said Georgy, thinking, what a tall order, but she knew that subjects from antiquity or the Middle Ages were now becoming popular.

'And needs much research! Our mutual cousin has promised to read it when it is completed. You have heard from him?'

'No, but they must by now be arrived in Florence – where as you know M de Lamartine is to represent France at the court of the Duke of Tuscany,' said Camille, bent over her work.

'Being in the country will give you time to finish your epic,' said Georgy. Why could she not help wanting to tease the poor man?

117

'Indeed,' said Louis-Marie not hearing anything ironic in her words.

'You could bring it along when you visit us with your friend,' said Camille. 'And now you must excuse me – I have to send a message to my bailiff.' She stood up, folded her embroidery and put it in the drawer of a bureau by the window. 'Will you stay to luncheon?' she asked.

'Alas, I should love to do so but have promised my great-aunt to accompany her to town this afternoon.'

'Do stay a little longer – you can recite your poem to Georgy.' With this, Camille swept out.

Georgy said, 'Yes, please do – I should be very interested.'

'I do not have the verses with me – I came over principally to see you. Amaury told me he had ridden in your direction and that you told him you would be pleased to see us both once Madame de Marceau had returned. I am afraid my friend is always off here there and everywhere – Paris one day, Lyon the next – but he agrees with me that a healthful ride in the woods is a daily necessity. Unfortunately, as I am not *chez moi* I cannot invite Madame and yourself to call on us, but I expect Aunt Hortense will return your hospitality eventually.' He took a breath after this long speech.

Georgy knew full well what a trial Camille found Aunt Hortense, so said only: 'That is very kind of her,' before adding in what she hoped was a casual tone of voice: 'Does Madame Bonaventure live – have a house – in Paris? Is Amaury Arnaud's father dead?'

Louis-Marie looked for once a little discomfited. Then: 'I believe my friend's mother is twice a widow,' he said. 'I think she was left with little money after the demise of her husbands. There are however relatives in Paris with whom my friend is on good terms.'

'Do they often come to Burgundy, then?' Georgy was emboldened to ask.

'It costs less than living in Paris,' he said shortly.

'It must be pleasant for him to have you as a friend,' she said diplomatically.

He drew himself up self-importantly. 'Amaury needs a mentor,' he said.

'Oh?'

'I believe his mother is relieved that he can rely on me to direct him in the paths of … duty.'

She had thought he was going to say 'righteousness', there was such a long pause between his words.

'I am sure,' she said.

'Also, his writing needs direction. I wanted him to meet Cousin Alphonse in Aix but he refused; he does not always see where his interests lie.'

She thought, there is a whole history behind all this. Cousin Alphonse, indeed!

Their conversation was interrupted at this point by the arrival of Thibault. There was no sign of his mother.

Nervously taking up his hat and riding crop, Louis-Marie added: 'Well, we shall look forward to your patroness's kind invitation.'

Her patroness! Louis-Marie was incapable of using the right word. What did he think she was here for? To write verse whilst looking into the sunset? No, he would not think that; girls were not put on earth to write verse. He must be puzzled that she was a sort of superior servant, a mixture of nanny and governess who was also treated as a member of the family. Maybe he was just being tactful? He was not such a bad old thing but she did find him more than a little ludicrous.

Camille appeared in the passage as he finally made his farewells at the front door before going round for his horse.

'Do tell Monsieur Arnaud he will be most welcome to visit – don't forget – Thursday you are both invited to luncheon!'

With that Georgy had to be content.

She looked forward to the Thursday with a delicious sense of mingled anticipation and excitement.

It was kind of Camille de Marceau to have ordered a specially good luncheon for the two young men.

Georgy realised that Jacques Cellard had also been invited to partake of the food and drink when he came out of Camille's small withdrawing room, having been closeted there with a sheaf of papers for well over an hour.

Louis-Marie and Amaury had arrived at noon, and consumed a bottle of cassis mixed with cold white wine as an apéritif. Célanie and Eglantine, along with a middle-aged servant, Régine, who still helped them out from time to time, had been commanded to produce artichokes with butter sauce followed by roast baby chicken and then salt beef. The meal finished with fresh local cheese, and blackberries as luscious and sweet as any Georgy had ever tasted, smothered in fresh yellow cream.

Throughout the repast, which was shared with the children, Georgy had to keep an eye on her charges. She could not relax whilst Thibault balanced peas on his knife or Lucie looked agonizedly at the too large portion of artichokes handed out to her. Camille was concentrating on the men, and appeared particularly interested in Amaury Arnaud, so Georgy listened, said little. Louis-Marie was giving the food his complete attention. For once he did not ask for milk. Monsieur Cellard kept his own counsel as he tucked heartily into the repast.

Georgy did wonder whether it was customary for the lady of the house to entertain three men whilst her husband was away from home. Her own mother might very well have done so, but Mama was not young, whilst Camille was still in her late thirties. Not that there was anything untoward or *louche* about the atmosphere – on the contrary it was light and civilized, but Georgy felt sure that they were all aware of the fact that such a meal would probably not have been undertaken if the master of the house had been at home. Madame de Marceau had seized her freedom and looked very handsome, cheeks slightly flushed, tendrils of well-dressed hair curling softly on her neck.

Amaury was in fine form, even showing off a little, but he did it so gracefully that nobody minded and Georgy was full of admiration. Louis-Marie looked relatively glum, but even Jacques Cellard smiled indulgently at the handsome Amaury.

Afterwards they were all to walk in the grounds.

'It is what we English call a "constitutional",' said Camille, and led the way with M Cellard, the children gambolling around them, running hither and thither, spending three times as much energy as the adults.

Georgy found herself alone at last with Amaury as they walked through a little thicket on the other side of the pond. He remarked, pitching his voice low: 'She is very kind, your cousin Camille – I am surprised my mother has not met her before but I expect she was in England when Mama was here last year.'

Georgy did want to talk about something other than their

hostess, so replied: 'Yes, you could write *vers de société* about her, couldn't you?'

'I believe the de Marceaus are very *minor* nobility,' he said. 'Not that I care a hoot for rank – but one must agree that she would probably be happier in Paris?'

'And is your mama happier there?' asked Georgy, since he obviously did not wish to discuss his poems.

'Oh, my mother is a law unto herself,' he replied.

'I am not used to "Society"' said Georgy artlessly. 'At home I suppose we have provincial worthies. Of course I met Camille and her family in London – but I don't care for wealth and fuss and rules—'

'Are all English women like you and Madame de Marceau?' he asked, slashing a bush with a hazel twig.

'What do you mean?'

'Well you are very proper in some ways but freer in others – I believe Louis-Marie is quite shocked at the freedom accorded the "governess"!'

'I am here to work, or I should not be here in France at all. I am not all that free at home, you know. We all have to observe the conventions, women most of all.'

'I expect Madame Camille can be quite haughty,' he said, on a different tack. 'They say her husband is a cold fish—'

Georgy was a little shocked that he should say this to her – and of her employer too. She changed the subject. 'At least we have good *poets* in England. Perhaps they write more freely than yours do here—'

'Oh, I have read your Wordsworth' – he pronounced it "Vordsvu" – 'and your Lord Byron!'

'Of course – everybody reads Byron – do you compare him with M de Lamartine?'

She wanted him to speak of matters that were of more importance to him than generalizations about national character. It was strange, when she was talking to him she could see him as quite apart from the image she had been carrying around with her. She sensed he was clever and combative, and did not take kindly to young women who challenged his own opinions.

'And what do *you* know of Lamartine, Mademoiselle?'

'I have ready many times the *Premières Méditations* and am struck how un-French they are—'

'Oh, he has not been technically adventurous!'

'Maybe not – I don't know enough to compare him with your earlier poets – he just seems a little like some of the English poets I love – but I can't really appreciate the language as I can my own.'

'They are elegiac, your English poets – you see I have read some too. Perhaps we need more rebellion here, a thorough cleaning up of old habits—'

'Do you mean in literature or in ordinary life? I thought your Revolution was supposed to do the latter?'

'*Eh bien*, it is time for a thoroughgoing literary one – or we shall all be back where we started. I see the elegiac rather than the passionate in M de Lamartine's verse.'

'Yet Lamartine writes of feelings that do not change – in spite of revolutions—'

'You mean he writes sentimentally of women – he is all heart.'

She wanted to say, what is wrong with that, but did not wish to venture upon the dangerous territory of talk about love. She wanted to say that when he wrote of his 'Elvire' it was of a love that came from the heart, was not just that of a young man's fancy . . .

'I agree,' continued Amaury, 'there is none better or more skilled when he writes of his states of soul. It is always a soul who is breathing in the summer air of early evening, is it not?'

'And that is very tender and beautiful—'

'He is always about to lose his love! Or has lost her. He seizes an impression but does not pursue it – he has an easy fluency— nothing appears to have been planned in his poetry.'

'But lyric poetry just – *gushes out* – I don't know the French word – he does not have to correct himself – it is all sincere and genuine—'

'He does not arrange his lines very well and he repeats himself—'

'It is a good thing *you* did not meet him in Aix or you would have disheartened him—'

'No, I should have said nothing to *him* – it is only to you I speak – or to my own friends. Nothing I could say would alter his way of writing—'

'You must admit that there has been no one to rival him in your country in the expression of true feeling.'

'But his feelings carry his style – how will he ever be able to write in a different style – as all poets must do to progress? He can be careless now – but how will he write when he is sixty? And it is not true that he has no rivals. I myself have met one of them—'

'Perhaps he will never be sixty. Byron will never be sixty – or even forty!'

'It may be a good thing for his verse that he died.'

'You are very cynical! I thought M de Lamartine such a nice man – and he gives the impression of great idealism.'

'Oh he is handsome, I agree, and talented, and has a charming personality, I am sure – but I have the feeling he will not wish to be a poet all his life.'

'Well, no; he has in fact gone to serve your country in Florence.'

'Really. There you see – he has delusions of power—'

'What are you two talking about?' asked Camille, strolling back with Jacques Cellard. Louis-Marie came up behind them looking hot and bothered.

'Oh, we were discussing poetry,' said Amaury Arnaud with a bow. 'And now I must talk to Thibault.'

'Yes, yes – I want to see your horse!' shouted Thibault.

Georgy was feeling excited by her conversation with Amaury, dazzled by his knowledge. At last here was someone to whom she could talk about what interested her. Yet in spite of that she also could not help wishing that they had got on to more personal things. Amaury probably saw her as a sort of junior aspirant blue-stocking. Oh well, she had asked for it, and it was better than making small talk.

Lucie came up to Georgy and put her hand in hers. 'I wish we could have visitors every day,' she said.

Georgy had so much to think about when the young men left at six o'clock that she wished she could go straight to her room. Unfortunately, the children had become over-excited and it was left to her to calm them down. Just before the men departed Amaury had told the women he was off to Paris at the end of the week.

'And you are taking Louis-Marie with you?' Camille had asked politely.

'No, I am going alone. I have to see my uncle – my mother's brother – and also to make a few enquiries about a little career for myself on a new journal. I hope to see you all again soon,' he said as he swung on to his mare. 'Thank you so much for your hospitality.' Georgy imagined his look had then lingered on her.

Jacques Cellard rode up on his black horse and waited for Louis-Marie to mount his steed. He was riding what could not truly be designated a horse, for it resembled a large pony. Could it be a mule?

Georgy thought she might have neglected Louis-Marie, so once he was safely on his mount, she said to him: 'You must bring Charlemagne next time.' He smiled stiffly. Maybe he did not feel too secure on his mount.

Camille said: 'Give our best wishes to your aunt. Go with Miss Georgina, children, it will soon be time for your milk and your beds.'

Georgy thought she had never seen Camille looking so well and happy.

How was she to meet Amaury again? They could only wait for an invitation from Aunt Hortense and she did not entirely trust Louis-Marie to acquaint his friend with that. Anyway, Amaury would soon be off to Paris.

She had reckoned without Camille, for a few days later that lady said: 'Jean has brought over an invitation from Hortense that we should all go over to Les Aisées tomorrow afternoon. She says she cannot entertain us to a meal – she is lacking servants, not being in her own home, but she would like to see us. I sent him back with a message that I hoped we would see M Arnaud – and perhaps his mother – before he departed to Paris.

So *you* like him too! thought Georgy.

They went over to Les Aisées in the second best carriage, driven by the groom, Paul. The drive was first of all through woodland, the trees a mixture of green and gold with a few already turning scarlet. Then they passed by water meadows on a narrow path by a river. Georgy had never realized how near this river was to the château. In the far distance they could see mountains, the Monts du Charolais, but they disappeared when they turned and came through another wood, this time on a broad path.

Camille pointed the way. 'Mademoiselle Vivier lives over there. She spends much of the year in the old house belonging to her sister's husband's family and they allow her to entertain now and then.'

'And Louis-Marie is often a guest as well?'

'Yes, he is related to them all and she likes him to visit. It would be boring for most young men but he is kind – or rather, I think he likes old people.'

Georgy thought, Yes, he can discuss their ailments with them!

At the end of the drive they came up to the house. It was sombre, larger than Pinac-Les-Saules, and quieter. Hortense Vivier, standing at the top of the shallow stone *perron*, was waiting to greet them at the central entrance. There was no sign of either young man. A middle-aged maid came up and led the way to the back of the entrance lobby, and then up a staircase that rose up two flights before they arrived at a landing on a long corridor.

Hortense waited for the servant to open the door and then they all trooped in. Here was Louis-Marie, sitting at a window seat in a deep embrasure.

Where was Amaury?

Georgy knew it was not her business to ask, so waited until Camille might enquire if anyone else were coming to this little gathering. The children looked a trifle intimidated by the long dark hangings in the room and began to converse in whispers. Aunt Hortense sat down in an uncomfortable looking chair by the unlit grate, and Camille and Georgy were given small chairs on each side of hers.

After some small talk, Camille asked casually: 'Is your new neighbour, Madame Bonaventure, not to visit us today then, Aunt?'

'She sent a message to say that Thierry, her little boy, was ailing with a cold and that she thought it wiser to stay at home. But her other son will soon be here, I should think.'

Louis-Marie got up and stood looking out of the window before turning and saying to the visitors: 'I have my epic here, Madame de Marceau, Mademoiselle Georgy! Shall I read it now?'

'That would be an excellent idea,' interrupted his doting aunt.

'But perhaps the children are not capable of appreciating it?' added Louis-Marie.

'Indeed, we should not like your recital to be spoiled,' said Camille. 'Why not take the children to a servant, Georgy, and then perhaps you and M des Combes could take a turn in the gardens? I wish to talk to Mademoiselle Vivier.'

Was Camille trying to manufacture an alliance between the two of them? Georgy suspected slight malice but then realized that this way Camille wouldn't have to listen to *Charlemagne*. It was her own fault for appearing eager to hear it!

'That would be delightful,' she said. 'Come, children.' Louis-Marie looked surprised but followed them down the stairs. An old servant woman was waiting in the hall, obviously posted there in case she were needed.

'Look – there's someone who will show you the garden, Thibault – and perhaps the stables!' said Georgy.

'*Bonjour, mes petits,*' said the woman. 'Come and see my doves!'

Louis-Marie made for a rustic bench under a spreading chestnut tree, saying: 'You might like some shade and then I can read to you.'

Georgy tried to look 'enthusiastic' but inwardly groaned. Still, she had asked for it.

'Is it your *Charlemagne* poem?' she asked politely, sitting down the bench as far away from him as would not be rude.

'Of course. It is hundreds of pages long. With me here I have only the part which I am working on at present. It is the story of Gunilda the heroine who sacrifices her life for one of Charlemagne's knights . . . .'

'A romance then?'

'An epic romance if you will – but I draw from life! Would you not wish, Georgina, to be the heroine of an epic? That is why I believe my verse will be popular among feminine readers.'

Georgy thought, no, I certainly do not wish to be the heroine of an epic! I am not the right woman for him to test reactions to his poem. I'd rather write an epic poem myself – though I think a lyric would be more my style. Aloud, she said: 'Please begin. I am listening.'

Louis-Marie began, and indeed after several minutes she did not see any way of stopping him. The verse was written in alexandrines, which she knew from her reading of the seventeenth century French tragedians, but, whether it was his voice or the monotonous regularity of the lines, she found her attention slipping.

'It is hard to understand by ear,' she finally interrupted him. 'Perhaps I could read your manuscript?'

He looked up, flushed with his endeavours. 'Alas, it is not yet in fit state to be read by another. But how did you like my *femme aux yeux de serpent?*'

'That was not your heroine, was it? Gunilda? I'm afraid I did not quite understand how this lady fitted in.'

'That is the difficulty of reading one's work in progress. She – Morven – is the embodiment of wickedness who enslaves one of Charlemagne's warriors and causes his death. Then Gunilda rescues Charlemagne from her deadly glance—'

'She is a kind of Medusa?'

'You have it exactly. You must read my description of Gunilda. Another day perhaps?'

'It is certainly – as far as I can judge – very cleverly put together – I mean your "quantities". It must be awfully hard to write the correct number of syllables in every line?'

Louis-Marie sighed, saying more humanly: 'The effort gives me a headache.'

'Then why not write something less formal?'

'Like our friend Amaury? Well, well, here he is!'

Georgy looked up and indeed saw Amaury Arnaud about to cross the parterre in their direction.

She wondered what he thought of Louis-Marie's efforts, though she had better not ask him in front of the scribe himself. She sensed Amaury was the sort of man who would speak the truth even if it wounded. All they had spoken of the other day about poetry came back to her mind and seemed to have nothing to do with Louis-Marie's effusions. But how was she to know whether Louis-Marie could write or not? Certainly the subject matter was alien to anything she found interesting. She had appreciated Lamartine and, before that, Ronsard, whom she had read with Edward Walker, but was she really qualified to judge in another language?

The thought of Edward Walker was strangely disquieting. Looking at Amaury now as he came up and leaned against the trunk of the chestnut tree, she thought how handsome he was, and young. If only *he* would read his own poems to her alone in the garden.

'And how does Mademoiselle find your verse?' he said teasingly to his friend.

'I find it very well – chiselled – and put together, but a little difficult for me to understand without my seeing the words themselves,' she said judiciously.

'Be careful or he will make you the heroine of his epic!'

Louis-Marie looked annoyed. 'You are never serious for a moment, *mon ami.* Georgy is an attentive listener – but now I feel we must go in to my great-aunt's chambers or she will be regarding herself as neglected.'

'Oh, Mademoiselle is a good listener,' said Amaury, and bent the full force of his greeny-grey eyes on hers as Louis-Marie put away his papers in a leather case.

'Are we not to be favoured with your own verse?' she asked, trying not to allow her voice to wobble. He would not like a lovesick maiden, she thought, and she must never let him know she found him so – so delightful. Edward Walker came into her head again. She remembered he had said she gave the wrong impression. Well, she was trying her best to be calm, cool, and collected though the very presence of this young man set her heart beating quickly.

'I have none with me – my style is different from that of the epic.'

'My friend follows Rousseau,' said Louis-Marie, looking up, 'but the subjects of his poems are abstract – revolution, rebellion . . . .'

'You have missed out loss and despair,' said Amaury, and she looked at him swiftly. That seemed out of character. But how Byronic he was, and young, and beautiful. Was he truly melancholy? Had he on the other hand the staying power of the noble lord?

'Come, come, you will frighten our guest,' said Louis-Marie testily.

'Oh I don't think Georgy is easily frightened,' he said.

They went up to sit with old Hortense in her faded rooms. Camille was still seated, eyes half closed, listening to some interminable tale from the past.

The children were delivered back by the old retainer as soon as she saw the three young people had returned upstairs. Once Thibault saw Amaury he jumped up and down with pleasure. Georgy felt much the same. But the children's return enabled her to study Amaury's face without being noticed.

'What a pity your lady mother could not accompany you,' said Hortense. 'She really must visit one day soon.'

'She is presently in Châlons,' said Amaury, 'with my little brother.'

The rest of the visit passed in small talk.

When they finally left, Louis-Marie came down the stairs behind Georgy and whispered: 'He is an improviser, you know!'

What did he mean? That Amaury told untruths or that his poetry was too informal, that of a dilettante?

Perhaps Amaury had heard him, for when they walked over to their carriage, Louis-Marie and his aunt waving from the *perron*, Amaury strolled over with them, and whispered to Georgy:

'Poetry is not written by men like Louis-Marie!'

Chapter 3

Georgy assumed that soon after his visit to Aunt Hortense Amaury would have left Burgundy to travel alone to Paris. It took at least five days to travel from Mâcon to the capital.

She had a note from Louis-Marie who wrote, among other things – and probably took some malicious satisfaction in the statement – that 'some people' could never settle down to work. She had no wish to be a pawn between the two men, one of whom she liked, the other whom she endured. It was not poor Louis-Marie's fault that she did not find him attractive. In any case, his remarks to her, apart from the jealous one on the stairs that afternoon, had hardly been those of an aspirant lover. Camille laughed at him, but said he was obviously impressed by Georgy.

M de Marceau had not yet returned from his own visit to Paris. One October afternoon Camille took the children in the carriage to Mâcon to arrange matters concerning Thibault's First Communion. She offered Georgy a free afternoon.

'I'm sure you have letters to write. I must occasionally go about my children's business!'

Georgy relished time alone; she owed Edward Walker a letter, having still felt reluctant to write a reply to his last that had now finally arrived. She opened her travelling desk and then went into a day-dream. Time passed. She decided to begin the letter, but the words did not come as easily as they usually did.

'I have met three poets so far,' she wrote – 'Monsieur des Combes, his friend Amaury, and M de Lamartine of course. The first two were both staying in Aix. The former is a sort of distant relative of the family, but his friend is a better poet, I think.' She shrank from describing Amaury, so confined herself to a slightly sarcastic portrait of Louis-Marie. Edward Walker seemed *so* far away . . . .

She got up and opened a few books, then walked to her window whose shutters were open in the mellow autumn sun.

From this upstairs casement she saw a flame-coloured dot on the lane to the château that wound through the park by the little lake.

A small figure on horseback was riding towards their big gate. When it dismounted the figure was seen to be that of a girl or young woman wearing a black jacket and black boots, a red riding-skirt and a cap the colour of a bright orange nasturtium. It was, Georgy thought, the new colour called 'Trocadéro' that had recently come into fashion. It reminded her of something, but she could not place it exactly.

A whip under one arm, the girl strode into the inner courtyard. Georgy could see she was slim and lithe. From under the cap peeped glossy dark curls. Whoever was she? She looked like a vision of freedom and energy.

She stopped at the outer door to the tower and rapped on it with her whip. Then she stood, head thrown slightly back, white teeth glinting in a sudden shaft of sunlight.

Nobody else seemed to be around, so, with some trepidation – but why? – Georgy ran down the stairs and unbolted the door. The girl looked surprised. Her eyes were of a dark ebony.

'I have come to find Amaury Arnaud,' she said in an abrupt tone.

'Amaury? But he is not here – he went to Paris some days ago, I believe—'

'Who are you? One of his girl friends?' She sounded scornful yet there was a slight tremble in her voice which Georgy, with her acute awareness of mood and excellent hearing, recognized.

'I am the governess here,' she said carefully. 'Monsieur Amaury is a friend of Louis-Marie des Combes who is related to the family I work for. Who are you and why do you ask for him? Why are you looking for him here?'

'Oh, I heard he sometimes visited this château ... he was to have come to fetch me – we were to leave for Paris tonight.' All this time her horse, or rather, pony, was wandering round the courtyard.

131

'I will see your horse is fed, and then perhaps you would like to come in and take a glass of wine—'

'Water is all I drink,' said the girl. She looked about seventeen.

Georgy called for Jean but it was the older man, Emile, who came out of the stables. He showed no particular interest in the horse but looked keenly at its rider before taking her steed.

'Please give it some hay,' said Georgy, somewhat at a loss.

The girl looked around her with interest as she followed her down the passage and they came out into the small sitting-room that looked out on to the herb garden at the back of the house at the bottom of the tower.

'The family is away. Monsieur de Marceau is in Paris, but Madame has taken the children to see the priest in the town. They'll be back this evening. There is only myself here and male servants. I was not expecting anyone to visit—'

'You know Monsieur des Combes well, do you? Perhaps *he* will know what has happened to Amaury.'

'He told us he would soon be off to Paris – that was all,' said Georgy.

'I can assure you that I would not be coming to look for him if it were not urgent. Amaury promised he would accompany me tonight. We were going to Lyon first of all – I even had his horse ready and I was waiting over by the river with a servant. They said at the inn that he had been seen recently at the château—' She spoke in this gruff, rather clipped, way but she appeared genuinely distressed.

'Hadn't we better introduce ourselves?' said Georgy. 'I am Georgy Crabtree.' She extended her hand. 'I am English, as you may have guessed.'

The girl gave a stiff little bow but did not take the proffered hand. 'Capucine,' she said.

Suddenly Georgy remembered where she had seen her before, though only in the distance, the night of the concert in Aix. Amaury's companion! Then it was true; he had a woman friend – possibly even a fiancée – and here she was. She remembered the tiny brooch in the shape of a nasturtium he was wearing that evening in his lapel. Like a Légion d'honneur. She must pluck up her courage to ask this girl more about him.

'Do sit down. Tell me, were you at a concert in Aix? In August? I believe I saw you there.'

132

It was perhaps Capucine's turn to feel jealous for she looked stony-faced but answered: 'I may have been. I do not remember you.'

'You were wearing a pelisse – or a cloak – of orange silk. I was not told your name.' And Amaury had a tiny brooch the colour of your cap, she thought.

'I don't wear such a thing as a pelisse,' said the girl scornfully. She was very fierce. But she sat down in a proffered chair.

'Well it must have been a dress then. I always notice colours.'

'Are you English always so – *personal*?' asked the girl rudely.

Georgy flushed. 'I didn't mean to be rude. I liked the colour. I was at that concert with Louis-Marie des Combes, who, as you must know, is a great friend of Amaury's—'

'That he is not! Louis-Marie is a fool,' said the girl emphatically.

'What is your real name?'

'I told you. My name is Capucine!'

'That is the name of a flower – an orange flower. The colour of the brooch Monsieur Arnaud was wearing that night.'

'You seem to have noticed everything about him! When did you see him last?'

'About a week ago – at the house where Louis-Marie's Great-Aunt Hortense lives – Les Aisées, is it? Amaury – Monsieur Arnaud – was staying with his mother not far away – at least he told us she was then in Châlons, but would presently return to the house she rented not far away. My employer, Madame de Marceau, has entertained him here though, it is true—'

'And he told you that he was off to Paris?'

'Yes. He did not say exactly when, but very soon, I thought.'

'Well, he lied!'

Or he has gone without you, thought Georgy. She said: 'Why not ask Monsieur des Combes? He will know, I'm sure, whether Monsieur Arnaud has left.'

The girl gave such an impression of physicality, of energy, of passion even. She was really very pretty, with curly black hair to match the piercing black eyes. It would not be surprising that Amaury Arnaud might be in love with her, thought Georgy, struggling to remain composed. After all, nobody knew that she herself was so desperately attracted to the young man. She had better remain cool.

'I'm sorry I can't help you. I am not closely acquainted with

Amaury Arnaud's movements,' she said, a little stiffly. 'Do go over to Les Aisées and see if Louis-Marie knows. There may have been some misunderstanding.'

'No misunderstanding – he has thought better of it!' muttered Capucine and shot out of her chair so suddenly Georgy recoiled in surprise. 'Men are all the same,' the girl went on. 'You just can't trust them! If you are the governess and are English, you ought to know that – haven't you ever read anything by your great revolutionary heroine?'

'Who?' asked Georgy in surprise.

'I don't suppose you've ever heard of her! though you might have heard of our French Madame Roland?'

'Tell me her name.'

'Wollstonecraft. She wrote about the Rights of Women!' Georgy could tell that Capucine pronounced the words as if they were capitalized. How interesting, and yet how odd!

She got up. 'No, don't bother letting me out. I know where my horse is. I'll go now,' she said. Then she added under her breath, so softly that Georgy was not sure she had heard right. '*Vive la République!*' and was off. She did not say: 'Thank you for your hospitality.'

Georgy watched her from the window as she galloped out of the stable yard, then turned in her saddle and waved with her riding crop. Such a strange visit.

She *had* heard of Mary Wollstonecraft the radical writer, though she had never read any of her writings. Edward Walker had mentioned her. She remembered he had once talked about female suffrage in connection with the great Condorcet and with some English Radicals. Not that she could remember any of the other names of women writers, though he might have spoken to her of them. 'Capucine' was decidedly an unusual person. What a vision of freedom and energy!

Later she was to wonder if she had dreamed the whole episode.

Camille and Eglantine and the children came back about six o'clock. The children were tired, Camille strangely quiet, so at first Georgy said nothing about the unusual visitor. But when the children had gone to bed Camille asked her to play cards with her for an hour or so, and she thought she had better mention the girl. Emile would certainly tell Célanie, who had been given the afternoon off, and she would tell Madame.

'Such a strange young woman called this afternoon,' she began.

Camille looked up. 'A gypsy? You must be careful—'

'No, I don't think so. She seemed educated.' Somehow she did not want to mention that she had seen her before in Aix. 'She was looking for Monsieur Arnaud.'

'Well, he doesn't live here.'

'I told her he had gone off to Paris – at least that is what he said last week. I advised her to ride over to Louis-Marie and enquire.'

'She came all alone? On horseback?'

'Yes. I should imagine she is an excellent rider. And very sure of herself. About my age – perhaps a year younger even.'

'I wonder who she might be. I thought I knew all our neighbours.'

'I had the impression she did not live in the district. I may be wrong.'

'Then M Arnaud is being chased by a young woman. How exciting.'

'She was wearing the most extraordinary little cap – that lovely new orange colour I remember was introduced in England this year – so it was probably in Paris last year – Trocadéro Orange—'

'Well, well. Are you sure you were not dreaming? She sounds like a ghost from the Revolution.'

'But then they wore scarlet, didn't they?'

'Better not mention it to my husband,' said Camille shortly and bent her head towards her cards.

No, decidedly, M de Marceau would not have approved of Capucine.

Or of Amaury Arnaud, Georgy realized.

Georgy wished she did know where Amaury was. The girl's sudden appearance and her questions had made her feel she did not know the man at all. Yet they had talked of poetry, and other things, and she had enjoyed the best conversation with him that she had so far managed to have since coming to France.

Next morning she heard voices in the garden and looked down from the schoolroom window to see Jacques Cellard talking to Camille.

The children had been telling her about the priest and their catechism: 'We have so much to learn that we might forget what we are learning with you, Mademoiselle,' said Lucie.

'Papa says the *curé* is more important than lessons,' said Thibault.

Lucie looked embarrassed. 'But Monsieur Cellard says it is just as important to learn your lessons as go to church!' she said.

Georgy had brought to France, along with *Le Petit Précepteur* and *Mangnall's Questions*, which had already proved themselves so useful, Maria Edgeworth's *Parent's Assistant* and Mrs Barbauld's *Evenings at Home*, books she had read herself at home in the Huntingore schoolroom. The English of Maria Edgeworth was too complicated for these children so she contented herself with retelling the stories more simply, but Mrs Barbauld was in small gobbets. Information, poems, stories – all invaluable! The French didn't appear to have books like Mrs Barbauld's, which was odd when you thought that the great Rousseau had written his *Emile* in French.

Georgy had already read *The Oak Tree* to Lucie and Thibault, and followed it up with what Rousseau called a *leçon de choses* – meaning a practical lesson. She had commanded the two of them to find an oak tree in the park, and they had much enjoyed this. She felt pleased that her lessons were going so well. She had not expected to enjoy them as much as she undoubtedly did, for she had uncovered in herself a mysterious talent for instruction. She would love to write to Edward Walker about this, but she had become a little embarrassed over the long missives she had sent him in her first few weeks in France and Savoy. She had used him as a kind of diary and had probably bored the poor man. Meeting Amaury, and dreaming as she did over him, had not only made her a little reluctant to write to Edward, but made her ask herself if she had acted honourably with him. She had not had any of those fantasies about Edward Walker that she had to try and stop having over Amaury, but perhaps Edward thought she had?

This morning however she felt little inclined for teaching. That was the trouble. You had to do things when you did not feel like them. She supposed that was what Louis-Marie might have meant by his *improvisateur*, and his talk of those who have no sticking power.

She took one more look at the garden, then went back to the

table. Camille and Jacques Cellard must have gone into the house.

She wondered when Monsieur de Marceau would return. When she thought about it she realized that Jacques Cellard seemed to visit only when Camille's husband was absent. He had visited Camille before they had all gone to Aix, after M de Marceau had already departed to Savoy.

Thibault echoed her thoughts when he said: 'I wish Papa would come back. I want to tell him that the priest said I was a very good boy.'

Georgy set them some work and found her thoughts returning to Capucine. There was some mystery about her, or was it just that the girl was determined to appear mysterious? She would have liked Edward Walker's opinion also about that young lady, but must use her own judgement.

Camille wanted to meet Amaury's mother, Madame Bonaventure, and perhaps ask her to dine at the château but the lady was as elusive as her son. When approached, Hortense gave it as her opinion that she too had gone to Paris, but Louis-Marie said:

'She doesn't normally visit people much, Cousin Camille – and I believe it would not in any case be a good idea.' When pressed, he blushed and said the rumour was she had had, long ago, connections with political leaders and that there was some mystery over Monsieur Bonaventure.

Monsieur de Marceau returned the following week so there was no further question of invitations to dine. That gentleman liked to keep himself to himself, shunned hospitality, since it had to be returned, and said family life did not need continual parties and dinners and guests. He appeared to be in a bad mood but Georgy noticed that Camille avoided any direct confrontation with him. She could very well have said, thought Georgy indignantly, that she had entertained his parents for two weeks, and been left alone in the countryside when he gadded off to Paris. But a husband's word was law in France, as in England. No wonder women were prone to small subterfuges when they needed a little freedom. She was more and more amazed that Augustin de Marceau had ever allowed his wife to employ an English girl – but she supposed she did not cost very much.

The leaves began to fall now, and went on falling. They were entering the dead end of the year. The harvest was over, and the hunting season; every small bird that could be slaughtered had been slaughtered. After a week or two at the end of October when the sun dazzled through the red and gold and yellow leaves of the hornbeams and beeches and ash trees, the weather turned suddenly colder and wood fires were lit in the salon and the downstairs rooms. Camille's small sitting-room was the cosiest but Augustin preferred his own quarters. Here he polished his guns and made plans for tree-felling with Emile and Jean. Georgy was wondering how they would celebrate Advent and Christmas. Catholics were said not to celebrate that festival very much. No holly or mistletoe for them. Yet Camille was English so perhaps she would give her children Christmas boxes? Georgy told the children about her Christmases at home with the Yorkshire waits and the plum pudding.

She felt at a loose end, not depressed but full of restless energy, not knowing where to put it. She felt the cold, even if her own home was situated in a colder clime than this château. The only way to get warm was to walk, and she could not expect the children to walk as briskly as herself.

She dreamed of Amaury Arnaud more than once.

Now it was winter and nobody had visited for weeks. M de Marceau was still preoccupied and irritable. Louis-Marie was back home in Lyon. There had been no sign of Amaury or the mysterious Capucine, and even Tante Hortense wrote to say she was confined to her rooms with a chill. For the first time since her arrival in France Georgy felt a little homesick, and it was not just the thought of the jolly Christmas she might have spent at home. She felt unhappy from the conviction that she would never see Amaury again. All her feelings were running to waste. Why, she would even have welcomed a chat with Louis-Marie! That made her realize she had better cut her losses and rouse herself, so she wrote again to Abigail Strang. Abigail had replied to Georgy's first letter with a rhapsodic description of the furnishings in the house in York that she and her soon-to-be-husband were planning.

On an evening in early December, once the children were in bed, Georgy wrapped herself in a blanket and settled down at the table in her room to reply to her old 'best friend'. Was an early marriage like Abigail's the only hope for her? She found it hard to sound enthusiastic about Abigail's chintz covers, and yellow striped wallpaper and silk cushions. Wouldn't *she* like to marry Amaury Arnaud? She considered this. Of course that would never happen, could not, for he was indifferent to her except as a conversationalist. And even if he fell in love with her – which would never happen either – she could not see herself a married woman like Camille. Where did all the passion go when people got married? In England, husband and wife were expected to love and respect each other, and have children, and if possible be good companions. She knew the marriage service well. It spoke of 'a remedy against fornication'.

The very words gave her a strange thrill. Would she ever want to be anybody's wife?

She bent back to her letter to Abigail. She could not write of this, and if you couldn't say such things to your best friend, to whom could you say them?

A few days later, Camille promised Georgy a visit to Dijon in the New Year.

'You have hardly seen anything of my adopted country,' she said. 'Only Aix – and that is not really French.' Perhaps she was frightened that Georgy might leave. 'We celebrate Christmas on the Eve,' she said. 'We have a Christmas log – the *bûche de Noël* – and Midnight Mass in the village church. Even the children go. You are welcome to join us. I shall invite Tante Hortense – if she can bear to tear herself away from her apartment.'

'Do you think Madame Bonaventure might come back to the country for the feast?' asked Georgy, trying to sound casual. She really meant, do you think Amaury might be in church? It was after all the nearest church also to Les Aisées and possibly to Amaury's mother's rented house.

'Yes. Célanie said yesterday that they were saying at the market that she is expected back.'

So Amaury might come along too? She could not see him worshipping in church, for she had gathered from what he had said during their long conversation about poetry that he was not a believer. Maybe his mysterious mother was not either? At least the possibility of his return to the district was something to look forward to. Georgy had always needed something to 'look forward to' and now there was the slight chance of Amaury's return.

It was still cold but the sun came out again in the week before Christmas and now Georgy felt more cheerful. On 20 December a carrier arrived from Mâcon with a large box wrapped in brown paper, sealed with her father's seal:

To Miss Crabtree, Chateau Pinac-Les-Saules par Mâcon

was repeated all over the box in large letters.

This *was* a surprise. Papa must have sent it weeks ago from London, and thence on the Mail to Dover and over the sea to Calais, and the long journey to Paris and Mâcon by diligence. She decided not to open it until the children opened their own presents on Christmas Eve the following Saturday. Her mother would not have sent anything perishable, she thought.

Christmas Eve dawned bright and frosty. Thibault was beside himself with excitement. Lucie had been busy for weeks sewing small presents for her parents and for Georgy. Camille told her that the women servants would be given a small sum of money on 'Boxing Day' because it was an English custom she liked to keep up. 'I do little enough *à l'anglaise* in an English way,' she said, and for the first time Georgy wondered if she regretted her marriage and exile.

'I wonder what Monsieur de Lamartine and his wife are doing,' she said to her mistress as she was helping to decorate the supper table with evergreens. They would eat and drink after the church service, tall *flûtes* for the champagne and a long white dish for the Christmas log. 'I expect they are enjoying a Tuscan winter. In Tuscany they have cribs in their churches just like some of our people do here. My sister Caroline was there one December. They celebrate the New Year more there – I'm told it's only in England and America that Christmas is sometimes the time for presents. Are you missing Yorkshire, Georgy?' Camille sat down, seeming to want to linger for a talk. 'Tell me what you do at home.'

'I do miss it a little. We have the waits come and sing for us and we put up holly and mistletoe. They light up the Minster at York on Christmas Day and sing the Yorkshire carol – that's "Christians Awake", you know. And we burn an ash log from Christmas Eve to Twelfth Night – they say the Norsemen brought us that custom. Where my father comes from they ring the church bells when the log is set alight and the children bang on their drums and blow toy trumpets! If people stay in, they play whist. Some old people still have their presents on the sixth of December—'

'The feast of St Nicholas—' said Camille.

'And then,' Georgy went on, unable to stop once she had started, 'then we eat Wensleydale cheese with our cake and drink mulled ale. And of course we eat frumenty.'

'What on earth is that?'

'Well, it's a sort of wheat with spice and sugar and you put currants in it and serve it with cream – and rum for the grown ups.'

'I remember your father once sent Caroline and her husband some pieces of Yorkshire Christmas pie,' said Camille. 'It had goose and game birds in a sort of thick pastry and they ate it cold with pickled pears and spiced oranges. We had never eaten anything like that before in London!'

'I suppose our customs are often quite local,' said Georgy.

'I suppose so – but I'm afraid you'll find our Christmas here rather tame! Wait till the New Year – the peasants celebrate that all right!'

Shortly afterwards, Tante Hortense arrived in a flurry of clothes and muffs and hats and boxes. She was to stay over until the New Year.

'Louis-Marie will be staying with his mama for the season,' she said, 'but he sends his kind regards.' She said *ses amitiés sincères* and Georgy felt relieved he was not to be of the party but sorry that he could not lead her to Amaury . . . . All the talk of home had upset her a little. She felt torn between wanting to return one day to where she had always belonged and the beckoning new world to which she was sure Amaury held the key. But then, it might all have been her imagination – which made her nostalgia for home more acute . . . .

At eleven o'clock that night she accompanied the family in the carriage to the village church. Camille and her daughter were wearing their best velvet pelisses which had made Georgy decide to wear her own precious new pelisse for the first time. Tante Hortense had decided not to accompany the family to church. The carriage journey to the château had shaken her up enough, she said, and the *curé* had called only last week at Les Aisées.

The village church was packed for the special mass. Candles glimmered in the gloom and the murmured Latin from the clutch

141

of priests was alternately soothing and mysterious. Georgy stayed in her chair next to Thibault when the others went up for the sacrament, and looked round eagerly for any sign of Amaury Arnaud. The idea of him seemed so far away, and that was a special pain. If talking about Yorkshire had made her long just to see them all again at Huntingore, even for only an hour or two, Amaury belonged to yet another different world, one she knew she had to learn about before she decided whether she wished to join it.

Then she looked up and saw a woman sitting on the side aisle who did not go up for the sacrament. She wondered if that could be Madame Bonaventure. But she did not know what that lady looked like, and you could not tell much from the back.

There was no sign of Amaury though, and when they came out of the church it felt much colder. The horses' breath was like rolling mist in the light from the lanterns the servants were holding.

Monsieur de Marceau had not said much during the journey there but as they were on the return journey he said, 'Remember, Thibault, at the next Christmas Midnight Mass you will be confessing your own sins.'

There should be others there, not just this family, Georgy found herself thinking as they opened the champagne and drank to the Nativity, yet she had never felt that at home. Christmas was a *family* festival. Was it that the de Marceaus did not feel like a family? Were Augustin and Camille de Marceau not happily married?

Lucie distributed her pen wipers and needle cases and received a large doll from her mother, and Thibault shrieked with delight over his new fort and soldiers. Georgy realized that both these presents were from their mother. Of course, French fathers did not give presents at Christmas . . . .

She opened her own large box before the sleepy children, full of their *bûche de Noël*, went to bed. A packet of books from Papa; new velvet ribbons from Mama and a box of crystallized fruit, and from her young cousins, John and Nathaniel a letter clearly written at Edward Walker's instigation. She would keep that for later. Edward himself had not yet replied to her last letter a sennight ago.

On Christmas Day Georgy woke as usual at half past seven and devoted some moments to thinking about what the family at home would be doing. There would be little cloth bags of money ready to give the servants on Boxing Day, and Christmas presents already there for the children. She should have thought ahead and sent something to her parents for her young cousins, and her brother Benedict, even if they did not expect them. Her brother Will was still away in the army but Benedict would be home. She had neglected Ben who had once been so close to her. She got up and looked again at the box of goodies that had arrived earlier. At the bottom she found a little book. Had Edward Walker smuggled a present to her? No. She opened it and on the flyleaf of *Rasselas* by Dr Johnson was written:

'*To my dear sister Georgy from her loving brother Benedict: Christmas 1825.*'

There was a good deal to be said for brothers. She would write to him straight away, but there was the day to get through first. She could already hear the children shouting from their rooms upstairs and she dressed hurriedly, told them to come down and went down herself to the *salle à manger* for her coffee and brioche.

Célanie was already there, bustling about, and carrying on a conversation with the other servant who was coming in from the kitchens with a large tray of steaming bowls of coffee: 'Just imagine – they say someone is living in that old shack down by Bourrons!' They were silent when they saw Georgy.

Célanie handed her a bowl of coffee. 'Lucie and Thibault ready for their milk yet? They were up late last night.'

'I forgot – happy Christmas – joyeux Noël – Célanie!'

'That's as may be – I've to take up the coffee to Madame Hortense – and the master and mistress will want theirs.'

Just then the children came bounding into the room. Oh dear, they needed their hair brushed and their hands washed. Might as well let them have their breakfast first.

'I want to play with my doll. I shall call her Bébette and I shall take her out for a pretend drive this morning,' said Lucie.

'Silly old doll,' said Thibault. 'I've got a better present than you.' Lucie looked at him pityingly and decided not to argue.

Georgy sighed. If only there were some new people coming for luncheon. Conversation with children could get a little wearying.

'It's very cold – we must wrap up well for a walk,' she said brightly. At least it would be a change to get out. The sun would not shine for long.

When Camille finally arrived downstairs Georgy had already taken the children out. Camille sat down meditatively to drink another cup of coffee. No use asking Augustin to go for a little drive, and she could find no excuse to take the carriage out herself.

Not for the first time Camille de Marceau was feeling like a prisoner in her own home.

Chapter 4

The day after Christmas, a servant rode over from Les Aisées with a message. Tante Hortense's great nephew Philippe, who had doubtless been pleased to feel someone else was keeping an eye on the old lady, had had his stable broken into. Nothing had been taken, but his best carriage horse had been let out into the yard in the middle of the night. Only the fact that he was wakeful in the early morning of Christmas Day and had gone down to investigate various whinnyings and thuddings had saved his horse from running away, and probably dying of cold.

Philippe Deriencourt asked his servant to tell his neighbour Augustin de Marceau to be extra careful. There were vagabonds, the servant said – and thieves – and gypsies – who might take horses next time.

Georgy crept into the domestic quarters. 'Why do you think they went into the barn at all?' she asked the Deriencourt servant, who was being regaled with a glass of mulled Burgundy. Camille's personal servants had received their Boxing Day coins that morning and the kitchen was in a good humour.

'They wanted shelter, Miss,' said the servant. 'My master thinks he wanted a bed for the night but was disturbed and left the big door of the grange open.'

'Our mistress knows,' said Célanie, 'that folk often sleep on our straw in summer, and do no harm.'

'But leaving a door or a gate open, that's different,' said Eglantine.

Augustin went round that night with Jean and Emile locking doors and moving ladders away from windows.

'Papa often gets unwelcome visitors,' said Georgy to Camille, 'but so long as they take nothing, he shuts his eyes. Once, a man took one of our horses but they never caught him. He'd have gone to York Assizes.'

As Georgy undressed for bed that night she thought, it might not have been a *man* who had left that door open! The image of the girl Capucine was unaccountably before her eyes. Yet it did not make sense, for the girl obviously loved horses. Was she about to steal one before she was disturbed? And she was probably miles and miles away in Paris, where she had been going that afternoon of her strange visit to the château. Oh, if only she could see Amaury and ask him about her. She might persuade Camille de Marceau to invite Madame Bonaventure to the château and to invite her son along with her. Wouldn't a middle-aged lady in the depths of the provinces wish to meet her neighbours?

In the meantime she might write to Louis-Marie. She could hint to him about the Capucine mystery as well as his relative's horse – and see what happened.

Dear Louis-Marie

I hope you spent an agreeable festive season? Or do you celebrate only at the New Year and Epiphany? In England that is called Twelfth Night. I wish you all good things for 1826 which will soon be upon us. It has been very cold here and the children have kept me busy but I was pleased that we did celebrate Christmas a little, since my mistress is English. She has promised me a visit to the capital of Burgundy in the New Year if the weather holds.

Have you been writing much? I hope I shall soon hear the rest of your epic ... (*What was a small white lie in such a good cause?*)

We have not seen your friend Amaury since we met him at Les Aisées and wonder if you have seen him? A few weeks ago we had the strangest visitor here: I was alone, as the others were in Mâcon, when a young woman on horseback wearing an orange cap arrived *looking for Amaury*! She said he had promised to start off that day with her to ride to Paris, and had then vanished. Do you know anything about her? I had the feeling that it might be the same woman who was accompanying him that evening we went to the theatre in Aix.

Recently there has been a break-in at Les Aisées. You may already have heard from your family about it. Nothing was taken but the door was left open and a horse nearly escaped in the middle of the night. I immediately suspected that young woman –

I don't know why. If you see Amaury, don't mention my suspicions, but tell him about the girl.

I hope you don't mind my writing to you, but she made such a strong impression on me.

We hope to see you soon. In the meantime, sincere good wishes for 1826, to which my employer, and your great-aunt, who is staying with us, add their own.

Your friend

Georgina Crabtree.

Georgy had told Tante Hortense that she had written to Louis-Marie, hoping that the old lady would not imagine she was pursuing him on account of any reasons of the heart. She would tell Camille later; she did not think Camille would mind her sending compliments of the season to Louis-Marie.

She gave the letter to Jean, who was going into Mâcon the following day. He would see that it was put on the coach that travelled each day to remoter parts of Burgundy, with mail and travellers. Louis-Marie's family home was near the border with the Franche-Comté. It might be some weeks before she received a reply. Tante Hortense said he might have already gone to Lyon to pursue his studies in law. This was the first Georgy had heard of the young man's law studies. He must work in a rather desultory fashion. Whilst she was waiting for a reply, she would casually introduce the name of Madame Bonaventure to Camille, hoping they might eventually succeed in meeting Amaury's mama.

One way of achieving this end was to be easier than she had expected, for it turned out that Jacques Cellard knew the lady, having done business with her when she rented her rather tumbledown house to the north of the forest. Camille mentioned this fact casually next day in conversation with Georgy, who tried not to appear too interested. Monsieur Cellard had not been seen in the house since Augustin de Marceau had returned, but she felt he was often in Camille's thoughts, without quite knowing how she knew. Madame Bonaventure must be an unusual woman to want to live in the back of beyond, she mused.

She was sitting with Camille who was looking silently out of the window of her small salon. Georgy was mending Thibault's nightgown, a job she dreaded, for her sewing was untidy. But she wanted to remain in Camille's good books – and in the good

147

books of Célanie who had quite enough to do without the children's mending. 'I suppose you knew whoever lived in that house formerly?' she observed aloud.

'No, *I* did not – it was empty for a long time. I believe it was once owned by acquaintances of my father-in-law, a family who also had to escape to London. But there was something he was not telling me, for I had the impression there had been some rift in the family over the events of 1794.'

Camille clearly knew nothing further. Georgy pondered what she had said. *Some rift* must mean that there was dissension on the family concerning the Royalists and the Revolutionaries. That girl Capucine looked like a rebel! Her cap was not scarlet – but some nasturtiums are red. Yet was it not over thirty years since these things had mattered? She yawned; she could so easily fall asleep over her sewing if she were not careful, for she had blown out her candle rather late the night before reading, and luxuriating in, Chateaubriand's *René*.

'I'd better fetch the children for their lesson,' she said, to wake herself up and banish idle speculation. She knew she was liable to let her imagination run riot when there was any sort of mystery in the air.

It was January now and colder, a wind whistling round the house, finding cracks and crevices and blowing through them to make the log fires smoke and the household shiver. Everyone was forced to wear their warmest clothes, and Georgy was glad her mother had insisted she take her old paisley shawl to France. It had protected her from the worst of the Yorkshire cold. Only the children did not seem to notice the change in climate, but their mother insisted they were dosed with tincture of cinnamon to ward off any chill.

'It is almost as chilly as Yorkshire,' said Georgy. She had not expected France to be so cold. In her imagination it had always been a warm sunny place.

'As soon as the weather improves I promise we *shall* go to Dijon,' said her cousin. 'There are things I need that I cannot buy in Mâcon. There's a good market there, and a stylish dressmaker and a milliner. And *you* shall see the wonderful old buildings and the churches. The Revolutionaries tried to destroy the cathedral but they say that, underneath, the crypt is still undamaged, though it will take years to clear it of the building above that had collapsed into it.'

'Are the tombs of the Dukes of Burgundy there?'

'No – they are in a special mausoleum about a mile away – there won't be time to see that. Perhaps another time. But there are many churches and towers, and the law courts and the old clock whose figures strike the hour over Notre Dame.' Georgy looked forward to all this, for she had seen some paintings of the old buildings of the Burgundian capital.

The next morning, before she could expect a reply from Louis-Marie, another letter arrived at the château, though it was not for her. She heard about it from Camille who was now treating her more and more as a sort of confidante, which sometimes made her a little uncomfortable. Augustin de Marceau had received a communication from Madame Bonaventure!

'She signed herself "Félicienne",' said Camille, a day or two later, and laughed a trifle unkindly. Georgy waited to be told what was in the letter, if Camille wished her to know. She did feel it was none of her business – except that this 'Félicienne' was the mother of Amaury, and anything to do with *him* intrigued her more and more. Did Monsieur de Marceau know that his wife discussed his private correspondence with her?

'It is nothing very interesting – or she would have written to me,' said Camille complacently. 'But it will perhaps be one way of getting her to come here. I could entertain a few people to luncheon. It is the usual story,' Camille went on, 'she wants Augustin to advise her when she writes to the government to try and reclaim some of her family's land that was confiscated under the Revolution.'

'Isn't it a bit late for that?' asked Georgy, who had heard a good deal about these properties. The old Count de Marceau had unusually managed to reclaim some of his land under Louis XVIII but he and his son Augustin were still occupied in endless lawsuits to get hold of more; this was the reason for which Augustin and his father were continually going to Paris, to argue for the restitution of those parts of their land and properties that had not been returned under the old king.

'Apparently, now that we have a new king on the throne they are all bent on trying again,' Camille went on. 'But I would guess that there is the extra problem of her being a widow who married again. I don't think she has much of a chance.'

Georgy was still confused about French politics. If only Edward Walker were here he could explain them to her. The de Marceau family were Royalists and Catholic, but Camille never seemed very enthusiastic about either the new king, Charles X, or his predecessor, who had been his elder brother, both of them the brothers of the poor guillotined Louis XVI. As Camille was English, she could hardly have ever been in favour of 'Boney', but Georgy had noticed that the attitude of the French to Napoleon was ambivalent, or at least, their attitude to his successes. Once he was seen to lose, and fail – and die in exile – it was a different matter. She had the feeling that Amaury had worshipped Napoleon as a child. Amaury was certainly no Royalist; he had been very scathing about the Lamartine family's Royalist sentiments and piety. But Amaury was young and he had told her he was a 'Romantic', and Georgy could not imagine that such a young man would ever adhere to any *ancien régime.* He would be what they called a 'liberal', she was sure. Mr Walker had said *he* had been a liberal too – but now he was older and more sceptical about 'progress'.

However, Amaury's mama might not agree with her son – especially if she was on the side of those who wanted the Revolutionary land settlement undone.

'The de Marceaus haven't yet given up hope of coming into their rightful inheritance,' said Camille, as though it was nothing to do with *her.* 'Augustin says they'll all be given a paltry sum,' she went on. 'You know there are seventy thousand of them – too many for them all to get their properties handed back. The people who have had them for the last thirty years will fight to keep them. I don't suppose Madame de Bonaventure will have any luck. I wonder where her husband's properties were.'

The arrival at the château – at noon, a few days later – of Félicienne Bonaventure in a closed carriage was for Georgy an anticlimax. The lady had accepted Camille's invitation to luncheon though Augustin had grumbled that she would be a nuisance and he had enough to do to see to his own family's survival without taking the problems of others under his wing.

Madame de Bonaventure obviously intended to discover as much as possible from her hosts. She carried a large linen bag like a barrister's bag of briefs. If it had been one it could not have contained more papers.

Georgy was watching with the children from the schoolroom

window. She was not invited to the meal because the children would only have been an encumbrance and her place was with them upstairs. She felt sure it was the same lady whose back she had studied the night of the midnight mass on Christmas Eve. Seeing her in daylight you could tell she had once been a handsome woman; she had an imperious air about her, her hair was dressed high, and she wore a dark ruby coloured pelisse. This was not really what Georgy had expected. But this *was* Amaury's mama, and she thrilled to the idea. She could not descry the features of the face in detail as the lady descended from her carriage, but if possible she intended to steal a look later from the stairs. Camille would be sure in any case to acquaint her with her impressions. Perhaps she might lead the conversation on to Madame de Bonaventure's son, once her husband had dealt with the business side of things. Augustin would make the best of it, would perorate at table. However reluctant he was to help anyone, he loved the sound of his own voice, especially when telling someone how foolish they were.

Georgy ate with Thibault and his sister in the schoolroom. They always served her with a glass of Burgundy – it kept her warm.

'Who is the lady who has come?' Lucie asked.

'It is Monsieur Arnaud's mother.'

'Why didn't he come too? I wish he would,' said Thibault.

So do I thought Georgy.

Later, she had the children well wrapped up and took them out into the grounds, keeping a weather eye on the drive in case the carriage should disappear. It was just as they were making their way back into the house that they heard voices and Camille appeared on the *perron* with their visitor. No sign of Augustin: he had – probably thankfully – escaped.

Amaury's mother was even more imposing when you saw her close to. She was a woman whom Georgy guessed to be in her late forties; tall and dark, not at all French looking, and not fashionably dressed. She was not exactly ugly, but strong featured, and the expression in her eyes was searching when Georgy was introduced to her. The strong jaw and jutting lower lip was allied with a guarded expression. Georgy could imagine the woman might be a plotter, aware of her rights and ready to pursue the path she wanted. Should she say she knew her son?

151

Camille decided for her. After introducing her children to Madame Bonaventure, Georgy hovering in the background, she said: 'This is my English cousin, Miss Crabtree. As I told you, she has made the acquaintance of your son Amaury.'

'Indeed,' said the woman a little frostily. 'My son is in Paris at present. He intends to study law.'

'That should be most useful,' murmured Camille.

Georgy thought, another lawyer! Camille means useful for the lady's 'crusade', I suppose. She said – daringly: 'He is also most conversant with literature, Madame.'

'That may be so – but verse never buttered brioches,' said the lady decisively.

'I hope your family will soon recover from their indisposition,' said Camille as the lady got into her carriage, which had been brought round from the stable yard. 'You must bring your small Thierry to play with Thibault,' she added.

'Oh, he is too young, I fear, to play with a big boy like Thibault!'

Thibault who was listening and patting the horse as he watched the coachman get up on to his seat, said: 'I would rather play with Amaury!'

The lady gave a bitter-sweet smile. 'Amaury has to work, little boy – as you will one day.' With a crack of the whip the rather broken-down old equipage that resembled an English gig trundled off.

'Tell him to come and bring his horse,' shouted Thibault.

'Hush, Thiby,' said Camille without much conviction. 'Well, well,' she added, once the carriage was lost from view and the children had gone into the house, 'what an unusual lady!'

'Did you like her?' asked Georgy.

'I don't know. I believe Augustin will have considered her rather rude and outspoken.'

'Not very lady-like?'

'No, yet I think she has had a most unusual life. She told us she had a child younger than Amaury, as well as the small boy of five. I got the impression that her second husband may *not* be dead.'

'Well, she would not want him involved in her first husband's lawsuit, would she?'

'No, but whether Monsieur Bonaventure is alive or has died she cannot apply for restitution of her first husband's lands for herself, only for her son Amaury. It was most odd, for she avoided any discussion of her second husband. She did say that Amaury's father was dead. But she did not say when he had died. Yet if she has a child of five it cannot be long since Monsieur Bonaventure was with her.'

Georgy thought, perhaps she was a Revolutionary who did not believe in Christian marriage. It made Amaury all the more interesting, to have such a mother.

'She was very interested in how my father-in-law got back some of his property, yet I had the impression she has no strong cards to play. Maybe Monsieur Bonaventure died in debt. Amaury has never mentioned lawsuits to me – or that he is a student of the law – I should imagine it is his mother who is bullying him into all that!'

Camille never treated her like a child. There were not many women who would talk so freely to a young unmarried girl of such things as second husbands and possible marital secrets.

She knew that Camille had secured her support and loyalty by acting in this way.

By the end of the month it was less cold and Camille said she could not put off her visit to Dijon any longer. They would drive there, stay overnight, she would go to her dressmaker, and see if the milliners or the *bonneterie* had anything she fancied, and meanwhile Georgy could look round the town. Célanie would stay with the children as M de Marceau was off to Paris once more, and Eglantine could accompany them to Dijon to carry parcels.

Thus it was that Georgy found herself on a crisp and sunny winter day in Dijon, standing in the square and looking up at the façade of the Eglise St Michel. She had already been to see the Palais de Justice and the Palace of the Dukes of Burgundy, and had admired the roofs of coloured tiles that made the town look cheerful amidst so much destruction of church buildings by the revolutionaries.

She had been to the thirteenth century church of Notre Dame, all of whose one hundred and eighty gothic statues of the life of the Virgin had been destroyed during the Revolution. She had liked the Jacquemart clock on the top of the church, brought there by Philip the Bold over four hundred years ago, and it had even had struck the hour for her. But she liked *this* church better – and it had survived the revolution, as so many buildings in the town had not.

Eglantine had gone into Notre Dame with her whilst her mistress was at the dressmaker's but now she had gone to the market and would later meet Camille to do some more shopping. Georgy was told to go into St Michel and wait there till they both came to fetch her. She was enjoying a few moments alone. No children, and no conversation to make.

Having had her fill of its wonderful richly ornamented Renaissance façade she decided to go into the church to see if there were any good statues and sculptures. Parts of the building were, she realized, seventeenth century, more recent than the other church or the cathedral. Edward Walker had once showed her pictures of Spain and she thought the outside had looked a little Spanish. She went in by the big central door.

She was disappointed by the interior; it was dark, and there were few pictures of any interest. She lit a candle and sat down. Not exactly to pray, more to think in peace. She liked the glimmering candles and the smell of recent incense.

She was startled when a voice said in her ear: 'Georgy?' A prickle of fear ran up and down her spine but in the split second before she turned she knew it was Amaury Arnaud.

'Sh,' he whispered. 'Can I come and sit next to you?' He had not expected her to refuse, for he came and sat on the long-backed chair next to hers. There did not seem to be anyone else in the church, except that occasionally in the long distance a priest could be seen crossing the nave at the front, genuflecting each time he passed the Host in its red light up on the altar.

'I thought you were in Paris!' she whispered. 'Your mother said you were!'

'My mother?'

'Yes – she came to lunch to ask Monsieur Marceau's advice concerning the reclamation of your father's property—'

'Oh, I had work here in Dijon,' he said carelessly. 'But I wanted to ask you a favour. I've been following you and that old servant round all morning!'

'Did Louis-Marie write to you then?' she asked.

'No. Why?'

'I told him his cousin's house at Les Aisées had been broken into – at least it was only the stables – but I was worried – and then I wanted to ask him about a young woman who visited us a few weeks ago – I think it was the same young woman with whom you attended a concert in Aix.'

He was silent.

'She was looking for you – she said you'd promised to accompany her to Paris, but you hadn't turned up. I don't know why she thought you might be at the château. Then it occurred to me that she was the sort of person who might be a gypsy – except that I was sure I'd seen her with you! Anyway I thought perhaps she let the horse out of the stable—'

'Georgy you are not making sense—'

'I'm sorry.' She thought, one sight of him and my mind is in a whirl, but I must discover if Capucine is his *petite amie.* 'Her name,' she said, 'was Capucine. Is that someone you know?'

'It might be. As a matter of fact I wanted to ask you something that might have to do with her.'

'And that's why you followed me?'

'Yes – well, it was just – that if anyone were to ask you about that … young woman … could you say nothing?'

'I have already told Camille – and the male servants saw her too.'

'Well, if anyone comes asking about her just say you haven't seen her recently, will you?'

'As you wish.' He must be besotted with her, but why had he not gone to Paris with her?

'I can explain it all later. Let's talk about something else.'

'Louis-Marie knows I saw her too – I told him—'

'Well, Louis-Marie is in Lyon at present, I believe.'

'She appeared to know you very well,' she said wistfully.

'Probably not all that well,' he answered after a brief silence. 'But she might need to escape those she regards as friends – and she is very young.'

Georgy immediately imagined Amaury trying to rescue a damsel in distress. Maybe her father was intent on marrying her to an old man she did not love? But why must she beware those she considered were friends? It was the reverse of her own situation where a father imagined a man had designs on his daughter and wished to prevent a possible engagement.

The young woman must be Amaury's lover! He would have to wait until she was of age to marry her.

'I liked her,' she said reluctantly. 'And I will do anything I can to help her if that is what you wish.'

'I knew you would! Georgy, I have missed you – you know?'

Her heart turned over. Could that be true? If he loved Capucine? Which she felt sure he did.

'If she asks for your help will you hide her and then let me know?'

'Does she often sleep in barns?'

'I hope that will not be necessary.'

'It all sounds very mysterious – is it to do with politics?'

'Why should you think that?'

'I don't know – everything unpleasant seems to have to do with that—'

'All I can tell you, and this in confidence, is that there are many – liberals – who are angry with our new King. Eventually there will be an uprising against him – and against religion.' He gestured round the church.

'I am not a Catholic, Amaury.'

'Do you think I don't know that?'

'Are *you* one of these liberals?'

'I might be. On the other hand, it is not very sensible at present to scheme against Charles.'

'If you sympathize with them, why should you be trying to get back your properties? – your father or grandfather must have been for the King?'

'Well, things have changed, and it is my mama, not myself who is, as you say, trying to get back property.' He took her hand. 'Don't let's talk any more about it – it's a boring subject – *ça m'ennuie.*'

She looked at him in the half light. Holding hands in a church was not something she had ever done before. Even if she was not a Catholic it seemed a little sacrilegious. But she did not care, and for the present she did not care that he was in love with that strange girl. It was enough to sit by his side and feel his hand. But Eglantine, or Camille, or both, would soon be coming for her. She told him this and he got up. She stood up herself.

'You need not tell anyone you saw me here. I hope to be back at my mother's next month. Don't forget what I told you if you see that young lady!' So Capucine was a young lady now!

Amaury bent his head and suddenly kissed her hand. Then he turned and went away and she watched as he went out through a side door.

She sat down again feeling shaky.

Camille had ordered a new pelisse to be made in blue velvet which would not be ready for some weeks. She also had her eye on a hat, a high-crowned elaborate affair with ribbons. 'I shall buy it next time,' she said.

Georgy wondered whether her housekeeping allowance stretched to such things. It was a good thing she did not long for fashionable clothes herself.

Eglantine had been busy buying 'superior' cassis, and cheese that could not be obtained in Mâcon. A cheesy smell permeated their carriage all the way back home. Georgy did not mind; she was abstracted, her mind full of Amaury – the way he had spoken, the way he had looked at her, the kiss he had left on her hand which she felt still like a burning spot on her skin. She was surprised the others did not notice her changed demeanour, but she supposed she had been so used to hiding her feelings at home with her family, and writing down the thoughts that were not for them to share, that her face probably belied her.

Camille herself appeared preoccupied on their return. Now was to be the worst time of winter: the weak sun that had, even so, caused the coloured tiles of the roofs of buildings in Dijon to glint in its rays, disappeared, and two weeks of more bitter cold and driving sleet followed.

There was no sign of Capucine and as far as Georgy knew, no further local break-ins. The weather was probably too bad even for thieves to move around the country.

Camille's husband remained in Paris.

It was almost the end of February when Georgy received a letter. Not from Amaury but in answer to her own from Louis-Marie. She had almost forgotten she had written to him, but realized on reading his letter that the young man had taken her letter as a sign of her interest in him rather than in his friend.

She realized also that Louis-Marie loved advising her; it was his way of demonstrating his interest *in* her – she hoped not his affection *for* her. The most pertinent parts of his letter were however to do with their mutual friend. After telling her at length where he had reached with his epic of Charlemagne (now to be called *The First Emperor*) and then thanking her for her news of the break-ins ('I shall write immediately to my father to ask him to make sure my uncle over at Les Aisées is taking all precautions,') he finally got round to mentioning Amaury:

'No, I have not seen our friend. I am, as you see in Lyon and I imagine he is still in Paris on a mission for his lady mother. I fear he is a trifle hot-headed and must not be taken too seriously. Some say that his whole family is mad – at least that is the general opinion among his friends here. I beg you, dear Georgina, to take the utmost care when you are abroad, for there are always robbers and brigands around and I fear that the young woman to whom you allude may be one of them. I think you must be mistaken about the woman you saw in Aix. As I am unfortunately short-sighted I did not see his companion very well.

I shall acquaint M de Marceau when I am next to stay in his delightful corner of Saône et Loire.

Your sincere friend
Louis-Marie des Combes.

Georgy did not hasten to answer this missive, for she was a little ashamed of having used Louis-Marie for possible information about Amaury. She would not tell him either that Amaury was not in Paris. Did she herself, *pace* Louis, really believe that the girl Capucine was a brigand? She obviously knew Amaury Arnaud. She was sure it had been the same girl – and there was that little favour he was wearing at the theatre that evening . . . .

Thinking and brooding about this, and what Amaury had said to her in the church, she began to be invaded with a most unpleasant feeling. It was some time before she gave it the name of jealousy. She must truly love Amaury if she allowed such feelings to take root in her? Capucine was his lover, or his fiancée; she had been with him in Aix as his accredited companion at the theatre. And Louis-Marie would not admit he had seen Capucine if she was the other man's *petite amie*. Even if he had, he would not mention the woman to her, for she was a respectable girl who was not supposed to know about such things.

All the ecstatic feelings that had followed upon Amaury's meeting her in the church, and sitting so close to her, and kissing her hand, suddenly vanished, to be replaced by a torturing uncertainty. He could not love *her* when he loved that other fascinating girl. She admitted to herself that she had found Capucine – whoever she was – fascinating. Another emotion then followed upon this one; if she too found Capucine beautiful and fascinating, she could not blame Amaury for doing so. She would adore them both then, for they were both strangely attractive.

She longed to see him again but tried to concentrate upon her work. The children were exhausting. They were bored indoors

and needed exercise. At the end of the month there was still nothing from Amaury, but instead, just when winter's grip was
loosening, Augustin de Marceau returned one evening from Paris.

He also bore news of Alphonse de Lamartine which Camille
recounted to Georgy over their early cup of coffee the next morning. 'Just imagine – the poet has fought a duel – in Florence!'

Georgy's heart stopped. 'A duel – but was he hurt?'

'Augustin says it was just ten days ago and the news was all over
Paris before he left. Apparently – but you may know more about
this than I do – it was in a poem where he was imitating Byron's
Childe Harold, and he said something rude about the Italians!
Anyway, they've all been up in arms! One of their colonels wrote
a pamphlet against Alphonse and this so enraged our poet that he
asked for "satisfaction".'

'What happened? Did he kill the colonel? Obviously he didn't
die himself or you wouldn't be telling me all this?'

'Well, they fought on the banks of the Arno – and Lamartine
had his right arm pierced by the fellow's sword.'

'So he lost the duel?'

'Yes, but apparently duels are forbidden in Tuscany – as you
know they are at home – and the poor colonel fellow was a political exile! So our poet interceded with the Grand Duke, who
decided not to prosecute the victor.'

'How noble of Lamartine!' breathed Georgy. 'Yet he was the
one who had wanted the duel – and if he hadn't said anything
rude about Italy the colonel wouldn't have written his pamphlet.'

'There, you see how stupid men are?' replied Camille.
'Augustin was all excited about it but I think it was *not* very noble
of M de Lamartine.'

'And poor Mary Ann – she must have been very worried!'

'Oh, they don't think about worrying their wives and children
when they do such things.'

Georgy was surprised at her employer, would have thought her
more 'romantic'. But the excitement over the duel – which even
invaded the torpor of M de Marceau – changed the next day into
a new excitement when a man on horseback brought a letter for
her.

It was from Amaury Arnaud.

Chapter 5

Georgy had certainly never received a letter in such a dramatic way. Fortunately she was still indoors, on the way back from a walk with the children. They had just turned into the stables in the courtyard for Thibault to look at the horses when the man came galloping up.

'Message from Monsieur Arnaud,' he said, doffed his cap and was off.

Nobody but Lucie and Thibault heard this or saw Georgy receive the missive, and Thibault was far too keen to indulge himself in his daily treat of horse-visiting to take much notice of anything else.

It must be something urgent for Amaury to send a rider with his message.

She did not open the letter until she could be by herself in her little bedroom up in the tower. Once she was there, and after quickly casting her eye down his angular script, she was puzzled. There was no mention made of Capucine or of any emergency. Instead, the letter appeared to have been written so that he might carry on their literary discussion of some months ago.

At the end there was no proper signature. Just a squiggle: *AA*. Perhaps he thought anything more would be giving too much away?

Chère Mlle Georgy

In the preface to his new collection of Odes and Ballads, a greater poet than your Lamartine writes that a poet must have only one model, *Nature*, only one guide, *Truth*. He must write with his *Soul* and his *Heart*. You may not have heard of Victor Hugo? He distils the whole of reality in his lyrical outpourings! I confess I thought him *plus royaliste que le roi* but now I sense something new in the air.

'Romantics' will eventually form alliances with liberals to bring about reform: as in style, so in the conduct of society. Things are very bad for the Common Man at present – more starvation, more misery, when our revolution of thirty years ago was meant to put paid to all that. Businesses are failing, money is short, even amongst my better-off friends. But all most of them can think about is getting back what their ancestors lost thirty years ago! Such people are an anachronism: an aristocracy who would like to believe the last century never ended. Or they are pious fools who look back even further – to the century before that! Your Lamartine's family is the same – and most of the people you will have met. I have to excuse my mother's attempts to get back her and my father's property, for she does it not for herself but for her children. She was once very different.

I shall shortly be *chez ma mère* and hope to ride over to see you next week. Perhaps you had better warn your employers in case they do not wish to entertain such a terrible fellow as myself.

Your devoted poet who would wish to follow his nature in revealing his heart—

AA.

What young woman would not have been fascinated by such a letter, especially a young woman with strong feelings, which Georgy undoubtedly possessed? Even so, she was left feeling slightly uneasy.

She had heard Amaury speak of a young poet called Victor Hugo but had not read anything he had written. If only Amaury would stick to poetry – and love – and not burden her with political thoughts. What good was it believing in revolutions? Or opposing them? It was all talk, and it was always the ordinary folk who had to pay for fine ideas. She must have got that message from Edward Walker, she supposed. She was sorry for the rich who had suffered so much thirty years before – but the poor, if they became the new rich – though she knew that was not likely – would be just as tyrannical, if given the chance. What would that woman Wollstonecraft have thought about it all? Were women just as bad as men in their political and material ambitions?

She stood at her window looking out at the park in the dusk, Amaury's letter in her hand. On her table was her little portable desk, in it Edward Walker's last letter to her. For weeks she had owed him a reply. She would so much value his advice now, not so much about Amaury, for the emotions she nursed in her heart were private, but about the correct attitude to political unrest and to the literary ideas Amaury was always talking about. Did Amaury believe in a new revolution, as Edward had believed in change when he was young in France over a dozen years ago?

Georgy had too much common sense not to be frightened of revolutions. She knew that Camille de Marceau liked Amaury, but how could she introduce him into her husband's house, when he was opposed to all that Augustin and his parents stood for?

The Poet Lamartine, whom Amaury appeared to despise so much, did not, she was sure, have quite the same beliefs as his own parents. Each generation changed the climate. She well remembered Edward saying that to her. It was natural to espouse change when you were young. In Aix, when she had first met Amaury, she had thought he had a generous spirit. Wasn't that more important than somebody's political stance? What good anyway had their 'Revolution' done? What had it brought but bloodshed and terror, to the innocent as well as the guilty?

Amaury had confessed that the ordinary people, especially the poor, amongst whom he did not count himself, were no better off now than before. It was true that Bourbon Louis XVIII and his successor Charles X had allowed a little more freedom to creep into the Constitution, and doubtless their successors would improve things even more, she hoped without another violent upheaval. Then she felt a little ashamed of her rational approach, aware that she might have such opinions because of the way she had been brought up. But I thought I was a rebel, she said to herself, and anyway Amaury is not a real revolutionary!

He doesn't like priests – but then neither does Edward Walker. He's a liberal – and despises Charles X – but then so probably would Edward.

Did Louis-Marie, Catholic and Royalist, understand his friend's position? And what had all these opinions to do with what Amaury – like his new poet – called the 'truth'? Was all religion hypocrisy? In spite of *his* religious principles Monsieur de Marceau was a gambler. Her own father, whom she suspected had no deep religious principles, would never have gambled with his wife's money – which she guessed the children's father did.

Georgy saw the moon was rising in the sky. Her thoughts turned away from the world of kings and revolutions and wars – and even ideas – and returned, as was their wont, to that other world of words, and feelings, and love.

The next day she said tentatively to Camille: 'I think Monsieur Arnaud is going to pay us a visit again soon.'

Camille was quick off the mark. 'You have heard from him?'

'Yes, he wrote a note to me and a man brought it over yesterday. I believe he is to stay with his mother again. He'd like to come over and see – me – us.'

'I shall have to ask my husband,' replied Camille. When Amaury had visited before, Augustin had been in Paris.

'He did not object to Madame Bonaventure.'

'No, but you know I have to be careful of the visitors I invite.'

'Yes, I know.'

Camille looked worried.

'You have been very kind letting me have friends here – I suppose I could ask Louis-Marie as well?' said Georgy.

'He is not at Les Aisées, is he?'

'No, but I expect he might be visiting his old aunt again soon.' She nearly said: 'and M de Marceau couldn't object to *him*!'

Camille said: 'There have been rumours about certain members of Monsieur Arnaud's family – not his mother, I don't think – people think she's peculiar but not dangerous. M de Marceau is always very aware of what is going on in this provincial society.'

In the event Georgy did not need to ask M de Marceau permission to invite Amaury to the château for he turned up one day unannounced. Fortunately, both Camille and Augustin were out of the house, the one on an errand for his father in Mâcon and Camille on another mysterious errand of her own. Georgy guessed that there were secrets in Camille's life to which she was not privy. For once the children were in the kitchens with the two servants, 'helping' them to bake the plain cakes that were to be consumed to alleviate their Lenten fast. Georgy had taken the opportunity to go for a little walk by herself. The ground was soggy so she did not intend to walk very far, but it was a good thing she had gone out, for as soon as she reached the pond and stopped at a gate, intending to walk over the field to the woods she heard a soft 'Pssst'.

She looked round in surprise. A horse had crept up behind her from the edge of the field behind the wood, his hoofs making no noise on the damp earth.

Amaury Arnaud jumped down from it, tethered his nag to a convenient tree and stood looking at her with the queerest expression on his face. She found herself trembling.

'Amaury! What are you doing here?'

'Well, I thought I wouldn't wait for an invitation but would make a little detour to see if you were free to talk to me for a few minutes!'

She thought she detected irony in his voice. 'You know that M de Marceau is unlikely to invite anyone here who nurses radical sentiments,' she said spiritedly, for he had given her a shock.

'You received my letter then?'

'Yes. I wanted to reply – but I was not sure where you would be. I didn't expect you to be here so soon!'

'Oh, there were reasons—'

'Not to do with that girl – Capucine? She never came again.' She blushed and hoped he had not noticed.

His face darkened. Whatever he felt for this Capucine it clearly disturbed him.

'No, she had to go away – for the present. But I think things are more settled.'

'And how is your mama?'

'I didn't come here to talk about my family,' he said rather roughly. 'I keep thinking about *you* – you ought to be flattered!'

'I thought of you too,' she said, not able to help herself speaking the truth to him.

'Dear little Georgy – come here!'

She was nervous, sure there must be some other reason for him being so affectionate.

'I can't stay out long – I only came out for air. I spoke of you to Madame de Marceau, and she said her husband did not like to entertain people of a radical persuasion.'

'Never mind – I'd rather see you like this – you must have guessed I'd be coming?'

'No, really I did not—'

There were already a few new green shoots of spring in the grass, and the mare began to nibble contentedly. But it was not warm, and Georgy shivered. Amaury put his arm round her.

'Are you frightened of me, Georgy? You are trembling.'

'No, of course not.' She drew away for a moment. 'I'm sure you could come again with your mother,' she got out. 'They had her for luncheon—'

'Yes, I know they did. Stop prevaricating Georgy – I came to see you, not your employers, or cousins or whatever they are. I came because I wanted to do this—' He took her in his arms and kissed her on the lips. Georgy was still bewildered – then kissed him back. How had he known what she felt for him? Or perhaps he did not. She would not tell him.

He kissed her again and she felt quite weak, and thought, I *shall* tell him eventually, for I am incapable of playing games with people. But she was determined to speak up for herself about other matters.

'Why did you say nothing to me before? You wrote only of politics – and Victor Hugo—'

'Did I? Well, I expect I was shy of writing down my feelings. I liked you when I first met you – remember – in the park at Aix with that fool Louis-Marie—'

'Oh, don't say that – he cannot help his manner – he might be a good friend to you, even though he surely knows of your political allegiances.'

'Oh don't talk of *them* – women need not concern themselves with all that.'

This was just what she had felt reading his letter, but coming from his own lips it annoyed her a little. In spite of his enormously exciting presence and the magnetic attraction he had for her she did not intend to pretend to be stupid.

'It's true I think there are more important things than wars and politics and governments – and revolutions,' she got out, 'but that is because I want to believe in—' she was going to say 'love' but knew she had better not. She substituted 'feelings', and added: 'What your Hugo calls the heart and the soul. In real life, I mean, not just in poems.'

'You are an original girl,' he said. 'But I would rather kiss you than hear you talk!'

'Not as original as Capucine!' she said. Now it was out. 'You love her don't you?'

'Georgy! How can you say such a thing when I have come all this way to embrace you? Which I willingly do again.'

165

She wished they could go indoors, sit down side by side, prolong a tender scene, but they could not – it was time for her to pull away.

'*Your* poet was like me, you know – Monsieur de Lamartine liked women!'

Of course he had liked women. What did he mean exactly? She thought, Amaury is even more handsome than Alphonse de Lamartine, because he is younger, and has winning ways.

'I meant – oh well, never mind. You are so young and innocent, Georgy. Are all English girls like you?'

She looked at him, at the naked desire she saw in his face. She had never seen such a feeling written on a face before, nor felt it for herself. It was all so sudden. She knew beyond doubt that if she went on knowing him she would be tempted one day to know him even better, in the way she had never yet known a man.

But she could not believe he 'loved' her. Not as she knew she had begun to love him.

'I must go,' she repeated.

'Promise me you will come here again – I shall ride round every day—'

'I cannot come alone usually,' she said. 'It will have to be with the children.' Who are chaperones, she thought.

'Then kiss me goodbye!'

She took his hand and kissed it and then she turned and ran towards the house. He stood looking in her direction for a long moment and then he mounted his horse once more, wishing he could spur the old animal into a gallop for he needed exertion and excitement if he could not yet have Georgy Crabtree.

She was too excited to walk back sedately to the château, but ran like the wind, her thoughts and feelings tumbling together in confusion. There was however no time to think calmly about it all, for the children were waiting for her to read them a story, and to be put to bed after that. She hoped nobody had seen her with him. Why should she be forced into a subterfuge? Another part of her whispered: You wouldn't really prefer to see him in the salon formally, as you see Louis-Marie, would you? If Amaury wanted their meetings to be a secret she would have to agree. She felt uneasy about it, for Camille de Marceau had been so kind to her. She was also uncomfortably aware that she was Camille's responsibility. She had never wished so heartily that she was older, responsible for herself, mistress of her own destiny.

As she mulled over all this after putting the children to bed that night, the old problem of what to say to Edward Walker came back to her mind. How she had hated her lack of freedom of action in the past. At least there was no Papa here to worry about her. The thought of Edward recalled to her mind his warnings of the difference between talk and action. He had said something about young men who thought young women of spirit were there for their delectation or taming. She remembered his very words: *You must not give the wrong impression because you are open and sincere!*

Did Amaury think she was a 'young woman of spirit'? Would his ardour cool once he had made a conquest? Wasn't that all nonsense? For the first time she realized that Mr Walker might have had his own reasons for saying what he did. She felt uncomfortable. What was wrong about the kind of good feelings she had for Amaury Arnaud? She must trust in her own judgement. Even to think of him – his face, his hands, his voice, made her want to weep with joy that someone like him existed – and that he liked *her*. The one person from whom she might have asked advice – Edward – was still the last person to whom she could open her heart.

She woke once in the night thinking of how Amaury's face had looked before he kissed her. Should she be frightened of him? Of her own passion? There was something unexpected in the way she had felt when he had been so close to her. Everyone would say she was wrong to encourage him. Yet she had not really encouraged him. Was it the image of Capucine that had made her rasher than she would have been? Amaury had appeared indignant when she had mentioned her – but had not denied that he loved her.

Georgy was to remember those last days of winter and early spring when her newly awoken feelings made every day into an excitement. Yet more than a week was to pass before Amaury managed to see her again. She thought: I might write to Louis-Marie and suggest he might pay us a visit – and bring Amaury with him. For some reason she wanted things to be above-board, even as she thrilled to the idea of secret meetings. But why not get to know another side to Amaury when other people were around as well? She took the bull by the horns and asked Camille if she might invite Louis-Marie over to the château when he came back from Lyon before Easter. Camille always seemed to be vaguely absent-minded now, but said finally:

'If you like, but I don't suppose he will be spending much time at home or with his aunt now he's back with his law studies.'

When, the next time Georgy saw Amaury, she approached him with this idea, he was scornful.

'We don't need *him* around, Georgy! We can be alone together soon – we can meet at night when it's warmer!' He sounded excited, had not dismounted.

She had only been able to slip out of the house for a moment this time, not really expecting to see him, but sure that he would ride over again soon if he had said he would.

'I came to say that my mother sends her respects to Monsieur and Madame de Marceau,' he stated, sounding bored. 'You can say I rode over but would not stay.'

'Is she intending to pay us another visit?' she asked.

'Please convey her respects – she invites both Monsieur and Madame de Marceau to come over to her little house next week. She suggests Tuesday – would you ask them?'

'Am I to come too – and the children?'

'All will be welcome. You and I can go for a walk by the river!'

'I'm afraid Monsieur de Marceau is away again, but I will ask Madame.'

'I can't stay very long today. I must be off now – I'm on my way to a doctor, my little brother is sick.'

'Thierry? Oh, I'm sorry – what seems to be the matter with him?'

'The usual childish fever. My mother does not trust the doctor over at L'Hermitage. Come here, Georgy!'

She went up and patted his mare who remained quite still.

'Come closer.'

She leaned against the warm body of the horse and Amaury bent down from his saddle and put back a tendril of her hair that had escaped from the white cap that covered her hair. She grasped his hands and kissed them.

He looked at her reflectively. 'You are so small – any man could easily crush you in his arms! But you don't want any man, do you?'

She looked up, and stared at him. It was true; she would be glad for those strong arms of his to hold her . . . .

168

'But I must go. Think of me, won't you – and try to persuade them to come over and see Mama?'

'I hope your brother will soon be better,' she said, stepping back.

He gave a slight tug of his reins and the nag moved away. He turned in his saddle as they entered the wood and blew her a kiss.

After this meeting she felt disconcerted. It had all been so different from the week before. She had the impression there was something on his mind and an even stronger impression that he did not intend to enlighten her about it.

She did not have the opportunity to ask Camille about visiting Madame de Bonaventure until the next day, for on the afternoon of Amaury's visit Camille said she had a headache and would keep to her room. Georgy told the children to play quietly and Lucie brought out her precious knitting. Célanie had taught her to knit and the little girl was making a scarf for her mother. Georgy managed to settle Thibault with his dissected puzzle. It was the picture of a horse, all in pieces to put together, and it kept him busy until his bedtime.

The next morning Camille came down to her sitting room looking wan but saying she felt a little better. At the first opportunity Georgy broached the subject of Amaury's mama.

'Madame de Bonaventure would like you and Monsieur de Marceau to visit her. She suggests next Tuesday afternoon. Amaury rode over yesterday morning and gave me the message in the garden,' she offered boldly.

Did Camille look at her rather sharply? Perhaps she was imagining it?

'Why can't the woman write a letter?' grumbled Camille. 'I'm sure my husband will have no intention of paying her a visit – and he will still be away next Tuesday.'

It went through Georgy's head that maybe Monsieur Augustin de Marceau was not 'about his father's business' in Mâcon or Paris, but gambling there, or elsewhere.

'I shall go over myself,' said Camille suddenly. 'It will do me good to get away a little now the weather is improving.'

'He did say we were all welcome – and the children—'

'I know a little more about his mother now,' Camille added. 'Monsieur Cellard tells me that Madame de Bonaventure was formerly for Napoleon, against the Royalists. It must have been her first husband who was the nobleman.'

'Amaury's father, then?'

'Well, after he died she married again but didn't manage to get back any property after 1814, unlike my parents-in-law. But why should she? Her first husband's family had lost money but had never been forced to emigrate. *She* took the fruits of Empire – and also remarried! There was some problem about her second husband too, but Jacques – Monsieur Cellard – was not sure about that. She may say she only wants the land back for her son, but it is not rightly hers to arrange.'

'And Amaury is no Royalist,' said Georgy before she could stop herself.

'No? Well, you had better not tell my husband that!' said Camille.

Georgy was mortified; she had spoken without thinking. But Camille did not appear disturbed on her own account. Had she any idea that Amaury Arnaud wanted to see her English 'governess' in secret?

Afterwards, she was to remember that Camille had called Monsieur Cellard 'Jacques', and to wonder whether there might not be an additional reason for her mistress making no personal criticism of young Monsieur Arnaud.

Augustin was not expected back before the end of the following week and Madame Bonaventure's invitation was for Tuesday. Camille once again consulted Monsieur Cellard and said they could combine their visit with a calling in on some peasant workers who were paid by the de Marceau estate.

Suddenly, Georgy wondered whether she really wanted to go to see Amaury's mother. Wasn't it the sort of conventional visit her friend Abby Strang's sister Louisa might delight in? As though she thought Amaury was 'interested' in her in an 'official' way. It was so difficult to remain neutral when the whole of society conspired either to keep you apart from young men or present you as rivals to their mothers' affections. She laughed at herself; she was really too absurd. She wanted to get to know Amaury in an ordinary way, know his character, not just carry on a clandestine affair of secret kisses. And yet, and yet … when she was near him, all these estimable wishes melted away and she just wanted him – needed him – to encircle her in his arms, or to let her 'drink in' his face, and absorb the whole of his masculine self through her pores. This had scarcely happened yet; her imagination, working on

170

their few meetings and the two occasions of kisses and embracing, had presented her with it as if it were a *fait accompli*.

If she could turn these imaginings into reality she might be able to ignore whatever was his involvement with Capucine. On other more ordinary occasions she must ignore her dreams to concentrate on his real-life presence – for, in spite of his talk about revolutions, she did like him, as well as finding him so attractive. The trouble was that on more formal occasions she would find her thoughts returning to that strange Capucine as if her own destiny were involved in hers.

On a windy day Georgy set off in the carriage with Camille de Marceau and the two children to visit Madame Bonaventure. They would pass through their own woods and then take a path that circled Les Aisées on a lane through the fields. At the bottom of these fields there was the shallow river which the path approached a little further along. Then it took its winding way through another wood and came out by a small village with a church. They did not stop there, but went on up a cobbled road bordered by a high wall. Behind the wall was the old house rented by their hostess. The drive was longer than Georgy had imagined; once they were through the high black gate in the wall and were driving along a rather muddy lane the house came into view.

She suddenly remembered as they neared the end of their journey that Amaury's little brother Thierry – she presumed he must be his half-brother – had been feverish the previous week. She was on tenterhooks lest he might still be ailing and might pass on his chill, or whatever it was, to Camille's offspring. She should have told her; she would never forgive herself if in her eagerness to visit Amaury she might have placed their health in jeopardy. Madame Bonaventure had not looked the sort of woman who might be concerned about other people's children. She did not know why she felt this, but she did.

All seemed to be well, however, when they were taken into a gloomy high-ceilinged hall, where a wild boar's head looked down from one of the walls, and their hostess advanced to greet them. She was followed by a strikingly handsome little boy who clung to the hand of a nursemaid.

Madame Bonaventure, now that Georgy was standing close to her, was seen to be a voluptuous woman in her mid to late forties with black hair, black eyes, cheeks that were slightly rouged

171

(Georgy decided) and with a few lumpy traces of smallpox. She was dressed in a long, décoletée crimson robe that swept the floor behind her, and when she finally shook hands with her Georgy felt the rings on her fingers. Amaury was nowhere to be seen.

'*Enchantée,*' murmured the woman. She turned to Camille again, saying: 'Do please call me Félicienne, Madame, I find the "older" manners freer, don't you? If I may call you Camille we shall be more comfortable.'

'Very well, Madame,' said Camille, but her expression remained guarded. 'May my children play in your stable yard?' she asked. 'They are so looking forward to seeing their friend Amaury!'

'Yes, he is a great favourite with infants. I suppose, having a small brother, he is used to them.'

Madame Bonaventure ignored Georgy, who was standing with the children, but said to the nursemaid, 'Take them out, will you, Estelle? Camille, my dear, we must find you a comfortable chair – the English have *such* comfortable chairs – and then you must taste my splendid cassis.'

Georgy moved away with the children as Camille was swept into a large salon whose rather tawdry gold hangings she glimpsed through a door set at an angle in the oak panelled wall.

Where was he?

She and the children trailed after Thierry and his nursemaid.

'Ask Thierry if he would like to play with you,' she urged Thibault, who looked sulky. He was a year or two older than Amaury's brother but the other child was tall for his age. 'Go on – he will tell you where the horses are.'

Then they all found themselves in the stable-yard, and there, mounted on a young chestnut gelding, was Amaury. Thibault whooped with glee whilst Thierry stood staring at him.

'Let me! let me ride him!' shouted Thibault.

Amaury dismounted. 'No, he's too big for you but I could just let you sit up there if you hold on to me,' he said.

'No – it's *my* horse!' said Thierry. Thibault looked daggers but held back. He knew what were the duties of a guest, even if the host was rather deficient in his own.

'Thierry, you can ride with me on the mule tomorrow,' said Amaury. Then he turned to Georgy and said in English: 'Ow splendid to see you, my dear.'

Lucie perked up. 'I understand English!' she said.

172

'Oh, I forgot. Then I am pleased you also 'ave visited my 'ouse.'

Lucie giggled and Georgy thought, I prefer him to stick to French. But perhaps *she* sounded just as foreign when she spoke in Amaury's language, though she hoped not.

Amaury lifted up Thibault and said, back in his own language: 'You hold him on the other side. There, you are on a very big horse now, Thibault!'

'My turn, my turn!' shouted Thierry, but Amaury, who was holding Georgy's hand behind Thibault as they both supported him did not immediately let it go.

'Let Thierry have a turn,' she commanded Thibault.

'Oh, he can do it whenever he wants – if I'm around,' said Amaury.

Eventually they jumped Thibault down and an old man came round and led the horse away.

'He doesn't really belong to us – he's been lent to my mother. She used to ride a good deal,' said Amaury without further explanation.

Georgy found she was full of questions to which she would like the answers. Had his mother known Amaury's father in The Terror? No, she was probably too young. But when had his father died? And when had she married again? Was her second husband dead too? Was he Thierry's father? She must suppress her inquisitiveness, though everything about Amaury interested her.

'Your mother says you are good with children because you have a little brother—'

'Yes, I had another half-brother, Rémy, who died, but he lived most of the time with his own father's family,' he answered, and then quickly changed the subject. 'Let's go for a little walk in the woods – the children can look for violets and primroses—'

So Thierry was not a Bonaventure?

'Isn't it a bit early for violets?' she asked him.

'I suppose so – but we can set the children to look. They might find a few celandines!'

She laughed. It was really impossible to talk privately to him with three children capering round them, and she knew there would be a limit to their patience in looking for spring flowers. But she liked to be with him, and squeezed his hand in return when he took hers, even as he spoke:

'I'm afraid I have to go again rather unexpectedly to Paris next week,' he said.

'Oh?'

'But I can come over to see you on Saturday – can't you get away for a little by yourself? There's that little hut at the bottom of the drive where we could go—'

She did not answer that but said instead: 'Camille once promised me a visit to Paris. I know Papa would send me the money if I needed to stay there. Monsieur de Marceau is still in Paris at present, I believe,' she added.

'Couldn't you persuade your cousin to go soon? Her husband might be pleased to see her!'

'I don't know, Amaury, she seems to prefer it when he is away. How long are you to stay there?'

'It might be several months!'

'Oh, no!' she said involuntarily.

'I'm afraid so, Georgy. If only we could be together in Paris! But I'll come and see you again before I go – you know the gardener's hut I mean?'

Amaury was a little strange, even off-hand, with her once he was in his mother's presence. She could not quite put her finger on it but he had not been the same man she had spoken to at the château, the man who had kissed her. Something was obviously preying on his mind. Something to do with Paris?

It was not until they all arrived home rather late that evening with two fretful children, for they had been obliged to call in on a farmer and his wife on the way back, that she wondered how he had come to know of the hut. She had seen neither Jean nor Emile working near it, but she knew where he meant. It was just off the path to the pond, and had probably been used for storing brushwood.

He had asked her to meet him the following Saturday. On Saturday morning she gave the children their last lesson until Monday, helped Célanie sort pots of conserve in the cellar, put down some eggs in isinglass and cut down some dried herbs hanging from the kitchen ceiling. Then she went up to her room and brushed her hair. It was understood she could have time to herself on Saturday afternoons. Camille usually took her children over to a friend of hers, one Henriette, who lived five miles away and who had two children of about the same age. Thibault always grumbled, and said the boy was 'stupid', and even Lucie would groan and say: 'Do we have to go?' But today Camille had promised them a ride in Jacques Cellard's cart which always pleased them, large carriages making them occasionally feel sick.

'We shall be back about seven. Have you anything for the diligence?' Camille asked her.

Georgy immediately felt guilty that she had not yet replied to Edward Walker. Last week she had managed a long letter to her mother who was now fretting over her absence.

Everything is dull here (her mother had written,) we shall be so glad when spring comes. Can't you be taken to Paris by the de Marceaus whilst you are over there? You've been away almost nine months and Papa is talking about our going to London this spring or early summer. I hear that your friend the Strang girl is to go to Paris on her honeymoon. She is getting married this week.

Well this was a surprise – she had heard nothing from Abigail.

'I shall pass by the coach office and might call in,' said Camille. 'They might have something for me and it would save paying a bigger frank. I shall ask also for you.'

At last they were off in Monsieur Cellard's cart. Georgy wondered at Camille preferring it to her own carriage, even if her children did.

She went back up to her room, and reread the letter from home, lifted her portable desk on to her lap and tried to begin a letter to Edward Walker but the words would not come. She would go out in half an hour or so and walk in the garden, pass by the hut. Amaury might not visit after all.

When she arrived at the hut, having taken the precaution of going there the long way round so as to put anyone off who might be looking out, there was almost complete silence, broken only by the call of a bird over the pond. The door was easily opened and once inside there was a wonderful smell of charcoal, and leaf mould, and the lingering scent of old summer flowers. There were rushes on the floor, and a worm-eaten old hammock hanging from the roof.

Of course Amaury would not come. He must already regret the ardour he had shown . . . .

She looked for somewhere to sit down. The hammock was obviously unsafe and the floor, in spite of the rushes, very dusty. There were a few sacks in the corner of the hut and she hoped there were no rats. Mice she could deal with, but not rats.

She looked round. There was a wheelbarrow on its back leaning against the wall and an old wooden rake. It did not look as though anyone used the place very much, except that when she pulled one of the sacks off the heap, to use it for sitting on, a piece of stuff fluttered out with it.

She bent down and picked it up off the floor. Red silk. Immediately she knew that Capucine had once been here, and that Amaury must have been with her. That was how he must know about the place; he had used it earlier for secret assignations! This sudden realization did not make her angry; it made her sorrowful.

And then suddenly, as she stood up and pondered this, she heard the neigh of a horse, and then footsteps on the path and there he was. Standing in the doorway, handsome, out of breath.

'Georgy!' he cried, 'I was not sure you would be able to come.' He moved quickly to her side and enfolded her in his arms. She thought, he smells of fresh air!

But she was not going to submit to his kisses again without trying to find out if he had been here before – and with whom. She pulled away.

'Amaury, tell me – this is not the first time you have been here, is it?'

He held her at arm's length whilst he smiled at her. 'What if it is not? Now *you* are here. Do you imagine I have lived at the Hermitage for the past two years like a hermit myself?'

She thought, freedom is what I believe in – and love – and *he* will have been in love before. I suppose I must just get used to the idea. But she could not resist saying:

'Was it with Capucine? There is the feel of her here . . .' She almost said: the scent of her, but she held up the little red handkerchief. 'It is just the kind of thing she would own, isn't it?'

'Georgy, I believe you are jealous!'

'You are still in love with her?'

His face darkened. 'Don't say that Georgy – it is not a fit subject for your curiosity. If I do know Capucine very well, believe me I only want to help her.'

He realizes I love him, she thought.

Then he was crushing her again to his chest, making her feel quite powerless. He kissed her lingeringly, little kisses brushing against her eyelids like moths' wings, and longer harder kisses on her mouth as if he was sculpting his lips to her own. She tried to resist, though every fibre of her body spoke a language that said : *Don't stop! Go on, go on!*

'Lie with me here!' he murmured.

'No—'

'But you will one day! In Paris – come to Paris and we can be free—'

'You are stronger than I am,' she said. 'And I am not a block of ice – but it is *love* that needs freedom – let us wait to see.' She spoke at random but he seemed to understand, for he said:

'You are a well brought up young English lady, Georgy, and I am an unregenerate Frenchman. Never mind. Shall I show you one day that I can love? I find you extremely attractive.'

She thrilled to these words. Why did the word 'love' make her almost ready to cast caution to the winds? Her upbringing and education seemed not to count when her body was in thrall to his.

'Forget Capucine,' he whispered. 'She is nothing to me. I must leave you now. I have written down my address, should you be able to escape to Paris.' He gave her a small piece of folded paper.

'Escape? I can't go there by myself – I have a hope that Madame de Marceau might take me there one day. Oh, Amaury, don't go to Paris yet!'

'I must – I shall stay till a lawsuit is over – possibly until July—'

It struck her that he had not really expected her to allow him to make love to her in the hut that afternoon. He must know she was as inexperienced in the arts of love as he was most likely an ardent practitioner.

Amaury Arnaud had made Georgy Crabtree understand the true nature of sexual passion. In some deep recess of her mind or heart she knew he did not love her. No matter. She would love him because she believed in him as much as she believed in the truth of his body that made hers feel like melting away.

Once his physical presence had been removed from her vicinity, a presence that acted like a magnet to her, she put the little scrap of red silk into her pocket, smoothed her skirt, and left the hut, thinking: well, at least he finds me attractive.

Chapter 6

It was late when Jacques Cellard brought Camille back from her friend Henriette's.

'I'm sorry, I was delayed,' she said, without further explanation. 'Look, in Mâcon there was a letter for me from England – they were going to bring it over next week.'

Georgy wanted to ask whether there had been a letter from Paris from her husband but it was not her business. If M de Marceau stayed there much longer, it would be more difficult for his wife to go herself as she had promised. Camille had left the children with her husband and the servants last summer but she would not want to leave them with only Georgy and the servants. On the other hand, once he had returned, he might object to his wife's going to Paris with Georgy. He might be averse to his wife's staying in Paris without him, even if she took the children with her to Paris, which would not be a good idea.

The next morning Camille was in a strange mood. As it was Sunday she sent the children to mass with Georgy but did not attend herself.

On their return she said: 'Now children, you will be able to tell Papa that you have attended mass regularly, won't you?'

'When is Papa coming back?' asked Thibault.

'I had a letter from him yesterday. He will soon be with us,' she replied shortly, and disappeared for the afternoon.

Célanie did not mince her words when Georgy went into the kitchens for a drink of milk for Lucie.

'So he's to come back next week? Say what you like, he neglects her – not that it excuses her – but—'

'What do you mean?' asked Georgy. Célanie was usually a fount of information.

'I have eyes in my head,' was all she added.

In the evening of the next day Georgy sat with Camille helping her with the accounts. Camille looked worried.

'M Cellard does his best but someone is still robbing us at the Soubrier vineyard,' she said. 'Augustin will have to ride over there next week to sort it out. Last year's vintage was good – the profit should have been higher.'

All this was a mystery to Georgy, whose mother never had to worry about farm prices, but she supposed the de Marceau land was potentially richer, with more opportunity for fraud.

Camille put down her pen and stretched her arms above her head. 'What did you think of Madame Bonaventure?' she asked.

Georgy's heart gave a thump. 'She was once a beauty? She gives the impression of being a hard woman, I think.'

'Oh, she was once a *grande scandaleuse*, I believe.'

'She must be quite old now, but she has that little boy—'

'She is forty six – she told me so! No longer, I would imagine, the object of men's admiration. She told me she once had a salon in Paris – she rather fancies herself—'

Georgy had never heard Camille be so rude about another woman before, but today she sounded bitter. Perhaps Madame Bonaventure was just a convenient object for her spleen.

'We women do not have power for very long,' Camille sighed. 'That is something I shall warn Lucie about when she is eighteen! One ought to be sorry for the poor woman.'

'Why? She has a handsome son—' and Georgy blushed, '– and other children, and she has had three husbands—'

'Oh I do not think she has had *three* husbands—'

'But the little boy – Thierry – was not Monsieur Bonaventure's – she said the two children of his lived with his family.'

'But that does not mean either that he is dead or that he was father to her youngest son!'

'Do women in France get divorced?'

'Very rarely. They tried it in the Revolution.' Camille was silent for a time, staring out of the window. Then: 'Women's reign is short – the years when you are sure of your attractions – but some women are attractive for longer than most.'

'I have noticed that Frenchmen look at you more closely than Englishmen do,' Georgy ventured.

'Yes. Young women speak silently to them, saying: "Notice me!"

179

You will find you will do the same if you go to Paris – you are young, *ma chère*. Youth however does not last.'

Had Camille some notion of her feelings for Amaury? Or was she reminiscing about herself? '*You* are still young – and beautiful,' she said to her shyly.

'That is very sweet of you, Georgy, but I am well over thirty, you know.' After a pause, during which Georgy regarded her earnestly, she added: 'Woman's life is a continual process of adjustment . . . . Forgive me – I don't know what I'm saying – I don't expect your mama talks to you about such things?'

'No – Mama is quite old—'

'I'll warrant she is no older than Madame Bonaventure!'

After a moment's thought, Georgy, completely amazed, said: 'You are right. Mama is only forty-six!'

'There you see – Madame Bonaventure has depended for her life on her looks, but your mama is happily married and does not need to try to look younger than she is.'

Georgy had once been told by her Aunt Charlotte in an unguarded moment that women were no longer the objects of male interest after about the age of forty. Men preferred very young women in their early twenties. She supposed she still had all that to look forward to. She had never applied these maxims about age to her mother. Married women were one thing; spinsters quite another. Englishmen liked young unmarried girls, but maybe Frenchmen liked older women and appreciated things in women other than beauty. Madame Bonaventure, however, had not seemed like a married lady.

Camille went on: 'Although I have never met her I have heard that your mama is a pretty woman – and a kind woman—'

'Yes, Mama is kind and good, I think, but she always does what Papa tells her to—'

'If his judgement is good, she follows it – that makes for domestic harmony, Georgy—'

'He is not always in the right – he thought my cousins' tutor – Mr Walker – was flirting with me, but he was not! I liked to talk with him, and he never took liberties.'

'Men are jealous of their daughters. I was not told the whole story but I knew your father wanted you to go away from home for a little time, as you did not "come out" in London society. But why did he not send away this Mr Walker if he suspected him of having designs on you?'

'Because Edward – Mr Walker – is the only person who can control my dreadful cousins! They live with us. Their father is dead and their mother constantly ailing.'

'Well, I am glad he gave you the chance to stay here. You have been a great help to me, so much so that I think you deserve a little holiday later in the spring. I hope we shall be able to arrange something.'

'Oh, I so long to go to Paris!'

After Camille's speaking so confidentially to her Georgy felt a certain reluctance to admit why she so much wanted to go there.

'I should like to go myself, to visit friends. When my husband returns next week I shall talk to him about it.'

Had Camille any money of her own? She must have, for Georgy could not imagine that Augustin de Marceau had ever been willing to pay for her sojourns in London. It was only to London that he did not appear to mind she travelled. He claimed he disliked the place, though he had spent his childhood there.

Georgy found herself wondering once again, before M de Marceau's return, whether Camille still loved her husband. She remembered having been told it had been a love match and that Camille had known him since their childhood in London, married him when she was twenty-one. Had her parents objected? Augustin was quite a lot older and of a completely different disposition. From servants' gossip Georgy knew he still gambled, which must worry Camille a good deal. Perhaps, however, it might give her a lever to insist she had a little freedom for herself, especially if it was with her money he was playing? Wives' fortunes belonged to their husbands, in France as in England, did they not? Or was there something in the *Code Napoléon* about separation of possessions? Women had to have dowries here. Could a wife keep some of her own money? Or only if her husband knew nothing about it? The Code was not written in the spirit of the Revolution; Napoleon had not been interested in equality for women! It was a reversal of the reactionary practices the Revolution had hoped to change.

Jacques Cellard called again on the Friday and he and Madame de Marceau were closeted for hours in Camille's sitting room. Georgy heard only what they were saying as he left: 'Then you must insist – I can call in accounts with the Soubrier family provided you can persuade him.'

'To set aside that sum? He may not have it now.'

Had Jacques Cellard some hold on Camille that he should speak so authoritatively? She had occasionally seen him looking at Madame de Marceau with what she imagined was undisguised admiration. Perhaps he too wanted her money.

As he was about to leave that evening, Georgy sensed a tension in the air. Monsieur Cellard was jovial with Thibault and Lucie, and always polite to her, but today he left without a greeting.

Then, curiously, he turned, came back and said, as she was about to take the children to their quarters: 'Have you seen young Arnaud recently?'

For a moment she was thunderstruck. What did he know about the two of them? She managed to stutter: 'I believe he is in Paris, sir.'

He gave her a long look, saying: 'He is a gentleman – but he is a hothead,' and then was off.

What business of his was it if she saw Amaury? She was indignant, but she hoped he would not communicate his reservations to Camille.

If she ever got to Paris, she *must* be allowed to see Amaury! She was already missing him terribly, feeling their love was threatened by partings and mysteries.

Warmer weather had arrived and it was fine enough and light enough to go outside with the children. She mooned alone in the garden when she got the chance, which was not often, and thought about sad things: the brevity of threatened love, and the refuge to be found in nature. Then she decided she was being silly, for Amaury wanted to see her and would soon write to her.

Before Augustin returned one windy evening at the beginning of March, a letter did arrive for Georgy. It was not from Amaury, but from Louis-Marie, to whom she had not written after Amaury's discouragement. She was so disappointed that the letter was not from Amaury himself that she left it to read in the evening, and by then M Marceau had arrived.

'Papa! Papa!' the children squealed when they heard his carriage wheels crunch on the gravel.

'Hush – your father will be weary after his long journey,' said Camille. She looked very nervous herself.

Their father greeted Thibault and Lucie perfunctorily, consenting to give them a watery smile. 'I hope you have been good?'

'Yes, yes! We went to mass every week!' said Thibault, aware of what might impress his papa.

Lucie put her hand in his. 'We have done many lessons.' Then she added: 'Mademoiselle Georgy talks to us only in English now!'

Augustin noticed Georgy standing quietly in the background. She sketched a minor curtsey.

'Take them up to bed soon,' muttered Camille when her husband had gone out of the room. 'We shall be busy talking over business tomorrow; see that they don't get in his way.'

Georgy felt uncomfortable, but took the two excited children to their rooms. What a shame their father could not show more love and interest in them both.

'Do you think he has brought me a horse from Paris?' asked Thibault, before he blew out his candle.

'I don't know, but I will bring you back a wooden horse if *I* ever go to Paris,' she said.

She escaped to her little bedroom as soon as possible after supper, for she sensed the atmosphere was still strained. Once there, she opened her letter. What could Louis-Marie have to tell her that was not an irrelevance? Could anything be worse than reading a letter from a man you did not love, when you longed for one from the man you did?

But as she read on she became interested. After a few platitudes concerning the weather and his health, and polite enquiries as to hers, he went on:

'I am off to Paris and shall come to my great aunt's a month after Easter which is early this year. I hope to see you at the château then for I have news of the *person* you mentioned as having paid you a visit earlier in the year. I cannot risk writing it. One never knows who might open one's letters. Suffice it to say that I think you had better be careful for I am told the lady is implicated in a most unwholesome affair – and is mad to boot.'

What *could* he mean? She had not thought Capucine unbalanced. Strange, fascinating, but not *mad*. Louis-Marie however, as a strict monarchist, most likely considered anyone who did not abase himself before King Charles X as having taken leave of his senses. She sat on her narrow bed and considered: he must know that Amaury is no monarchist – and Amaury is his friend. But how do I know that he really likes him?

She resolved to let nothing pass her lips inadvertently to Louis-Marie about Amaury's feelings for her, and she would never speak to Louis-Marie about her own feelings. That would be vulgar. But she might unintentionally betray them!

A few days passed with no communication from Amaury. Georgy was not worried, for the mail was sporadic in this rural backwater. Even if he had written to her the moment he arrived in Paris it would take ten days or so for anything to arrive at the château.

A letter from England arrived on the following day for M et Mme de Marceau and Georgy recognized her father's hand. What could he be writing to them about? She hoped it was not to say she must now come home. By the same messenger however there was a letter for her from Paris, her old friend Abigail Strang.

She knew that Abby was now married, and had delayed writing to her, not knowing where to send her letter. This letter was a surprise indeed for it was written in Florence.

'You will by now, I expect have received a letter from your father. Hugh and I are to be in Paris for two weeks on the way home from our honeymoon, and I suggested to your papa before we came here that you might be spared for a few days from yr. duties to meet us in Paris for a little holiday. It seems so long since you and I had a good talk and we have all missed you . . . . I earnestly hope it can be arranged.'

Was this what her father was writing to the de Marceaus about? If she could only go to Paris! She looked again at her friend's letter; Abigail was to be in France in a few days. But how could she pay for her own board and lodging in Paris? She could not expect Abigail's new husband to pay for his wife's old friend! Would her father really be willing to help her?

Camille had taken her letters and her *Journal de Modes* up to her room, so she must possess her soul in patience. How slowly the morning passed.

After luncheon, having sent her children to Célanie in the kitchen, Camille asked Georgy to come to her sitting room. 'I have received a letter from your father,' she began.

184

Georgy was on tenterhooks but did not interrupt.

'He thinks you might be in need of a holiday, and apparently your friend Miss Strang is very soon to be in Paris for her honeymoon—'

'Yes – she wrote to me—'

'Your papa says he will send you money to stay in Paris with your friend who will arrange an hotel lodging for you. As you know, I was hoping to go to Paris myself, but it may not be possible. Would you like to go? It would be quite soon – in only a week's time? Monsieur Cellard has to go there next week, and could accompany you in the diligence.'

'Oh, yes!' breathed Georgy.

She would see Amaury; she was sure she could escape from the newly-wed couple now and again.

'Your friend must be indeed fond of you if she wants to see you on her honeymoon!' added Camille with a laugh.

Georgy thought: Abigail would just like to talk to me – I don't doubt her future husband has been cajoled into this. Aloud, she said: 'But could you spare me? It might be awkward for you.'

'I think the children can miss their English lessons for a week or two!'

She showed Georgy the letter, addressed to Monsieur and Madame de Marceau, signed with a great flourish – *Your Sincere Friend Christopher Crabtree* – and sealed with her papa's big seal.

Why hadn't he asked her first? Or written to her? It was usually Mama who wrote. But Papa would guess she would be overjoyed to see Paris. Maybe he was feeling a little guilty about having insisted she stay a year in France.

'I hope your friend's husband will be able to make good arrangements for you. However, as it is not usually done for a young lady to travel alone, I am wondering if Monsieur Cellard might also bring you back. The diligence that leaves Mâcon for Lyon and Paris is quite swift – it takes only five days in good weather.'

'Then you would allow me to go, ma'am?'

'I think you do deserve a little holiday – and there are things you could purchase for me in Paris. I *might* even be able to join you there – though I doubt it. But Jacques – Monsieur Cellard – often goes there on business.'

Camille was very practical. Augustin de Marceau might be not so willing. Papa was to send money for her journey and upkeep so he would not be out of pocket. It soon transpired that M de Marceau, who was in and out of the house all week, was too occupied with his own finances to give much thought to her. Camille told him only that Georgy's father had made arrangements for her to go to Paris for a stay of around ten days.

'I hope you're not thinking of accompanying her?' he said crossly. Augustin did not want his wife to go anywhere at present. It was easy for him to gad off to Paris, but not poor Camille. Soon too, she might have to go on a visit to Monsieur's parents, along with the children. That would solve the matter nicely, for Georgy would not truly be welcomed at the Count's. Augustin raised no objection to her plans. Georgy felt that he hardly noticed her in any case.

The children were a different matter. Lucie did not like the idea at all. 'But who will teach us? Will you come back? Promise you will come back!'

Georgy looked again at the address Amaury had given her and which she had folded up and put in her jewel box. She would have to make sure he knew she was coming and make secure plans to see him, plans that would not arouse the suspicions of Abigail. But her friend, as she well knew, did not have a suspicious mind.

Apparently Amaury was lodging on the rue Vaugirard. Knowing nothing of Paris she asked Camille if there were a map she might consult. 'I must prepare my holiday,' she said glibly. But she did feel a little guilty.

She wrote to Amaury, telling him where she would be staying herself, thinking he could reply to her there. She did not wish to appear too 'enthusiastic'.

She was not exactly relishing the prospect of a five-day journey accompanied by Jacques Cellard, with whom she always found it hard to carry on a conversation. It had turned out he needed to set off for Paris on 13 March, and was perfectly amenable to accompanying her on the journey.

She would have borne anything to get to Paris and see Amaury. She hoped M Cellard would not turn up later in her vicinity in Paris.

Now all that remained to do was to write to her father and to Abigail, pack the clothes she would need, and wait.

She would arrive in Paris on 18 March.

Part Three
Paris

Chapter 1

Jacques Cellard did not utter a word to her on the first leg of the journey, until they had almost reached Mâcon. Then he said: 'Is this more comfortable than your English Mail?'

She answered after due deliberation: 'I think our seats are more comfortable but this equipage feels lighter.'

'Are your roads good?' he asked.

This enabled her to make an effort, and for a time she chattered about the new turnpikes.

Mâcon was a thriving country town with a large open market. The busy river Saône ran by the side of its streets, and when they changed horses Georgy glimpsed many boats, and on the river banks great barrels of wine ready for transportation.

They left Mâcon for Dijon in the diligence, to spend another night there before continuing north. In the evenings it became quite chilly on the road and she was glad of her old paisley shawl to wrap around her. The following days' travel were tedious. Later, she wished she had taken more notice of their route but she had preferred to shut her eyes and think about Amaury, and she was too lost in her dream of him at night to notice whether the beds at the inns were comfortable.

She eventually asked M Cellard about Paris, for he knew it well, having spent some time there in his regiment, he told her, 'years ago'. She was surprised. He was not curmudgeonly but apparently shy. *Par délicatesse* she avoided mentioning Camille de Marceau again, having seen how he coloured up when she told him how kindly she had been treated by that lady. She wondered if he was married.

The mid-March air was already fragrant with an early spring as they came north, with the forest of Fontainebleau not far away from the road that led to Paris on the last lap of their journey.

'The children will miss you,' he said.

'Oh, Lucie will – I have had to swear I shall return in two weeks.' She thought, what if Amaury wants me to stay with him?

'Madame will miss you too,' he got out after a pause.

Another surprise. Did the bailiff imagine she was there as a companion also for Camille? But perhaps she was.

'She gets lonely,' he added.

'It is true Monsieur is much away,' she said without thinking. After that M Cellard was silent.

She fingered Amaury's address that was in the pocketbook she kept in the capacious pocket of her second best pelisse. She knew it off by heart: 22 rue de Vaugirard. She even knew where that was. Near the gardens they had laid out for Marie de Médicis in the seventeenth century.

On the last day of the journey, by the time the coach had passed through Charenton and, two hours or so later, rattled into its final staging post, it was almost dark.

All along the crowded streets they lurched, and then they came through a high gate painted black and into a cobbled yard with a lamp shining through the leaves of chestnut trees, and the diligence stopped.

'It is one of the offices of the customs-house,' said her companion.

What would she do if Abby and Hugh were not there? In her trunk was the present she had bought for her friend – a length of blue silk from Lyon that she had saved all her meagre salary to afford.

M Cellard helped her get down and they waited as the trunks were taken from the roof, and borne away from the yard by two stocky individuals.

Now she followed the others into a sort of restaurant where on the ground floor all was bustle.

And here was Abigail and her tall top-hatted husband waiting in an inner room. A swift introduction to Jacques Cellard, who saluted the English couple, before rapidly disappearing, and then Hugh Thompson ordered one of the men to follow them with her trunk and basket, and here they were at last in a carriage that would convey them to the rue St Honoré where was

190

situated the hotel of the newly-weds.

She looked round eagerly as the hackney coach clattered and bumped on cobblestoned streets amongst enormous crowds of people. There were even large mastiffs pulling hand-carts!

'Is it a feast day here?' she asked Abigail, who smiled and said: 'No, it is just Paris. It is always like this.'

They passed along a narrow shop-lined street, people milling around on the pavement, when a pavement existed, for not every street had one, and also sauntering along in the middle of the road. She noticed too that in one street along which they slowly progressed there was an open gutter running down the middle that looked like a sewer. How strange. Were there no drains?

At the end of the next street, outside a café, there were tables laid in the open air, and a tinker was sitting just round the corner with the tools of his trade.

'They are always pulling down houses and rebuilding them,' said Abby. 'And you fall over the builders' bricks and things if you choose to walk rather than drive.'

'A good thing they are rebuilding,' said her husband. 'Many of these old houses look dangerous, and at night most of the side streets and the back streets are very dark. They've got gaslight only on the show boulevards and streets!'

They arrived at the rue St Honoré, and there was the usual bustle of unpacking. Hugh disappeared. Georgy was glad, for she felt dirty and needed to comb her hair. Abby was her usual peaceful self. Marriage had not so far changed her demeanour; of course she had been married only three weeks.

And here Georgy was – at last – in Paris. Had *she* changed a little from what her friend remembered? Abby said she would be tired and left her to rest before coming down for supper.

'Here are two letters for you,' she said.

One was from Amaury Arnaud. The other was in Edward Walker's more familiar hand.

Once she was in her room, she opened the letter from Amaury. Written from the address in the rue Vaugirard which she already knew, it appeared to have been hastily penned, for it was full of blots and scratchings.

Spring has come and you will have arrived. I cannot see you before next Wednesday the 22nd for I am employed doing something I cannot divulge. Suffice it to say that I have met V. Hugo! He is a near neighbour, but it is not a district it is advisable for a young lady to visit, even though very near the famous garden of the Luxembourg. I shall therefore, when advised by you, call upon you at your hôtel – 'with the blessing of Madame de Marceau,' I think you should say to your English friends – and take you to walk in the Tuileries or on a longer drive. They say Versailles is much neglected or I should suggest it as the subject both of an outing and lyric poem on the vanished glories of the past. Who do you think I saw yesterday in a café on this very street? Old Louis-Marie! He says he is resting from his labours, but I suspect he frequents duchesses!

Georgy knew that there were parts of the old Paris which one should in no circumstances visit, for Camille had impressed this upon her. There were gambling dens and vice in the arcades and houses of the Palais Royal. She had also been warned that most of Paris was filthy, only the newly built parts being pleasant to visit. Amaury's letter disappointed her a little, though she could not have said exactly why. But she would love to walk with him in the Tuileries gardens which were said to be fine and pleasant – and clean.

It really did feel like spring here when she opened the shutters of her small but pretty room and looked out on the rue St Honoré. Hugh had told her on the way that the British Embassy was not far away, where the British Foreign Minister and his clever wife Harriet reigned in great splendour. Apparently, Harriet Granville's soirées and Saturday mornings were the talk of Paris society. Flowers in great profusion grew in a 'gallery', a kind of interior conservatory planted around the garden end of the magnificent white and gold reception rooms, with divans placed for comfort. There was even a little grove of orange trees and lilacs, and on the tables baskets of moss and violets. Hugh and Abby had read about it, not being of the requisite Highest Society to be invited to such a place.

'Of course, Anglo-French relations are at a low ebb,' Hugh had explained in a wise voice, and Georgy forbore to ask why. Something to do with the British foreign minister, she guessed.

But she did know that the Harriet Granville he had mentioned was the sister of Lady Morpeth, who had but recently become the new Countess of Carlisle at Castle Howard. The great palace was near York and she had been taken there as a child at a time when the old Earl had allowed people to be shown round his land.

She stood for a moment at the window, remembering that day, and her school in York – and her friendship with Abigail . . . .

She had better go down to her now and see how she could introduce the subject of Amaury into their conversation. Abby would probably want a long chat after dinner, though Georgy was fearful of intruding upon her and her husband. She would take her cue from her friend. It was gratifying enough that Abby had insisted she make this special visit.

It was after dinner. Hugh Thompson, who seemed to have perfect manners, though he said little, was attentive to her as well as to his young wife.

Abigail looked very happy, and Georgy was relieved. At first she had wondered how they could get back on to the level of their old friendship, what with a year having passed, and their both being in a foreign country, and her friend with a husband to boot, but when they began to talk of home, Abby was full of gossip and even Hugh joined in.

'She's been longing to see you – I think she misses home,' he said. 'Apart from missing her kettle to make tea!'

Georgy laughed. The kettle was one item the French did not seem to have heard of.

The couple were full of the fine sights they had seen in Florence, but Abby confessed to finding travel tiring and to look-ing forward to starting life in her own place. She had always been a home bird; she it was who had sobbed night after night at school in York, whilst Georgy had perforce to comfort her. Georgy of course had not sobbed but enjoyed being away, even if she missed her brothers and her dog Patsy.

Abby had not changed, unless she was more serene now that she was married to a respectable man. What would she think of Georgy's plans to meet Amaury, who might or might not be respectable?

'Tell me about the wedding-breakfast,' said Georgy, and Abby was pleased to oblige with more details than Georgy really wanted. Then it was her turn to tell them of her life in Burgundy. She described meeting the Poet but they had never heard of him.

She brought down her wedding-present before telling them about her next week's visitor. The blue silk from Lyon was much admired. Hugh said he was going out for a stroll and to smoke a cigar and would leave the girls to talk.

'It is so kind of you – and your Madame de Marceau is kind too, allowing you to come and stay here with us – I cannot imagine how I would manage with two French children,' sighed Abby when he had gone out.

'They do speak English. I enjoy teaching them – and I am not to stay in France for ever.'

Abby was not properly apprised of the reasons for her departure to France and Georgy did not think she would enlighten her at present. It had all been ridiculous, a storm in a teacup. But then Abby said, as if divining her thoughts:

'Your cousins' tutor came to our wedding breakfast. He is a gentleman, isn't he.'

'Oh – Edward Walker? Yes, I suppose so – though he works for a living. Who invited him?'

'My father did,' replied Abby. 'He knows a relative of his, I believe—'

'How very odd. I always gathered from Edward – from Mr Walker – that he came from an excessively poor family, and that is why he had to become a tutor.'

'Well, perhaps that was his story,' said Abby sagely. 'Maybe he quarrelled with his family.'

'A friend of Madame de Marceau is to visit me here next Wednesday,' said Georgy, plunging in after a short pause. 'He is a young man whose mother she sometimes entertains at the château – and he is working in Paris. He would like us to take a walk in the Tuileries gardens.'

'Oh, that will be nice for you,' said Abby amiably and unsuspiciously.

But how was Georgy to escape before this? She fully intended to explore a little of Paris for herself, especially around the rue Vaugirard.

*

Not until the May of 1826 did Alphonse de Lamartine return from Florence to France for a holiday in his native land, where he stayed at home for two months. He had just inherited from his father the Château de Montculot, but he was not to return to live near Mâcon until two more years had passed. He was now thirty-six, the life of young man about town abandoned when he married six years before. Neither did he need any longer be the penniless poet. Money might be short, but the reason was his chronic addiction to gambling, as well as his generosity towards both himself and others.

His rival Hugo, twelve years younger than Alphonse, was already enormously prolific, distilling the whole of how he felt about life and the world in lyrical outpourings. He was at that time living in Paris on the same street as Amaury Arnaud, the old rue Vaugirard that starts near the Luxembourg Gardens and winds round Napoleon's sixth and fifteenth *arrondissements*.

Rue Vaugirard was not a street which Abigail and her new husband Hugh Thompson would be likely to visit on their honeymoon, even in a closed carriage, for like most tourists they stayed put in the fashionable district of the city. Even there though, some less salubrious quarters made Hugh shudder with distaste. It was true that the very newest buildings and gardens in Paris were splendid – the Tuileries gardens above all – and to those gardens they walked along with Georgy on the first morning of her stay with them, a Sunday which did not seem like one.

There was a notice which seemed to say you must walk in these gardens only for pleasure and leisure and not use it as a short cut to the market. How odd!

'You can come here again with Monsieur – I forget his name,' said Abby.

'With Monsieur Arnaud? Yes, it is very pretty and pleasant.'

And indeed it was, very lovely. All was spanking new and modern. No feel of the past here, thought Georgy. There were smooth gravel walks, and fountains with swans and goldfish, and statues, and raised terraces. They were just about to plant out the little orange-trees that had been kept over the winter indoors in the Orangery. An officer of the National Guard was walking along keeping an eye on the crowds in the gardens, though they were all behaving very well.

'A pity we are too early to see the flowers,' said Abby. 'They say the beds have been planted with every variety of bloom.'

'Well, my dear you should have waited to marry me,' said her husband, and they both laughed. Georgy thought they were going to be happy.

They stood for a moment in front of the Louvre, and looked across the river. The golden dome of the Invalides was shining in the distance in the spring sunlight. Tomorrow they were to visit the museum's *Grande Galerie*.

It was very pleasant walking in Paris, thought Georgy. No distance appeared too great. She preferred it to what she had seen of London the previous year. She had noticed all sorts of little things that made Paris so different from the London she had seen on her visit to Cousin Caroline. But you could not really get to know a place unless you visited people in their own homes. The French people she knew had strange ideas of England but perhaps some of them were not entirely wrong. They said the English dressed badly and that was most likely true, for the women here were neat and fashionable but not dressy. Only the very rich were *haut ton*. Their gloves and hats and boots were elegant and well chosen but the men often affected moustaches and beards. But the very worst thing about this most beautiful city was its drains – or rather, lack of them.

This morning, they returned by way of the Place Louis Quinze. A few carriages and hackneys and carts, a few riders on horseback, ambled across the sanded paths, and children and dogs hung around near a little open-air shop that was nothing more than a table set up to sell wine from a carafe.

'This square is going to be altered and extended,' said Hugh, who seemed to have done much preparation concerning the sights of Paris for his visit. 'They guillotined the French king – Louis XVI – just over there!' He pointed at the other end of the square.

'Why don't they pull down all the dirty old parts of Paris – especially that Ile de la Cité?' asked his wife, who had passed some terrible sights during some of their carriage drives. 'As you saw on your way here, there aren't usually any footpaths,' she said to Georgy, 'so your carriage just crawls along, with people getting in the way all the time. We should not have gone there if we had known.'

'I expect they will soon demolish a good deal,' said Hugh, 'and you can't complain of the Place Vendôme.'

Georgy wanted to see more of the less fashionable parts of Paris. Was the street where Amaury lived as bad as described by Abigail? Could she not just walk across the bridge, and continue in the direction of the Faubourg St Germain? She could see on the map that it was not very far away. There were so many people around all the time – indeed the streets were crowd-packed, so what harm could she come to if she went on a little expedition alone? She wanted to do a little prospecting around Amaury's neighbourhood in daylight without his knowing. The more difficult problem was how to make her escape from her two friends.

Chance was to put an opportunity in her way on the first Tuesday of her holiday, the day after they visited the Théâtre Français to see *Le Misanthrope* with Mlle Mars in the role of Célimène, a wonderfully polished production but not always easy to understand.

Abigail had knocked at the door of Georgy's room on the Monday morning. She had a letter in her hand.

'It's such a nuisance,' she began. 'Papa's old aunt who married an American is living in St Germain-en-Laye – that is some miles from here. She's very rich. Papa wants us to visit her, and she has asked us for tomorrow. Of course, he didn't realize how long it would take for his letter to arrive so there's nothing for it but to go tomorrow. Apparently, she entertains only on Tuesdays. And the Tuesday after that we shall be gone. Papa *could* have remembered before – it would be very boring for *you*—' She was too polite to say that Georgy had not been invited by the old lady.

'Oh, never mind,' said Georgy with a smile, her heart giving a great leap. 'I shall be perfectly all right here. You forget I am quite used to France – and there are some shops near the Place Vendôme where I promised Madame de Marceau I would enquire about muffs for winter.' She was hastily extemporizing, finding in herself an unsuspected talent for telling fibs. 'I can eat here in the hotel – you must not bother about me—'

'Well, if you're sure?' Abby looked doubtful. *She* would certainly not want to spend a day by herself in Paris.

'Of course I'm sure. You go along and be entertained by your rich relation!'

'She's about ninety!'

They both giggled.

Hugh appeared to accept the arrangement and also thought it politic to go along with his father-in-law's plans. He must keep in with Mr Strang, and in any case it would be a pleasant drive there through lovely woods and hamlets, though they must set off early and return late.

At last Tuesday morning dawned. Georgy had made her plans. She would walk to the rue Vaugirard, which would be easy to find as it ran by the side of the Jardins du Luxembourg. She might even go into the gardens whilst she was so near. She did not intend to reveal herself to Amaury, only to look at the house where he was living and get a general picture of the district.

Abby and Hugh left early. Georgy drank a cup of coffee with them and then waved them off. She went back to her room to have another look at the map that Camille had lent her. She must cross the river by the Pont Royal to the Quai des Théatins and then she had worked out the route from there to the Luxembourg Gardens: she must walk down to the new Institut de France, down the rue Mazarine to the St Germain district, and then make for the large church called St Sulpice which was quite near the Luxembourg Gardens and the street where Amaury was lodging. A walk of about a mile and a half, that was all, and on a lovely spring morning. She dressed in her dark pelisse and took a basket with her, borrowed from one of the hotel maids, to make it look as though she was off to market in case anybody stopped her *en route*.

All went well until the rue Mazarine turned itself into another with the name of the rue de l'Ancienne Comédie, a narrow lane with many young men lounging around its cafés. Georgy ignored the pointed remarks made to her, though she was aware of a sort of galvanism running in her veins that made her want to be noticed, and pleased, if a little frightened, when she was. She knew she was being admired for her face and youth, and the knowledge seemed to bring with it a sort of power, of which she was also a little ashamed.

But she made her way south, trusting her general sense of direction, glad she had her basket and her old pelisse. She tried to look as if she knew where she was going but had one or two false turns before finally coming very suddenly upon an entrance to the Luxembourg Gardens, quite missing out the church she had thought she must pass. She must have walked a little further to the east than she had intended. On the way back she must find St Sulpice so as to be sure of the quickest way back.

She heard bells ringing for a mass; they sounded quite near and must be from that church. It had taken her little more than half an hour but she felt she was in a different city now. She must find the rue Vaugirard before allowing herself to look in at the Luxembourg Gardens.

There were young women coming and going, alone through the gates, young women with baskets, who must be real maidservants, unlike herself. They gave her courage for she was suddenly mindful of all the stories of possible dangers – robberies, seizures of girls from the street, told her by Camille – and even, since her arrival in Paris, by Abby. It was not safe, they said, for respectable ladies to walk alone. Yet she presumed it was no less dangerous than in London.

She wished she did not have to hurry; she had not been able to linger on the way and there had been so many old buildings she would like to have studied more closely. If she were a young man she would have strolled along and not felt vulnerable, although it was true that young men sometimes provoked fights with strangers.

She consulted her map again by pretending to look in her reticule where she had copied the part she needed. It would not do for her to look lost. Where *was* the rue Vaugirard?

Then, as she looked up, she realized that she must be actually standing on the very street. Here it followed the walls of the gardens. She crossed it and looked at the houses there. They looked old and a little crumbly. Over one high *porte-cochère* was the number 19. Now she must find 22.

She remembered that the houses on the Paris streets that run parallel to the river are numbered from east to west, and those at right angles to the Seine take their number from whichever end is nearest the river. She fancied it had been, of all people, Edward Walker who had once told her all this. But whether even numbers followed odd, or were on different sides, she was not sure. Number 22 however must be a little further along on the other side for she knew this rue Vaugirard ran pretty well parallel to the river.

She walked along and just before another street that plunged down a slope to the right, she saw a faded sign with the number 22 painted in blue. Now that she was actually in the right place she wondered what to do next. She certainly did not want Amaury to see her. But there was nobody at present in sight and no one at an open shutter. She stared at the house from the other side of the street. It was tall and thin and there were many closed shuttered windows; it must be divided into many small apartments.

She recrossed the street. Just before number 22 there had been a café with faded gilt lettering: '*Tabourrey-20*' it had said.

This would be where Amaury and his friends lingered to discuss their literary progress! If she'd been a young man she'd have pushed open the door and gone inside for a glass of wine or a cup of coffee. But Georgy, though bolder than most in such matters, was quite sensible enough to know that young women with any pretensions to respectability did not go alone into cafés. Only prostitutes – *filles de joie* – went there. This was not Aix where a crowd of young ladies and gentlemen might meet quite innocently.

She decided now to go into the Luxembourg Gardens, and was astonished at their extent. Long *allées* wound round under groups of trees in the distance and there were flower-beds, as yet rather empty, and children playing on the paths under the trees. Over it all she sensed an air of palpable neglect. It did not look as if it had yet recovered from the Revolution. The place she had just passed had, under The Terror, been used as a prison. The building looked innocuous enough now, if in need of rebuilding.

It was all in great contrast to the Tuileries which were so open and bright and fashionable. This park did not look fashionable – but she liked it.

There were groups of students walking along puffing at their pipes and a few poor women trundling little carts. Under a beech-tree that was just about to come into leaf she saw a wooden bench. Dare she sit down? There were a few hungry sparrows pecking in the dust underneath.

She shifted her basket to the other arm and advanced towards the empty bench. Just as she was about to sit, having put down her basket, another person came walking briskly from behind the alley of lime-trees, obviously making for the same bench. Oh well, there was room for two, and fortunately it was a young woman.

Yes, it was a young woman.

It was the young woman who called herself Capucine! Georgy recognized her immediately. She was not wearing the orange cap, but had instead a scarf of the same colour, flapping over a dark green *redingote*. Oh dear, she had better have a story ready. Obviously, Capucine must have been visiting Amaury. She would not expect the English girl to be in Paris, but even so, Georgy turned her face away just in case and was astonished and not a little frightened when the girl said, 'We have already met, Mademoiselle.'

She feigned astonishment. 'Why, Mademoiselle, I do remember you! You came to the Château de Pinac in autumn. You said you were off to Paris, if I remember rightly?'

'What brings you here yourself? I'll wager it is the handsome Monsieur Arnaud?'

'Oh, no,' lied Georgy. 'I am in Paris with dear friends from England who today must visit an aged relation. So I decided to take a little walk through the more interesting parts of the capital. I hear that the longest street in Paris starts from here—'

'You are surely not staying on the Left Bank, Mademoiselle? English tourists usually stay near the Place Vendôme, I believe?'

'That is true, we are at the Neuncies hotel, but I prefer the district my feet have brought me to this morning.'

'Sure you are not looking for someone?' mocked the girl, but she did not look cross.

'Who could I be looking for? I know no one in Paris—'

'Monsieur Arnaud – as I said, he lives near here.'

And I suppose you visit him, thought Georgy. Aloud, she said: 'I know that students and writers do live in this district – I expect it's cheaper. Actually I was looking for St Sulpice.'

'You like Catholic churches?'

'Not especially – but I find the religion interesting.'

Capucine stared at her. Then she sat down next to her, Georgy moving over a little to give her more room on the bench.

'Did you know what Amaury's friend Hugo called the twin towers of that monstrosity?' asked Capucine conversationally.

'No – how could I know?'

'He said they looked like two clarinets that don't quite match!'

'Well, if you don't mind, I must be getting along if I am to see that church before my return—'

'Have you heard of Madame Récamier?' asked Capucine suddenly, ignoring her remark. '*She* lives near here too. All the young men visit her – but they say she remains chaste. Of course now she is very old.'

'No, I've never heard of her – but I remember you once mentioned my compatriot, the writer Mary Wollstonecraft. Since then I have remembered she was the mother of the woman who married my favourite poet.'

'You have read Frankenstein?'

'No, but I intend to.'

'The mother was a great woman – she was in Paris over thirty years ago. My grand-father was young then and actually met her.'

'The *Vindication of the Rights of Women*,' murmured Georgy. Had those 'rights' all disappeared now, after Terror had overwhelmed the Revolution, and then destiny given France first to the Emperor Napoleon, and finally back to the Bourbon relatives of those not long ago put to death? 'Thirty years ago – it seems so long ago, doesn't it? Did your Revolution really change anything?'

'It was a better generation,' said Capucine, looking at her with more interest. She was silent for a moment and then asked abruptly: 'Do people in England read about the Rights of Women?'

'No, the woman you mentioned is not much read at home. I only heard of her because I had a tutor who agreed with her. They do read her daughter's "Frankenstein" though!'

Capucine said: 'You were lucky with that tutor.'

'Oh, Edward is quite unusual – not many Englishmen live for long in your country, but he did.'

Capucine was silent for a moment and they both watched a pigeon strutting around on the gravel. Then even more abruptly she changed the subject again: 'How much does your hotel cost here in Paris?'

'We can live for a *napoléon* a day, I believe. That is less than an English pound.'

Capucine whistled. 'A labourer has to live for more than a week on that!'

'Well, it's an exceptional visit for me – my father is paying for me to stay with some English friends – in England it would cost more—'

'He is rich, your papa?'

'No, just "comfortable" – and I work for my living at present, as you already know.' Capucine's tone annoyed her. And she did not believe either that Capucine was poor, but that she chose to live in poverty – if that was what she did.

'These gardens were built between 1615 and 1627 – did you know that?' asked the young woman.

'I knew they were designed for Marie de Medicis,' replied Georgy standing up. 'Now I really must go—'

'Oh, well, then, I expect I shall see you again soon,' said Capucine.

'Why, are you returning to Burgundy?'

'Possibly – I have not yet decided. What I should really like to do would be to go to England.' Her face seemed to cloud over as she added wistfully: 'I feel I should be free over there.'

'You always seem to me to be very free.'

'If you can call having to run away being free!'

It was on the tip of Georgy's tongue to ask her to explain but Capucine must have realized she had given away too much for she said hastily: '*Au revoir*, then.'

They shook hands rather formally, and Capucine whisked off along the path and through the far gate. Georgy could hardly get up and follow her though she suspected she was going straight over to Amaury's lodgings.

Why was the running away? From what? She had kept quiet about why she was in Paris herself, at the same time as being clearly very curious about Georgy's presence so near Amaury's lodgings.

Georgy decided she had not acquitted herself too badly in this unexpected encounter. Should the young woman mention to Amaury whom she had seen in the gardens, he might be surprised, but surely not angry? Unless he was still carrying on a love-affair with the strange girl. Had it all been on the girl's side? Georgy was reluctant to believe her adored Amaury could ever have acted duplicitously. If there had ever been anything between him and Capucine it was surely over? She suddenly felt angry with herself. Why hadn't she just asked the young woman if she were seeing Amaury and also made it clear she was soon to see him on her own account? Next time she saw him, she would certainly insist on finding out from Amaury more about her, for if Capucine was running away, it could not be from Amaury.

Just for now she would walk back to the Right Bank by St Sulpice whose towers she was now suddenly glimpsing as she turned the corner of the rue Napoléon . . . .

She stood for some time in the square by the fountain, gazing at the twin towers of the vast church that looked too large for what she had assumed was a humble quarter of Paris. It was true, they did not match – one was unfinished – and they *did* look a little like two clarinets, or 'clarionets' as they pronounced the word in Yorkshire.

Amaury had already written and spoken warmly of Victor Hugo, and Capucine must also have met him, or seen Amaury recently enough to be told of his remark. Was Amaury now establishing himself in a circle of poets that included Hugo? Did Lamartine know of his young rival? She must try and find a book of the man's poems, since everyone was talking about him. She'd seen one or two little open-air bookstalls on the quay by the Seine on the way here.

She went into the vast church. The organist must be practising, for organ music was pealing through the gloom. There were a few chairs – no pews as there would have been at home – so she sat down at the back of the nave to listen to it.

A young man who had been standing before a statue of the Virgin in a distant side-chapel nearer the altar, began to walk in her direction towards the big door at the back.

The morning had not finished presenting her with surprises, for who could it be but Louis-Marie des Combes. Then she remembered he had said he would shortly be in Paris – she had quite forgotten, so full had her mind been with Amaury. She also remembered what he had written about Capucine in his letter: that she was mad – or dangerous – or both. She wouldn't tell him she had just seen her.

She remained seated, thinking: why should I have to make excuses for being in Paris? He might think it odd that I am by myself – but that is not his business.

How strange to meet two people she already knew in a place where she had never been before. Was it just coincidence? I was looking for Amaury, she thought, and wherever *he* is, that girl will eventually turn up. As for Louis-Marie, he has not yet seen me, and she bent her head as if in prayer, uncertain whether to acknowledge him or not, yet not wishing to act in a cowardly fashion. As he was about to pass her she raised her head and looked at him full in the face with an attempt at a smile. It was his turn to be astonished.

He stopped and said: 'Mademoiselle Georgina! What are you doing here?'

She thought of replying, 'Have I no right as a poor benighted Protestant to frequent one of your Catholic masterpieces?' but discretion won and she said meekly: 'Why, I am here in Paris with English friends—'

He looked round for them.

'No – they are away today – I decided to walk round by myself.'
'Alone?'
'Why not? It is an interesting quarter here, is it not?'
'At least they did not use this church as a saltpetre factory in the Revolution!' he said grimly.
'Which one was used for that then?'
'St Germain des Prés – not far from here – they hated religion.'

They were whispering but when she rose he began to make his way out, looking over his shoulder to see if she were following him. They arrived by the immense outer door; Louis-Marie turned and genuflected in the direction of the altar, and Georgy was almost tempted to trail her fingers in the holy-water stoup.

Once outside, she said: 'I had forgotten you said you were coming to Paris. I'm sorry I never replied to your last letter—'
'I must escort you back to where you are staying.'
'Oh, that is not necessary. I shall walk back the way I came.'
'Have you been seeing Amaury?'
'Why – is he here too?' she asked in feigned astonishment. She was determined she would not let slip her meeting with Capucine. Yet she would like to hear more about her from this man.
'He is not far away, I believe, getting himself mixed up with the Hugo crowd.' He sounded cross.
'Oh, I have heard of Monsieur Hugo – I expect you prefer Monsieur Lamartine as a man and a poet?'
'Amaury has no judgement,' he said curtly. 'Hugo does not have *le bon ton* – he certainly does not write for young ladies!'

She thought she had better ask him how his own epic was going on.

He bridled, and said: 'Paris is very distracting – I am not staying here long. I came to sit a law examination.'
'Then I hope you have passed?'
'I do not yet know. When are you to return to Burgundy? Or do you return home with your English friends?'
'I have been here a few days and hope to stay another few days,' she replied.

He stopped suddenly as they were walking along towards the river. 'Do not get mixed up with Amaury – he can be very – injudicious.'
'I expect you are talking about politics?' she asked in what she knew was a *faux naïf* tone of voice.

205

'It is not just that. There are plots around everywhere – people who want to get rid of the King. They should be careful – we had enough of the liberals before. The Emperor delivered us at least from *them*—'

'I did not know Amaury was *such* a radical,' she said, thinking instead of Capucine. Louis-Marie had not yet mentioned her and she hoped he would not.

She thought, this man is just jealous! She did not flatter herself that he nurtured any real feelings of *tendresse* towards her but she guessed he was jealous of both Amaury's success with women and his friendship with published poets.

'I shall be perfectly all right now. My friends will be back soon,' she said, after he had piloted her across an especially muddy street which turned into one of the quays by the side of the Seine.

'Then I hope to see you back in the château – I am soon to leave Paris myself,' he said, and raised his high hat. She inclined her head and escaped before he could change his mind.

Well, she had discovered nothing more about Capucine; she would have to ask Amaury. Oh, if only it had been Amaury she had come across in the church or in the gardens; he might have been flattered she had come to look at his abode. She would have to be patient until he arrived at her hotel, and then there would be the necessary introductions to Abby and Hugh.

On the way back she stopped on the Quai Voltaire and saw the book shops there, whose windows displayed wonderful books she would love to own – if she were suddenly possessed of a fortune.

She crossed over to the little *bouquinistes* and looked at their more humble wares, but could find no poetry by anyone she had ever heard of.

Chapter 2

The happy couple had not yet returned when Georgy finally arrived back at the rue St Honoré, so she settled in the salon of the hotel with a cup of coffee and a book. She could not concentrate, so she gave herself a quick mental examination, a habit she had learned from Lucie who had been told how to examine her conscience before she went to confession.

It was odd, she was as much intrigued by Capucine as by Amaury, when she ought to dislike her 'rival' if that was what she was. Was it because Amaury might love the young woman that she too found her interesting? Disturbing but interesting. Anything to do with Amaury was interesting of course. Amaury *must* be 'carrying on' with her – or have done so once?

Perhaps Capucine was nursing a broken heart and that was why she was always running away. Louis-Marie had not mentioned her this time; she wondered why. Maybe his friend had sworn him to secrecy. She knew from one of her brothers that men had a certain idea of loyalty to each other where women were concerned, and could keep secrets if they must. But Louis-Marie's constant references to 'radicals' and 'danger' must surely have been more about Capucine than about Amaury Arnaud who, as far as she knew, was involved in nothing more perilous than his mama's law-suit, in spite of his occasionally extreme attitudes.

She thought about what Capucine had said about Mary Wollstonecraft and the *Vindication of the Rights of Women*. That might by why Capucine was seen as 'dangerous' by Louis-Marie. But what had that to do with Revolution, or overthrowing the King? Why was it so shocking? Women, like men, were human beings.

When she gave her mind to it, as she was now trying to do, seated in the half dark on a spindly-legged chair in the little gilt sitting-room, with its gas brackets and hard sofas, the idea came to her that men would not easily give up their dominion over women. The Wollstonecraft woman had written in no uncertain terms that men must change. So must women change too. The trouble was, many of them didn't want to. Would Abby want more 'freedom'? No, in a dangerous world she'd rather be under the protection of dear Hugh. Married ladies had few rights, but if they were happily married, did that matter?

Did she herself want Amaury to be any different? What did *he* think about such writings?

Louis-Marie would certainly abhor the lady. At least you knew where you were with Louis-Marie.

She really knew so little about Amaury. Perhaps Capucine had managed to convert him to her way of thinking?

She remembered Edward Walker telling her something about Shelley, who had drowned, and Mary Shelley's father, and how they were all atheists, or something like that. And she had said – it must be two years ago now that they had had this conversation – 'How can such a man who writes such marvellous poems be an atheist?' She so loved Shelley's lyrics. But what must it have been like to be married to such a man? Mary, his wife, wasn't a poet, though she was a writer. She was so young and Edward had told her she had lost not only her husband but also all but one of her children.

Women had it hard. Was that God's fault, or Nature's, or men's? Here in France women were not laughed at for being learned, or a little 'blue', so long as they were married. But young women of her own age were much less free than in England, and of course she did not know many working women apart from the servants – and they probably had more freedom than little Lucie would ever have after the age of twelve. Parents found the husbands for their daughters here. Girls were married off young – and then the fun could begin! That must be why the old de Marceau couple did not like Camille: *They* had not chosen her!

She sat on alone until it was dark and she heard the sound of carriage wheels in the courtyard and knew the travellers had returned. She would tell them she had been for a short walk by the Seine.

Now all she had to do was wait for Amaury to arrive. How she longed to see him, so she could forget all the talk and the ideas and the struggles, and just enjoy his presence.

Amaury Arnaud came round to the hotel on the rue St Honoré the next afternoon, a Wednesday. Georgy and Abigail were in the salon writing letters when he was announced. Immediately Georgy's heart beat fast and loud but she tried not to let her excitement show. She had still not told her old friend anything of her real feelings for the young man.

Introductions were made and Amaury, speaking his fractured English, was clearly charming Abby. When Hugh came in, Amaury became sober and serious and discussed the French financial situation with great aplomb if in even more fractured English.

Then he said: 'Well, am I to take Mademoiselle Georgy for a little walk in the fresh air?'

Her friends raised no objection to Georgy's going out for a little promenade with him; they nurtured no suspicion, she was sure, that she might be with a man she loved.

The sun was shining brightly that afternoon as they walked along by the river; the trees on the Ile St Louis where he led here were all in bud, and there were flower-sellers all along the way. There were couples sitting on benches looking at the Seine, girls wearing the ubiquitous cashmere shawl, for there was still a nip in the late March air, or showing off their brightly coloured turbans, with apron and kerchief to match.

Georgy and Amaury had so far been silent, but once they had sat down on an iron bench near a little bridge he turned to her, saying:

'I hear you have already been out looking for me!'

Was it Louis-Marie or Capucine who had told him?

'Oh, I went for a little walk without my friends,' she replied. 'I thought I might see you but instead I saw Louis-Marie – in the church – St Sulpice.'

'I cannot take you back to my lodgings,' he said, taking her hand and holding it loosely.

'I don't care if it is proper or not,' she said boldly.

He ignored that, and went on: 'We could go for a longer walk. I could take you to the Bois de Boulogne tomorrow – where the

209

convent of Longchamp was – they say the nobility will all be driving in that direction in their carriages this week, as next Sunday is Easter Sunday. Would you like to go there?'

Oh anywhere, anywhere, she thought, anywhere with you. She was trying not to gaze at him but he really was so handsome. 'Why should they go there because of Easter Sunday?' she asked, trying to sound intelligent.

'Because before the Revolution, during Passion Week, people used to go to the convent. Then The Terror razed the building to the ground but all the smart people still see the place as sacred.'

'Oh.'

'I would like it to be possible for you to stay with me here in Paris,' he said, 'but it is not feasible. I expect you will have to return soon to Madame Camille?'

She did not say, I thought you said we could be together in Paris, and that was why you would not make love to me in the hut . . . . 'Alas,' she said. 'But I would like to share your life here – meet your friends, be part of your life – enjoy your future fame . . . .'

He was silent and she went on: 'I expect your friend Capucine shares your life a little?' She could not help sounding a little envious.

'You call her that – or did she tell you that was her name?'

'A sort of nickname, I suppose. I find her very – interesting.'

'Oh yes, but she is a rebel, you know – doesn't care a fig for conventions.'

Oh those *convenances*, she thought. It was her turn to be silent.

He added: 'Not like you, Georgy. You are a good girl, I am sure.'

She raised to him a face so stormy that he laughed. 'You need not be jealous of her,' he said.

'I am not jealous – why, should I be?'

'She knows me well,' he replied.

Then he put his arm round her waist and planted a chaste kiss on her cheek and another on her forehead. She wished he would kiss her mouth again, but today he appeared to have enormous reserves of self-restraint.

'I will come back to your lodging, if you wish,' she said suddenly, hardly aware of having put her desires into words.

'You know, Georgy, that we Frenchmen do not have women

210

friends of the platonic kind. If you became my *petite amie* you would have to tear yourself away from your family and from your kind Madame Camille and they would come running after you. You are not free, you see.'

Neither is Capucine, she thought. But I am free to *marry* you! Then she felt horrified at her own conventionality. But it was true, she *would* like to marry Amaury and be with him for ever. Did he not know that? If she told him such a thing, he would most likely run away, as most men were said to do from too passionate girls who believed love lasted into eternity. But if he really loved her, wouldn't he want her with him for ever? Why should she pretend she did not care?

Edward Walker had always told her not to wear her heart on her sleeve because it might give the impression of someone far less 'serious' than she really was – but what did *he* know about her? If Amaury thought she was a 'good girl', she must have given him the impression of a Georgy far more strait-laced than she really was. Certainly someone very different from Capucine.

She found herself wishing once more that she were a young man. She smiled at the thought, for if she were, she would not be in love with Amaury and he would not be attracted to her. And it was an odd thing to be thinking of when the man you loved was holding your hand.

'Why are you smiling?' he asked her.

'Oh I was just wondering why you consider me so "good".'

'Because I am *not* good,' he replied.

'I don't care.' I do care if he is in love with another woman, she thought. Or if there is another woman at his lodging. He has told me he finds me attractive, said that he will show me one day that he can 'love', but has he ever said he 'loved' me? Did that word *amour* mean something different in French? Well, I don't care if it does, she thought. I want that too.

But she must have looked sad for he said: 'Men are not like women, Georgy.'

How could she say: *Do you love me?* No, she could not. But she could say: *I love you.* So she did: 'I love you, Amaury.'

He searched her face then, and said: 'I will take you to the Bois tomorrow. When do you return to the château?'

'Next week – on Tuesday. I am waiting to hear from Madame de Marceau.'

'Your holiday is not very long. Who is to accompany you back?'

'Camille said that Jacques Cellard was coming to Paris in any case and would take me back. But I'd be perfectly all right travelling alone. There is nothing very terrible about a woman travelling alone, you know!'

'You did not come alone.'

'No. Monsieur Cellard happened to be travelling to Paris—'

'Then I tell you what – you might tell Madame de Marceau *I* could travel back with you – maybe Cellard has better things to do? In any case, I have to return to my mother soon for a short time so I could accompany you on the journey.'

'Oh, that would be wonderful!' But even as she spoke she wondered if it was just a whim of his and nothing would be done about it.

'It's getting late. I have to see a friend at six. I'll walk you back now.'

She was disappointed that their walk was to be so short and it did not escape her that Amaury was not at all desirous of her visiting his lodging. Why? Had he some little milliner concealed there? Or was it Capucine who had some empire over him? But he had offered to accompany her to Burgundy – and if that were possible it would give them a good long time together.

He kissed her again and she shut her eyes. He smelled of a faint pomade mingled with the fresh breeze from the river and his cheek was cool, his lips gentle.

When she returned to the hotel she felt so in love with Amaury that she had to make an effort to jerk herself back to reality and hide her feelings.

Over dinner she said casually: 'Tomorrow, Monsieur Arnaud is to take me along with some of his friends to the Bois de Boulogne.'

'Has he his own carriage?'

'I believe his friends have a fine one,' she lied. 'It would be nice to have a bit more fresh air. I shall need my stout shoes if there is to be much walking,' she added, knowing they would be pleased to be alone for another afternoon. 'Would you like to come too? He extends the invitation to you both.' How easy it was to tell small lies.

'Oh no, Georgy – we don't speak French and it can be so

awkward, but you could invite him to dine with us before we leave.'

'He is to return to his mother's soon,' she said. 'So he may travel back in the diligence at the same time.'

In bed that night she felt her earlier love for Amaury enhanced by thoughts which were a mixture of longing, and excitement, permeated with other thoughts she could not seem to banish, thoughts about the brevity of love and the threats that might encircle it. Why, though, should she feel melancholy? Amaury was here in Paris; she was not alone; she was, if not as independent as Capucine appeared to be, quite free – whatever Amaury had said.

The day dawned in a clear sky. Georgy woke early, got out of bed, opened her shutters and looked out across the cobbled street. Over the rooftops of shops and houses she could see the Louvre, and even the river, for her room was in a mansard, high up.

Today she was going to walk out with Amaury. She dressed in her best mauve cotton dress with its pattern of sprigs of violets, and its green ribbons, shook out her paisley shawl and brushed her old pelisse in case the day was not as warm as it promised. Paris streets were so muddy and the bottom of pelisses and mantles and skirts trailed in mud. She had her strong boots with her and put them on in readiness for when Amaury called for her at eleven o'clock. Then she brushed her hair and arranged a few ringlets over her forehead. She had admired the rich Parisian ladies with their high-piled hair and elaborate hats, but they were not for her. In her reticule she put a pocket handkerchief and her purse. Now she was ready and would take a cup of delicious Paris coffee with Abigail and Hugh. They had decided last night to go shopping in the morning for they were determined to take back as many presents as they could pack, to thank all those who had given them wedding-presents. Then they would sample one of the many crowded restaurants near the Louvre – people here all ate their midday meal in restaurants, even quite ordinary people, and Abby wanted to try the food.

Georgy had breakfasted and was sitting by the window of the inner courtyard of the hotel when she heard the rattle of carriage wheels. She went outside and through the door that led to the cobbled outer yard. A sort of post-chaise had drawn up there and Amaury jumped down from it.

There was just time for him to greet Hugh and Abigail who were already dressed for going out shopping. Abigail looked most fetching in a long brown mantle and straw hat.

'I am on my way to meet my friends,' said Amaury. 'I thought, I will come for Georgina first.'

'It looks a delightful day for a drive,' said Abby innocently.

When they had departed and Georgy was seated in the post-chaise by Amaury's side she said: 'I did not know we were to meet some of your friends?'

'We are not,' he said with a laugh. 'At least, we may see some of them, but I thought it made our little outing sound more respectable. They don't seem to expect you to have a chaperone?'

'Well, I never did at home—'

'English girls!' he said with that look of bemusement and slight puzzlement.

They came up to Napoleon's Arc de Triomphe and drove under it.

There were a few elegant equipages – private carriages owned by the *beau monde,* all seemingly going in the same direction.

'The Passion Week excursion,' Amaury said complacently. 'But most of them arrive at three o'clock to pretend they are going to visit the convent at Longchamp. I told you it was burned down in the Revolution.'

'Yes, how sad,' said Georgy without thinking.

'Oh, it is only on the last three days of Lent for two or three hours – even Englishmen come on horseback, and the women show off their new fashions.'

They sent their own hired driver away until the late afternoon when he was to collect them from the top of the *Allée de Longchamp* and drive them back to the centre of Paris.

Amaury appeared to know the place well. 'It all used to be a forest around us – duels are still fought here,' he said. 'These people in their carriages drive to the ruined convent, then, when everyone has seen them, they drive back. We shall not go in that direction!'

'Some may even walk here, like us?'

'A few. They say that some people come to kill themselves here.' She shuddered. Amaury went on: 'It's not properly laid out around here,' he said. 'There is talk of making something of the place, there could be a waterfall, and a lake with an island where people could eat their suppers by moonlight. How romantic that

214

would be!' She thought he sounded cynical. 'But at present, apart from this week before Easter, smart people don't come here. It's a little too – wild – at present for Parisians.'

'We have Hyde Park in London,' she said. 'But that's more civilized, I think.'

'I thought, at least it would be a little bit of country where we could walk.'

There were small buildings, and a few windmills scattered around the grass knolls and thickets and forest rides, and she glimpsed one larger building. All was peaceful with the sun slanting through the newly green trees, as they continued to walk along the sandy lane. Other walkers were out too on this delightful spring day, but they did not look like rich people. She noticed that elegantly-hatted men were absent. There were not many carriages on the nearer rides, either.

Amaury struck off down a path through a thicket and she followed him. 'We didn't come here to be plagued by crowds,' he said. 'There is a little place at the end of this ride. We can sit and talk, if it is not too cold.' Quite a stiff breeze was blowing, and after all spring had only just arrived.

Georgy wanted more than anything to ask him about Capucine. She knew it was not wise, but she was consumed with curiosity, especially when she realized that many of the young women she had seen out with their beaux looked like *midinettes*.

Amaury put his arm around her waist when she came up to him, saying: 'Well, well, Georgy, I have been longing to see you away from the crowd.'

'We could sit for a while on that grassy slope,' she suggested boldly, pointing to a little further along the path.

'All right.'

They walked up a slight slope and saw in the far distance, on the principal ride, a few barouches and prancing horses.

'I like this hint of wildness better,' she said, sitting down on the grass. 'Hyde Park is always terribly crowded.'

'Here at least we are sheltered,' he said and sat down beside her on the grass in front of a few low bushes. 'You know, in the Revolution they used many of the trees here for firewood – and after our defeat at Waterloo your army camped here.'

'You always sound so involved in the past!' she could not help replying. The Revolution had been over for a generation and even Napoleon himself had been dead for five years, long after he had lost power, but Amaury was always harking back. Wasn't he supposed to be a Radical?

'Well, perhaps the rose-gardens are still here,' he said. He turned towards her and pulled her roughly towards him and kissed her on the lips. But she felt he was expending an emotion that was nothing to do with her. She pulled away.

'I want to ask you something,' she said.

'Well?'

'Have you been – are you here in Paris with – someone else? Another woman?' She blushed, her heart beat fast and her voice quavered as she spoke, but she must know. Had Capucine told him she had seen her?

'Why do you ask that, little Georgy?'

She took her courage in both hands and said, looking into his face as she spoke: 'Because I went for a little walk the other day – near where you live – and I saw – that girl—'

'Which girl?'

'You know, the one who calls herself Capucine! She knew you were going to see me, I'm sure.'

He sat up, 'Yes, she told me!'

'Then you *are* seeing her.' She felt flat, hurt.

'If I see her, it is not because I am in love with her, you know. Am I not to speak to any other woman? I also heard that you saw Louis-Marie in the church. Am *I* to be jealous of *him*? Come, come Georgy this is all nonsense!'

'I'm sorry. I thought you might be – fond of her – or why does she always follow you around? If I were a man I'm sure I would find her very fetching.'

'I have known her a long time,' he said slowly, 'and believe me, she is not a rival for my affections – or not in the way you might think. Now, give me a kiss and stop torturing yourself. You know I am fond of you – and you are a very pleasant person to kiss!'

He matched the words with another kiss, this time a more tender one, and she felt she would melt away, but still there was a harder centre in her of emotional discomfort.

Why could she not be like a man and take the moment as it came? Why not 'gather ye rosebuds while ye may'? She looked steadily into his beautiful eyes, and almost without volition murmured, 'I feel there is such a mystery about her.'

216

He sighed. 'If there is, I do not want you to become involved in it.'

'But you wanted me to help her – before—'

'Yes, because there was no other way. In the end your help was not needed.'

'Oh.'

'I am not betraying you with Capucine,' he said again, firmly.

She knew that if she persisted he would become cross and she would forfeit any further kisses. The sound of other visitors had faded away and all was silent. They might be in a wilderness. Did she want him to seduce her in this remote place?

She would like to lie down in his arms. All she could hear was the beating of her own heart and she wanted to hear his through his thin jacket. Why could she not stop asking him questions?

Amaury sighed, saying: 'I think we should go to a little place I know for a warm drink.'

What was he thinking?

'If you like. I am sorry if I was too curious.'

'You know, Georgy – about my plan. I really could accompany you back to Burgundy next week. It would give us time to be together. Have you thought about it?'

She guessed he must be thinking of staying at an inn with her. Well, she would show him she was not some silly jealous girl. She loved him and wanted him as her lover! But clearly today was once again neither the time or the place. She would throw in her lot with his on the way home.

They walked further along the edge of a little wood and came out in the courtyard of a farm where there was a notice, looking incongruous, advertising glasses of wine and plates of bread. They sat down at a wooden bench, and held hands, eyed by an old man in a dirty uniform.

For the rest of their trip they spoke no more of Capucine or of the past but chatted about poetry and about Amaury's new friend Victor Hugo. Amaury retailed the gossip about Louis-Marie, who was said to be paying court to a rich Catholic widow, and also told her of an American who lived not far from him, a big solid chap who wanted to be a poet.

'I think I might go to America,' he said meditatively.

'I think you will be an entrepreneur – a business man,' she teased him. 'You will build a pleasure garden in the Bois—'

'You don't believe in my poetry,' he said.

'I do – but you may do other great things too!'

'Why do you love me, Georgy?'

'Because you are a poet.'

'*Ce n'est pas une raison.*'

No, it was not, she knew. She was attracted to his youth, his strength, his body, whilst still knowing little of his mind. He kissed her again, there was nobody in sight and no other visitor to the farm, and she had the sudden thought that if she succumbed to him his ardour would cool, once he had made a conquest of her.

This was an unpleasant thought, and when he said: 'Old Lamartine was once like me, you know. He adored women – had plenty I am told!' She was startled.

But she replied: 'Oh, so *you* adore women, do you?'

'Certainly – and for the present I find you *très attirante* – very attractive.'

She was tempted to say there and then that she would give in to his desires. Tempted yet frightened, for some other counsel was also working strongly in her. *For the present*, he had said. She did not want to love Amaury Arnaud *for the present* but for ever.

He was charming and amusing and she blossomed when he told her she was intelligent and had fine eyes and that her French was now almost indistinguishable from that of a true Frenchwoman, but she found she did not trust him.

'Why are you looking so soulful?' he asked her.

'I did not know I was. I was thinking, perhaps, that love should last—'

'Oh, love does not last,' he said lightly. 'If you knew anything about it you would know that.'

'But I *do* love you!' she cried.

Today he must be trying to be especially honest for it was his turn to look sad as he said:

'You will prove it then when we stay together on the way back to Burgundy! Much as I should like to seduce you here and now, it is not the time and place, *chère amie.*'

This made Georgy suddenly rebellious, and she kissed him passionately.

'No, no,' he said, and half pushed her away. 'It is time to return. I hope you have enough energy left to walk back to the *Allée de Longchamp?*'

Why could he never be serious for long? Was it necessary for her to become his for him to feel free and easy with her?

'You love someone else, I think?' she said in a small voice.

'No – or not what you girls mean by love.'

'And what is that?' she asked boldly.

'Oh, you want fellows to plead for all eternity – but I am too honest for you all!'

They turned and walked back together, silent at first. He appeared sunk in thought, and Georgy was disturbed, unsure of herself, even if she was sure she had wanted Amaury to make love to her and thereby put an end to all this talk.

They arrived at the place where they had been dropped that morning and the covered chaise came up soon afterwards. Once in it Amaury pulled up the blinds and kissed her all the way back to the rue St Honoré.

They arrived at six o'clock at the hotel, and he said: 'Will you write to your Madame Marceau and tell her I can accompany you back home?'

'I could do that, but Monsieur Cellard will most likely have already left Mâcon. I'd have to leave a letter for him at the hotel. Oh I do so want to go with you!'

'Were you to stay until your English friends left?'

'Yes – they leave on Monday and I was to wait until Tuesday or Wednesday when Monsieur Jacques Cellard would collect me.'

As they said goodbye he kissed her lightly on the cheek and murmured: 'One day you will know what a self-denying man I am.'

'Am I not to see you tomorrow? Or Saturday?'

'Let me know as soon as you know when Cellard will arrive and then I can come for you. You can send a servant with a note – you know my address. I'm afraid I shall be rather busy over the next day or two.'

Georgy trailed into the hotel full of conflicting emotions.

Chapter 3

Georgy was able to talk to Abby alone that evening, for Hugh went to the Palais Royal with a friend from England who had just arrived in France on business.

'I told him to entertain Mr Rushforth and that I'd have an early night,' confessed Abigail. 'Hugh has been everywhere here with me – and I know that men like an occasional holiday from women.'

'Well, I hope neither of them will lose his money,' said Georgy. 'That place houses a gambling hell, you know. My employer mentioned it to me. I fear her husband – Augustin de Marceau – gambles there.'

Abbey looked shocked. Then: 'I don't think Hugh would gamble,' she said complacently. 'He's far too sensible.'

'You are really happy, aren't you?' said Georgy. 'With Hugh.' Somehow she did not connect Hugh's and Abby's relationship with romance, more with the comforts of home.

'Well, I do love him,' said Abby simply.

'And I'm sure he loves you.'

How lucky some people were.

'I wish you could find a husband as kind as mine,' said Abby. 'But you'll be back home soon and we shall have some dinner-parties with lots of Hugh's friends.'

Clearly Abby did not envisage her friend falling in love with a Frenchman. But Georgy knew that if she ever married it would have to be a man a little more complicated than a country solicitor like Hugh.

How presumptuous that is of me, she thought, but she knew a man like Hugh would never set her pulses racing.

Abby was obviously wanting to find out if she had any young

220

man waiting in the wings, so Georgy cleverly turned the conversation to fashion and the differences between London and Paris, not all to the advantage of the latter.

The next morning she was about to write the difficult letter to Camille de Marceau explaining that she might not be there when Monsieur Cellard came to fetch her back to the château, when a hotel servant bearing a brass tray knocked at her door. On the tray was a letter.

'For me?'

Who could be writing to her care of Mrs Thompson? It took her a moment to realize that Abby was Mrs Thompson. Then she saw that it was Camille's own writing and was franked Mâcon. She paid the acceptance fee and told the servant to take it down to the courier.

She slit open the paper, which was folded and sealed with Camille's pink seal and read:

I am to arrive a little later in Paris on Thursday March 30th accompanied by M. Cellard. We have to collect the settlement of a debt owed to my husband.

Please look out for my arrival – I shall come straight to your hotel. We can then accompany you on our return to Pinac a few days later.

In haste
Camille de M.

Abby and Hugh were to leave on Monday night and Georgy had told Amaury she would return with him after that, on whichever day he chose. He was supposed even now to be enquiring about seats in the diligence.

Now what was she to do? She would have to tell Amaury their trip was off. It was too late to write to Camille to explain she was returning with him. Mme de Marceau must have decided to leave several days ago and would now be on her way. There was no way of avoiding returning with her. No, there was nothing for it but to let Amaury know, and he would not be pleased. But might she pretend to Mme de Marceau that the second letter from Burgundy had not arrived, and then return immediately with

221

Amaury? The hotel would pass on any message from her to Camille if the latter arrived to find her gone. She couldn't ask Abby to tell Camille she had gone, for the Thompsons would have left before Camille arrived, and in any case she could not implicate the innocent Abby in her plans.

She regretfully decided she could not act so discourteously towards her employer who had been so kind to her; she was not ruthless enough. It would worry Camille terribly if she came to Paris and found Georgy gone.

She hastily scribbled a note to Amaury and sent it with the servant who had brought her the letter from Camille.

Mon très cher Amaury

Our plans will have to be abandoned. Mme de Marceau herself is to arrive in Paris next Thursday! She wishes me to travel back with her, so I shall not be able to wait to go with you. My English friends leave on Monday morning. Can you come and see me after they have departed, before Camille arrives? If you can't, then please tell me when you will be returning to Burgundy, and where we can meet next. If you have gone to the trouble of reserving a place for me in the diligence, pray cancel it. Should they make a fuss, tell them I was suddenly called back earlier.

> Your loving
> Georgina.

Abby was looking forward to her return to England and making plans for all the hundred and one little things to be done: moving into a new home, settling furniture, linen, and cutlery. Indeed, Georgy had the impression that her friend found just as much pleasure planning all this as in the honeymoon with her Hugh. Georgy tried to simulate an interest in all Abby's talk of table linen, and plants for the garden, and the price of coal, but she was on tenterhooks waiting for an answer from Amaury. More than once, she decided she must walk to the rue Vaugirard again to look for him. What if he had not received her letter? But the maid said she had left it with 'the young gentleman' and with that Georgy had to be content.

On Easter Saturday Georgy helped Abby shop for more small presents to take back to family and servants, whilst Hugh saw that their trunk was taken off in a cart to the customs house to be shipped on the same packet as themselves from Calais. On the Sunday they all went to high mass in Notre Dame. The cathedral was completely packed. 'It is like a theatre!' whispered Abby to her friend.

When the actual moment came next morning to say 'goodbye', Georgy felt both sad and relieved. But at last she could now await a visit from Amaury with equanimity.

'You'll be back home soon, dear, won't you?' urged Abigail, and Georgy had not the heart to say she had no intention of returning home just yet. There were still at least two months to go of the year she had promised Camille de Marceau.

She walked by their carriage as far as the *porte-cochère*. Abby was leaning out of the equipage, looking anxious.

'You are sure you will be all right until your lady comes for you?'

'Of course, Abby – it will not be long.'

And then they were gone, and at first it was slightly unnerving to be alone. She imagined the servants looked at her a little askance. She went back to her room to write her journal and a few letters. It was definitely not the done thing for young ladies to stay unaccompanied in hotels. But she had paid for her room up to date and made a big fuss about waiting for her friends from Burgundy. She tried to relax, and in the afternoon went into the salon to read.

As she was drinking her coffee there, congratulating herself at least upon having followed the noble path of duty and renounced her *voyage de noces* with Amaury – she had been under no illusion as to what kind of journey *that* would have been – a maid came into the room and up to her with another letter.

Hurrah! Amaury had written at last? They would have two days together before the others arrived for her.

But no, it was not from Amaury. It was addressed to *Miss Crabtree care of Mr Thompson*. It had an English look about it.

She took it from the maid, who waited until she found the change to pay the boy, and then she opened it and spread it out on the table.

Her mother's sprawling inimitable hand said:

Dearest – your father is ill – a stroke – you must return at once. I imagine you may accompany Hugh and Abby. I am all at sea myself

but am writing this immediately to ask you to come or it may be too
late. Your loving

Mama.

Georgy felt her hands become cold and her mouth go dry. What
was she to do? The others would be well on the way to Calais by
now and they were to take the *paquebot* early the next morning.
Too late for her. She'd have to return alone. Then she remembered that Mme de Marceau would be arriving on Thursday
afternoon. She's have to explain the position to the manager, and
leave a message with him for Camille. But she could not leave
France without letting Amaury know what had happened . . . .
there was nothing for it but to write to him again. He might even
offer to accompany her back to England. No, she must not think
of that if Papa was dying. Oh, if only there were a way of getting
messages quickly across land and sea.

She sat down and penned a swift note to Amaury, giving him
her Yorkshire address. It was now four in the afternoon, she could
not risk looking for him; he might not even be in. Then she'd
order a carriage to take her tomorrow morning the same route as
her friends had just taken today. She should have just enough
money to get across the Channel. She had some English sovereigns sewn inside her stays by her mother; it seemed aeons ago,
and until now she had forgotten all about them.

She did all these things, with the help of the servant who had
taken her first note to Amaury, and who now went off with a
second one. Then she asked the manager to book her in a chaise
that would take her and her luggage to the point of departure of
the Calais diligence the next morning.

When she finally sat down, her packing having been completed
– thank goodness she had not brought very much to Paris – she
read and reread her mother's short note, and tried to think about
her father. Mama had as usual omitted to put a date on her letter.
Papa might already have perished?

The servant came back to say that the young gentleman had
not been there but she had given the letter to a lady at the same
address who said she would hand it on. Georgy had no heart to
wonder who this young lady was.

She was not hungry, but knew she had better eat something.
Tomorrow, she'd have a journey lasting a whole day to Calais and

then, even if a small boat was ready and waiting to take passengers to the *paquebot*, a voyage next day across the Channel of eight or nine hours.

It was late when she finally lay down on her bed in her underclothes ready to dress again quickly in the morning. Oh, if only Amaury would come, or just send her a message!

She was woken from a restless doze by a knocking at her door. She sat up immediately, her heart thudding.

'Mademoiselle! Mademoiselle!'

All she could think of was that her father had died and somebody had come to Paris to tell her.

She leapt out of bed and pulled her morning gown over her shift. 'Who is it?'

'The young lady who took your note, Mademoiselle.'

'What time is it?'

'Just after midnight – shall I let her in?'

She recognized the voice of the servant who had taken the letter to Amaury.

Then another voice: 'Georgy it's me – Capucine. I come with a message.'

'Yes, I will open the door.'

She did so. The servant melted away with a shrug of her Gallic shoulders and Capucine pushed her way into the room, flinging off her voluminous brown cloak to reveal that she was wearing a kind of man's waistcoat, a cravat and black boots.

Georgy stared at her.

'It's all right. I know what has happened. I am sorry – I read your letter to Amaury,' she said without preamble.

'How dare you!' Georgy was angry.

But Capucine sat down, saying: 'Please don't be angry – it is a matter of life and death. Not just your father – I mean I am very sorry about that – but I have to come to England with you tomorrow.'

'Why?' Georgy managed to get out.

'Because I must escape – if I don't, I shall die.'

'To escape from what?'

'It's better you know nothing about my reasons. I promise I'll tell you one day when I am out of danger.'

'Does Amaury know you are here?'

'No – he is away from Paris. Don't worry, I left both your letters for him to read when he returns. It's a good thing I read them first!'

'How do *you* know where he is or what he is doing? You have no business to read my letters to him. How long has he been away?'

Capucine ignored all these questions and said: 'Nobody knows I have come to you. Amaury does not. Believe me, I don't wish to harm you. I am not dangerous, Miss Georgy – but I must leave France.'

'And you won't tell me why?'

'I'll tell you this now – Mary Wollstonecraft would have been proud of me!'

Was she mad?

Georgy felt suddenly weak and tired. 'You know why I am travelling home tomorrow,' she said with a catch in her voice. 'You are welcome to come along with me, but have you money for the journey?'

'Yes, I have enough. I want to travel as your servant. Some people are looking for me everywhere, so if you don't mind, I shall be your English maid.'

'Well, shall I talk to you in English then?' Georgy could not forbear commenting a little acidly.

'Oh, I do speak English – better than Amaury does. Now we both need to sleep – I will tell you more on the journey. Please trust me.' And Capucine sat down in the only armchair and shut her eyes.

Georgy lay back on the bed.

Strangely enough, she did trust her.

For a woman as young as Georgy Crabtree was on that spring day in 1826, the idea of a journey, even one undertaken for possibly tragic reasons, was as of an Odyssey. Even with Camille, on their way to France a year ago, she had talked to fellow travellers and looked eagerly at all the sights – the last of England and the first of France. There was something so exciting about travel to a place you did not know, where people spoke another language.

Now she was going in the opposite direction and knew more or less what awaited her, but she could not stop herself trying to imagine what the French people on the boat – if this was their first trip to perfidious Albion – would think of Dover when they finally arrived.

She was surprised what a pleasant companion Capucine was turning out to be. She had packed away her masculine attire with no explanation as to why she had been wearing it, and dressed herself in a long silk apron under the cloak. A crisp white cap, and the same elegant boots, completed the effect. She was a good actress and in every line of her being she looked like, walked like, and spoke like a maidservant. Georgy wanted to clap.

But Capucine had said little of import so far, had not vouchsafed any further information as to why she had to go to England. Whilst they had been in the diligence to Calais, once she had ascertained that she need fear nobody who was sitting with them in the dusty old coach, she had talked a little of Paris. She had reeled off the names of the poets and novelists and critics who frequented the Café Tabourrey.

'Yes, I saw that café the day I was on the rue Vaugirard and saw you in the Luxembourg Gardens,' said Georgy, trying to take an interest, when all she was really concerned with was the whereabouts of Amaury.

'There is even an American poet who haunts the place,' Capucine went on. 'His French is execrable but he's a good fellow.' Yes, thought Georgy, Amaury mentioned him too. Perhaps he was a Republican. She forbore to ask whether Capucine had been accompanied by Amaury on such occasions. She could have been?

'He has a funny name in English – Longfellow!' continued Capucine. 'There are so many young men who want to write – and critics too – but they know nothing of life.' After this she lapsed into silence until they arrived in Calais.

There was not much opportunity for a proper conversation whilst they were involved in all the fuss attendant upon arrival: finding a bite to eat and a drink of coffee in the middle of the night, the necessity of holding on to their small items of luggage, the haggling over fares, and all the weary waiting. Then there arose the problem of finding a place in one of the boats that had to be rowed out to the steamer that lay further out in the harbour.

Georgy had been half hoping that Hugh and Abby might still be in Calais but there was no sign of them. Obviously they had taken an earlier steamer.

But at last they and their boxes were on board the *paquebot* and were riding the waves until it should leave at dawn. Only then, having arrived on deck in the early hours, and surrounded by people of all shapes and sizes, did Georgy feel that Capucine might perhaps reveal a little more on the subject of herself. She did not want another discussion of the merits of American poets and French critics.

They were both well wrapped up and chose to stay on deck, at least to begin with, rather than be stuffed into the hold where most passengers were packed. She could see that the people on deck or going into the cabins were mostly Englishmen returning from their tour of Europe, or tradesmen, probably of both nationalities, and even some Frenchwomen crossing the Channel to look for work in England.

It was an English boat. When Georgy heard her own language in the mouths of the seamen, it forcibly reminded her that her time in France was over, and brought to the forefront of her mind her worries about her father. Since the arrival of her mother's letter she had scarcely had time to think of him, for Capucine's sudden eruption into her life had driven the reason for her journey out of her head.

Now she contemplated the dreariness of a return to Yorkshire in the Mail, with no way of alerting her family as to her whereabouts. Had Camille arrived yet at the hotel on the rue St Honoré? Where was Amaury?

Amaury! He had been lurking in her mind as a sort of sensation accompanying her journey, and now she must speak to Capucine about him.

They found a coil of rope and sat down on it. Nobody disturbed them. Most of the other passengers were now probably asleep but Georgy did not feel sleepy.

The moon was shining, a brilliant disc above the inky sea. Slowly the last of the passengers was helped up the ladder on the side of the boat, and eventually peace reigned. Georgy drew her pelisse round her and tucked her feet under it.

Capucine was wearing her little orange cap, that now looked like a pennant in the slight breeze. She had her arms crossed inside her brown cloak. What a sturdy creature she was. How to begin?

'What will you do when we arrive? *I* shall have to find the coach

228

to London – we came on one called The Rocket – and then in London I must find the York Mail – it will be very tedious.'

'You could stay with your relatives in London for a night?' suggested Capucine.

'It would only take up time. I must get to Papa as soon as possible.'

'I may go north straight away myself,' Capucine went on, looking directly at her travelling companion. 'Don't worry, not to be a nuisance to *you*, but I have the name of a person who might help me. I have met Republicans from your country, you know.'

'Then you have escaped for political reasons?' enquired Georgy, trying to sound polite though her own words sounded outlandish.

'No, not exactly. I am not in a plot at present to remove that stupid Bourbon Charles from the throne. My fears are more – personal.'

'Are they to do with Amaury Arnaud?' asked Georgy timidly. 'Is it Amaury you want to marry?'

Capucine laughed. 'No, Georgy, you will not get that idea out of your head! But if I told you the truth you would not believe me.'

'Try.'

'I can tell you that Amaury knew perfectly well that you thought he loved *me* – he was using me to make you jealous, you see!'

'No!'

'You see, you *don't* believe me! If you think I am his *petite amie* you are wrong. But you ought to know that he does have a mistress in Paris. That's why he didn't want you to visit him on rue Vaugirard – only I am not that woman. I wanted to tell you before but I knew you wouldn't believe me.'

'He never explained to me who you were or what he was doing with you. You *were* at that concert with him – and he knew about your coming to the Château de Pinac that afternoon – and there were other things . . . . Then you turn up near his lodgings in Paris! Oh, where is he?' It was all too much! Georgy felt like weeping.

Her father was most likely dead, and there was nothing for her anywhere. She made an effort to control her thoughts. She must keep going. Never had she longed so much to be home in her own little bed with nothing changed – or to be back walking in

229

the Bois with Amaury. Why had he not written or come to her? Had he really gone away from Paris? Had he perhaps sent Capucine to her?

'Hush,' said Capucine, 'your father may rally – and I am prepared to tell you my connection with Amaury if you will promise not to betray me.'

'Well, tell me why you had to leave France. Why should I betray you? I like you.' As she spoke, she realized it was true. She *did* like Capucine.

'I had to leave my country,' Capucine began, 'because my father has been trying to force me to marry a man I do not love – an old man – a rich man – who will save the family fortunes! Also, my family knows that I am a Republican like my grandfather, and a thorn in their side! I don't want to marry anybody, but if I did it would be a rational marriage to a man who was a friend to me and who would want me to be an independent being.' She spoke passionately but looked out to sea with a melancholy face.

Georgy was horrified. 'But they can't make you marry a man against your will, can they?'

'You forget, Georgy, that in my country parents decide whom their daughter will marry – it's taken for granted. You remember the great Mary Wollstonecraft said that women were not created merely to gratify the appetite of man, or to be his upper servant who takes care of his linen and provides his meals? Well, this man wants me for just that.'

'But surely parents couldn't force you to marry a man you could not love? Most girls are encouraged to marry *young* men, aren't they? How old is this man they want you to marry?'

'He is fifty – and wants an heir to his estates. I hate him!'

'You said your grandfather was a Republican – surely his descendants would not be bigots?'

'Oh, Georgy, you are very naïve – we have had so many changes in France and some people have kept up with them all. My mother was brought up in Revolutionary circles – she was only a little girl, but her father, my grandfather, was a friend of the great Revolutionary philosopher, the aristocrat Condorcet – who died in prison. My mother was brought up to believe in the Revolution – that was only at the beginning, of course. Afterwards, her family suffered so much she decided to put herself first. Her first husband was also an aristocrat, and a lot older than she was, but he died after only a year or two. When Napoleon became First Consul she married a man who had never been a revolutionary and only changed his Royalist convictions when it was to his advantage to swear loyalty to the new Emperor. Under the Empire he became a colonel in the Imperial Army and for a time she turned herself into an Imperial creation. Later, after the Restoration, she turned into a Bourbon – or tried to pretend she had – but if we ever get rid of Charles she'll be on the side of his successor, whether it's a Republic or another monarch!'

'It's all so confusing,' said Georgy. 'I've never been able to follow all that has happened in France during the last thirty or forty years.' It was better to concentrate on this than to allow herself to think about Amaury.

Now she was remembering something that had taken place ... where had it been? And to whom had it happened? Suddenly it all came back. 'That reminds me of Madame Bonaventure, the lady who is Amaury's mother.'

'Exactly!' said Capucine simply.

'You mean – ?'

'Yes, I am her daughter.'

This was such a shock that Georgy felt the hair on her scalp rise.

'You are Amaury's *sister*? But then, why – ?'

Suddenly a great weight lifted from Georgy's shoulders but it was to be followed by the terrible knowledge that she had never known the real Amaury. Why should he have kept the true state of affairs from her?

'His *half*-sister. He is the son of Count Arnaud and I am the daughter of her second husband, Colonel Blaise Bonaventure.'

'You are – Mademoiselle Bonaventure?'

'Suzanne, *dite* Capucine. Yes, that is my name. I don't like it. A year ago, I ran away from my father's house and found my mother again. My mother had been unfaithful to him, you see, so I had not been allowed to live with her. She had had another child, my other half-brother Thierry.'

'Yes I remember him. Only a little boy.'

'I thought my mother would save me from my father's plans, but no, she thinks I should marry his choice for me and make the best of it. She is poor now, and has no moral rights over the children she had with my father, Colonel Bonaventure, and no power to alter his wishes even if she wanted to.'

'Because she ran away from him?'

'Yes, she is *hors de société.*'

'But surely Amaury can't want you to marry this old man?'

'Amaury wants to get his hands on his own father's estates. He will do nothing to sully his own reputation for respectability.'

'I will stand by you,' said Georgy firmly. 'I will not let them take you away – if you came to Yorkshire you could live with me.'

'I told you, I know an English family who might help me,' said Capucine with dignity. 'I do not wish to involve you – I can ask them for help and they will hide me.'

'Capucine, where is Amaury now?'

She did not answer at first. Then she said: 'I trusted him, and he followed me to Paris, as I had followed him last year. Then he turned against me – said I should marry well. My father might even take my mother back if I did, he said, and I would inherit a fortune when my old husband died. Two days ago he told me had decided to tell my father where I was hiding. I was in Paris with an old woman of eighty whom my grandfather used to know. Amaury was still trying to persuade me to "see reason". When he saw I would not – and that I did not consider the marriage had anything at all to do with "reason", he decided to take me back home to my father. I escaped before he could, I expect he is now looking for me.'

'He would never think of looking for you with me, would he?'

'No, since he thinks you believe I am your deadly rival for his affections!'

'But I do love him,' Georgy burst out. 'He is perhaps only trying to be a good brother to you – the world is a harsh place and he must care for you.'

'Yes, he wishes I had a dowry to marry with. He thinks my father ought to provide me with one and does not believe me when I tell him that Papa has no money whatsoever. My father lives for past glories, Georgy, he'd like the Emperor back!'

'Too late for that!'

'Yes, but if I had a dowry I would not need to wed the man my father wishes me to – an old friend of his from the Imperial army. But, Georgy, the money Amaury is also trying to recover for my mother would eventually belong to me just as much as to Mama or him! It was the fortune left by *Mama's* parents – my mother was called after her own mother – Félicienne de Crespigny – it was an old and noble family. Their land was confiscated after the Revolutionaries disowned my grandfather. I told you, he was an aristocrat – even if he was also a Radical.'

It was getting chilly now on deck, and a little predawn wind was rising. Georgy felt full of despair on her own account but also filled with compassion for her companion. What were her own problems with Papa last year – or even her sadness about Amaury's real intentions – when compared with a father who was hounding his daughter in order to force her to marry against her will?

'Let's go below deck,' she suggested, 'and then you can tell me more.'

Capucine rested her brown hand on Georgy's cold face for a moment. 'You are kind,' she said. 'I would willingly have you for a sister – and you would do my brother good!'

'I have a confession to make,' said Georgy. 'I have thought ill of you in my mind – even suggested it to others. When there was a break-in at Les Aisées and the stable door was left open I suspected you! But of course you love horses too much to do that. And then –' she hesitated – was it fair to mention the hut and the little scrap of red stuff? She took courage. 'There is a hut in the grounds of the château where Amaury wanted us to meet – and I found – a little scrap of red silk there. I thought it must be from your dress. But it wasn't, was it?'

'Gracious me, Georgy. If Amaury knew of the hut it would be because he'd taken some girl there, I assure you! And I am not the only person to wear flame-coloured garments, you know!'

'I'm sorry,' said Georgy humbly. 'I just suspected you because I was sure Amaury was in love with you. How was I to know who you were?'

'He ought to have told you – but he loves mysteries,' said Capucine.

Georgy thought, well in that he is like his half-sister! But she was fearful, if also curious, to find out more about this 'mistress' of Amaury in Paris. She decided to try to avoid any further discussion of the matter at present with his sister. She was just as curious about Capucine's strange mother, had never before set eyes on a woman with such a chequered past.

They went down the companion ladder and found a small cabin dimly lit by a swaying oil lamp. Only one other person was

233

in occupation – an old woman, fast asleep on a bench under the porthole. They arranged their bags and loosened their scarves and outer garments. Already down here you could sense the motion of the waves; even on this new steam-ship it would be a long voyage.

'Your mother – did she leave her husband because she fell in love with Thierry's father – or kept falling in love with other men? Or did he leave her?' Georgy finally plucked up the courage to ask.

Capucine turned the full glance of her black eyes upon her. 'What is "love"? she asked. 'You say you are in love with my brother and I grant you he is a handsome fellow, although you are too intelligent for him! Women ruin their lives through love. That's one thing my mother has taught me – though she does not know it – and I intend to avoid men and remain independent.'

'But without money how can a woman be independent?'

'By working.'

'I know, but poor women are not free either.'

Capucine knit her brows. 'In a different sort of society it could be managed. I still believe in my grandfather's first principles!' Then she added softly: 'Even my heroine Mary was abandoned by her lover.'

'I thought she married that philosopher?'

'Oh, that was later – and then she died after childbirth.'

'So a woman cannot win – either Nature, or Men will defeat her?'

'I was told by someone who knew her that Mary tried to kill herself twice when she lost the love of a man,' said Capucine. 'In that way, you see, she was weak.'

'Yet she believed in being rational and independent?'

'It is one thing to believe in those virtues but harder for women not to follow the dictates of their heart. My mother's first husband, Amaury's father, died, though by then they were separated. She committed several "indiscretions" when *my* father was away fighting for Napoleon. I remember well that there were men around her. Much later she fell in love with Thierry's papa. By then my father was back in France and cast her off. She did not want to lose me – but by her actions she did.'

'It is wrong that a woman must lose her child if she commits adultery.'

'Or even if she does not. She could be a perfectly innocent person – but a woman has no jurisdiction over her legitimate husband's children. I was forced to go to my father, and he took no interest in me. It was only to score a point that he insisted I live with him at the Restoration.'

'He had previously had no hand in your upbringing? Did you miss your mama?'

'What do you think? I was only six – it was terrible. Whatever Mama had done wrong I did not deserve to lose her. Amaury stayed with her, of course. I resolved I would run away when I was older and I made careful plans. Amaury helped me at first but now he has cold feet. He must be *respectable* and it is not *respectable* to come between a father and his daughter.'

'He spends a good deal of time over your mother's lawsuits – at least that is what he told me he was doing in Paris. Your mother even tried to get Monsieur de Marceau to help her – but I thought it was about her first husband's land, not her father's.'

'Oh, he is undertaking both. Mama has changed. Life does change people. All these plans to recover land and gold for the ex-émigrés make me angry. Mama's father was never an émigré, just a man who came to his senses when The Terror began. My grandmother had money too. But Amaury's father lay low and died of natural causes.'

'Well, now there is indemnity to all former émigrés. The de Marceau family fled to England and they too are fighting to recover all that was taken away from them.'

'Yes – the desire for money and possessions is as strong as love for many people.'

'But what if this present king is turned off his throne? That's what you want, isn't it? That Charles should go?'

Capucine lowered her voice. 'Only if he were to be followed by a liberal Republic! At present there are many murmurings against the priests, and much contempt for Charles – but nothing is actually being done to change things.'

'Why not wait for change to happen and in the meantime stay in England?'

'I want to help with those changes. England is terrified of revolution, even of change. I could not stay there for long.'

'But if Amaury has turned against you – and now wants you to marry your father's choice – why not perhaps marry an Englishman?'

'I don't want to marry anybody, Georgy. I just want to earn my living and to stop being persecuted.'

'Anyway, Amaury is not a Royalist. I should have thought he would be on your side.'

'Men are all the same – he even told you lies to cover up what he was doing in Paris!'

Georgy swallowed. She had firmly resolved not to pursue the question of the absent Amaury but dare she ask Capucine if Amaury *loved* this other woman? Why should he have wanted her to suspect he was in love with his own sister?

'Why did he not tell me who you really were?'

'I told you – he likes intrigue,' said Capucine flatly. 'He has had many *petites amies* – I'm sure he is fond of you, Georgy – but he is entangled at present with this older woman.'

'Maybe that will soon be over?'

'Probably. He is like Mama – always falling in "love", though he does not make himself miserable. I am sorry, Georgy, you do not have to believe me. Perhaps I am mistaken in his feelings for you.'

'He never spoke of marriage – and that was not what I was thinking of either! We were going to stay together – at inns on our way back to Burgundy – I had agreed on that.'

'I am convinced you love him – but if you became his lover he would never marry you – and that is really what you want, isn't it? Wait for him to get in touch with you. English girls are so idealistic about men.'

'Tell me more about his present attachment,' said Georgy miserably.

'Don't worry, he won't be marrying *her*!'

Georgy realized what Capucine meant but decided not to pursue the matter. She would try to get some sleep.

Both young women finally dozed.

When the ship moved away from Calais, and all through the long voyage, until they went on deck eight hours later and saw the white cliffs, before the pilot vessel helped them dock in Dover, nothing more was said about Amaury. But they both knew that in spite of possible difficulties in future they were now friends.

Chapter 4

The passengers had collected themselves at the harbour master's office, waiting for their baggage. Through the window they could already see the London coaches waiting for them, several of which they had been told would leave in the late afternoon. Now Georgy was assembling her forces for the next long leg of the journey, with thoughts for no one but her father. Capucine had stated she would accompany her to London and so Georgy had let the matter rest.

They were called up for their baggage, in order to hand it over to whichever coachman could take them, and then went outside to wait.

Suddenly Georgy saw none other than Abigail Thompson waiting by a smaller carriage behind two coaches on the dusty street. She gave a start of surprise, then waved frantically.

Capucine looked at her interrogatively. In spite of her exhaustion Georgy's mind moved quickly. Rapidly she whispered:

'It's my friend Abby, with her husband, who left the day before us for England. They must have been delayed. Don't worry, I shall say you are a French friend who is travelling north. They have met your brother – but better not mention that. I'll call you Marie, if you don't mind.'

Abby had caught sight of her and now Hugh had joined her and they were both rushing up to the crowd of arriving travellers.

'Georgy – what's happened? Why are you come?'

'It's my father – Mama wrote – the letter arrived only after you'd gone – he's ill, Abby, and so I had to come straight away—'

'All by yourself?' said Hugh. 'If only we had known, you could have travelled with us.' His tone said that it was certainly not done for a young lady to travel alone.

'No – my French friend Marie here accompanied me – she has family in Yorkshire,' replied Georgy quickly.

Capucine played her part well, shook hands demurely and murmured: '*Enchantée.*'

'I have ordered a private carriage,' said Hugh with a lordly manner. 'We shall find you both room with us – we were just stowing our own luggage away.'

'You were delayed, then?'

'Yes, our boat was delayed several hours,' replied Abby. 'But all's well that ends well – we shall be taking the Northern Mail tomorrow morning.'

Hugh was a kind man, thought Georgy; he might certainly not relish the company of two women all the way home.

'I am so sorry about your father – but won't your Madame de Marceau be worried when she arrives to find you gone?' asked Abby.

'I left a message with the manager at the hotel – it all had to be arranged very quickly after Mama's letter arrived.'

Hugh now took charge and ordered a harbour servant to put the young women's bags in with their own. Georgy found she felt relieved. There was something to be said for a husband after all. Capucine looked faintly sceptical but had obviously decided that discretion was the better part of valour, so said little. They would assume her English was scanty, Georgy decided.

At last, after Hugh had opened his *pique-nique* basket and passed round cups into which he poured a golden tot of brandy for each of them from a leather bottle, and had then insisted they sample the box of sweetmeats Abby was carrying, their driver came up. Eventually they set off before the two larger coaches for the long journey on the Dover Road through Kent. Georgy settled back into the upholstered carriage with a sigh of relief. Capucine shut her eyes and pretended to be asleep.

Capucine had pretended to be drowsy all the way to London and indeed when they arrived there, once again in the middle of the night, Georgy did not have to pretend. But her dreams were full of passion and sorrow and insecurity and she knew even in the dream that she was dreaming of Amaury Arnaud with an unknown woman.

She woke though in good time for a breakfast of dry toast and tea at the Maidstone coaching inn. When she opened her eyes she saw that Capucine was already up and dressed.

'I'm off now. I can't risk accompanying you all the way – your friends might talk. Tell them my cousin came for me. I'm going to find a horse – I have the money.'

'To ride all the way? But surely that is dangerous!'

'No more dangerous than being discovered by my father, I assure you. I will write to you when I arrive.' She was wearing her waistcoat, cap and boots, looked every inch a young boy.

'But where do your friends live?'

'Near Leeds. It's a family called Naylor my grandfather once knew. I promise I will come to see you when matters are arranged, but you will have to say I am a French girl you met in Paris – I can be Marie again if you like!'

Now in the cold light of day and back home in England all Capucine's story seemed outlandish, odd.

Georgy sat up. 'Oh, Capucine, please don't go! I am worried. Have you been to England before?'

'Yes, when I was a little girl. Don't worry, Georgy. My nine lives are not yet up!' Then she lowered her voice and sat on the little truckle bed and said: 'Promise you will not tell him where I am if he comes for me!'

If Amaury came to the hall looking for her, Capucine would not be in danger, but Georgy did not think he was likely to do that.

'I don't even know where you will be. I promise I won't tell anybody the name of the family you are visiting, but if you are in any difficulty you must come to us at Huntingore Hall. Fifteen miles from York – my father is well known—'

Then she remembered he was ill, might already have died. But she was sure Capucine would still be welcomed by her family, so she hastily scribbled the name and directions of the hall on a piece of paper from her journal which now travelled with her wherever she went, and gave it to her friend.

'*Merci*, Georgy – and now I'm off. It's not their business but tell your friends someone came for me.'

'Thank you for trusting me, Capucine – I will stand by you.' Georgy had tears in her eyes. On seeing them, Capucine looked away.

'It will all work out for you, I know,' she said. Then she picked

Loving and Learning

up her *sac à main* and after lightly pressing Georgy's hand slipped out of the room.

Georgy was not hungry, even for the toast.

Another day and night were to pass before Hugh Thompson's own carriage drew up on the gravel drive of Huntingore Hall. They had left the Mail in York where his carriage was waiting, and he had insisted on sending a rider ahead to the hall with news of Georgy, and then taking her on there. Abby stayed at home to talk to her own mother about the wonders of Europe.

Georgy jumped down from the carriage. Her mother was waiting at the top of the flight of steps, and there too was Benedict her brother.

'Mama – is he . . . ?'

The two fell into each other's arms.

'Thank God you are here, Georgy! Oh, I hope I did the right thing – but he is much better – really much better though still weak and cannot move his left hand. I have very much missed you, dear – we will go and see him straight away – he's up in the Arbour Room. Oh, Mr Thompson, how can I thank you enough? I should never have asked her to come back alone, but no harm done and you have been so kind—' Ben took Georgy's other arm and they passed into the house.

She thought, it is like a dream. Mother no longer knows the old Georgy, but *she* is just the same. I am glad to be back. I must see Papa … and then, will Edward Walker be here still? I wish I could tell him all that is on my mind. She dared not ask her mother, who knew nothing of the clandestine correspondence they had conducted over the past year, or at least during the first six months of her stay abroad. She found she had a need to see him, but felt embarrassed at the thought of him.

When she went into the Arbour Room she found her father propped up in his bed looking weak and pale but, they said, no longer in danger. His speech was still slurred but his eyes showed her how glad he was to see her. Georgy knew there would be no further allusion to the reason for her year away.

In the evening, a long conversation with her mother brought her up to date with all the recent events at the hall; and her mother was put in the picture about as many of the events in Paris as Georgy thought suitable for her ears.

'I am very concerned that Madame de Marceau will be looking for you – oh, I do hope the manager of your hotel will have given her your explanation. I should not have asked you to come, I suppose, but we did not think your father would live—'

'Hush, Mama, of course I didn't think twice about coming – Camille will send on my things, I expect. She was going to take me back to the château, but I intended in any case to come home in June.'

This was not strictly true. She would have stayed in France so long as she could see Amaury.

Before she went up to bed in her little old room with its flowery paper and chintz covers, she plucked up her courage to ask Ben if the tutor was still working there. There had been no sign of him.

'The boys are away – their mother wanted them for Easter. Walker has – most suitably – gone on a walking holiday for a few days,' he replied.

Georgy laughed. It was nice to be back speaking English, but it would take her some time to acclimatize herself. Back home she was the daughter whose life was arranged for her.

In the meantime, where was Capucine? Tomorrow she must mention to Mama the possibility of her arriving at the hall in case she suddenly turned up.

She went into her father's room to say goodnight, but he was asleep, the nurse sitting by his bed sewing. Georgy felt too tired to write her journal that night and slept for ten hours, waking to the sun streaming through the window of her old room. No shutters here.

The next morning she made a late breakfast of tea and toast with her mother. Mrs Crabtree was still caught up in her husband's illness and so was more than usually absent-minded, finding it still hard to concentrate on anything else. Georgy tried to insist she now took a rest; she was back home and could supervise the servants if necessary.

Apparently Benedict had been 'a tower of strength', and the house 'a haven of peace' once her two nephews had gone home – but Ben must now carry on with his vacation study and the boys were supposed to be returning after Easter. This ought to have given Georgy the opening for an enquiry as to the whereabouts of Edward Walker, but somehow the enquiry stuck in her throat. She realized she was still a little annoyed by the way her parents had assumed she was the object of his dishonourable intentions. But with all the upset of her husband's stroke her mother might even have forgotten why her only daughter had been sent away?

'The doctor calls every day – and we have a very good nurse – you saw her – a Mrs Bennett – so you must rest from your own journey, dear. Perhaps later on in the summer you may visit London and stay with my cousin Caroline. Of course we ought to have told you to come on home after your little holiday in Paris – I'm sure Papa never intended you to stay on so long with that Madame de Marceau – but your letters seemed to show you were enjoying yourself.'

'Oh, I was! And in Paris too. By the way, Mama, I must entertain Abby and her husband once Papa is out of danger.'

'He is out of danger now, I believe, only he may not regain the strength in his leg and arm. It is good to have you back – though I expect our life here will seem dull to you after all your excitements.'

'But Mama, I was mostly teaching the two children. I shall miss them. I *would* like to visit Cousin Caroline again if it can be arranged. I have made other friends too, who might even wish to visit me here.'

She was thinking of Capucine, in the reality of whose existence it was harder and harder to believe as she sat on with her mother over their tea and eggs and toast. Mama had not changed at all; she had suffered a shock but she had overcome it and the even tenor of the house might perhaps be disturbed by the return of her errant daughter. Ben agreed when a day or two later she put this to him.

'They are getting older and do not like change – I believe they became used to life without any of us "in residence"!'

'Had Papa been overdoing it?'

'You know what he is like – always active – and it will be hard for him in future.'

'Is Mr Walker intending to return with the boys?'

'I expect so. He is a decent chap. He was even helping father with the home farm accounts, I think. I never believed that servants' tittle-tattle, you know – about him ogling you—'

'But I liked him – and that was wrong?'

242

Ben made a grimace. 'It got you time abroad! Are you sorry to come back? I mean, apart from Papa—'

'Yes I am, a little. It is lovely to be home and see all unchanged – or little changed – but I shall lack occupation.'

Talk passed to her other brother Will who was now in garrison in Suffolk.

'He was here when Papa first collapsed but there was nothing he could do and he had to return.'

'There is little I can do either now I am here, Ben, except be a companion to Mama!'

'You seem older, Georgy. You have grown up. If I were you, and Caroline Bond invited me to stay in London, I'd go. Or perhaps you'd prefer to go back to France?'

'I shall have to wait and see what Madame de Marceau wants. I believe she was planning to visit her sister again this summer, so perhaps she will bring the children with her next time. I liked being a governess, Ben!'

Talking to her brother about France was making Georgy more and more sad and despairing about Amaury. Had he never loved her, even a little? The idea that all she had felt for him – and was still feeling – had been in her mind alone, that her passion was unrequited, did not remove her anguish but intensified her yearnings, a mixture of remembered passion, and overarching sorrow. She took to walking alone in the meadows, which in this northern clime were only just waking from their winter coma. Now Lamartine's words of elegy and exile from love began to take over her thoughts. Before, she had thought she understood them, but now the truth of the poet's own grief at the loss of a beloved, fed her own fears. Because one person was absent there was nobody left in the world who mattered, and the world was a desert!

But she returned always to the fear that she might have imagined he loved her. There could be some explanation for his not writing: the mails were sporadic, or he was still away from Paris, had not yet received her letter. This feeling of insecurity only added to her depression.

She was waiting also for a letter from Camille, uneasy that nothing had yet arrived from her either. She tried to banish from her mind the idea of that 'other woman' about whom Capucine had been so specific.

She must try to recover her old sense of self. Could one not choose to forget? Then, back into her mind would come the thought: Why had Amaury never revealed to her his true relationship to Capucine?

She puzzled greatly over Capucine, for she feared for the girl's safety. At least it took her mind off Amaury. Where was Capucine now?

If only she had someone to whom she could communicate all her recent experiences – except for her feelings for Amaury, which she would nurse privately. Who was there but Edward Walker?

Papa was looking less grey now. He could still not articulate his speech very well but it was clear that he had not lost any of his intelligence. She must not worry Papa with any further problems over Edward, yet when Edward did return she must speak to him in private. He would tell her what to do about Capucine, might even help to trace her. Edward understood French politics: after all, he had once lived in France. They said the tutor was soon to return, and every day she waited for the sight of a post-chaise bringing him from the town. For a week she was each day disappointed. Then, one afternoon, when she was in her grandfather's library trying to concentrate on Dr Johnson, but finding her mind wandering untethered hither and thither, she heard the sounds of wheels on the gravel and a shout of 'Whoa there!'

That morning Mama had received a letter from her Cousin Caroline but had so far not communicated its content. Did it contain an invitation for her to spend some time in London? Anything would be better than sitting eating her heart out missing Amaury, except that she felt she could not leave Yorkshire so long as Capucine was somewhere near and might even come to the hall.

She got up and looked out of the side window that looked on to the drive. A chaise was just turning round with more 'whoa-ing' and exhibitionist brandishing of a whip in the air.

She went to listen at the door that led into the big entrance hall. There were the sounds of someone lugging boxes upstairs. No children's voices. Was it Edward arrived alone? She'd go to see if her mother was in the small sitting-room, or upstairs with Papa. In the afternoon Mama often read to her husband. Georgy had offered to do this, but Mama said Papa liked his wife to be there sitting by the bed.

Ben had gone to visit friends for a week and the house was quiet. Dare she go to the top floor to see if it had been Edward who had arrived in the chaise? Mama had said nothing at breakfast – she had been too immersed in her letter.

Georgy crept up first to her father's dressing-room and heard the drone and occasional chuckle which signified that Miss Edgeworth's *Castle Rackrent*, a book both her parents had enjoyed in their younger days, was being read aloud to her father by his wife.

She continued up to the next floor and heard two of the maids chatting to each other. They came out of Edward's old room and she quickly went back down the stairs. She could not very well show too much interest to the servants so she decided to wait.

She took her little white cape from her own room, then went downstairs and out through the door of the conservatory. The sun had been shining on to the glass and she sniffed the warm pungent smell of moss and peat. Robinson the gardener had threatened to grow pineapples here but had so far not been successful. She stopped to crumble a leaf from the geraniums he was 'growing on'; soon they would grace the parterre in front of the house.

She turned by the hedge and went on to the nearer lawn where several lilacs were waiting to bloom. Then she walked round by the orchard to the old swing. It was quite dry so she sat on it and moved lazily round and round. Somehow, Nature, or the garden, had raised her spirits a little. It was probably the sun. Amaury was still far away.

Edward Walker came upon her there.

He was striding along, book in hand, determined not to waste such a lovely spring afternoon, and he stopped in surprise.

'Georgy! I did not know you were back.'

Evidently he had not yet spoken to his employers. She got off the swing.

'No, they wrote when Papa fell ill and I returned last week. How are you?'

'More to the point, how are *you*? I am well. I shall enjoy the break before my charges arrive. By the way, you realize that Hargreaves left us last year?'

'I thought she must have done. Thank goodness!'

Now she felt a little shy. How to begin? She must not mention Amaury. 'We could take a walk by the river,' she suggested. She did not care if she were seen. She was grown up now. Let them dare insinuate. Unless Edward Walker thought it imprudent?

He did not appear to, for he fitted his stride into hers and they walked along, a little distance between them, in the direction of the water meadow where a tiny tributary of the Wharfe bubbled along.

'And how is your French? Much improved? What are your charges to do without you?' The humour in his tone made her realize how much she had missed his irony. He went on, 'I looked forward to receiving your letters, you know.'

She realized he was nervous and decided to put him at his ease. 'Oh, it would take a week to tell you all I had not time to write. But I have a problem – you might help me with it?'

'I hope I can—'

'It is about a girl – a French girl I met in Burgundy – and later, not long ago, when I was in Paris with the Thompsons. You see, what would you do if you knew someone whose father had ordered her to marry a man she did not care for, came to you, having escaped her pursuers and asking to be taken to England?'

He gave a slight start and looked at her carefully. Then: 'How old is she?'

'Oh a year younger than me – but even if she were twenty-five they could still make her marry against her will, she says. France is a very fine place and they talk a lot about liberty, but young ladies there are more under their parents' thumbs, I think. This young woman is extraordinary – she is a real revolutionary, like someone out of the 1790s! I like her very much so I travelled to Dover with her and then she said she would go north herself as she knew an English family up here. Since then I have not seen her and I am worried she may have been kidnapped—'

'Surely not?'

'I would put nothing past her family! She has the most extraordinary mother – a woman who has been married many times – well, two *at least*, as far as I know – and who has changed her political complexion as often as she has changed her hairstyle. We met her in Burgundy. Madame de Marceau – I told you about her, she is very kind – even had her to lunch. But this girl does not live with her mother – she was forced to live with her father when her mother left him – at least that is the story and I believe her.'

'What is she called, this lady?'

'Well, she was called Madame Bonaventure when she was married to Cap – to the girl's father. I'm not sure now if she is married to anyone but she has turned against her own daughter. All she can think about is money – getting back the estates of her own parents and her first husband.'

'But why should the girl not ask to wait till she is of age?'

'Because she is determined not to marry anyone, Edward. She is very brave and she hates her father, I think. I feel responsible. What should I do? Should I try to find her and offer her protection?'

'What protection could be offered a Frenchwoman, not yet of age and not in her own country? Your father could do nothing.'

'Well, think about it, will you. I'm sure there must be something I could do.'

'She seems to have impressed you.'

'Yes, more than anyone else I met over there.'

And Georgy knew that was true.

More even than Amaury.

They wandered back to the house.

Edward Walker cleared his throat and said: 'I do not wish to go against your father's wishes Georgina – Georgy – but I think if you are to stay here at the hall I should state plainly that I wish to talk to you now and then! Your father is confined to bed now but when he gets up I shall say this to him. I imagine however that you will be visiting away soon? Thank you for telling me of your friend's dilemma.'

'Thank *you* for listening to me. Mama has asked her London cousin, Caroline – Camille's sister – if I may stay with them again – but so far I have heard nothing of it.'

'It is so good to see you again, Georgy.' He smiled, then bowed, and Georgy watched him as he walked briskly back to the house. There was a spring in his step, though he had always gone about purposefully.

Things were not going to be easy. A whole year away and nothing appeared to have changed. But it had been good to talk to him. Her father's illness had changed matters perhaps. What the eyes could not see the heart could not grieve over. She surprised herself with her own callousness. Mama might notice if she talked overmuch to Mr Walker, but she was still too caught up with her husband's recovery to bother about it. Papa would not be told until he saw for himself that she and Edward Walker were still friends, or until Edward spoke to him about it.

When Georgy came into early dinner with her mother, at five o'clock in the little dining-room, Mrs Crabtree looked up from her chair where she was sitting, hands folded, and said:

'Georgy, I was looking for you everywhere – I have heard from Cousin Caroline and they invite you to stay in London with them. There is news about Madame de Marceau – she received your letter and there is a little note from her too. Apparently she has suddenly come to London herself.'

'Good heavens! She was not to come before June. I wonder what can have happened? Are the children with her?'

'I do not know, but my letter was written only three days ago. Here is yours.' She handed over a thin sheet of white paper. 'Read it now – Lizzie won't be bringing in our meal for a few minutes.'

Georgy unfolded the paper and recognized Camille's spidery script:

Dear Georgy,
We received the message you left for us and spoke also to M Lamennais of the hotel. I pray you arrived home safely and that your papa has rallied? Please convey my concern to your mama and give her my kind regards. I am here in London unexpectedly, and I should be glad if you were to accept my sister's invitation to London. I am hoping the children will soon be brought over to me by Célanie. They missed you a good deal when you were in Paris.

For the present I am your sincere friend,
Camille de Marceau.

Georgy looked up. 'She sends her regards to you and hopes Papa is improving. She would like me to stay at Mrs Bond's because Lucy and Thibault may soon be joining her.'

'Georgy dear, have you not had enough of governessing?'

'Well, I was to stay until the summer, Mama, it was only for Papa that I returned. It would be pleasant to see the children – and there are things of mine I left at the château when I went to Paris

248

that the maid might bring over for me. But perhaps I should wait?'

She was thinking of Capucine. How to leave a message for her if she turned up at the hall? There had been nothing from her, nothing. She could not stay home for ever. If she went to London she could return to France eventually with Camille – and see Amaury . . . .

'But, my dear, you would not wish to return to France? I had hoped you would settle down here with me and your father now. They are talking of new concerts in York at the Festival Concert Room – just think, it can accommodate two thousand people! And then there are the balls at the Assembly Rooms—'

'It was not my idea to go away!' said Georgy rebelliously.

She found she could no longer bear the idea of staying at home. Visiting different members of the Crabtree and the Newby families, shopping in York, sewing new clothes, spending hours sticking items into her scrapbook, or writing in the albums of friends had no appeal, nor even walking in the surrounding countryside or boating on the Ouse. Mama would not want her to spend her day reading, that was clear. She would rather be a humble governess!

The maid came in just then so she bit back her next remark which had been to point out that Edward Walker was returned and that she had no intention of giving him the cold shoulder.

'Yes, dear, I do see the difficulty,' said her mother mildly. She must know that Mr Walker had returned – but Georgy was not going to ask her. 'Well, think over a little visit to Caroline,' said her mother as they finished their meal in silence.

'Yes, Mama.'

That evening Georgy wrote a letter to Amaury which she decided to send to Paris. In it she said nothing of Capucine, only that she had been so sorry to miss him in Paris and to forego the journey back to Burgundy with him.

> I am to go to London where Madame de Marceau is already with her sister. I may return to France with her.

She added her London address just in case . . . . She had wanted to write him a love-letter but had felt constrained. What excuse could he have for not writing to her after she had left France? She remembered very clearly that she had once given him the address of her parents. Of course he might be still out of Paris – but where? Might he know nothing of her return? Might he be worried, even frantic?

Next morning she sealed the letter and took it to a servant she could trust who shopped once a week in York where it could be taken to the Mail. The collection from their village was only a weekly one and the only day had already passed. Then she went to the schoolroom in search of Edward Walker. The boys were to return on the morrow and she found him there sharpening pencils and unpacking books.

'I am to go to London in a few days,' she began. 'I wanted to ask a favour of you.'

He put down the parcel he was unpacking.

'I am sorry – I am always asking you to help me but there is nobody else.'

'What is it, Georgy?' he asked quietly.

'Only that if that girl came here looking for me, you would tell her where I could be found in London.'

'Is it wise? What if her family is looking for her in London already? They may guess she might escape across the Channel?'

'Well I don't want her to think I have abandoned her. Will *you* help her?'

'Yes, but this is not my own house, Georgy. I could not put your parents into a difficult position—'

'Then you think I should not go to London?'

'No, I do not think that at all. You must go – you have your life to lead. If *my* wishes had anything to do with it, Georgy, I'd like you to stay here and for us to take up our lessons again, but that is not possible. In any case,' he added with an attempt at a joke, 'you are now too old to learn anything! No, you must make new friends. I dare say you have already made some – apart from the girl. What is she called, by the way?'

Georgy hesitated for a moment, did not answer his question about new friends, then: 'Her name is Capucine. Really, it is Suzanne, but she prefers Capucine—'

'A little flower, is it not? An orange flower, that, in French?'

'Yes, a nasturtium.'

He laughed. 'She is inventive, your friend!'

'She wears a little cap that looks like a flower – an orange cap. If she comes here, *will* you tell her, Edward, where I have gone? I want to see her and she would be safe at Mrs Bond's.'

'I will do as you ask, Georgy, if you promise me you will not take any foolish risks yourself.'

'Oh, I am very cautious! Thank you.'

When she had gone he remained a long time lost in thought. He should not have spoken as he had. But she had probably not realized what he meant. He had behaved so well, so effectively covered his tracks, that it had never entered her head throughout the past year that he loved her. How he had looked forward to her letters – which had slowly dried up since Christmas.

As for 'Capucine' . . . .

He sighed, and returned to his work.

Georgy left on the Mail for London three days later, accompanied by Hugh Thompson who happened to be going there himself on business. She was angry that she was not allowed to travel alone after doing that very thing all the way from Paris to Dover, alone with Capucine. But she must behave as a young lady should. She found herself wishing she could have asked Edward about Amaury.

There was nobody else to talk to about love.

At least in London she could talk to Camille.

Chapter 5

If it had been possible to drive thoughts of Amaury Arnaud out of Georgy's head, the situation she found in London at her aunt Caroline Bond's would have done the trick. It did not – but it led her among other things to a reappraisal of her own situation.

At first everything seemed much the same as on her visit the previous year. On her arrival at the house in the afternoon Camille was still out shopping, according to Caroline, who received her warmly.

'Camille is so looking forward to seeing you,' said she, and her uncle Clive added:

'My, how you have grown!' This was odd for she had not grown even half an inch for two years. Clearly he wished to convey something.

Camille arrived back about five o'clock and sent a message by her sister's maid for Georgy to come to her chamber. Georgy had finished unpacking and was sitting by the window that looked out on to the backs of some other grand houses, thinking how different was the atmosphere of London from that of Paris.

As soon as she received the summons she hurriedly brushed her hair and checked her appearance in the glass. She must not look as if she had reverted to her former English hobble-de-hoyness.

Georgy's knock at her chamber door brought Camille to open it herself. Georgy was surprised to find the lady's appearance was somewhat dishevelled. Camille kissed her cheek in the French way, and said:

'Sit down. There is much to tell you. But first, here are some of the clothes you left behind at the château!' The ever practical

Camille had brought with her Georgy's best pelisse which she had scarcely worn in Burgundy.

'Did you have your best frilled cotton evening-dress with you in Paris? You could wear it here in London unless the weather is too cold.'

'Yes – I wore it in Paris.' She well remembered wearing it the day she had gone to the Bois with Amaury. 'Thank you for bringing the pelisse dress. Mama would have been very upset if I had left it behind!' Truly Georgy had scarcely given thought to her clothes or all she had left behind in Burgundy. It was typical of Camille to settle practical matters first. Georgy sat down and waited for the rest.

'Has my sister said anything to you?'

'What about? Oh, Madame de Marceau, how are Lucie and Thibault? I do miss them – did they miss me?'

'Georgy, you may call me Camille now we are back home. As for the children, I am hoping that Célanie will bring them across very soon. But there are, problems ... oh, dear this is very difficult—'

Georgy waited politely.

Then Camille switched her tone, saying: 'I hear your dear papa is much better? What an adventure for you to cross the Channel alone – but I expect you managed very well – as you always do.'

It was on the tip of Georgy's tongue to say that as a matter of fact she had not been *quite* alone, but discretion prevailed. Thank goodness she had never written that letter to Camille to say she intended to return to the château with Amaury Arnaud.

'Yes, I enjoyed the crossing – and when I arrived home I found Papa had taken a turn for the better. I am sorry it was all such a muddle – the manager at the Hôtel Neuncies was helpful – and I hope no harm was done?'

'We arrived next day. I was with Monsieur Cellard, as you know. In fact he has accompanied me here to London and is staying with a friend, a wine importer in the City.'

She paused, and Georgy asked herself if she was supposed to draw any conclusions from this announcement.

'How useful that he could accompany you on the voyage,' she said demurely.

Camille got up and began to pace round the room. She looked distracted. Suddenly she turned and said: 'My husband – de

Marceau – has lost my dowry at the gaming house – he has gambled away my fortune! I have left him!'

This was not what Georgy had expected to hear. 'But – have you no redress? And the children?'

Camille burst into a loud sobbing, and Georgy stood horrified. This was worse than anything she had imagined.

'A wife's fortune no longer belongs to her – he is even in debt—'

'But Count de Marceau and his wife – surely they will help him?'

'They think of nothing but repossessing what was theirs. It was on their account he probably took the chance he did. At the Palais Royal. I have no redress,' she repeated.

'You must send for the children.'

'Even the children do not belong to me! Yet I feel he will let them come. He does not like his peace of mind disturbed and the servants cannot always control them well . . . . My marriage is over, Georgy – whatever the Church or Society says, I shall not go back.'

'Has he tried to make amends?'

'No. I discovered what had happened just before I – we – decided to come to Paris. When I wrote to you I did not know the truth. Oh, if it were not for Jacques I should have to live on my sister's charity, but he will not allow that – he is finding work over here – he knows a good deal about wine, and the English are importing more Burgundy now.'

'Well, I am glad he is here with you.'

'If Augustin discovered he was here in London it would mean my children could not come over to me – even though he is in the wrong! He may even go to prison for bankruptcy. I implore you to say nothing to anyone about Monsieur Cellard—'

'Of course I shan't.'

Georgy was now becoming more convinced that Jacques Cellard and Camille de Marceau were conducting an affair. She had nursed her suspicions before, but suppressed them. Many married women of a certain social rank in France did have affairs with other men, she knew that, but Camille had also been a good wife.

'I think you must just ask for the children to be brought over to see your family. You can decide what to do when you have spoken to your husband again.'

'You think so? Yes, I shall have to talk to him again – when his parents are not hovering round him. I shall tell him you are here to look after Thibault and Lucie.'

She seemed all of a sudden pathetic. How was Georgy, a girl of only nineteen, to advise a worldly woman?

'You must not let anyone know about M Cellard,' repeated Camille with a watery smile. 'Once I have the children I shall apply for a separation order on account of my husband's dereliction of duty. Jacques is not living here – there is nothing underhand – but I wanted to tell you he was here in London, in case you saw me with him.'

'Is your sister acquainted with him?'

'She knows I have had to lean upon our bailiff and that he is working on my account. I bought a vineyard in my own name last year – he helped me.'

So that was why they had spent so much time together. Georgy remembered the long discussions when Augustin de Marceau was away. Perhaps she was wrong and it was only a business relationship – though nobody would believe that.

'I would not mind if Augustin took Thibault. Boys need a man around – but little Lucie must live with me,' Camille went on, her mind jumping from one aspect of the situation to another. 'I am in despair Georgy – what should I do? Jacques loves me – well, you ought to know!'

She burst into tears again. Georgy got up and awkwardly patted her shoulder.

'You are a good friend to me,' said Camille sniffing into her lacy handkerchief.

Later, when Camille had calmed down, Georgy agreed she would say nothing to Caroline unless she was asked, in which case she would laud the business talents of Monsieur Cellard and wax indignant over Monsieur de Marceau.

She did not need to do the latter for sister Caroline was angry and indignant on behalf of her sister and appeared to have no suspicions concerning the man who had accompanied her to London.

Georgy saw that Camille must first of all regain her strength and equanimity. She must not panic; she had every right to be disgusted by her husband's folly. Had he, though, any idea of her relationship with Monsieur Cellard, whatever that was?

'I'll write myself to Lucie and Thibault,' she offered. 'They will feel things are back to normal if they hear from me.'

Madame de Marceau was closeted in all the next morning writing to Augustin. In the afternoon she went to Gray's Inn Square to see her own lawyer. Monsieur Cellard kept well out of the way, but Georgy was to see them the following day in the street before they disappeared into a carriage in the direction of the park. Did Caroline really not suspect what was going on?

Amaury had still not written to her and, as the shock of Camille's revelations faded, Georgy felt once more anxious on her own account. It was wonderful how someone else's troubles took the mind off one's own. Camille had not broken down again and had remained calm in her sister's and brother-in-law's presence, which was a relief. They had been given a bare account of her husband's financial problems, but they were not matters her sister Caroline would think suitable for discussion at the dinner table, especially not to a young unmarried cousin. Caroline did say to Georgy that her arrival appeared to have cheered her sister up.

A week after her arrival Georgy received an unexpected letter, forwarded to her by her mother in a packet that included a letter with good news of Georgy's papa.

> The doctor promises he will walk again one day soon. Today he stood for several minutes holding on to the chair.

The other letter, short and to the point, was from Capucine.

> I hope your father is improving? I am writing to say that I shall not stay long in Yorkshire for I cannot find work here. Please write c/o Mr R Naylor, Park Place, Leeds. I believe I could more easily lose myself in London. I have the impression that my family spies may already have discovered where I am staying at present. If I do not hear from you within the week I shall go to you at the Hall.
>
> Amitiés – Capucine

Georgy immediately told Camille about Capucine, sparing her the details of her persecution but revealing she was Amaury Arnaud's sister. Camille suggested she ask her sister Caroline if she might give a bed for a night or two to a French lady whom she had met at the château. Georgy was surprised that Camille was willing to enter the subterfuge and pretend Capucine was a family friend but Camille was no stranger to intrigue and obviously thought it was a plot for Georgy to keep in touch with Amaury.

'Has he not written to you? Or that Louis-Marie? Men are hopeless correspondents – I expect the sister will soon return to France.'

Georgy had completely forgotten about Louis-Marie and it suddenly entered her head now that he might be spying on the family on behalf of Colonel Bonaventure. Then she dismissed this as an ignoble suspicion.

Caroline proved agreeable to her inviting 'a young French friend' to stay. 'Any friend of yours or my sister's is a friend of the family, my dear,' she said kindly. Georgy lost no time in replying to Capucine, telling the young woman not to go to the hall but to come and stay in Montacute Square.

The next day Georgy came down to her toast and tea and found Camille reading a letter that had just arrived from Augustin.

'Is he about to send the children to you?'

'He says he is to bring them himself! He pleads for my "understanding". I do not wish him to come here and I must have Lucie—'

Georgy realized Camille had no choice if Augustin wished to come to London. It was awkward. Monsieur Cellard would have to be kept well out of sight.

'My sister and her husband will support me. I am surprised he would dare show his face here.'

That afternoon Camille was in a strange mood. They were together in the little dining-room nibbling macaroons and sipping tea and Georgy was wishing she might ask her advice about Amaury. Camille however, a woman who appeared to have made an unfortunate marriage, was not perhaps the best person to advise her. What on earth had made her marry Augustin de Marceau?

'I once thought I loved my husband,' she said suddenly.

Georgy waited for more.

'I knew nothing of his gambling,' Camille went on. 'I knew the family had lost their estates and much of their money, except what they had managed to bring over here as émigrés. But I thought I knew Gus quite well. I'm sure if we had stayed on in London it would have worked out.'

'Did he not gamble over here?'

'Hardly at all as far as I know – it was only when we returned to France and he found he had the responsibility of a wife – and then the children. He used to say he loved me – and I believed him,' she said.

'I'm sure he must have loved you,' said Georgy earnestly. It was not so easy being someone's confidante. Camille might regret her words later.

'Women have to get men on their own terms,' continued Camille. 'If you are clever, you succeed. Men want women and for women to give them children – and to show off their wives to their friends. I don't deny he once found me attractive. But he has changed. My – affections – were engaged, so I wanted to be married. But that was the mistake . . . .'

'Don't most girls want to be married?' said Georgy. She wondered, was it because there was really no alternative? No! – she had day-dreamed about being married to Amaury, being part of his life. But it had been a dream, akin to her notions of becoming the kind of woman who ran a salon and met interesting people who had profound conversations. In reality there was not much scope for an unmarried woman as young as herself, even in Paris. Unless she was original, exceptional. Like Suzanne Bonaventure – Capucine.

Her thoughts were reverting to Capucine when Camille said: 'It *could* have worked out, but the day I saw he cared less for his children than his gambling was the day my love for him died in my heart. Men want from women what people call The One Thing – I should not be saying this to you, I don't suppose – but you see women want it too and that is what I meant by a bargain – on your own terms – since women usually want children too.'

Georgy poured her another fragile cup of tea in silence. Camille began to say more, then stopped, then sipped her tea, then put the cup down and said in a strangled voice:

'I think I told you before, Georgy, that our reign over the passions of men is short – even the men who adore us do not want to think of our growing old. Oh, that magnetism in the veins possessed by most young women – it vanishes so quickly!'

Georgy remembered how she had felt in Paris when young men looked at her: *Notice me!* her instincts had said. 'You might marry a man who was also your friend, who liked the same things – so you could explore them together,' she said now. 'Or with whom you were just comfortable.' She was thinking of her own parents.

'Oh, I fancy that is another sort of bargain,' said Camille.

'Well, look at Monsieur Lamartine and his wife,' suggested Georgy. 'He is awfully attractive and handsome, and I'm sure he is very fond of his wife. But I imagine he has had *hundreds* of lovers!'

'My point exactly,' said Camille. 'His *wife* has not!'

'I know what you mean by magnetism,' said Georgy after a silence. 'It is a power – but we don't always have it for the person we'd like to attract, do we?'

'Yet sometimes we do when it is too late,' said Camille, and Georgy knew she must be thinking of Jacques Cellard, who must be madly in love with her. Was it too late? 'That is why it is important to choose the right man,' said Camille. 'Girls marry when they are scarce out of the schoolroom, and what do they know about men?'

'Well, it is perhaps better not to marry – or at least not a man you love – and then you will not be disappointed.'

'What a little cynic! Forget this conversation, Georgy. My sister would be horrified ... I'm sure *you* will find the right man.'

Later, Georgy thought that passion always brought tears and despair in its train. But if Amaury arrived at the door, might she forget all that and fall into his outstretched arms?

It was not Amaury who arrived three days later but his sister. Capucine looked perfectly composed as she pulled on the big bell in the porch of the handsome house and was let in by a parlour-maid. Georgy was hovering on the front stairs. She had calculated it would be this afternoon that her friend arrived in London. She rushed towards her and they embraced. Capucine looked quite respectable, no longer wearing the breeches and waistcoat and boots Georgy had last seen on her in Kent, but with a dark pelisse and gloves.

'You look very smart,' she whispered.

'My friends insisted I look *comme il faut*. It is kind of your cousin to take me in – but I do not think it will be for long.'

Georgy saw that she looked pale and tired, but then a long journey in the Mail taxed the sturdiest of people.

'You must stay as long as you want. It's a pity we can't explore London a little together.'

Georgy had been secretly planning for Camille to take on Capucine as a sort of amanuensis. Or Mr Cellard might like someone who spoke English to help him in the wine business? Even if Lucie and her brother arrived from France she herself did not intend to stay for ever as governess. Being abroad had made the hard work more of a pleasure, but it would not be the same in England. If Amaury chose to come for her she intended to return like a shot to France! But it would surely be an ideal position for Capucine.

She did not ask Capucine where she had been and with whom. If she wished to have secrets she would not poke around to discover them. 'As long as you remain in this house you are safe,' she said and led her friend to a small room next to her own that had been prepared for her.

'I may have changed my mind about what to do about my situation,' said Capucine when she had taken off her mantle and gloves.

'Let us take a dish of tea – they make it well here – and then we can talk. But first I must introduce you to Mrs Bond. You have not met Camille – Madame de Marceau either, have you?'

'Oh, I may have seen her in the distance,' replied Capucine vaguely.

Georgy hoped her friend would rise to the occasion and behave like a nice well-brought-up young lady. In truth *she* now felt more nervous than Capucine looked. Maybe she was so used to hiding her nerves, or had none.

Caroline Bond was already sitting behind a silver teapot in the small dining-room when the young women went down. Georgy performed an introduction and saw that her middle-aged cousin's initial impression of her friend was favourable. No doubt about it, Capucine knew how to behave – and if that was also how to dissemble, what did it matter? She chatted politely in her fluent if accented English.

'Oh, yes Georgy and I met in Burgundy and came across each other quite by chance in Paris.'

Paris was then discussed: the ices at Tortoni's; the concerts where some women could go without escort; the terrible old streets that so shocked the English visitors.

Georgy put in her oar: 'You know it is quite the done thing in France, Cousin Caroline, for ladies to show they have read books and can discuss ideas – not just play the piano and sketch ruins!'

Caroline laughed. 'Indeed? Well, I wonder if my sister would agree? But, my dear, there must be people at home who do not object to women being learned?'

'And in France it is only *married* ladies who are allowed opinions,' said Capucine with a smile.

Caroline, perhaps suddenly remembering why her cousin's daughter had been sent to France so summarily the previous year said hurriedly: 'Well, so long as ideas are not imposed upon the conversation of others. I'm sure there are plenty of learned ladies in London – and even amongst the country gentry – why, there are many writing women in our country.'

'Just as there are in France,' interposed Capucine. 'But the English do not like many of our French writers – they find them too cynical.'

'I hear you have friends in Yorkshire?' said Caroline, changing the subject, as she poured out a second cup of tea for herself and Georgy. Georgy's throat felt parched – she had felt so nervous about Capucine's ability to present a bona fide story about herself.

Capucine meanwhile was nibbling biscuits. 'Yes, my parents knew some English people some years ago and we kept in touch with them. But,' she added, looking at Georgy, 'I think I shall have to return to see my brother very soon. It is extremely kind of you to allow me to stay in your magnificent house.'

Don't overdo it, prayed Georgy.

When tea was over they went up to Georgy's room again. Camille had not so far put in an appearance.

'What was that about your English friends?' Georgy asked as soon as the door was shut. 'I never know whether you are telling the truth!'

Capucine laughed. 'It is true that my grandfather knew some English people before The Terror – and later my mother met English people. Of course, *she* did not give me their address – she

261

knew nothing of my intention to go to England – but I got Amaury to look for it.'

Amaury. Where was he in all this?

'Are you really going back to see him? I thought you were running away from him?'

'Then you have not seen him at all? Has he not written to you? He wrote to me – he knew where I'd be – and said he had changed his mind and would no longer help my father find me. But what do you think of my new idea? We tell my father I have married in England and so cannot be married again!'

'But who would marry you? And you said you would never marry!'

'Well I don't intend to, of course, it's just to make him think he can't browbeat me any longer! Would it be better to say I have a wealthy protector over here?'

'Capucine, please be serious. I have not seen Amaury, neither has he written to me.'

'Oh dear, *quel dommage*! But you are right – my ideas are not very good. Yet I believe in my brother – he will help me to evade Papa.' Then she was silent and moved over to look out of the window.

Georgy said nothing to Capucine about Camille and Jacques Cellard, nor yet about Monsieur de Marceau's gambling. But she imagined the sharp eyes of her friend would detect anything untoward when she finally met the lady. This she did at dinner when Camille arrived, pale but dry-eyed. If Capucine had now decided to return to France it seemed as if Camille would have to look elsewhere for a governess should her children come to be with her in London.

Georgy could not help thinking of Amaury. Why had he not written? He had written to Capucine! Had she been completely deceived and the whole story was a fabrication on the part of Capucine? Was she really his sister? Georgy felt wretched thus to doubt her – but she *must* see him.

Camille looked with interest at Capucine who had decided to plunge into a version of the truth.

'Georgy tells me you have met my mama?' she said, when the three of them were taking coffee after the meal. Caroline was thankfully out of the room or she might have wondered why Camille had not met that mother's daughter before this.

'Madame Bonaventure—'

'Hm,' said Camille speculatively, then rested her glance upon Georgy who looked away.

'I live with my father,' said Capucine. 'They are separated—'

'But your mother keeps his name?' said Camille with interest.

'Yes.'

'And your brother? He is not Bonaventure?' asked Camille who knew full well Amaury's surname.

'No, he is my half-brother. My mother's first husband died.'

'Georgy and I have both met your brother, Mademoiselle. And another little brother too, I believe—'

This time Capucine looked away. Fortunately, Camille was too tactful to ask whether he too went by the name of Bonaventure.

'Your mother was much exercised with lawsuits over her husband's estates – my husband could not help her, I'm afraid. His family too is still negotiating.'

'Yes, my brother is undertaking all that.'

As they spoke, Georgy felt ashamed at having doubted her. Of course, Capucine was Amaury's sister! Camille even remarked upon the likeness, one which Georgy could not discern. Shortly afterwards Camille said she was tired and went up to bed. Georgy too felt exhausted from her longings for Amaury. There would be a perfectly valid explanation for his not writing, but if only he would come for her! He had her address in London – unless he had not been back to the rue Vaugirard for his letters.

What she would do if he did, what she would say to her kind hostess was another matter. She would just have to elope! Camille, another of love's victims, might even help her?

Chapter 6

The next day dawned windy and cloudy, one of those days of a
London spring when it seems as if the season that has been waiting in the wings for only a few days has forgotten its lines and
decided to depart. Blossom was falling from the trees in Kew
Gardens and the ladies who had put away their winter mantles
thinking they might now wear their new pelisse-robes in the street
had perforce to bring out the warmer wear once again.

'Paris can be just as cold,' said Capucine when Georgy
complained of English weather.

'But surely not as changeable?'

They were in the white-panelled morning-room where a fire
had been lit. Georgy was trying to read but Capucine was restless.
Camille had offered to take them both shopping at the Quadrant
in the carriage in the afternoon. 'To take my mind of my troubles,' she said, with a watery smile.

Georgy thought, well she must have some money of her own in
England or she could not shop. I hope her papa did not give away
all her fortune when he gave away his daughter.

She was just deciding she had better write some letters when
Camille burst into the room waving a letter:

'It has just arrived – from Augustin. He has sent the children
ahead with Célanie – they are to arrive this very afternoon!'

'Oh, I am so glad!' said Georgy. 'It will be very good to see them
again.'

After this, nobody could settle. Georgy dared not ask Camille if
her husband was likely soon to follow his offspring, but Camille
answered her unspoken question.

'I shall believe he is not come, only when I see Célanie and the
children arrive in a carriage at our door without him.'

By the middle of the afternoon they were rushing to the window that looked out on the square every few minutes. Georgy went up to the room the children were to occupy and found two of Caroline's maids making beds and hanging fresh curtains.

Coming down the stairs she heard from below a sudden murmur of voices. A cold wind flew up the stairs as the great door was closed.

Was not that the sound of a man's voice? She hurried down the last flight of stairs. Camille was standing with Thibault in her arms and Lucie was dancing up and down. When she caught sight of Georgy she screamed:

'Mademoiselle Georgy!'

And then Célanie appeared, and behind Célanie, a man.

A man in a green jacket.

Amaury Arnaud. Had he come for her at last?

Where was Capucine?

Georgy rushed towards the group who now looked as if they belonged to a frozen tableau.

Amaury did not open his arms for her to rush into his embrace. Not at all: he bowed to Camille, then he *bowed to Georgy* and it was left to Célanie to do the explaining. She turned to Camille who was hugging Thibault. Georgy took Lucie's hand and the little girl squeezed it.

Célanie said: 'Monsieur – whom I have met before at Madame's – was on our boat and helped me with Thibault when he was sick – such a storm! – and he has this very address from Mademoiselle Georgy! *Et voilà* – I said he may share our hansom. He says he is come for his sister,' she explained in rapid French.

Caroline now appeared: 'Come children, to your rooms – and we shall give you a nice warm drink, for you look perished!'

Camille looked at Georgy as she said to Amaury: 'Your sister was here – she seems to have disappeared—'

'No, I am here,' said a voice and Capucine materialized by the door to the drawing-room.

'Bonjour, Amaury.' She smiled at him.

Georgy stood as still as a statue. Then: 'Hello, Amaury,' she said herself in a small voice. 'I am glad you received my letter, for I was worried about you.'

'Take your brother into the morning-room,' said Camille. 'I must see to my children.'

Célanie turned and shrugged her shoulders in Georgy's direction as she climbed the stairs behind her charges who were now subdued.

Georgy hesitated, then decided that Capucine might need her support, so she followed the two into the room.

Capucine said: 'You two have many things to say to each other. I shall leave you to say them and I shall return in ten minutes.' And she was off.

Amaury remained standing in the middle of the room. To do him credit he did look slightly embarrassed. Their last meeting had been such a tender one. What had happened since to make him so different?

Georgy decided to speak first. It was odd speaking French again and she felt she could have better expressed herself in her own language.

'Amaury, why didn't you write? Did you not receive my letter about Papa? I sent it to your lodgings. Capucine read it but she left it for you to read, she says . . . .' Now he looked stern. She went on: 'I gave you my address in Yorkshire in my letter – oh, I was so worried I might never see you again...!' Suddenly she remembered the 'Other Woman' but she wasn't going to mention *her*. 'I was looking forward to going back to Burgundy with you. If Papa had not fallen ill so that I was obliged to leave Paris, would you still have gone with me?'

At last he spoke.

'I *would* have travelled to the château with you, Georgy, but then other things happened and I had to leave Paris. I was going to write to you then, but your own letter came before I could. And see, here I am now!'

'Yes, but you've come for your ... sister, not for me. She must have told you where I would be? Or was it just Célanie on the boat?'

He did not answer this but said, after a moment's silence: 'Still jealous?'

This was so unfair and made Georgy so angry she thought she would like to lash out at him there and then! It was just as she had felt in childhood when brother Will had accused her unfairly of something. But she controlled herself, saying:

'Your sister and I are good friends. She says you are now reconciled to her not marrying her father's choice. Oh, yes she's told me all about that!' She saw a mixture of emotions cross his face. She did not want to dislike him so she said: 'Let us not quarrel, Amaury.'

He looked uneasy now, and she knew in her heart of hearts that the 'other woman' had discovered his plan and made a fuss. Had he ever wished to do anything but seduce her, make a conquest of a lovesick girl? And yet he was an attractive man, a man who bothered to talk to children, one who had charmed her and amused her as well as leading her senses astray. Also, he had *not* seduced her. For whatever reason, he had behaved 'honourably'. Perhaps she had never needed to fear the destruction of her honour and future happiness through what was called 'erotic vice' – the fate meted out to all young women who succumbed to their lovers.

Then she thought: it was easy for him to have behaved 'honourably' – he had never been passionately attracted to her! She had been self-deceived and now felt humiliated . . . . Yet he had kissed her, had said those words to her ... had it all been to pass an idle moment or to notch a conquest?

He was at present searching her face, across which he could see these several emotions passing.

'You see, Georgy I began to worry myself that you would – not to put too fine a point on it – want to be more to me than a – a sweetheart. And if I took you back to the château, Madame de Marceau would soon discover and then I should be expected to ... commit myself . . . .'

'Which you were not prepared to do. You should never have asked me to travel with you, Amaury!'

'I know I should not. It seemed an amusing notion at the time. On the other hand I did take you out in Paris, did I not?'

Georgy went pale. An amusing notion! Her dreams of sleeping together in the great four-poster beds of inns, lying in each other's arms, waking together . . . .

It was most extraordinary. She stood there and saw Amaury change before her eyes into ... just another young man. Handsome, it was true. But not a genius, not another Lamartine . . . .

She even rubbed her eyes as if a mote in them had affected this transformation, realizing even as she did that the change was in her. At the same time she knew there would be a lot of misery before what she had seen was accepted by the other parts of herself that would do anything to keep his affection – if it had ever been that.

He was still staring at her. Perhaps she looked deranged. He seemed to be waiting for a reply, so she said: 'I see.' Then: 'Did Capucine tell you to come here?'

'No, but I knew where she would be! I guessed you would help her. My sister is very ... persuasive. I even knew where she would go in Yorkshire – odd, wasn't it, that the person to whom she addressed herself was from your own part of the world? Mistère Robert Naylor.

She wanted in spite of everything to laugh. The solid Yorkshire name sounded so outlandish in Amaury's heavy accent.

'*You* found her address – her grandparents had been friends of an English family—'

'But now she wants to come home with me.'

'How do we know you will not take the side of her father? Can she trust you?'

He looked very ill at ease.

It was no good Georgy saying that if he reneged on his promise he would never see *her* again for it was obvious that would not distress him as it would have distressed her, up to five minutes ago . . . .

'You cannot make a woman marry against her will, Amaury. You are a liberal, a man who hates tyranny.'

'My sister needs stability in her life – she has led a strange life for the past year – it is time for her to settle down.'

'Then you are going to deceive her!'

'No more than she has ever deceived me – young women need marriage. Georgy—'

'Oh really? Capucine does not wish to marry *anyone*—'

'Do not meddle in matters that are not your affair.' He was angry now, but so was Georgy.

'I see that your free thinking, your – revolutionary sentiments do not extend to women! Capucine is right. Men, however liberal, are tyrants—'

'Do not speak of things you do not understand. I am only accompanying my sister to see her mother whom she has neglected. Her mother knows far more about these things than you do—'

There were footsteps and Capucine came back into the room.

'Capucine – do not believe him – he will take you to your father – if you go back to France now you will never escape! Please stay here – or go back to your friends in Yorkshire, this Mr Naylor – your father will understand that he cannot force you—'

Capucine looked from one to the other, then she said, 'I do trust my brother – he has always helped me in the past. It was only in Paris that I suspected he had received orders from my father. Now I know he was away for quite other reasons. Do not worry, Georgy, I can look after myself.'

'You are going now – this afternoon? Please wait until tomorrow – please, Capucine.'

But Capucine took Georgy's hand and said: 'No – I must face my future, not run away. I have been running away for too long. I shall show my father I am resolved never to marry. Amaury wrote to say he was beginning to change his mind and that the man he had in mind for me was perhaps too old.'

Georgy did not understand her friend. But Capucine was resolved and Amaury stood there with a slight smile on his face. She thought, he had sounded exactly like Louis-Marie!

'Then we must explain to my cousin that you are leaving,' she said briskly, her tone of voice scarcely betraying her feelings. It seemed the only way to bear them. 'She will think it rather odd, but you can say *your* father needs you now!'

Caroline was introduced to Amaury, 'my friend's brother' and told he had come to escort his sister back to France.

'What a shame, my dear, there is so much to see in London, but if your mama needs you, we must let you go,' she said pleasantly.

Camille, when she came down from settling her children, for they were both exhausted and needed a sleep, was less cordial. She suspected something, Georgy thought, for she stared long and hard at Amaury and asked Capucine if it was really a matter of urgency that she left England that very evening.

'My brother has made all the arrangements,' said Capucine.

'Thibault has asked to see Monsieur Arnaud before he goes,' said Camille. 'If you do not object?'

Georgy wanted very much to speak alone to Capucine before she left and knew she would have to be quick about it. 'I will come up to your room and help you pack,' she said. The children were on the floor above, so the length of their conversation depended upon how long Thibault could spin out a conversation with his hero.

'Oh, I have very little to pack,' said Capucine, avoiding her eyes. But Georgy insisted and as soon as they reached the room, she whispered, 'Do you really wish to go? Is Amaury forcing you?'

'Yes, I think it best for me to return,' said Capucine. 'I was putting myself too much in the wrong by escaping. It would be different if I had another suitor ready to take me away! If I appear reasonable now, they will not insist upon the marriage. Amaury thinks that Papa will allow me to stay with *Maman* for a time and I think I must do that—'

'But what has changed?' cried Georgy.

'This has changed,' said Capucine and thrust two letters from her baggage into Georgy's hand. 'Do not read them yet awhile – but it will explain why. Tell me, Georgy, you do not regret too much that my brother is not in love with you? I do not mean to be cruel but that is the case, *n'est-ce pas?*'

'I thought I loved him, but it is not to be,' whispered Georgy. 'But I must say farewell to *you* and that makes me sad.'

For answer, Capucine said: 'You will marry one day, Georgy. *I* shall not. Come back to Paris one day and see me – and – *vive la République!*'

They embraced. Then Capucine took up her bags and Georgy darted into her own room for a moment to put the letters somewhere safe. What could they be about? She thrust them under her pillow, then followed Capucine downstairs.

Amaury was now being polite to the two ladies but as soon as he saw that his sister was ready he made his goodbyes, shaking hands with Camille and Caroline and uttering many expressions of gratitude, but refusing their carriage.

'A walk will do us both good,' he said. He shook Georgy's hand too and looked for a moment into her eyes with an unfathomable expression, but she thought she saw calculation there. Would Lamartine have behaved like this? It was an inopportune moment but she suddenly realized that Amaury was a poet who never wrote; she had never seen any of his productions, had even seen more from the pen of Louis-Marie than from him. Oh, he had discussed other poets, talked a lot about poetry, sketched out his ideas, but what had he ever written? He was a critic.

And then the brother and sister went through the door into the square. She watched them out of the window as they walked away. Amaury had taken his sister's bag in one hand and his sister had hooked her arm in his, and Georgy thought: they look more like lovers than brother and sister! But they *are* brother and sister, I am sure of that.

She had no opportunity to read the letters until after dinner, a meal during which Camille said little, though Caroline was clearly trying to distract her from her own troubles by making sprightly conversation about 'our French friends'. Georgy pleaded tiredness and went up to her room after coffee.

Dear Georgy

I have little time to write, but you deserve an explanation. When I came to England it was to find the man whom I thought might be my real father – an Englishman who had known my mother years ago. But I was wrong, completely wrong, and I have decided to go back to France where I belong. I shall fight for a Republic – for true Liberty and Equality – and Sorority! For all the French. I told the man in question – Robert Naylor – about your kindness to me. Lo and behold, he knows you! It is all most peculiar. He has written to you and I enclose his letter.

Farewell, dear Georgy, do not forget

Your Capucine.

But she did not know a Robert Naylor. Georgy searched her memory. Naylor was a Yorkshire surname, true; maybe she had met the man at one of her boring cousins' boring house-parties in the East Riding? But he would not be the sort of person to know a Revolutionary.

The other letter was folded twice and the name of Miss Georgina Crabtree printed carefully on the outside. She opened it carefully, and started with shock. She certainly knew 'Robert Naylor'.

Dear Georgy

All I write now is in the utmost confidence.

I knew "Capucine's" mother, Félicienne de Crespigny, later Arnaud, later still Bonaventure, when I was a young man in my early twenties. I was in France for a short time after the capitulation of Paris at the end of March 1814 before I returned to England at the restoration of the Bourbons. All this was before Waterloo, of course.

Félicienne was more than ten years older than me, but much more worldly-wise. She had been obliged to be so, for she was the daughter of an intellectual Revolutionary and a lady of the Bourbon *noblesse*. Her first husband was a rich aristocrat who had been forced to flee The Terror, and had changed his name from d'Aubigny to Arnaud. She had a son by him, a boy called Amaury who was about twelve when I knew the family. Monsieur Arnaud, the boy's father, must have died when the boy was very young for she had remarried. Her second husband was a Colonel Blaise Bonaventure, who had followed Napoleon on almost all his campaigns, and she had a daughter by him – Suzanne, and a little boy who died. It was whilst the colonel was away that she had liaisons with several men, including myself, a callow youth who thought he was in love with this splendidly sensual woman. Suzanne was about six years old and very attached to me. Indeed once she called me Papa and I had to tell her I was not her papa. She knew me as Robert Naylor.

My full name is Robert Edward Walker-Naylor. My father, recently deceased, was a rich West Riding worsted manufacturer. In 1811 I, his only son, had espoused the cause of the Luddites! He was very angry with me. I had just achieved my majority so I decided to make my own way, went abroad, and refused to touch my father's fortune or accept any money from him. He had been quite a Radical in his own way, was a follower of Wilberforce and in his personal life a man of high principle, and I could not understand why he could not agree with me about the new machinery.

After Waterloo Madame Bonaventure returned to her second husband, but if what Suzanne has told me is correct, he must have discovered her various infidelities and left her soon afterwards. By then of course I was back in England.

I had no idea that after I left France Suzanne went on believing that I was her real father! She never liked her father. He reciprocated and took out on her the animosity he felt for her scapegrace mother, and his grief at losing a son, whose death he blamed on his wife. He insisted on taking the child in 1816 to spite Félicienne.

Later, Félicienne must have had another liaison, for Suzanne tells me that she has yet another brother, still a small boy. (Thierry, thought Georgy.) None of Félicienne's children was mine, Georgy. Please believe me.

Madame Bonaventure now appears to have nobody left except

her children. Her son Amaury is, Suzanne tells me, devoted to her: 'always running around doing her bidding,' to quote the young lady. I tried to explain that it was because her mother had not kept to the normal conventions that she was now alone and almost penniless and that I thought Suzanne should not make her own life more difficult. She was once fond of her mother who was – and still is, I expect, a difficult – but brave woman.

Suzanne – I gather she now calls herself Capucine – probably takes after her grandfather. He was a friend of the great Condorcet, you know. I always think that you too with your love of literature must take after your own grandfather.

Suzanne is a woman of strong passions and a tendency towards impetuosity. Who can blame her? I presume you must have met her half-brother, Amaury? From what she has told me, I judge that her brother has more of an eye to the main chance. It's true that he searched his mother's papers for his sister in order to find my name and old address, and this enabled her to trace me.

I was grieved to disappoint her in her paternal hopes but I had to tell her the truth: if Bonaventure was not her father I certainly was not! I have encouraged her to return to France, for I believe – maybe too optimistically – that her father will not wish to court great unpopularity by obliging, nay forcing, her to marry this elderly friend of his. A letter from her big brother arrived whilst she was staying in Leeds at my father's old house (there is a house-keeper) telling her he had arranged matters and she could return to her mother and no longer be forced to marry.

I am aware that all the revelations in this letter to you would not be regarded as suitable for the eyes or ears of a young lady and if I have offended you I apologize. But I thought it might be time for me to speak out. Your father has no idea of my provenance. I expect I may have to enlighten him one day. I wished to make my own way in the world without any reference to my own family, but I feel that the time will soon come for me to reveal that I am – alas! – not some worthy weaver risen through the ranks of society, poor but honest, for my father died whilst you were in France, bequeath-ing me a goodly fortune along with a letter saying he had forgiven me my conduct but hoped I had now 'come to my senses'. I am scarcely a gentleman's son – but neither is your father! We come from similar layers of society, the hard-working 'business' end. Your father would have approved of mine, indeed he has probably met him. I had changed my name on returning to England – if he had known who I was, he would have treated me differently, but I thought it best to dissemble, and to earn my bread, if not by the sweat of my brow, at least through honest toil of another sort.

Now I can be myself. I have a great regard for you, Georgy. Your letters from France buoyed me up. I shall say no more at present but I look forward to a reply from you. I have done my best for Suzanne – who, by the way, also has a sincere affection for you.

Your old friend
Robert Edward Naylor-Walker

Georgy put the letter down, her heart beating rather fast. It would soon be time for her own confession and she half dreaded, half looked forward to unburdening herself. But perhaps Capucine had told Edward of her friend's passion for Amaury?

She could not get to sleep that night; her mind was full of Amaury and Capucine. When she finally dozed off, it was almost dawn, and she dreamed of Amaury, with whom she was having a long conversation. In the dream she was no longer angry with him, but she woke with tears running down her cheeks. If only he loved her! She knew that he did not, and probably never had.

Did she still love him? You could not suddenly discard all your good and tender feelings for someone, and there was a lot of good in Amaury. But her feelings for him had certainly changed. She realized that she would have been prepared, in order to be his lover, to have thrown over all the principles that had been inculcated in her. But unless love were mutual it did not last. Someone was always left yearning for what they could not have. You might spend your whole life like that.

She was sure now that Amaury's radicalism would never extend to women, that whatever his political opinions he had very proper ideas about the role of women in the lives of men. How could you blame him? He was like most men, and must also have disapproved of his mother's emotional vagaries. He also had some hold over his sister, she was sure. Or Capucine was fonder of him than she had ever admitted. Amaury, however, might not do what she wanted, might even now be planning to take her back to her father, or not raise a finger against her being married off.

She got up and tried to continue the conversation she was

274

having with herself. This must be what it was like to fall out of love.

He only wanted me to listen to him, never to listen to me. I was there to be kissed and dallied with, yet all the time he had another woman in Paris . . . . And he was cold and unpleasant to me yesterday. I had done nothing to deserve that. Not one kind word, not even a smile. He never took me seriously; if I had told him that I too had written some verse, would he have shown any interest? I doubt it . . . .

That afternoon she sat down to compose a letter to Edward Walker. It felt strange. The last time she had written to him she had been in France and still besotted with Amaury. It took many hours and much effort before she was satisfied with what she had written.

Dear Edward,

Thank you for writing to me. I don't suppose one receives such a surprising letter more than once in a lifetime. Is it not strange that you and I were both involved with the same family? I have to tell you that I had met, and become rather fond of, Amaury Arnaud before Capucine came looking for him at the Château one day last autumn and found me instead.

I do not think I ever mentioned the name Bonaventure to you in my letters, or you might have realized it was the lady you once knew. Of course you would not have expected her to be renting a house in the depths of rural Saône et Loire! When I saw you a week or so ago in Yorkshire you must already have seen Capucine, so you knew about whom I was speaking. It must have been a shock for you when she mentioned *my* name! I know you have been kind to her, but what could you do? Will she ever escape to the kind of life she wants, even needs? I cannot see her staying with her mother and acting the good daughter at home. Neither can I envisage her returning to her father. Or even in a household of her own, for she deserves a better fate than a domestic one. She is so brave, far braver than me, yet I believe she had personal motives as well as political ones. Or they were mixed, as probably her mother's were? Like her mother, as far as I can read between the lines of your letter, the daughter is a woman of extremes. Her brother is not.

She looked up. Could she yet say to an old friend that she had been in love with a young man, a man at least ten years younger than her correspondent?

She had deliberately said nothing about Amaury in her letters to him from France, not after the first meeting anyway, but had even then felt uncomfortable when writing to her old tutor. For not quite the first time she began to wonder what Edward Walker's real feelings for her had been. Had she been blind? She had thought of him as a platonic friend, her best friend – and she was sure that he also had considered her that at least. Never had he committed the slightest impropriety but it must have been galling for him when she was sent away as if he *had*. She continued:

Both the brother and the sister fascinated me – as the sister still does. It is difficult to explain, but do you know that word 'glamour' used by Scott in one of his novels? I find Amaury and Capucine 'glamorous'. I suppose I found Monsieur de Lamartine glamorous too for I once imagined that Amaury Arnaud was a poet in the same mould. I do not think so now. But he is a good critic, and a fine talker.

After long conversations with Capucine, I have come to the conclusion that Politics are less important for me than Poetry and human feelings. She made me see how different I was from her, and also made me uncomfortably aware how our lives depend upon little strokes of fate: on who we are, how we were brought up, whether we were loved . . . . If Capucine cannot escape her fate, I think she will die! Please do not say I am being melodramatic. In the present state of Society she should have been born a boy.

She took courage now and wrote:

You have 'confessed' your old passion to me when you did not have to do so, therefore I will tell you that Amaury might have accompanied me back to Burgundy from Paris, if I had not suddenly had a letter from Mama. Now I am relieved I did not, though I am also sad. So you see, my reputation has been saved! I tell this to no one but you.

I believe I now need a little time of rest and reflection. I have not yet explained to you that my employer has left her husband, whether temporarily or permanently I am not sure. Her bailiff accompanied her to London and now her children are arrived here – on the same boat as Amaury Arnaud. If Camille de Marceau asks me to, I shall stay on in London for the time being to help her with the children. Not much time for 'rest', you will say, but looking after children at least stops one becoming too concerned with oneself.

Now that you are back at the hall I give you full permission to tell my parents we are in touch with each other, should you wish to do so. I am tired of being treated as a child and I must acknowledge you as a friend. I think also you should tell Papa who you really are. I shall eventually write to Mama.

During the next few weeks Georgy, with all the elasticity of youth, was to get over her feelings for Amaury Arnaud. She would never forget him, but she was determined not to mope over her first love. She decided to keep the pages of her journal in which she had described her feelings. There had been nothing wrong with feeling them, after all.

She decided one afternoon to find out more about the *Vindication of the Rights of Women*, looked in her cousin's library and found the notorious lady's book. She was sure neither Clive nor even his wife had read it; it must once have been fashionable to possess a copy. When the children were in bed she read a chapter of Mary Wollstonecraft, and then, as she was still not sleepy, a few pages of Mary Shelley's *Frankenstein*, thinking, a mother and a daughter, but very different kinds of women. Madame Bonaventure and Suzanne, were perhaps rather *alike?*

Camille gave her *Pride and Prejudice* in French, as a little thank-you present. Georgy enjoyed it just as much as when she had read it for the first time in her own language. How *would* its author have got on with la Wollstonecraft? Camille was still uncertain about her husband's intentions. Caroline would provide her sister with board and lodging but Camille had little cash of her own as yet – until Jacques Cellard's negotiations on her behalf bore fruit. She wrote to Augustin to tell him she intended to keep the children with her in London for the time being, and awaited his reactions. He replied saying his parents were 'mortally wounded' by her attitude and that he required Thibault back at the château by September. In the meantime he was consulting his lawyers. But Camille had also consulted lawyers, though nothing was yet settled. Georgy realized that Camille was really very intelligent but had learned to hide it.

The day was to come in the autumn when Augustin, never yet having visited her at her sister's – he was probably frightened of showing his face to the family he had defrauded – received notice from his wife's lawyer asking for an official separation. Camille was going against the advice of one lawyer and even of her own family, but it had the effect of Monsieur de Marceau's eventual arrival in London and many further visits to solicitors when family matters were at least partially arranged. Augustin had received a letter from his bailiff in the summer to apprise him of his new post with a large firm of vintners, but with no mention of England. It had been quickly apparent to Caroline how matters stood with Camille and Jacques Cellard but she thought Augustin could have no proof of adultery. So long as the English family stuck together and supported Camille . . . .

Lucie and her brother were happy to be spoiled all summer by their aunt and uncle and overjoyed that Mademoiselle Crabtree was to stay with them for a time. But in October Thibault returned to France with his father to stay with his grandparents, who had moved into the château. Célanie stayed on in London, whilst the other servants remained with their master. Camille hated to lose her son to her husband but it was the only procedure that would enable her to stay on in London.

A year was in fact to pass before any permanent settlement between the de Marceau husband and wife was affected, a year in which Camille was terrified her husband would discover what her real relations were with M Cellard, who now went between London and Mâcon but never called upon her husband. He had actually found him a new bailiff!

And Georgy?

She and Edward were now writing each other long, detailed letters. After several months their correspondence had taken such wings that she began to wish they could talk rather than write.

There came a day in November when Edward declared himself:

I have loved you ever since I set eyes on you, when you were barely sixteen – *à l'âge ingrat*. Tell me I may have a little hope! I know you are not a stranger to the passion of love ... (Had Capucine also told him about her love for Amaury?) ... and I do not expect to be the object of such a passion. I can only offer you my own, for I would also wish to look after you, and walk hand in hand with you towards the same horizon. Even if you need years to make up your mind, even, should you decide in my favour – we had to wait until you were of age, unless you tell me to go away, I shall wait for you. If you give me this little hope, I shall soon no longer be able to conceal my feelings and intentions from your parents. I look forward with impatient delight to your arrival at the hall for Christmas. At last I shall see you again and you will have the opportunity to know if you could feel for me a tenth of what I already feel for you.

Somehow the truth of his old relations with another woman had made Edward more attractive to her rather than less. He knew about love and about passion; he had suffered on its account; he was no dried-up bachelor but one who had experience of the body of a woman, and that curiously excited her. But what was truly amazing was that he loved her, really loved her. Her love for Amaury had been all in her own mind. Was Edward's the same, or did women have to wait for love, for a man to declare himself first?

A few days later Georgy wrote to her mother in one of her regular family missives, telling her that she and Edward Walker were still good friends and respected each other, and that Mr Walker had something to tell her father as soon as he was well enough to hear it. Yes, she would be coming home soon: she missed them all.

The day arrived – just before the Christmas of 1826 – and Georgy was ready to return home. 'Miss Lucy', now to all intents and purposes an English girl, needed the companionship of other children and Camille had found a little school in Fulham for her, so Georgy's help would no longer be needed in the New Year.

She told Edward of her decision to return 'in hope', which was the signal for Edward Walker to ask to see Christopher Crabtree. Georgy's papa was continuing to make good progress, and Georgy's two cousins, Nat and Jack, were to be sent away to school, which would necessitate Edward's leaving the hall. Now was the time to settle things.

Here was the dear old place! There was even snow on the ground to welcome her; she had always loved snow. There would be parties and dances as well as the family festivities but she did not care about them unless she might go with Edward. She would accept the invitation from Abby and Hugh to visit them in their new house. Abby was already expecting a baby.

She and Edward had agreed not to be seen together until they had had time to talk, but Edward would let her know straight away how his interview with her father had gone the day before.

She waited anxiously as the carriage stopped and she climbed down, the wind whipping her cheeks. She was wearing her best pelisse dress of deep blue silk lined in white, and she felt it made her look a little French. The padded hem still weighed her down a little but she had better get used to wearing such things, she supposed.

Her mother and father were waiting at the top of the flight of stone steps and she ran up them and was swept into their arms.

Her father was now able to speak. He clasped her tightly. 'Georgy love – so many surprises!' he said.

Her mother squeezed her hand, saying: 'Oh, you look so fashionable dear!'

Nothing more important was added just then, and Georgy went up to her room to unpack, the whoops and shouts of her two boy cousins echoing distantly. Then swiftly she crept down the back stairs that led to the library floor, for they had agreed to meet there the minute she arrived.

Yes, he was there. For a moment they both hesitated and then Georgy went up to him and put her hand in his. He took it to his lips. She felt a great sense of relief for she had worried lest all his words and all her words would vanish in a puff of wind should she suddenly find his physical presence less attractive. But he held her hand steady, and his eyes were deep and serious, and the smile at the corner of his lips told her she had 'come home'.

'We may speak to each other then?' she asked.

'Your father is willing – he is too surprised at my family revelations to object. So if you will let me, Georgy, I shall try to prove I am worthy of you.'

'Indeed you are – but it is strange to be together after so many letters. It is like the old days in the library!'

They remained looking at each other, scarcely moving, until Edward released her, saying: 'You must go to your parents now – the boys are to be here over Christmas, so my services are still required. The good news is that your brothers may also arrive tomorrow.'

'Oh I am so happy to be back – and to see you, Edward,' she said shyly.

Georgy had missed her English Christmas last year so it was two years since she had been home for the season, and she enjoyed it all. The Christmas festivities lasted over till Twelfth Night and never had the hall resounded to so many young persons and so much happiness. Will had invited his fiancée, a blushing girl from Suffolk, and Ben talked twenty to the dozen to Edward about magnetism and revolution and Kant and Napoleon and the slave trade. Even the two boys were not too annoying. Perhaps their noise blended in with everyone else's.

On Twelfth Night Edward asked to speak again to Mr Crabtree. It was not enough that they were now allowed to speak to each other freely. He must ask formal permission from her father to court his Georgy.

'We can ask *her*!' said Crabtree.

Georgy, who had been sitting with her mother awaiting her father's summons, rose with alacrity.

'Are you sure, dear?' murmured Adelaide Crabtree. 'He is a lot older than you—'

'That is one of the very good reasons I *am* sure,' replied her daughter coolly. She knew her mother had always liked Edward Walker.

Her father and Edward were sitting before the library fire when she went in. Edward rose.

'Are you willing to give him a chance then, daughter?' asked Papa, looking uncertain. His speech was still a little slurred. 'Mind you, it is only so you can get to know each other a bit better. Nothing is promised – you are a free woman,' he added.

'Yes, Papa. I am willing.'

'You are very young – but I suppose you know your own mind?'

'Yes, Papa, I do – and I give Edward complete permission to persuade me he can make me happy – so long as he is also a free man who can change his mind.'

'I shan't do that, sir,' said Edward, and smiled.

281

'So long as I can make you happy too,' added Georgy softly as they toasted the New Year and each other, and Mama came in to join them and then brother Ben. Will had already returned to his barracks.

Later that evening Georgy and Edward looked out together at the snowy landscape, and it was before the long window at the front of the hall that Georgy received her Edward's first kiss.

'Your father has quite melted towards Mr Walker,' said her mother that week. 'I suppose it was discovering he came from a good family – but I always guessed he did.'

Indeed Edward was discovered to have been left a goodly sum of money by his grandfather Fred Naylor whose investments had been accruing interest year after year. Edward had never touched the money before but if he were to take on Georgy and the possibility one day of children he would have to swallow his scruples.

Georgy accepted Edward's formal proposal in the spring of the year 1827 and they were married in the summer of that year.

Capucine was invited to the small wedding breakfast but did not come.

In the autumn of 1827 Georgy and Edward continued their honeymoon abroad. They had found no difficulty in coming to an agreement over their destination, for what could be more fitting than the Lac du Bourget?

Georgy knew that by its shores she would find the joy she already took in Edward's company renewed and strengthened. Edward knew that the lake meant more to her than a beautiful place, or even a beautiful piece of poetry, for Aix still contained a memory of first love, yet was also where she had begun to find her feet as an independent creature.

Edward always claimed that their mutual happiness and love was not purely a 'romantic' happiness; but neither was it a tamed and domesticated form of passion. It also included a rare friendship, and a meeting and marriage of two minds that also belonged to day-by-day existence.

Georgy felt her own happiness was like that of the bluebirds on the cups and plates of the pension: simple, and true. Nothing she might have imagined could have improved upon reality.

As they stood one sunny day by the shore of the lake, Edward took her hand and said: 'I had to let you grow up – I dared not hope you would ever return my love. I am too lucky!'

They looked across to the other shore which even on a summer day could appear dark, covered as it sometimes was with the shadow of the mountain, and Georgy thought of Lamartine and his love for Elvire. Although it had been cruelly snatched away from him by death, had he not swiftly found solid happiness with his English wife? But nobody ever knew the sadnesses life might throw at them.

As though echoing her thoughts, her own lover said: 'Our love may not be the kind that poets write about, Georgy, but I rather fancy writing a lyric describing the lake and the clouds – everything I see is transformed when you are by my side.'

Even so I would not have had her miss the miseries of unrequited love for Amaury, he thought, a love resembling my long-ago passion for Amaury's mother, Félicienne. For a time romantic passion might have overwhelmed us both, yet we have found each other and know we are alike.

I'd wager her 'Poet' had other loves even after his Elvire died, though he might have settled for marriage in the end . . . . For me though, marriage is not a settling but a triumphant new beginning.

He did not say any of this to Georgy just then, but instead took her hand. 'I regret that I am not a good poet, dearest – you must forgive me,' he said instead. He smiled as he spoke. His earlier words had charmed and touched her. She felt her cup overflow.

She too had her unspoken thoughts, on much the same lines as Edward's. Her love for Amaury had not been happy. She had imagined she might be worshipping an ideal, an ideal Young Poet, a new Lamartine, when in reality she had been sensually infatuated by Amaury's looks and youth.

Edward was not so handsome but his tenderness was genuine, and no one could have been more passionate. And Edward loved her.

Of all those she had met in France, she thought it had been the elusive Capucine whom she had really loved.

That evening they were strolling in the square observing the fashionable crowd who had come to take the waters when suddenly

Georgy gripped her husband's arm, saying: 'Look! I'm sure that is Louis-Marie! Over there!' A young man was walking along in their direction accompanied by an old lady. 'It's Tante Hortense Vivier!' As they came up, Georgy stopped and Edward waited to be introduced.

'Why, it is Mademoiselle Georgina!' said Louis-Marie raising his hat. 'You remember her, Aunt – the little English girl?'

'Good evening, my dear,' said Hortense, looking slightly reserved. No wonder – she would doubtless have heard lurid stories about Camille de Marceau.

'This is my husband, Edward Walker,' said Georgy demurely. 'How nice to see you again. How are you?'

'It goes not too ill with me,' said Louis-Marie, looking immediately unwell. 'Are you here for the cure yourselves?'

'Oh no. I am come just for the sake of old times,' replied Georgy mischievously. 'My husband wished to see Savoy.'

'Oh yes, it is magnificent,' murmured Edward, taking his cue from her.

'We are here for the baths,' said Louis-Marie. 'Shall we all go for a sirop? It would be pleasant to have a chat.'

Edward agreed so they went into a café under one of the pensions and ordered fruit and water. Both Georgy and Edward were wondering if Louis-Marie would mention Arnaud or his sister. He did not, and Georgy was not going to.

'Have you finished your epic?' she asked Louis-Marie. His face brightened.

'Indeed – and it was published in Paris in March!'

'Oh, do send us a copy,' she said. 'I would love to read it!' He looked most gratified.

Edward was talking to the old lady and getting on with her like a house on fire. Her face was wreathed in smiles. She had probably not had any conversation with a man who was not a relative for many years.

Louis-Marie leaned conspiratorially towards Georgy. 'It is better for women to marry men of their own nationality,' he said approvingly. How sententious he was.

When later on in the autumn his epic arrived in England for them, Georgy was amazed to find it rather good.

Epilogue

Amaury Arnaud married a much older woman, a rich lady. They had no children. Unlike Lamartine, he had always been very good with money, so when in 1852 Paris began to be rebuilt, Amaury was one of the backers of Baron Haussman. He had recovered some of his grandfather's and father's estates after the death of his mother, and he later inherited money from his rich wife. He had long ago ceased to write verse.

His mother, Félicienne Bonaventure, had always adjusted her sails to the prevailing wind, and was in middle and old age to flourish under different dispensations. That she had once been connected with the old Revolution gave an ageing woman added mystery; that she had once been a follower of Napoleon gave her glamour in the eyes of the romantic; and that she had suffered under the Bourbons who had refused her rightful claim to her parents' – or first husband's properties – reports were now vague – gave her both popular and fashionable support.

The year after Georgy and Edward visited Savoy on their honeymoon, Alphonse de Lamartine returned to Mâcon, but Georgy never saw him again. In 1829 he privately recognized his sixteen-year-old bastard son Léon, the child of his old lover Nina de Pierreclau. Nina had returned with Léon from a long stay in the Argentine, whereupon her old lover found a post for her as post-mistress at Pauilhac.

In 1836 Alphonse was to change his mind about introducing Nina into his writing and to use her in connection with yet another of his heroines in his epic poem *Jocelyn*. By then he had been for three years a member of parliament.

In the preface to his play *Hernani* in 1830, Victor Hugo called poetry 'the intimate essence of all that is'. He was of the opinion that Romanticism was no other than 'liberalism in literature'. Georgy and Edward would discuss these ideas, both political and literary. Both Lamartine and Victor Hugo had by now joined the liberal faction.

In July 1830, the struggle between the anti-monarchists and Charles X was won by the liberal opposition, among whom was Capucine and some of her friends who had formed themselves into the *Jeune France* Republican movement. After three days of fighting in the streets in Paris, the Bourbon monarchy, first restored in 1814, was overthrown. The same year, the Place Louis Quinze where Louis XVI had been guillotined was renamed the Place de la Concorde.

Georgy and Edward discovered only some months later from Louis-Marie, with whom they had kept in touch and who strongly disapproved of any revolution but a spiritual one, that Capucine Bonaventure, disguised as a boy, had been killed in the vicious street fighting of July 1830.

When Stendhal brought out his *Le Rouge et le Noir* in 1832, Georgy, who was always an avid novel reader, recognized in the traits of Julien Sorel – albeit in masculine guise and with not quite the same political principles, the temperament and almost a similar end to that of Capucine Bonaventure.

As was to become customary in that turbulent century, in 1830 the King, this time old Charles X, fled to England. Another monarch, one Louis-Philippe, regarded as the 'bourgeois' king by what remained of the old *noblesse*, followed him on the throne, to be known as the King of the French rather than the French King.

Lamartine never went into exile but his old age was sad after the brilliance of his youthful poetic career and the bravery of his political life. He had always been an optimistic gambler, but gambling caused his partial ruin. He was forced to produce a constant succession of *belles-lettres*, biographies, memoirs, novels, histories, histories of literature and political memoirs in an attempt to pay off his many debts and keep the wolf from the door. He wrote fewer and fewer poems as he grew older.

After the old count's death in 1832, Augustin de Marceau, like his distant cousin Alphonse, had also continued to gamble in the

286

Palais Royal, but had restricted his life to that of a minor country gentleman, living with his parents. His separated wife continued to live in London, not seen in 'Society' on account of her living with her lover, Jacques Cellard, a well-known London wine merchant and importer of Burgundy.

Lucie was to marry an Englishman. Thibault however stayed in France, and joined the new king, Louis-Philippe's court. After Louis-Philippe lost the throne in 1848 – in yet another 'revolution' – and went across the Channel to exile in England, Thibault eventually nailed his colours to Napoleon the Third. Victor Hugo was to spend fifteen years exile in the Channel Islands during this Second Empire.

By this time Georgy and Edward's daughter Susan was eighteen, and a passionate girl.

As her mother knew well, it was no good expecting your children to learn from your own past mistakes.

Throughout her long life Georgy was often to turn to a poem by Sir Walter Raleigh.

She had always thought that one verse described Amaury Arnaud, another verse her husband.

> *Know that Love is a careless child,*
> *And forgets promises past;*
> *He is blind, he is deaf when he list*
> *And in faith never fast ...*

When she reached the end of the poem she read:

> *But true love is a durable fire*
> *In the mind ever burning;*
> *Never sick, never old; never dead,*
> *From itself never turning.*

This she trusted was her love for Edward, and his for her.